About the Authors

Michelle Douglas has been writing for Mills & Boon since 2007, and believes she has the best job in the world. She's a sucker for happy endings, heroines who ve a secret stash of chocolate, and heroes who know ow to laugh. She lives in Newcastle Australia with her n romantic hero, a house full of dust and books, and eclectic collection of sixties and seventies vinyl. She es to hear from readers and can be contacted via her bsite www.michelle-douglas.com

estselling author **Nancy Robards Thompson** has a gree in journalism. She worked as a newspaper orter until she realised reporting 'just the facts' was ng. Happier to report to her muse, Nancy has found ana writing women's fiction and romance full-me. Critics have deemed her work, '…funny, smart observant.' She lives in Tennessee with her husband their crazy corgi. For more, visit her website at cyRobardsThompson.com

A® Award-winning author **Leah Ashton** never cted to write books. She grew up reading everything m pony books to cereal boxes at breakfast. One day discovered romance novels – and one day, much r, wondered if she could write one too. Leah now es happy-ever-afters for heroines who definitely t need saving. When she's not writing, Leah loves ay breakfast, rambling conversations and laughing she cries. She really hates cucumber. And scary movies.

D0417832

Mavericks

Mavericks: Resisting the Rebel

MICHELLE DOUGLAS

NANCY ROBARDS THOMPSON

LEAH ASHTON

MILLS & BOON

First Published in Great Britain 2020
By Mills & Boon, an imprint of HarperCollins*Publishers*
1 London Bridge Street, London, SE1 9GF

MAVERICKS: RESISTING THE REBEL
© 2020 Harlequin Books S.A.

The Rebel and the Heiress © 2014 Michelle Douglas
Falling for Fortune © 2014 Harlequin Books S.A.
Why Resist a Rebel? © 2013 Leah Ashton

Special thanks and acknowledgement to Nancy Robards Thompson for her contribution to *The Fortunes of Texas: Welcome to Horseback Hollow* continuity.

ISBN: 978-0-263-28218-4

MIX
Paper from
responsible sources
FSC® C007454

Printed and bound in Spain
by CPI, Barcelona

THE REBEL AND
THE HEIRESS

MICHELLE DOUGLAS

For my little brother, Kyle, who's always been a
rebel in his own way.

CHAPTER ONE

RICK BRADFORD STARED at the Victorian mansion elegantly arranged in front of him and then down at the note in his hand before crumpling the piece of paper and shoving it in his jeans pocket.

He'd checked with his friend Tash earlier. 'You're sure you got that right? Nell Smythe-Whittaker rang and asked if I'd drop round?'

'For the tenth time, Rick, yes! It was the Princess all right. And no, she didn't mention what it was about. And no, I didn't ask her.'

For the last fortnight Tash's brain had been addled by love. His lip curled. Not that he had anything against Mitch King and it was great to see Tash happy but, as far as he could tell, her street smarts had all but floated out of the window. Why hadn't she asked the Princess what this was about?

Because she was viewing the world through rose-coloured glasses, that was why. His lip curled a little more. He wasn't sure he could stand being a third wheel in her and Mitch's hazy, happy little world for much longer. It was time to move on. Tomorrow he'd head up the coast, find work somewhere and…

And what?

He lifted a shoulder.

First he'd find out what Nell Smythe-Whittaker wanted.

You won't find that out by standing here on the footpath like some dumb schmuck.

Blowing out a breath, he settled a mantle of casual, almost insolent assurance about himself. The people from Nell's world—probably including Nell herself—looked down on the likes of him and he had no intention of giving them, or her, the satisfaction of thinking he cared two hoots either way.

Would Nell look down that pretty autocratic nose at him? He hadn't spoken to her since they were ten years old. He could count the number of times he'd seen her since then—and only ever in the distance—on one hand. They'd never spoken, but she'd always lifted a hand in acknowledgement. And he'd always waved back.

It had never felt real. It had always felt somehow apart from the daily humdrum. He scratched a hand across his face. *Stupid! Fairy tales!* He was too old for such nonsense.

You're only twenty-five.

Yeah? Well, most days he felt as if he was fifty.

Clenching his jaw, he pushed open the gate and strode up the walk to the wide veranda with its ochre and cream tessellated tiles. With an effort of will, he slowed his strides to a saunter and planted a devil-may-care smirk on his face.

Up closer, he could see that Nell's fancy castle needed some attention. Paint peeled at the window trims and flaked here and there from the walls. One section of guttering leaned at a drunken angle and the wider garden was overgrown and unkempt. Here and there he caught sight of the silver wrappers of crisp packets and chocolate bar wrappers winking in the sunlight.

So…the rumours were true then. The Princess had fallen on hard times.

Ignoring a doorbell he had little faith would work, he lifted his hand to knock on the ornately moulded front door when voices from the partially open French windows further along the veranda halted him. Words didn't just drift out on the summer air. They sped.

'You won't get another opportunity like this, Nell!'

A male voice. An angry male voice. Rick's every muscle bunched in readiness. He hated bullies. And he really hated men who bullied women. He stalked down to the windows.

'You are a sleazy, slimy excuse for a man, Mr Withers.'

He paused. Her voice held no fear, only scorn. She could obviously deal with the situation on her own.

'You know it's the only answer to the current straits you find yourself in.'

'Is that so? And I suppose it's a coincidence that this particular solution is one that will also line your pockets?'

'There isn't a bank manager in Sydney who'll loan you the money you need. They're not going to touch that business plan of yours with a bargepole.'

'As you don't happen to be a bank manager and I no longer have any faith in your professionalism you'll have to excuse my scepticism.'

Rick grinned. *Go, Princess!*

'Your father won't be pleased.'

'That is true. It's also none of your concern.'

'You're wasting your not inconsiderable talents.' There was a silence. 'You're a very beautiful woman. We'd make a good team, you and I, Nellie.'

Nellie?

'Stay where you are, Mr Withers. I do not want you to kiss me.'

Rick straightened, instantly alert.

In the next moment a loud slap rang in the air, followed by scuffling. Rick leapt for the window, but it burst open before he could reach it and he found himself pressed back against the wall of the house as Nell frogmarched a man in a shiny suit along the length of the veranda, his earlobe twisted between her thumb and forefinger, and all but threw him towards the gate. 'Good day, Mr Withers.'

The suit straightened and threw his shoulders back. Rick went to stand behind Nell, legs planted and mouth grim. He folded his arms and flexed his biceps.

The suit gave the kind of smirk Rick would give a lot to wipe off his face…except he wasn't that kind of guy any more.

'I see you've your bit of rough. So that's the way you like it?'

'I'm afraid, Mr Withers, you're never going to find out how I like it.' She glanced behind her and met Rick's gaze, her green eyes…beautiful. 'Hello, Mr Bradford.'

Her voice reached out and wrapped around him like a caress. 'Hello, Princess.' He hadn't meant to call her that; it just slipped out. Those eyes widened and continued to stare into his until the breath jammed in his throat.

'Well, you needn't think your bit of rough is going to get you out of your current jam and—'

'Oh, do be quiet, you horrible little man.'

Those green eyes snapped away and Rick found he could breathe again.

And then he looked at her fully and what he saw made him blink. Nell looked as if she'd just stepped out of some nineteen-fifties movie. She wore a dress that made every male impulse he had sit up and stare. It had a fitted bodice that was snug to the waist and a skirt that flared out to mid-calf. It sported a Hawaiian beach print complete with surf, sand and palm trees.

'Mr Bradford is ten times the man you are and what's more he has manners, like a true gentleman.'

He did? In the next instant he shook his head. They were reading from different scripts here.

Without another word, Nell turned and took his arm. 'I'm so glad you could drop around.' And she led him back along the veranda, effectively dismissing the other man. 'I'm terribly sorry. I'd take you through the front door—I don't want you thinking I'm taking you in via the tradesman's entrance or some such nonsense—but I can't get the rotten thing open. I'm also afraid that you'll have to excuse the mess.'

She led him through the French windows into a large room—a drawing room or parlour or music room or something of that nature. Whatever it was, it wasn't the kind of room he'd had much experience with and, despite her words, it wasn't ridiculously messy, but there were haphazard piles of boxes everywhere and piles of papers on the only piece of furniture in the room—a small side table.

'Why can't you get the door open?' He detached his arm from hers. Her warmth was…too warm.

'Oh, I don't know.' She waved a hand in the air. 'It's jammed or swollen up or something.'

Why hadn't she had it looked at?

None of your business. He hovered by the French windows until he heard the clang of the front gate closing behind the suit. He glanced behind to make sure anyway. He turned back to Nell. 'What was that all about?'

Those green eyes caught fire again. 'He's an estate agent who wants to sell my house, only I'm not interested. In more ways than one! He turned out to be a seriously sexist piece of work too. I can tell you now, Mr Bradford, that if you try any of the same tricks you'll meet with the same fate!'

She was a slim blonde firecracker. In a retro dress. He wanted to grin. And then he didn't.

The fire in her eyes faded. She made as if to wipe a hand down her face only she pulled it away at the last moment to clasp both her hands lightly in front of her.

She was so different from the last time he'd seen her.

'I'm sorry, that was an unforgivable thing to say. My blood's up and I'm not thinking clearly.'

'It's all right,' he said, because it was what he always said to a woman.

Nell shook her head. 'No, it's not. I have no right to tar you with the same brush as Mr Withers.'

That was when he noticed that behind the blonde princess perfection she had lines fanning out around her eyes and she wasn't wearing lipstick. 'I'd prefer it if you'd call me Rick.'

The hint of a smile played across her lips. 'Are you up for a coffee, Rick?'

And, just like that, she hurtled him back fifteen years. *Come and play.* It hadn't been a demand or a request, but a plea.

He had to swallow the lump that came out of nowhere. He wanted to walk out of those French windows and never come back. He wanted…

He adjusted his stance. 'I thought you'd never ask.'

She smiled for real then and he realised that anything else that had passed for a smile so far hadn't reached her eyes. 'C'mon then.' She hitched her head and led him through the doorway into a hallway. 'You don't mind if we sit in the kitchen rather than the parlour, do you?'

'Not at all.' He tried to keep the wry note out of his voice. His type was never invited into the parlour.

Her shoulders tensed and he knew she'd read his tone. She wheeled around and led him in the other direction— back towards the front door—instead. She gestured into the large room to the left. 'As you'll see, the parlour is in a right state.'

He only meant to glance into the room but the sight dragged him all the way inside. In the middle of the room something huddled beneath dust sheets—probably furniture. It wasn't that which drew his attention. Plaster had fallen from one of the walls, adjacent to an ornate fireplace, and, while the mess had been swept up, nothing had been done about the gaping hole left behind. A rolled-up carpet leant against another wall along with more cardboard boxes. The light pouring in at the huge bay window did the room no favours either. Scratching sounded in the chimney. Birds or a possum?

He grimaced. 'A right state is the, uh, correct diagnosis'

'Yes, which is why I currently prefer the kitchen.'

Her voice might be crisp, but her shoulders weren't as straight as they could be. He followed her into the kitchen and then wasn't sure if it was much better. The housekeeper had obviously upped and left, but how long ago was anyone's guess. A jumble of dishes—mixing bowls and baking trays mostly—teetered in the sink, boxes of foodstuffs dominated one end of the enormous wooden table and flour seemed to be scattered over the rest of its surface. It smelt good in here, though.

She cleared a spot for him, wiped as much of the table down as she could and he sat. Mostly because it seemed the most sensible and least dangerous thing he could do. He didn't want to send anything flying with a stray elbow or a clumsy hip. Nell moved amid the mess with an ease and casual disregard as if she were used to it. He didn't believe that for a moment, though. The Princess had grown up in a world where others cleaned up the mess and kept things organised. This was merely a sign of her natural polish.

Or unnatural polish, depending on how one looked at it. She'd lacked it as a ten-year-old, but her parents had obviously managed to eventually drill it into her.

The scent of coffee hit him and he drew it slowly into his lungs. 'So…you're moving out?'

Nell started as if she'd forgotten he was there. She sent him one of those not quite smiles. 'Moving in, actually.'

Moving in? On her own? In this great old empty mansion?

None of your business.

His lips twisted. Since when had he been able to resist a damsel in distress? Or, in this case, a Princess in distress. 'What's going down, Nell?'

She turned fully to stare at him and folded her arms. 'Really?'

He wasn't sure what that *really* referred to—his genuine interest or his front in asking a personal question. He remembered his devil-may-care insolence and shrugged it on. 'Sure.'

She made coffee and set a mug in front of him. Only when he'd helped himself to milk and two sugars did she seat herself opposite and add milk to her own mug. The perfect hostess. The perfect princess.

'I'm sorry. I'm so used to everyone knowing my business that your question threw me for a moment.'

'I've only been back in town for a fortnight.' And he and she came from two different worlds, even if they had grown up in the same suburb.

Even amid all the disrepair and mess, she shone like some golden thing. Him? He just blended in.

'I did hear,' he ventured, 'that your father had fallen on hard times.'

Her lips tightened. 'And nearly took the livelihoods of over a hundred people with him in the process.'

Was she referring to the workers at the glass factory? It'd been in the Smythe-Whittaker family for three generations. Tash had told him how worried they'd been at the time that it'd go down the proverbial gurgler, that more unemployment would hit the area. But… 'I heard a buyer came in at the last minute.'

'Yes. No thanks to my father.'

'The global financial crisis has hit a lot of people hard.'

'That is true.' He didn't know why, but he loved the way she enunciated every syllable. 'However, rather than face facts, my father held on for so long that the sale of the factory couldn't cover all of his growing debts. I handed over the contents of my trust fund.'

Ouch.

'But I've drawn the line at selling Whittaker House.'

Her grandmother had left it to Nell rather than her father? Interesting. 'But you gave him your money?'

She rested both elbows on the table and stared down into her mug. 'Not all of it. I'd already spent some of it setting up my own business. Though, to be perfectly frank with you, Rick, it never really felt like my money. Besides, as I was never the daughter my father wanted, it seemed the least I could do.'

'But you're still angry with him.'

She laughed then and he liked the way humour curved her lips in that deliciously enticing manner. Lips like that didn't need lipstick. 'I am. And as everyone else around here already knows the reason, I'll even share it with you, tough guy.'

He leaned towards her, intrigued.

'Besides the fact he had no right gambling with the factory workers' livelihoods, his first solution was to marry me off to Jeremy Delaney.'

His jaw dropped. 'Jeez, Nell, the Delaneys might be rolling in it, but it's a not-so-secret secret that he's…' He trailed off, rolling his shoulders. Maybe Nell didn't know.

'Gay?' She nodded. 'I know. I don't know why he refuses to be loud and proud about it. I suspect he's still too overawed by his father.'

'And you refused to marry him?'

'Of course I did.'

He flashed back to the way she'd frogmarched the suit out of her office earlier and grinned. 'Of course you did.'

'So then my father demanded I sell this house.'

It wasn't a house—it was a mansion. But he refrained from pointing that out. 'And you refused to do that too?'

She lifted her chin. 'As everyone knows, I gave him the deeds to my snazzy little inner city apartment. I handed over my sports car and I signed over what was left of my trust fund, but I am not selling this house.' Her eyes flashed.

He held up his hands. 'Fair enough. I'm not suggesting

you should. But jeez, Nell, if you don't have a cent left how are you going to afford its upkeep?'

The fire in her eyes died and her luscious lips drooped at the corners. And then he watched in amazement as she shook herself upright again. 'Cupcakes,' she said, her chin at *just* that angle.

'Cupcakes?' Had she gone mad?

In one fluid movement she rose, reached for a plate before pulling off a lid from a nearby tin. 'Strawberries and Cream, Passion Fruit Delight, Lemon Sherbet, and Butterscotch Crunch.' With each designation she pulled forth an amazing creation from the tin and set it onto the plate, and somehow the cluttered old kitchen was transformed into a…fairyland, a birthday party.

She set the plate in front of him with a flourish and all he could do was stare in amazement at four of the prettiest cupcakes he'd ever seen in his life.

'I do cupcake towers as birthday or special event cakes in whatever flavour or iced in whatever colour the client wants. I provide cupcakes by the dozen for birthday parties, high teas, morning teas and office parties. I will even package up an individual cupcake in a fancy box with all the bells and whistles…or, at least, ribbons and glitter, if that's what a client requests.'

He stared at the cakes on the plate in front of him and then at the mountain of dishes in the sink. 'You made these? You?'

His surprise didn't offend her. She just grinned a Cheshire cat grin. 'I did.'

The Princess could bake?

She nodded at the cupcakes and handed him a bread and butter plate and a napkin. 'Help yourself.'

Was she serious? Guys like him didn't get offered mouth-watering treasures like these. Guys like him feigned indifference to anything covered in frosting or cream, as if a sweet tooth were a sign of a serious weakness.

He didn't stop to think about it; he reached for the nearest cupcake, a confection of sticky pale yellow frosting with a triangle of sugared lemon stuck in at a jaunty angle and all pale golden goodness, and then halted. He offered the plate to her first.

She glanced at her watch and shook her head. 'I'm only allowed to indulge after three p.m. and it's only just gone two.'

'That sounds like a stupid rule.'

'You don't understand. I find them addictive. For the sake of my hips and thighs and overall general health, I've had to put some limits to my indulging.'

He laughed and took a bite.

Moist cake, a surge of sweetness and the tang of lemon hit him in a rush. He closed his eyes and tried to stamp the memory onto his senses and everything inside him opened up to it. When he'd been in jail he'd occasionally tried to take himself away from the horror by imagining some sensory experience from the outside world. Small things like the rush of wind in his face as he skateboarded down a hill, the buoyancy of swimming in the ocean, the smell of wattle and eucalyptus in the national park. He'd have added the taste of the Princess's cupcakes if he'd experienced them way back when.

He finished the cupcake and stared hungrily at the plate. Would she mind if he had another one?

Rick stared at the three remaining cupcakes with so much hunger in his eyes that something inside Nell clenched up. It started as a low-level burn in her chest, but the burn intensified and hardened to eventually settle in her stomach. It was one thing to feel sorry for herself for the predicament she found herself in, but she'd never experienced the world as the harsh, ugly place Rick had. *And you'll do well not to forget it.*

She had to swallow before she could speak. 'Scoff the

lot.' She pushed the plate closer. 'They're leftovers from the orders I delivered earlier.'

He glanced at her and the uncertainty in his eyes knifed into her. He'd swaggered in here with his insolent bad-boy cockiness set off to perfection in that tight black T-shirt, but it was just as much a show, a fake, as her society girl smile. Still… She glanced at those shoulders and her mouth watered.

In the next instant she shook herself. She did *not* find that tough-guy look attractive.

He pushed the plate away, and for some reason it made her heart heavy. So heavy it took an effort to keep it from sinking all the way to her knees.

'How…when did you learn to cook?'

She didn't want to talk about that. When she looked too hard at the things she was good at—cooking and gardening—and the reasons behind them, it struck her as too pathetic for words.

And she wasn't going to be pathetic any more.

So she pasted on her best society girl smile—the one she used for the various charity functions she'd always felt honour-bound to attend. 'It appears I have a natural aptitude for it.' She gave an elegant shrug. She knew it was elegant because she'd practised it endlessly until her mother could find no fault with it. 'Who'd have thought? I'm as surprised as everyone else.'

He stared at her and she found it impossible to read his expression. Except to note that the insolent edge had returned to his smile. 'What time did you start baking today?'

'Three a.m.'

Both of his feet slammed to the ground. He leant towards her, mouth open.

'It's Sunday, and Saturdays and Sundays are my busiest days. Today I had a tower cake for a little girl's birthday party, four dozen cupcakes for a charity luncheon, a hen party morning tea and a couple of smaller afternoon teas.'

'You did that all on your own?'

She tried not to let his surprise chafe at her. Some days it still shocked the dickens out of her too.

His face tightened and he glanced around the kitchen. 'I guess it does leave you the rest of the week to work on this place.'

Oh, he was just like everyone else! He thought her a helpless piece of fluff without a backbone, without a brain and probably without any moral integrity either. *You're useless.*

She pushed her shoulders back. 'I guess,' she said, icing-sugar-sweet, 'that all I need to do is find me a big strong man with muscles and know-how…and preferably with a pot of gold in the bank…to wrap around my little finger and…' She trailed off with another shrug—an expansive one this time. She traded in a whole vocabulary of shrugs.

A glint lit his eye. 'And then you'll never have to bake another cupcake again?'

'Ah, but you forget. I like baking cupcakes.'

'And getting up at three a.m.?'

She ignored that.

He frowned. 'Is that why you wanted to see me?'

It took a moment to work out what he meant. When she did, she laughed. 'I guess you have the muscles, but do you have the know-how?' She didn't ask him about the pot of gold. That would be cruel. 'Because I'm afraid I don't.' She bit back a sigh. *No self-pity.* 'But no, that's not why I asked you to drop by.'

His face hardened. 'So why did I receive the summons? If you knew I was at Tash's, why couldn't you have dropped by there?'

She heard what he didn't say. *Why do you think you're better than me?* The thing was, she didn't. He wouldn't believe that, though. She moistened her lips. 'I didn't think I'd be welcome there. I don't believe Tash thinks well of me.'

He scowled. 'What on earth—?'

'A while back I went into the Royal Oak.' It was the hotel where Tash worked. Nell had been lonely and had wanted to connect with people she'd never been allowed to connect with before. For heaven's sake, they all lived in the same neighbourhood. They should know each other. She was careful to keep the hurt out of her voice. She'd had a lot of practice at that too.

There you go again, feeling sorry for yourself.

She lifted her chin. 'I ordered a beer. Tash poured me a lemon squash and made it clear it'd be best for all concerned if I drank it and left.'

Rick stared at her, but his face had lost its frozen closeness. 'And you took that to mean she didn't like you?'

She had no facility for making friends and the recent downturn in her circumstances had only served to highlight that. 'Yes, I did.'

'Princess, I—'

'I really wish you wouldn't call me that.' She'd never been a princess, regardless of what Rick thought. 'I much prefer Nell. And there's absolutely no reason at all why Tash should like me.' Given the way her parents had ensured that Nell hadn't associated with the local children, it was no wonder they'd taken against her. Or that those attitudes had travelled with them into adulthood.

He looked as if he wanted to argue so she continued—crisp, impersonal, untouchable. 'Do you recall the gardener who worked here for many years?'

He leant back, crossed a leg so his ankle rested on his knee. Despite the casual demeanour, she could see him turning something over in his mind. 'He was the one who chased me away that day?'

That day. She didn't know how that day could still be so vivid in her mind. 'Come and play.' She'd reached out a hand through the eight-foot-high wrought iron fence and Rick had clasped it briefly before John had chased him off. John had told her that Rick wasn't the kind of little boy she

should be playing with. But she'd found an answering loneliness in the ten-year-old Rick's eyes. It had given her the
courage to speak to him in the first place. Funnily enough,
even though Rick had only visited twice more, she'd never
felt quite so alone again.

That day John had given her her very own garden bed.
That had helped too.

But Rick remembered that day as well? Her heart started
to pound though she couldn't have explained why. 'Yes,
John was the one who chased you away.'

'John Cox. I remember seeing him around the place.
He drank at the Crown and Anchor, if memory serves me.
Why? What about him?'

'Did you know him well?'

'I'm not sure I ever spoke to the man.'

'Right.' She frowned. Then this just didn't make any
sense.

'Why?' The word barked out of him. 'What has he been
saying?'

'Nothing.' She swallowed. 'He died eight months ago.
Lung cancer.'

Rick didn't say anything and, while he hadn't moved,
she sensed that his every muscle was tense and poised.

'John and I were…well, friends of a kind, I guess. I liked
to garden and he taught me how to grow things and how
to keep them healthy.'

'Cooking *and* gardening? Are your talents endless, Princess?'

She should've become immune to mockery by now, but
she hadn't. She and Rick might've shared a moment of
kinship fifteen years ago, but they didn't have anything
in common now. That much was obvious. And she'd long
given up begging for friends.

She gave a shrug that was designed to rub him up the
wrong way, in the same way his 'Princess' was designed

to needle her. A superior shrug that said *I'm better than you*. Her mother had been proficient at those.

Rick's lip curled.

She tossed her hair back over her shoulder. 'John kept to himself. He didn't have many friends so I was one of the few people who visited him during his final weeks.'

Rick opened his mouth. She readied herself for something cutting, but he closed it again instead. She let out a breath. Despite what Rick might think of her, she'd cried when John had died. He'd been kind to her and had taken the time to show her how to do things. He'd answered her endless questions. And he'd praised her efforts. The fingers she'd been tapping on her now cold coffee cup stopped.

'Nell?'

She dragged herself back from those last days in John's hospice room. 'If the two of you never spoke, then what I'm about to tell you is rather odd, but...'

'But?'

She met his gaze. 'John charged me with a final favour.'

'What kind of favour?'

'He wanted me to deliver a letter.'

Dark brown eyes stared back at her, the same colour as dark chocolate. Eighty per cent cocoa. Bitter chocolate.

'He wanted me to give that letter to you, Rick.'

'To me?'

She rose and went to the kitchen drawer where she kept important documents. 'He asked that I personally place it in your hands.'

And then she held it out to him.

CHAPTER TWO

EVERY INSTINCT RICK had urged him to leap up and leave the room, to race out of this house and away from this rotten city and to never return.

He wanted away from Nell and her polished blonde perfection and her effortless nose-in-the-air superiority that was so at odds with the girl he remembered.

Fairy tales, that was what those memories were. He'd teased them out into full-blown fantasies in an effort to dispel some of the grim reality that had surrounded him. He'd known at the time that was what he'd been doing, but he'd wanted to hold up the promise of something better to come—a chance for a better future.

Of course, all of those dreams had shattered the moment he'd set foot inside a prison cell.

Still...

The letter in Nell's outstretched hand started to shake. 'Aren't you going to take it?'

'I'm not sure.'

She sat.

'I have no idea what this John Cox could have to say to me.' Did she know what was in the letter? He deliberately loosened his shoulders, slouched back in his chair and pasted on a smirk. 'Do you think he's going to accuse me of stealing the family silver?'

She flinched and just for a moment he remembered wild eyes as she ordered, 'Run!'

He wanted her to tell him to run now.

'After all, I didn't disappoint either his or your father's expectations.'

Those incredible eyes of hers flashed green fire and he wondered what she'd do next. Would she frogmarch him off the premises with his ear between her thumb and forefinger. And if she tried it would he let her? Or would he kiss her?

He shifted on the chair, ran a hand down his T-shirt. He wasn't kissing the Princess.

'If memory serves me correctly—' she bit each word out '—you went to jail on drug charges, not robbery. *And* if the rumours buzzing about town are anything to go by, those charges are in the process of being dropped and your name cleared.'

Did she think that made up for fifteen months behind bars?

A sudden heaviness threatened to fell him. One stupid party had led to…

He dragged a hand down his face. Cheryl, at seventeen, hadn't known what she'd been doing, hadn't known the trouble that the marijuana she'd bought could get her into—could get them all into. She'd been searching for escape—escape from a sexually abusive father. He understood that, sympathised. The fear that had flashed into her eyes, though, when the police had burst in, her desperation—the desperation of someone who'd been betrayed again and again by people who were supposed to love her—it still plagued his nightmares.

His chest cramped. Little Cheryl who he'd known since she'd started kindergarten. Little Cheryl who he'd done his best to protect…and, when that hadn't been enough, who he'd tried to comfort. He hadn't known it then, but there wasn't enough comfort in the world to help heal her. *It hadn't been her fault*.

So he'd taken the blame for her. He'd been a much more likely candidate for the drugs anyway. At the age of eighteen he'd gone to jail for fifteen months. He pulled in a breath. In the end, though, none of it had made any difference. That was what really galled him.

Nell thrust out her chin. 'So drop the attitude and stop playing the criminal with me.'

It snapped him out of his memories and he couldn't have said why, but he suddenly wanted to smile.

'The only way to find out what John has to say is to open the letter.'

He folded his arms. 'What's it to you, anyway?'

'I made a promise to a dying man.'

'And now you've kept it.'

She leaned across, picked up his hand and slapped the letter into it. She smelled sweet, like cupcakes. 'Now I've kept it.'

A pulse pounded inside him. Nell moved back. She moved right across to the other side of the kitchen and re-filled their mugs from the pot kept warm by the percolator hotplate. But her sugar-sweet scent remained to swirl around him. He swallowed. He blinked until his vision cleared and he could read his name in black-inked capitals on the envelope. For some reason, those capitals struck him as ominous.

For heaven's sake, just open the damn thing and be done with it. It'd just be one more righteous citizen telling him the exact moment he'd gone off the rails, listing a litany of perceived injuries received—both imagined and in some cases real—and then a biting critique of what the rest of his life would hold if he didn't mend his ways.

The entire thing would take him less than a minute to read and then he could draw a line under this whole stupid episode. With a half-smothered curse he made deliberately unintelligible in honour of the Princess's upper class ears, he tore open the envelope.

Heaving out a breath, he unfolded the enclosed sheet of paper. The letter wasn't long. At least he wouldn't have

to endure a detailed rant. He registered when Nell placed
another mug of coffee in front of him that she even added
milk and sugar to it.

He opened his mouth to thank her, but...

The words on the page were in the same odd style of all
capitals as the envelope. All in the same black ink. He read
the words but couldn't make sense of them to begin with.

They began to dance on the page and then each word
rose up and hit him with the force of a sledgehammer. He
flinched. He clenched the letter so hard it tore. He swore—
loud and rude and blue—as black dots danced before his
eyes.

Nell jumped. He expected her to run away. He told himself he hoped she would.

'Rick!' Her voice and its shrillness dive-bombed him
like a magpie hostile with nesting instinct. 'Stick your head
between your knees. Now!'

And then she was there, pushing his head between his
knees and ordering him to breathe, telling him how to do
it. He followed her instructions—pulling air into his lungs,
holding it there and releasing it—but as soon as the dizzi-
ness left him he surged upright again.

He spun to her and waved the balled-up letter beneath
her nose. 'Do you know what this says? Do you know
what the—'

He pulled back the ugly language that clawed at his
throat. 'Do you know what this says?' he repeated.

She shook her head. 'I wasn't there when he wrote it. It
was already sealed when he gave it to me. He never con-
fided in me about its contents and I never asked.' She gave
one of *those* shrugs. 'I'll admit to a passing curiosity.' She
drew herself up, all haughty blonde sleekness in her crazy,
beautiful Hawaiian dress. 'But I would never open someone
else's mail. So, no, I haven't read its contents.'

He wasn't sure he believed her.

She moved back around the table, sat and brought her

mug to her lips. It was so normal it eased some of the raging beast inside him.

She glanced up, her eyes clouded. 'I do hope he hasn't accused you of something ridiculous like stealing my grandmother's pearls.'

He sat too. 'It's nothing like that.'

'Good, because I know for a fact that was my father.'

He choked. *Father*. The word echoed through his mind. Father. Father. *Father*. In ugly black capitals.

'And I'm sorry I've not tracked you down sooner to give that letter to you, but John died and then my father's business fell apart and…and I wasn't sure where to look for you.'

He could see now that she hadn't wanted to approach Tash to ask how she might find him.

He wasn't sorry. Not one little bit.

'But when I heard you were home…'

He dragged a hand down his face before gulping half his coffee in one go. 'Did he say anything else to you when he gave you this?' The letter was still balled in his hand.

She reached out as if to swipe her finger through the frosting of one of the cupcakes, but she pulled her hand back at the last moment. 'He said you might have some questions you'd like to ask me and that he'd appreciate it if I did my best to answer them.'

He coughed back a hysterical laugh. Some questions? All he had were questions.

Her forehead creased. 'This isn't about that nonsense when we were ten-year-olds, is it?'

He didn't understand why she twisted her hands together. She wasn't the one who'd been hauled to the police station.

'I tried to tell my parents and the police that I gave the locket to you of my own free will and that you hadn't taken it. That I gave it to you as a present.'

She stared down into her coffee and something in her face twisted his gut.

'I thought it was mine to give.' She said the words so softly he had to strain to catch them. He thought about how she'd handed her apartment, her car and her trust fund all over to her father without a murmur. So why refuse to hand over Whittaker House?

She straightened and tossed back her hair. 'That was the moment when I realised my possessions weren't my own.'

But for some reason she felt that Whittaker House was hers?

'I told them how I wanted to give you something because you'd given me your toy aeroplane.'

It was the only thing he'd had to give her.

'Which, mind you, I absolutely refused to hand over when they demanded me to.'

That made him laugh.

She met his gaze squarely and there wasn't an ounce of haughtiness in her face. He sobered. 'I've never had the chance to say it before but, Rick, I'm sorry. My mother and father were so angry. And then the policeman frightened me so much I...I eventually just told them what they wanted to hear. It was cowardly of me and I'm truly sorry if that episode caused a lot of trouble for you.'

It'd caused trouble all right. It was the first time he'd come to the police's attention. It hadn't been the last time he'd been labelled a thief, liar and troublemaker by them, though.

They'd just been two kids exchanging treasures and trying to forge a connection. Her father, the police and his background had all conspired to blow it out of proportion.

But none of it had been Nell's fault and he'd always known that. 'Don't sweat it, Princess.' He used the nickname to remind himself of all the differences between them, to reinforce them.

She sat back, her chin tilted at that unconsciously noble

angle that made him want to smile. 'Don't worry. I was let off with a caution, but I didn't know the police had questioned you too.' The poor kid had probably been terrified. He had been.

She nodded to the letter balled in his hand. 'But John hasn't hassled you about any of that?'

He shook his head and her shoulders slumped in relief. She straightened again a moment later. 'So…do you have any questions?'

She looked as puzzled and bewildered as he felt. He wondered if she was counting down the minutes until this interview ended. Did she find it awkward and wrong for him to be sitting across the table from her? Or did it feel weirdly comfortable?

He shook off the thought and set the crumpled letter on the table and did what he could to smooth it out.

'*I won't beat around the bush,*' he read, '*but you might as well know that I'm your father.*'

Nell's mug wobbled back to the table. She stared at him. Her mouth opened and closed. 'But he chased you away.' And then her eyes filled.

Rick knew then that she'd had no notion of what John's letter contained.

He glanced back at the letter and continued reading. '*I may be better served taking this knowledge to the grave as it's brought me no joy. I don't expect it to bring you any either.*'

Nell's intake of breath reverberated in the silence.

'*I have no faith in you.*'

Her hands slapped to the table.

'*But you might as well know you have a sibling.*'

She practically leapt out of her chair. 'Who?' she demanded, and then forced herself back down into her seat. 'Really?' She frowned. 'Older or younger?'

He raised an eyebrow. 'I think I'm the one who's supposed to be asking the questions.'

'Oh, yes, of course.' She sat back and folded her hands in her lap. 'I'm sorry.'

'I'm not going to tell you who it is. If it matters to you then you'll have to prove it.'

Her jaw dropped. 'But that's… How…how can he be so hard and cold? He's supposed to have looked after you and…' She swallowed and sat back again. 'Sorry.' She smiled, a weak thing that did nothing to hide her turmoil. She made a zipping motion across her mouth.

Rick shrugged. 'He ends by simply signing it *John Cox*.'

She shook herself, frowned. 'I know the questions belong to you, but, Rick, I have no idea how to answer any of them. I haven't a clue who your sibling could be. I had no idea John was your father. I've never seen him with either a woman or a child. I—'

He handed the letter to her. He watched her face as she read the remaining lines. It darkened, which gladdened his heart.

And then it went blank. Rick eased back in his chair and stared up at the ceiling, not knowing whether to be relieved or disappointed.

Nell ignored the first lines John addressed to her in the letter. *Miss Nell, if you think Rick is in any way redeemable and you can find it in yourself to help him…* She snorted. What kind of nonsense was that? What kind of father just turned his back on his child? She thought about her own father with all of his demands and bit back a sigh.

'You'll find a clue where the marigolds grow.' She turned the letter over, but there was nothing written on the back.

'Any idea what that might mean?' Rick asked, slouching back in his chair as if they were discussing nothing more interesting than the weather.

She opened her mouth. She closed it again and scratched her head. 'My best guess is that, as he was a gardener and this is where he gardened, it refers to a garden bed some-

where on the estate, a garden bed where he grew marigolds, but...'

'But?'

Rick sounded bored. She glanced at him, tried to read
his face, but couldn't. She lifted one shoulder. 'The thing
is, I don't recall John ever growing marigolds. Apparently
my mother didn't like them.'

She stabbed a finger into the Passion Fruit Delight cupcake, glowering at it. 'Why couldn't he have just told you
who your sibling is?' She stabbed it again. 'Why couldn't
he have told you the truth from the start and been a proper
father to you?' Stab. Stab. 'I'd never have guessed any of
this in a million years and—'

She pulled herself up and collected herself. None of this
was helping. She wiped her finger on a napkin. 'Okay, so
what else could marigold mean?'

Rick picked up the Strawberries and Cream cupcake
and pushed nearly half of it into his mouth. She watched,
mesmerised, at the way his lips closed around it, at the appreciation that lit his eyes and the way his mouth worked,
the way his Adam's apple bobbed...the way his tongue
flicked out to seize a crumb from the corner of his mouth.

She wrenched her gaze back. 'It could be a girl's name.'
Her voice came out strangled.

'Do you know a Marigold or two?'

The words came out lazy and barely interested. Didn't
he care? She tried to focus on the question he asked rather
than the ones pounding through her. She frowned, thought
hard and eventually shook her head. 'I don't think so. I
don't even think I know any Marys.' She leapt up, seized
her address book from the sideboard drawer and flicked
through it...and then searched the list of contacts in her
mobile phone. Nothing.

She stood. 'Okay, maybe there's marigold wallpaper
somewhere in the house or...or moulding in the shape of a
marigold...or an ornament or a painting or—'

'Princess, you've lived here your whole life. Do you really need to go through this mausoleum room by room to know whether it has marigold wallpaper?'

No, of course not. She sat. She knew every room intimately. She could remember what it looked like ten years ago as if it were only yesterday. There hadn't been any marigold paintings on any of the walls. There'd been no marigold wallpaper or bedspreads or curtains. No marigolds. Anywhere.

She glanced at Rick again. She could deal with his devil-may-care teasing and that tough-guy swagger. In fact, those things gave her a bit of a thrill. Considering she didn't get too many thrills, she'd take them where she could. She could even deal with the cold, hard wall he retreated behind. She could relate to it, even if she did feel he was judging her behind it and finding her lacking. But this… This nothingness hidden behind mockery and indifference. She was having no part of it.

She folded her arms. 'Don't you care?'

'Why should I?' He licked his fingers clean.

'Because…'

'What did he ever do for me?'

'Not about John!' She could understand his indifference and resentment of the other man. On that head it was John's stance that baffled her. She leaned across the table until its edges dug into her ribs. 'Don't you care that you have a brother or sister somewhere in the wide world?'

One shoulder lifted. He reached for the last unmangled cupcake. A dark lick of hair fell across his forehead. Nell pushed away from the table to stare, unseeing, out of the kitchen window, determined not to watch him demolish it with those delectable lips, determined not to watch him demolish it the way he seemed hell-bent on destroying this chance, this gift, he'd been given.

She pressed her hands to her chest. To have a sibling…

She stilled. She glanced back behind her for a second

and then spun back. Rick *hadn't* left. He hadn't read John's letter and then stormed out. He *had* shared the letter with her. Rick could feign indifference and couldn't-care-less disregard all he wanted, but if he really didn't care he'd have left by now.

Her cupcakes were good, but they weren't that good.

She sat again. 'I wish I had a brother or sister.'

'And whose image would you most like them cast in?' He leaned back, hands clasped behind his head. 'Your mother's or your father's?'

She flinched. He blinked and for a moment she thought he might reach across the table to touch her. He didn't. She forced herself to laugh. 'I guess there is always that. A sibling may have provided further proof that I was the cuckoo in the nest.'

'I didn't mean it like that.'

The hell he hadn't. 'It's okay.' She made her voice wry. 'You've had a shock, so it's okay to say hurtful things to other people.'

He scrubbed a hand across his face. 'I didn't mean for it to be hurtful. I'm sorry. I just refuse to turn this into a "they-all-lived-happily-ever-after" fairy tale like you seem so set on doing.'

He didn't want to get his hopes up. She couldn't blame him for that.

He rose. 'I believe I've long outstayed my welcome.'

Nell shot to her feet too. 'But…but we haven't figured out what marigolds mean yet or—'

'I'm not sure I care, Princess.'

She opened her mouth, but he shook his head and the expression on his face had her shutting it again. 'Good girl,' he said.

Her chin shot up. 'Don't patronise me.'

He grinned a grin that made her blood heat and her knees weak and she suddenly wanted him gone. Now. 'You know where to find me if you decide to investigate this issue further.' And then she swung away to dump the used coffee grounds into the kitchen tidy. When she turned back he was gone. She sat, her heart pounding as if she'd run a race.

Rick let himself into Tash's house, his head whirling and his temples throbbing. What the hell was he supposed to do now?

What do you want to do?

He wanted to run away.

But...

He pulled up short, dragged in a breath and searched for his customary indifference, but he couldn't find it. Too many thoughts pounded at him. And one hard, implacable truth—he might not be able to do anything with the information John Cox had belatedly decided to impart. Marigolds might remain unsolved forever.

In which case he could jump in his car—*now*—and head north without a backward glance, without a single regret. Except...

What if Nell does work out what it means?

He had a brother or a sister. He rested his hands against his knees and tried to breathe through the fist that tightened around his chest.

'That you, Rick?'

Tash's voice hauled him upright. 'Yep, just me,' he called back, shoving aside the worst of his anger and confusion. Tash might be his best friend, but he wasn't sharing this news with anyone.

He just hoped the Princess would keep her mouth shut too.

He forced his feet down the hallway and into Tash's living room—still full of sun and summer, and all he wanted to do was close his eyes and sleep. One glance at him and Tash's eyes narrowed. 'What did Nell want?'

He swung away to peer into the fridge. 'Soda?'

'No, thanks.'

He grabbed a soda and then sauntered over to plant himself in an armchair.

Tash folded her arms. 'She's obviously pushed your buttons.'

'Nah, not really.' He shrugged. 'She wanted to know if I had the time and the inclination to do some work on Whittaker House.'

'Oh, Lord, you're going to make the Princess your next project?'

He stretched out a leg. 'I haven't decided yet.' He took a long drink. The cold liquid helped ease the burning in his throat. 'Mind you, the place is going to rack and ruin.'

'It's a shame. It's such a nice old place. Gossip has it that she only moved back in this week so she's not wasting any time getting things shipshape again.' Tash sent him one of her looks. 'Rumour has it that she's far from cash-happy at the moment.'

'I kinda got that impression. What else does rumour say?'

Tash managed a local pub—The Royal Oak. Lots of workers from the glass factory drank there. What Tash didn't know about local happenings wasn't worth knowing.

'Well, apparently there's no love lost between Nell and her father.'

She could say that again.

'Old Mrs Smythe-Whittaker left the house to Nell and I'm not sure how these things work, but it was left in trust for her father to manage until Nell turned twenty-five.' Tash's lips twisted. 'Nell turned twenty-five earlier in the week. She moved in and...'

'Her father moved out?'

'Bingo.'

Before he could ask any more, Mitch came striding into the room. 'Hey, gorgeous.'

'Hey, doll,' Rick murmured back, but neither Tash nor Mitch paid him the slightest attention.

Tash flew out of her chair to launch herself at the big blond detective. 'Catch any bad guys today?'

Mitch thrust out his chest and pounded on it with one hand. 'Loads.'

For a moment it made Rick grin. Mitch the shrewd detective and Tash the take-no-prisoners barmaid in love and flirting. A miracle of miracles.

He rose and set off back down the hallway for the front door. 'I'm eating out tonight,' he tossed over his shoulder.

He needed time to think.

He pushed out of the front door, his hand clenching into a fist. This whole thing could be an elaborate hoax, a nasty trick.

Or you could have a brother or a sister.

Could he really walk away from this?

He lengthened his stride but the thoughts and confusion continued to bombard him. Damn it all to hell! Why did this have to involve the Princess? She'd been trouble fifteen years ago and hard-won wisdom warned him she'd be trouble now.

There was something about her that set his teeth on edge too.

Somewhere inside him a maniacal laugh started up.

The next afternoon, Nell swiped a forearm across her brow and stared at the mountain of dishes that needed washing.

Staring at them won't get them done. If she were going to take a half-day on Mondays then she needed to use that time productively. She started to move towards them when a knock sounded on the back door.

She spun around and then swallowed. Rick. In worn jeans and another tight black T-shirt. And with that bad-boy insolence wrapped tightly around him. She didn't know whether to be relieved or something altogether different— like apprehensive.

She wiped her hands down her shorts. Instinct warned

her that the less time she spent in Rick's company the better. Better for her peace of mind and better for her health if the stupid way her heart leapt and surged was anything to go by. She tried to swallow back her misgivings. Her family had done this man no favours. She owed him for that.

With a sigh she waved him inside, kissing goodbye to the notion of a clean kitchen followed by a soak in a hot tub with a good book. 'Good afternoon.'

He just nodded as he took the same seat at the table as he had the previous day.

'Can I get you anything?'

'No, thanks.'

Neither of them spoke and the silence grew heavy. Nell moistened her lips. 'I...' She couldn't think of anything to say.

Rick's gaze speared to hers. 'Shall I tell you what occurred to me overnight?'

Her mouth dried though she couldn't have explained why. She gave a *please continue* shrug.

'I wondered if there was the slightest possibility that by staying here it meant John Cox had the chance to remain close to his other child?'

It took a moment for that inference to sink in. In a twisted way, she could see how he could make that leap. Without a word she went to her important documents drawer and pulled out a folder. She opened her mouth to try and explain its contents only to snap it shut. She shoved the folder at Rick instead. The contents could speak for themselves.

He stared at her for a moment and then riffled through the enclosed sheaf of papers. A frown lowered over his face even as his chin lifted. For a moment he looked like a devil. One who'd cajole with dark temptations that could only end in destruction and ruin. Her heart kicked in her chest.

She swallowed and looked away.

'This is a paternity test your father had done...twelve years ago.'

'That's correct. He arranged for that test when he and my mother divorced. As he said at the time, he had no intention of being financially responsible for a child that wasn't his.' Only the tests had shown beyond a shadow of a doubt that she was his daughter.

And that he was her father.

Rick slammed the folder shut. 'God, Nell, that man's a nightmare of a father!'

She turned back and raised an eyebrow. 'Snap.'

He rocked back and then a grin crept across those fascinating lips of his and a light twinkled in those dark eyes and some of the awkwardness between them seeped away. 'Okay, you got me there. I'll pay that.'

And then he laughed, and the laugh completely transformed him. It tempered the hard, insolent edges and made him look young and carefree. It made him breathtakingly attractive too, in a dangerous, thrilling way that had her blood surging and her pulse pounding.

She swallowed. 'On that head, though...' She nodded at the folder. 'I can't say I blame him. My mother isn't the kind of woman who has ever let the truth get in the way of a...good opportunity.'

Her mother was in the Mediterranean with husband number four the last she'd heard, which was about three times a year. Oh, yes, her family—they were the Brady Bunch all right.

Rick clasped his hands behind his head and leaned back. She wondered if he knew precisely how enticing that pose was to a woman—the broad shoulders on display, those biceps and the hard chiselled chest flagrantly defined in the tight black T-shirt angling down to a hard flat abdomen... and all in that deceptively open, easy, inviting posture.

She bet he did.

Even with all of that masculine vigour on display, it was

his eyes that held her. He surveyed her until she had to fight the urge to fidget. She reached for another shrug—a *pray tell, what on earth do you think you're staring at?* shrug. She was pretty certain she pulled it off with aplomb, but it didn't stop him staring at her. A ghost of a smile touched his lips. 'I'm starting to get the hang of those.'

She squinted at him—a *what on earth are you talking about?* squint. 'I'm sorry, you've lost me.'

He lowered his arms. 'For all of these years, here I was thinking you had the best of everything.'

She flicked her hair over her shoulders. 'Of course I did. I had the best education money could buy. I had designer clothes, piano lessons and overseas holidays. I had—'

'Parents who were as good at parenting as mine.'

She swallowed. 'One shouldn't be greedy.' Or self-pitying. 'Besides, they were merely products of their own upbringing…and they had their good points.'

'Name one.'

'We've already uncovered one. They didn't betray each other so badly that I was the cuckoo they thought I might be. I'm not John's secret love child and therefore I'm not your mystery sibling.'

'Just thought I'd ask.'

She hesitated. 'I did wonder…'

'What?'

'Would your mother be able to tell you anything that might be of use?'

She didn't like to ask about Rick's mother—she'd been a prostitute. Nell had a lot of bones to pick with her parents, but she'd never had to watch her mother sell her body. She'd always known where her next meal was coming from. She'd had a warm bed to retreat to. She'd been safe. She gripped her hands together. She was *very* grateful for those things.

Rick shook his head. 'She developed dementia a few years ago. It's advanced rapidly. Nine times out of ten, she doesn't recognise me these days.'

Oh. Her heart burned for him. 'I'm sorry.'

He merely shrugged. 'What are you going to do?' He said it in that casual, offhand way, which only made her heart burn more fiercely.

She clapped her hands together in an attempt to brisk the both of them up. 'Well, I had another thought too. We should go and check out John's cottage. It's been empty since he went into hospital. I mean, I know it was cleaned, but maybe it'll contain some clue.'

'It could all be a hoax, you know?'

'For what purpose?' She didn't believe it was a hoax. Not for a moment. And when she made for the door, Rick rose and followed.

They picked their way through the overgrown garden— across the terrace to the lawn and then towards the far end of the block. Whittaker House had been built on generous lines in more generous times. The house and grounds sprawled over the best part of a city block. No wonder her father wanted her to sell it.

She wasn't selling! But it all needed so much attention. She bit back a sigh. It was all she could do not to let her heart slump with every step they took. It had all been so beautiful once upon a time.

'Hell, Princess, this looks more like years rather than months of neglect.'

'John was sick for a long time before he had to go into the hospice. He had a young chap in to help him, but...' She shrugged and glanced around. Her father hadn't maintained any of it. 'There are a lot of vigorous-growing perennials here that have self-seeded and gone wild. It looks worse than it is.' She crossed her fingers.

'Do you see any self-seeding marigolds?'

He'd adopted that tone again. 'I'm afraid marigolds are annuals not perennials. They need to be replanted each year.'

'Why go to all that bother?'

'For the colour and spectacular blooms. For the scents and the crazy beauty of it all. Because—'

She slammed to a halt and Rick slammed right into the back of her. 'What on earth—'

He grabbed her shoulders to steady her, but she didn't need steadying. She spun around and gripped his forearms. *'You'll find a clue where the marigolds grow.'*

His face lost some of its cockiness. And a lot of its colour. She couldn't concentrate when he stared at her so intently. She sat on the edge of the nearest raised bed and rubbed her temples. 'When did I find out my mother didn't like marigolds? John told me when I wanted to plant some of my own.'

Rick sat beside her, crushing part of a rampant rosemary bush. The aroma drifted up around them.

'And why did I want to plant marigolds?' *Oh, but...* 'He couldn't have known, could he?'

'Couldn't have known what?'

She turned to him. 'After he chased you away that day he gave me my very own garden bed to tend.'

'And you grew marigolds?'

She shook her head. 'I wanted to, but I didn't. You see I had this old chocolate box tin and it had pictures of marigolds on it and I showed it to John and told him that's what I wanted to grow.'

Beside her, Rick stiffened. 'A tin?'

She nodded.

'What happened to the tin, Nell?'

'I put all of my treasures in it and...' But it had been a secret. John couldn't have known. Could he?

'What did you do with them?'

'I buried them here in the garden. After the policeman left. I snuck out in the middle of the night and buried them when nobody could see what I was up to.' She turned to meet his chocolate-dark eyes. 'And I never dug it back up.'

He swallowed. 'Okay, so all we have to do is try to find

where you buried it.' He leaned back on his hands as if he hadn't a care in the world, but she'd seen beneath the façade now. 'I bet you've long forgotten that?'

No. She remembered. Perfectly.

She leaned back on her hands too, crushing more rosemary until the air was thick with its scent. She drew a breath of it into her lungs. 'Doesn't that remind you of a Sunday roast?'

He didn't say anything.

'What are you afraid of?' She asked the question she had no right to ask. She asked because he kept calling her Princess and it unnerved her and she wanted to unnerve him back.

'Where I come from, Nell, Sunday roasts weren't just a rarity; they were non-existent.'

He said her name in a way that made her wish he'd called her Princess instead.

He leaned in towards her. 'And what am I afraid of? I'm afraid this isn't some hoax your gardener has decided to play and that everything he's said is true. I'm afraid I have a thirteen-year-old brother somewhere out there growing up by the scruff of his neck the way I did and with no one to give him a hand.'

Her stomach churned.

'I'm afraid he's going to end up in trouble. Or, worse, as a damn statistic.'

She pressed a hand to her stomach and her mouth went so dry she couldn't swallow.

'Is that good enough for you?'

It wasn't good. It was *horrible*. Her parents might not have been all that interested in her, but she hadn't been allowed to roam the streets unchecked or at risk of being taken advantage of. Her parents might not have been interested in her, but she had been protected.

'I remember exactly where I buried it, Rick.'

He stared and then he half laughed. 'You're full of surprises, aren't you?'

She leapt up and dusted off her shorts. 'We'd better hope John put it back in exactly the same spot or we're going to be spending a lot of time digging.'

She led the way to the garden shed. She grabbed a spade, secateurs and a couple of trowels. And gloves. Rick merely scoffed when she asked if he'd like a pair too. 'On your own head be it,' she warned. 'We're heading for the most overgrown part of the garden.'

He took the spade and secateurs before sweeping an elegant bow. 'Lead the way, Princess.'

It was crazy, but it made her feel like a princess. Not a princess on a pedestal, but a flesh and blood one.

She led him across to the far side of the garden. 'I'll trade you a trowel for the secateurs.' He handed them to her and she cut back canes from a wisteria vine gone mad. 'That's going to be a nightmare whenever I find the time to deal with it,' she grumbled. She cut some more so he had room to move in beside her. 'Believe it or not, there's a garden bed there.'

She trimmed the undergrowth around it, found the corners. It wasn't as big as she remembered, but that still didn't make it small.

She moved into the centre of it, stomping impatiens and tea roses. She closed her eyes and shuffled three steps to the right. She took a dolly step forward and drew an X on the ground. 'X marks the spot,' she whispered.

CHAPTER THREE

RICK STARED AT the spot and cold sweat prickled his nape. What the hell was he doing here?

To run now, though, would reveal weakness and he *never* showed weakness. In the world where he'd grown up weakness could prove fatal.

Not showing weakness and acting with strength, though, were two different things. When Nell took one of the trowels from his nerveless fingers, he couldn't do a damn thing about it. He couldn't move to help her. He couldn't ask her to stop.

'The spade will be overkill, I expect. The ground is soft and although it felt like I'd dug for a long time I was only ten so I expect the tin shouldn't be buried too deeply.'

It was only when she dropped to her knees in the dirt that Rick was able to snap back to himself. 'Princess, you'll get dirty.'

She grinned, but she didn't look up. 'I like getting mucky in the garden.'

She certainly knew how to wield a trowel.

'Cupcakes aren't the only things I'm good at, you know?'

'I didn't doubt for a moment that you'd be a gardening expert too.' He wondered if he should climb into the garden bed and help her. Except she looked so at home and he had a feeling he'd only get in the way. 'Can I help?'

Her grin widened. 'Nah, you just stand there and look pretty.'

He couldn't help it. He had to grin too.

'I can cook other things too. I'll cook you a Sunday roast some time and then you'll know what I meant about the scent of rosemary.'

Something hard and unbending inside him softened a fraction. Digging in the garden, grinning and teasing him, she was the antithesis of the haughty, superior woman she'd turned into yesterday. He could see now that he'd done something to trigger that haughtiness because Nell used her supercilious shrugs and stuck her nose in the air as a shield. The same way he used his devil-may-care grins and mocking eyebrows.

As he continued to stare at her, some parts of him might be softening, but other parts were doing the exact opposite. He adjusted his stance and concentrated on getting himself back on an even keel.

He wasn't letting a slip of a girl—any girl—knock him off balance.

'Princess, I admire cooking and gardening skills as much as the next man, but it's all very domestic goddessy.' A bit old-fashioned. He was careful to keep the judgement out of his voice and the mockery from his eyebrows. He didn't want her getting all hoity-toity again.

'Oh, that'd be because—'

She froze. It was only for a second but he was aware of every fraction of that second—the dismay on her face, the way the trowel trembled and then the stubborn jut of her jaw. She waved a hand in the air, dismissing the rest of whatever she'd been about to say.

He frowned. *What on earth...?*

Metal hitting metal made them both freeze. With a gulp, Nell continued digging. Rick collapsed onto the wooden sleeper that made the border for the bed and tried to ease the pounding in his chest.

Within a few moments Nell had freed the tin, brushed the dirt from its surface along with the dirt from her knees.

She dropped the trowel at Rick's feet and settled herself beside him. The tin sat in her lap. They both stared at it as she pulled her hands free of the gloves. She reached out to trace the picture on the lid.

'Marigolds,' he said softly.

She nodded.

'Why didn't John let you plant marigolds here?'

'Because my mother didn't like them, remember?'

'Nobody would've seen them all the way down the back here.'

She lifted a shoulder. 'I found it was always best not to make waves if one could help it.'

'I decided on an opposite course of action.'

She glanced up with a grin, her green eyes alive with so much impish laughter it made his chest clench. 'You did at that. I'm going to take a leaf out of your book and fill this entire garden bed with marigolds.'

Good for her.

She held the tin out to him. 'Would you like to do the honours?'

His mouth went dry. He shook his head. 'They were your treasures.' He couldn't help adding, 'Besides, you could be wrong and maybe John never knew about the tin.'

'I'm not wrong.'

Her certainty had his heart beating hard and fast.

She sent him a small smile. 'Well, here goes.' And she prised the lid off.

An assortment of oddments met his gaze. Silly stuff one would expect a ten-year-old to treasure. And from it all she detached a small gold locket that he recognised immediately. She held it out to him and his heart gave a gigantic kick. 'When I buried this I swore that if I ever had the chance I'd give it to you.'

'Nell, I couldn't—'

She dropped it in his hand. 'Even now it brings me no

joy. It reminds me of the trouble it caused. Throw it away if you want and spare me the bother.'

His hand closed about it and his heart thumped. In kid-speak their exchange of gifts had been a token of friendship. Not that the adults had seen it that way. But the locket shone as brilliantly for him now as it had back then.

'While I keep this.'

She held up the tin aeroplane he'd given her and a laugh broke from him. He took it from her and flew it through the air the way he used to do as a boy. 'You really did keep it.'

'I wasn't a defiant child. I generally did as I was told.' Her lips twisted. 'Or, at least, I tried to. This was the one thing I dug my heels in about.'

Along with this big old relic of a Victorian mansion. He wondered why it meant so much to her.

'I should've dug my heels in harder about the rest of it too, Rick. I'm sorry I didn't.'

He handed her back the plane. 'Forget about it. We were just kids.' And what chance did a timid ten-year-old have against bullying parents and glaring policemen?

'Hey, I remember those—' he laughed when she pulled out a host of cheap wire bangles in an assortment of garish colours '—the girls at school went mad for them for a while.'

'I know and I coveted them. I managed to sneak into a Two Dollar Shop and buy these when my mother wasn't looking, but she forbade me from wearing them. Apparently they made me look cheap and she threatened to throw them away.'

So instead Nell had buried them in this tin where no one could take them away from her…but where she'd never be able to wear them either. Not even in secret.

She dispensed quickly with a few other knick-knacks— some hair baubles and a Rubik's Cube—along with some assorted postcards. At the very bottom of the tin were two stark white envelopes. The writing on them was black-inked capitals.

One for Nell.

One for him.

With a, 'Tsk,' that robbed the moment of its ominousness, she handed them both to him and then proceeded to pile her 'treasures' back into the tin and eased the lid back on. 'Do we want to rip them open here or does it call for coffee?'

'Coffee?' His lip curled, although he tried to stop it.

'You're right. It's not too early for a drink, is it?'

'Hell, no. It has to be getting onto three o'clock.'

'I don't have any beer, but I do have half a bottle of cheap Chardonnay in the fridge.'

'Count me in.'

He carried the spade, the secateurs and the letters. She carried the trowels and the tin. It touched him that she trusted him with her letter. He could simply make off with both letters and try to figure out what game John Cox was playing at. But the gold locket burned a hole in his pocket and he knew he wasn't going anywhere.

Besides, Nell had been the one to decipher the clue and dig up the tin. So he helped her stow the garden tools and followed her across the weed-infested lawn, along the terrace and back into the kitchen. He set both letters onto the table. Nell washed her hands, collected two wine glasses and the bottle of wine.

He took the bottle, glanced at the label and grinned. 'You weren't joking when you said cheap, were you?'

'Shut up and pour,' she said cheerfully. 'When it's a choice between cheap wine and no wine…'

'Good choice,' he agreed, but a burn started up in his chest at all this evidence of the Princess fallen on hard times.

He handed her a glass, she clinked it with his and sat. He handed her the letter. She didn't bother with preliminaries. She set her glass down, tore open the envelope, and scanned the enclosed sheet of paper.

Rick remained standing, his heart thudding.

With a sound of disgust she thrust it at him. 'I don't like these games.'

Rick read it.

Dear Miss Nell,
If you think he's worth the effort, would you please pass these details on to him?
Yours sincerely,
John Cox.

She leapt up and snatched the letter back. 'He calls you "him" and "he's".' She slapped the sheet of paper with the back of her hand. 'He doesn't even have the courtesy to name you. It's…it's…'

'It's okay.'

She stared at him. She gave him back the letter. 'No, it's not.' She took her seat again and sipped her wine. She didn't grimace at its taste as he thought she would. In fact, she looked quite at home with her cheap wine. He'd have smiled except his letter burned a hole in his palm.

'And just so you know,' she added, 'the details there are for his solicitor.'

Rick didn't think for a moment that John had left him any money. It'd just be another hoop to jump through. Gritting his teeth, he slid a finger beneath the flap of the envelope addressed to him and pulled the letter free.

At least it was addressed to him.

Rick
If you've got this far then you have the approval of the only woman I've ever trusted and the only woman I have any time for. If you haven't blown it, she'll provide you with the information you'll need for the next step of the journey.

It was simply signed *John Cox.*

He handed the letter to Nell so she could read it too. It seemed mean-spirited not to. She read it and handed it back. 'Loquacious, isn't he?'

Rick sank down into his chair.

'The solicitor, Clinton Garside, is wily and unpleasant.'

'Just like John Cox.'

She shook her head and then seemed to realise she was contradicting him. Based on all the evidence Rick had so far, 'wily and unpleasant' described John to a T. 'I never knew this side of him. He was quiet, didn't talk much and certainly wasn't affectionate, but he was kind to me.'

Maybe so, but he still hadn't let her plant marigolds.

Nell glanced at Rick and it suddenly hit her that he was only a step or two away from abandoning this entire endeavour.

She didn't know why, but instinct warned her that would be a bad thing—not bad evil, but bad detrimental. That it would hurt him in some fundamental way. As the messenger of the tidings she couldn't help feeling partly responsible.

You have enough troubles of your own.

Be that as it may. She owed Rick. She owed him for what had happened fifteen years ago. She owed him for letting herself be browbeaten, for not being strong enough to have defended him when that had been the right thing to do. She might only have been ten years old, but she'd known right from wrong. She had no intention of making the same mistake now.

She straightened. 'Clint will give you the runaround. He'll tell you he won't be able to see you for weeks, and that's not acceptable.'

'Nell, I—'

'If you have a sibling out there who needs you—' she fixed him with a glare '—then it's unacceptable.'

His lips pressed together in a tight line. He slumped back in his seat without another word.

Nell pulled her cellphone from her handbag and punched

in Clint Garside's number. 'Hello, it's Nell Smythe-Whittaker. I'd like to make an appointment to see Mr Garside, please. I know he's very busy, but it's rather important and I was hoping to meet with him as soon as possible.'

'I'll just check his appointment book,' the receptionist said.

'Thank you, I appreciate that.' She searched her mind and came back with a name. 'Is that you, Lynne?'

'It is, Ms Smythe-Whittaker.'

'Please, call me Nell. How's your husband coming along after his football injury? Will he be right to play the first game of the season? All the fans are hoping so.'

'We think so, fingers crossed. It's nice of you to ask.'

Exactly. And in return…

'There's just been a cancellation for Wednesday afternoon at three-thirty. Would that suit you?'

'Wednesday at three-thirty,' she repeated, glancing at Rick. He shrugged and nodded. 'That's perfect! Thank you so much, Lynne. I really appreciate it.'

She rang off and stowed her phone back into her bag. 'Three-thirty Wednesday,' she repeated.

'So you're intent on holding my hand?'

An edge had crept into his voice. She sat a little straighter and lifted her chin. 'It'll speed things up.'

'Why are you so intent on helping me get to the bottom of all this?'

She reached out to clasp the stem of her wine glass, twirled it around and around on the table. She lifted a shoulder. 'There are a few different reasons. Guilt, for one. Your father has been dead for eight months and I've only found the time to give you his letter now.'

'If he was my father.'

If.

'You had no idea what that letter contained. If you did…'

'I'd have tried to deliver it the same day! And I'd have quizzed John to within an inch of his life, but that's beside the point. I should've found the time to deliver it to you sooner.'

'You've had a lot on your plate these last eight months. You've no need to feel guilty.'

'The locket,' she whispered. 'It caused you so much trouble.'

'We were just kids, Nell. None of it was your fault.'

That wasn't true. 'I still feel badly about it.'

He reached out and for a moment she thought he meant to take her hand; at the last moment he pulled his hand back. 'I wish you wouldn't.'

He hadn't touched her but warmth threaded through his eyes. His mouth had lost its hard edge, replaced with a gentle sensuality that threatened to weave her under its spell. She knew in her bones that Rick would know how to kiss a woman and mean it.

It took all her strength to suppress the thrill that rippled through her. She fumbled to find the thread of their conversation again. 'The police labelled you a thief and a liar,' she forced herself to say. 'They thought you bullied me into handing the locket over. Those labels stuck.'

'Not my fault, Nell. And not yours.'

Because he seemed to want her to, she nodded.

'Anything else?'

'John,' she sighed. 'I can't help feeling he'd want me to help you and...I don't owe him, but he was kind to me.'

He shot back in his chair, his eyes cold.

Her heart thumped. 'I'm not trying to justify his behaviour to you. That's shocking and unforgivable.' But Rick would never have found the marigold tin without her help and what if there was further nonsense to be endured during the solicitor's appointment?

All of the hard angles had shot back into Rick's face. A lazy devil's smile hovered about his mouth, but it didn't reach his eyes. She pulled herself up, lifted her chin and gave the most speaking shrug in her armoury. 'Of course, if you'd prefer I didn't attend the appointment on Wednesday, obviously I won't.' She reached for her glass and took a sip, pretending it was something French and priceless.

Just like that, Rick laughed and the devil leached out of him. 'What a pair we are.'

'What are you talking about?'

He dismissed that with a flick of his fingers. 'If you think it'll make the meeting more profitable then I'd appreciate your presence.'

She took another sip, glad this time that it was just plain old Chardonnay. 'Okay.'

'What's more, I'll thank you in advance and mean it. Thank you, Nell.'

'You're welcome.'

'This, however—' he lifted his glass and drained the last mouthful '—is awful.'

She feigned outrage, but he only grinned. 'I know where Garside's office is. It's on the high street, right?' She nodded. 'Would you like to grab a coffee beforehand?'

'Oh.' Her face fell. 'That's a really nice idea, Rick, but—'

'You have other plans. No sweat.' He rose as if it were of no consequence. She wished it felt that way to her. Coffee invitations had been few and far between these last few months. 'I'll see you out the front at three-twenty-five.'

She rose too. 'Right.'

'Correct me if I'm wrong, Nell... You don't mind if I call you Nell, do you?'

Nell suppressed a shudder at the wet smile Clint Garside turned on her. 'Not at all.'

'I was under the impression that the business you wished to discuss concerned yourself.'

She forced her eyes wide. 'Oh, but it does, Mr Garside. It's just before we get to that I was hoping we'd be able to clear up this little matter for Mr Bradford and my family's former employee, the late Mr John Cox. It's been such a weight on my mind.'

'Well…of course, of course.'

He smoothed his hair back and sent her another greasy smile. He barely glanced at Rick. She'd forgive him the smarminess, but she wouldn't forgive him for ignoring Rick. He had no right to his snobbery. He had no right thinking he was better than Rick.

'You have to understand, however, that it may take my staff and I some time to locate the file. It's an older case and I'm sure you appreciate—'

'Oh, I do hope not.' Nell crossed her leg and smoothed a hand down the bodice of her dress. 'Once that document is found I was hoping to discuss the possibility of selling Whittaker House with you. I wanted to know if you'd be interested in handling the conveyancing of the property for me?'

She traced fingers along the V-neck of her dress, drawing the solicitor's eyes there, and she could've sworn that beside her Rick was trying not to laugh. She didn't dare glance at him for fear that a fit of giggles might overtake her.

She tossed her hair back and assumed the most superior posture she could. 'Of course, I couldn't possibly consider that while I have loose ends like this one hanging over my head.' She sighed and made to rise. 'Perhaps you'll be so kind as to call me once you've found the relevant documentation and then we can take it from there.'

'Oh, please sit, Nell. Let's not be too hasty.' Clint Garside rushed around the desk and urged Nell back into her seat. 'Let me just have a quick look to see if they're near at hand after all.'

'Why, of course.' She beamed at him. 'I can't tell you how much I appreciate all the trouble you're taking.'

Rick snorted. Clint glanced at him sharply and Nell reached out to touch the solicitor's arm and recapture his attention before elbowing Rick in the ribs. 'The file?' she reminded him gently.

'Oh, yes.' He was all smarmy smiles again. He patted her hand before trotting over to a filing cabinet on the other side of the room. *Ugh!* Behind his back, she wiped her hand down her skirt. The man had a touch like a dead fish.

'Bingo!' Clint turned with another wide, wet smile and held a file aloft. And for no reason at all her heart started to hammer. Was this the moment Rick would discover the identity of his sibling?

'So…' Clint sat across from her at his desk again, the file closed in front of him '…about Whittaker House…'

Beside her, she could feel Rick bunch up with tension. 'Yes, it's such a responsibility owning a house like that, but…' She gave a delicate little cough and glanced sideways to indicate Rick. 'Perhaps we can take care of this matter first and then…talk in private?'

His eyes gleamed. 'Why yes, of course.'

He opened the file and glanced at what she supposed must be John's instructions. 'There's nothing too difficult here. The late Mr Cox left a letter for Mr Rick Bradford should Mr Bradford ever come to collect it. The letter will need to be signed for, of course.'

'Of course,' she echoed.

'But, before that can happen, Mr Bradford has to provide a password.'

The air left her in a rush. Her entire body slumped like a deflated balloon before she had the foresight to shake herself upright again. She turned to Rick, trying to swallow her panic. *A password?*

'You will only get one chance, Mr Bradford.'

Acid burned her throat. 'Oh, Rick…'

He merely grinned at her, those dark eyes dancing. 'Don't sweat it, Princess.' He turned to the solicitor. 'The password will be Marigold.'

'That's correct.'

Marigold? He was a genius!

'All you now need to do is sign here.' Clint handed Rick

a pen without looking at him and indicated where he should sign. His lack of courtesy grated on her. Hadn't the people around here heard that Rick's name had been cleared?

Ah, but there's no smoke without fire. Her lip curled at the narrow-minded pettiness of it all.

Rick read the short statement, signed and took the letter from Clint's outstretched hand. He clasped her shoulder briefly. 'Thanks, Nell.'

And then he left. She wondered if she'd ever see him again.

Seven and three-quarter minutes later Nell made her escape from Clint Garside. With what she hoped was a breezy wave to Lynne, she shot outside to drag a breath of air into lungs that had cramped.

'Hey, Princess.'

She spun around to find Rick leaning against the wall just outside the door. One leg slightly raised, knee bent so his foot rested on the wall behind too. The epitome of casual indolence and she had to swallow to contain the leap of joy her heart gave at seeing him.

Slowly, she eased a breath of air out of lungs that had cramped up in an entirely different way. Rick wore a pair of dark denim jeans and a white business shirt, top button undone—no tie—and with the sleeves rolled up to his forearms. He looked like a model for a jeans commercial.

'Everything okay?'

She should be the one asking that. She swallowed and nodded and tried not to swoon in relief that he'd waited. 'I wasn't sure if you'd still be here.'

'Why not?'

That intent dark gaze watched her as if…as if she were worth watching, she realised. As if he liked not just what he saw, but…her. As if he liked *her*.

No doubt it was all just a trick of the light. And if it wasn't it'd just be smoke and mirrors. Rick had a reputation where women were concerned. Flirting would be as natural as breathing to him.

'I thought you might like to be alone to read John's letter.'

He glanced away and she took a step closer. 'What did it say?'

One of those broad shoulders lifted. 'I haven't opened it yet.'

She stared at those shoulders and bit her lip. A hum started up in her blood. She stretched out her toes to prevent them from curling.

'The street didn't seem like the right place. I'd prefer more privacy than that.'

Did he want to go home? Or maybe he wanted privacy, but didn't want to be totally alone? 'You could come back to Whittaker House with me if you like.'

One corner of his mouth hitched up. It made her blood chug. 'You're dying of curiosity, aren't you?'

'Absolutely,' she agreed. 'But there are cupcakes at my place. There's a Salted Caramel with my name on it.'

'Is there one for me?'

She gave an exaggerated roll of her eyes. 'Of course there is. I would never be so cruel as to eat one in front of company without offering them around first. You can have the Cherry Cheesecake and the Bubblegum if you like.'

'Sold!' He pushed away from the wall and fell into step beside her. 'Did you drive?'

She shook her head. 'It's only a five-minute walk— did you?'

'Nah, it's only about two minutes from Tash's.'

They walked along in silence. She was aware of the heat and magnetism he gave off, of the grace with which his tall body moved and the confidence in his strides—shortened to match hers at the moment. With each step she took, her awareness of him grew.

'You were magnificent back there, you know?'

'Me? You were the one who guessed the password!'

'You had that slimy solicitor eating out of the palm of your hand.'

She snorted. 'That was nothing more than him being overtaken by his own greed.'

'You played him to perfection. I went into that meeting determined to stamp my mark on it, but…'

She pushed a strand of hair behind her ear and dared to meet his gaze. 'But?'

'You were an absolute delight to watch and I didn't want to interrupt you. I can't remember the last time I enjoyed myself so much.'

Her cheeks warmed. 'I was pretty good, wasn't I?' she said because she didn't want him to see how much his words touched her.

He threw his head back and laughed. 'Did you crush him like a bug when I left?'

'I was tempted to, but no.'

He eased back to survey her. 'Why not?'

She kept her gaze straight ahead. 'It doesn't do to make enemies.' She had enough of those as it was. 'He thinks I'm exploring my options and that he's number one on my go-to list. Besides, I didn't want to burn our bridges where he was concerned until after you'd read your letter.' Who knew when they might have to consult with him again?

He didn't say anything so she forced herself to smile up at him. 'I'll save squashing him for another day.'

Her heart started to thump. Hard. She had to tread carefully—very carefully. She was in danger of turning this man into her Sir Galahad. Just as she'd done as a ten-year-old…and throughout her early teens—the fantasy boy who'd ride up on his white charger and rescue her.

She scowled and picked up her pace. Well, she was no damsel. And Rick Bradford wasn't a Sir Galahad in anybody's language.

CHAPTER FOUR

Nell bustled about the kitchen, putting the coffee on to percolate, arranging some of those sugary confections with their over-the-top frosting and decorations onto a plate and setting it on the table.

While Rick was aware of Nell's activity, all he could focus on was the letter he'd placed on the table. Sun poured in through the windows over the sink and a warm breeze wafted through the wide open back door and the kitchen gleamed in spotless—if somewhat crowded—cleanliness. And yet none of it could hold his attention.

The envelope sat on the table and the black capitals seemed to sneer at him. He deliberately turned to Nell. 'When did you move back in here, Princess?'

'Friday.'

His head snapped back. 'Friday? As in five days ago?'

'That's right.' She poured out two mugs of steaming coffee. She wore another frock. This one was white with cherries printed all over it and she had a red patent leather belt cinched at her waist.

She'd moved in on Friday, met all of her weekend orders, had dealt with the suit *and* had found the time to help him out too? And she hadn't complained. Not once. She hadn't made him feel as if he were in the way or as if she had more important things to do.

Why?

Because of a silly incident fifteen years ago and a sense

of responsibility to a dead man? He dropped into a chair, his chest heavy.

She sat too. She glanced at the letter, but she didn't ask about it. Instead, she selected a cupcake and cut it into quarters, sliced one quarter in half and with the crumb delicately held between thumb and forefinger she brought it to her mouth. Her lips closed about it and she let out a breath, her eyes half closing.

He swallowed. If the taste and texture of salted caramel did that to her, he wondered what she'd look like if she licked whipped cream from his—

He shot back in his chair, hot and hard. Hell! Where had *that* come from? Gritting his teeth, he tried to shake his mind free from the scent of sugar. He gulped coffee instead and scalded his tongue.

'Ignoring it won't make it go away.' She broke off another crumb. He averted his gaze as she lifted it towards her mouth. She was silent for a moment. 'You really aren't sure yet if you do want a brother or a sister, are you?'

He'd already told her that. 'You don't get it?' Why he'd expected her to understand he couldn't begin to explain. They might've grown up in the same neighbourhood, but they came from completely different worlds.

'I think I do. You're afraid this unknown sibling will reject you.'

Her candour sliced into the heart of him. He held himself tight so he couldn't flinch.

'I'd be afraid of that too.'

The simple admission eased some of the previous sting. 'Who in their right mind would reject you, Princess?'

'I know. It's inconceivable, isn't it?' She lifted her nose in the air and gave an elegant shrug, but it was so over the top he found himself biting back a grin.

He let a part of the grin free and reached for a cake.

'You're afraid your history—having been to jail and

whatnot—will mean they won't want anything to do with you.'

He bit into the cupcake, barely tasting it.

'And yet you're also afraid your sibling could be on the same path you were, that he or she may need help.'

It took all of his strength to swallow without choking. Acid churned in his stomach.

'There's no easy answer to any of that, is there?'

He couldn't bear to look at her. He wasn't sure he could stand the sympathy he suspected he would find in her face. He pushed his chair back and sat side on to the table.

'You do know you don't have to address those concerns yet, though, don't you?'

Very slowly, he turned back to her. Her face wasn't full of sympathy, but rather no-nonsense practicality.

'You can find out who this sibling is and then make the decision about whether to approach them or not.'

She had a point. In fact she made a very good point. He straightened. If all was well and good in his sibling's life, he could walk away without a pang.

Liar.

If all weren't well, maybe he'd find a way to help them anonymously.

Or maybe he'd introduce himself. Maybe he'd give family another shot and—

He clenched his eyes and closed his mind to that possibility. It was too soon to think about it, too soon to get caught up in the fairy tale Nell harboured—that this would end well for everyone. This was the real world and, more often than not, in the real world things didn't work out.

That didn't change the fact that on this point she was right—he didn't need to make every decision at this current moment in time. He went to reach for the envelope when she said, 'It's also occurred to me…'

She bit her lip. It made her look incredibly young. He pulled his hand back. 'What?'

She grimaced. 'What if John left a letter for your sibling with sleazy solicitor Garside—to be opened at some future date?'

He stiffened.

'What if at some time in the future this sibling turns up on your doorstep? Wouldn't it be better to…' She trailed off as if she didn't know how to finish that sentence despite all of her surface polish.

His hand clenched to a fist. 'You're saying forewarned is forearmed?'

They stared at each other for a moment. Eventually she shook her head. 'I don't know what I'm saying.'

Her chin lifted. 'Yes, I do. I'm saying read the darn letter, Rick, and then maybe you'll enjoy your cupcake.'

It surprised a laugh out of him. The Princess had changed from the shy little kid and the awkward teenager. He wanted to ask her about the transformation, only he suspected she'd chide him for changing the subject and avoiding the obvious.

And she'd probably be right.

He tore open the letter. He tried not to think too hard about what he was doing. It didn't stop the skin of his scalp tightening over until it became one big prickling itch.

The envelope contained a single sheet of folded paper. His hand trembled—just for a fraction of a second—and that sign of weakness make him want to smash something. He glanced at Nell to see if she'd noticed, but she was intent on reducing her cupcake to a pile of crumbs. He let out a breath and unfolded the sheet of paper.

He stared and stared.

And then he let loose with the rudest word he knew.

Nell jumped. Her chin shot up. 'I beg your pardon?'

'Sorry,' he growled. Not that he felt the least bit remorseful.

She moistened her bottom lip and he was suddenly and ravenously hungry. For a moment it seemed that if he could

lose himself in her for an hour he'd find the answer to ease
the burn in his soul.

As if she'd read that thought in his eyes, she drew back,
but pink stained her cheeks and her breathing had grown
shallower. If he wanted, he could seduce her. Right here,
right now.

If he wanted...

A harsh laugh broke from him. Oh, he wanted all right,
but there was always a price to pay for seducing a woman.
The price for this woman would be too high.

He leapt out of his chair and wheeled away, his hands
clenched to fists.

'Please don't punch a wall. I already have enough holes
to mend.'

Her words couldn't drag even a ghost of a smile from
him.

'I take it, then, that you recognise the name John has
given you?'

Name? *Ha!* He wheeled back and thrust the letter at
her. With a wary glance up at him she took it. She stared
at him for two beats more, looked as if she wanted to say
something, and then with the tiniest of shrugs turned her
gaze to the letter.

She frowned. She turned it over and then back. She
held it up to the light. The frown deepened to a scowl. She
slammed it down to the table. 'But this doesn't make sense!'

'It's obviously some kind of code.'

'A code?'

She swore then too and it surprised him so much his
head rocked back.

'Of all the mean-spirited pieces of spite!' She leapt up,
hands clenched and eyes narrowed, as she paced up and
down beside the table. 'Not only does he spend your *entire* childhood ignoring you—' she flung an arm out '—but
now he plagues you with nonsense and taunts you with a
carrot he keeps whisking out of reach.'

She ended on an incoherent growl of frustration. Rick eased back to lean against the wall. The Princess wasn't just cross—she was hopping mad. In fact, she was a great big ball of boiling rage.

She stabbed a finger in his direction. 'If I could get hold of him now I'd make his ears burn, let me tell you.' She slammed a hand to the table. 'Well, we'll just crack that code! And to hell with him!'

She glanced at Rick, stilled and then rolled her shoulders. 'What?'

'Who are you really angry with, Princess?'

The colour leached from her face. 'I don't know what you're talking about.' She took her seat and crossed her legs, polished and smooth once more.

He sat too. Even though he knew he should leave.

She pushed the sheet of paper back across to him. 'All of these letters and numbers—they have to mean something.'

Did he really want to bother with any of this? He raked both hands through his hair and fought the exhaustion that washed over him. If he walked away now, what would be the worst-case scenario?

The answer came to him too swiftly. He reached for a cupcake, needing the sweetness to counter the bitterness that rose up through him. The worst-case scenario would be at some point in the future to come face to face with a younger version of himself—a kid he could've helped. A kid he'd chosen to reject in the same way John had rejected him. How could he justify walking away to that kid when he'd had the chance to discover the truth?

Could he live with that?

Maybe, but in his bones he knew he didn't want to.

Damn it all to hell!

He came back to himself to find Nell copying the code onto a notepad. 'What are you doing?'

'Making a copy.'

'Why?'

She'd taken this too personally—as if John had lied to her.

'I'm going to do an Internet search on codes tonight to see what I can find out.'

'Nell, this isn't your problem.'

'That's not what it feels like.' She finished and pushed the letter back towards him. 'Besides, it won't hurt to have a copy.'

He supposed not.

'C'mon.' She rose. 'We haven't checked John's cottage yet. There might be a box or two of his belongings left behind, something that might give us a clue.'

He rose. What he should do was thank her for her help, and tell her this was no longer her problem. Except…it wouldn't hurt to check out where John Cox had spent over thirty years of his life. It might give him a sense of the man. He'd take anything to gain some leverage in this wild goose chase.

And then he could leave.

For good.

He couldn't prevent a sense of déjà vu when they stepped out of the back door and made their way across the terrace. The yellow heads of dandelions waved in the breeze. Nell pointed to one. 'I've always kind of liked them. They're cheery, don't you think? I must've spread a whole forest of them throughout the garden. I loved it when they turned puffy and I could blow their seed heads and set them free. I used to think if I could blow the entire seed head off in one breath and make a wish it'd come true.'

'Did your wishes ever come true?'

She lifted an eminently elegant shoulder. 'I expect one or two must've, I made so many. Law of averages would suggest so.'

She was lying. He wasn't sure how he knew. Maybe it was the way she lifted a hand to her face to brush an imaginary strand of hair back behind her ear. Maybe it was the way she studiously avoided meeting his gaze.

And maybe he was watching her just a little too closely? Gritting his teeth, he forced his eyes to the front.

They passed the garden shed. They moved beyond Nell's first flowerbed until they reached the very back of the property. Nell pushed open a gate in a six-foot-high bamboo fence to reveal a cottage on the other side. Rick followed. 'You'd have no idea this was here if you didn't know about it.'

'That's the point. Heaven forbid that one should catch a glimpse of where the hired help live.'

He couldn't tell from either her voice or her bearing whether she subscribed to that view or not. She didn't give him the time to figure it out either, but strode up the two steps leading to the cottage's veranda and reached for the door handle…and then came up short when it didn't budge. She turned back to him with a shrug. 'Locked. I wonder where the set of master keys for the property can be?'

He knew how to pick a lock…

Nell moved back down the steps, dropped to her knees and reached beneath the veranda. When she drew her hand back she held a key.

It hit him then that he wouldn't be able to just walk away. Nell knew his father and this property like no one else did. If he wanted to solve this mystery he was going to need her help.

Nell was going to be the key.

Nell tossed the key to Rick.

He caught it as if he'd been catching curve balls all of his life. Which was probably true. She bit back a sigh. She couldn't change Rick's past any more than she could change her own.

'You can do the honours,' she told him.

'Why?'

She blinked. 'What on earth do you mean—why?' She didn't feel like explaining her ambivalence. 'Because you're closer.'

'Was closer,' he corrected.

How was it possible for this man to divine her private moods so accurately? *Who are you really angry with?* She shied away from that one. 'As far as I know, this place hasn't been disturbed in months. If there're any creepy-crawlies in there you can encounter them first.'

'I'm not buying that for a moment, Princess. I just saw the way you stuck your hand beneath the veranda. You're not afraid of spiders or insects.'

'What about ghosts?' The words shot out of her before she could pull them back. She grimaced at his raised eyebrow. 'Not a literal one. Ghosts from the past.'

She ruffled out the skirt of her dress to give her an excuse not to look at him. 'This area was always out of bounds to me when I was a child. I'm still not feeling a hundred per cent easy being here.'

'Princess, you own this cottage. It's yours. You have every right to be here.'

She lifted her chin and considered him. He raised that eyebrow then, as if daring her. She plucked the key from his fingers, stuck it in the lock and turned it. 'I don't even know if the power's still connected.' She swung the door open, but when she tried the switch, light flooded the room.

She stepped inside with Rick at her heels. The door led straight into the living room. 'I've never been in here before,' she murmured, 'so I don't know the layout.'

This room and the adjoining kitchen were sparsely furnished but, other than a faint layer of dust, it was remarkably clean and tidy. She strode across to the kitchen area and hunted through the cupboards. 'There's some crockery, cooking utensils and cutlery, but there doesn't seem to be anything personal,' she said, turning back to the living area.

'Not much in here either,' Rick said, closing the drawer of the sideboard.

'Maybe we'll have more luck in the bedrooms.'

But, other than a bed, a mattress encased in plastic—presumably to protect it from the dust—and some linens, they found no trace of John Cox's presence in either of the two bedrooms. It was as if he'd been washed away when the cleaners had come in. Whoever her father had hired, they'd done their job to perfection.

Nell dropped to the wooden chair that sat at the desk in the smaller of the two bedrooms. Had John used this room as a study? If so, what had he studied? What, other than gardening, had he been interested in?

Other than avoiding his paternal duties, that was.

She glanced at Rick. She couldn't tell what impression the cottage had made on him. If any.

He turned as if he'd felt the weight of her gaze. 'You were hoping we'd find something.'

'Of course I was. Weren't you?'

'I thought it a fool's mission from the beginning.'

Oh, great. She glared at the ceiling. So not only was she a spoiled little rich girl, but she was a fool too? She straightened when she realised what she was staring at. 'A loft hatch.' She rose and set her chair beneath it and then gestured for Rick to investigate further.

'If there's anything at all up there, Princess, it'll only be porn magazines.'

'Look, I'm not tall enough to reach it properly so just humour me, okay?'

He didn't move. He just stared at her instead. She lifted her arms and let them drop. 'If I have to go and get the ladder from the shed to do it myself I will.'

With a smothered something she was glad she didn't catch, Rick hauled himself up on the chair and pushed the loft cover to one side. Pulling himself up, he peered inside.

Nell surveyed the way his forearm muscles bunched

and the promise of bulging biceps. Not to mention the long clean line of his back. Her heart pitter-pattered. Her fingers curled into her palms, even as her tongue touched the corner of her mouth.

Rick had been a good-looking youth, but it was nothing to the man he'd become. And in those jeans there was no denying that he was all man.

And the stupid fluttering in her throat reminded her that she wasn't the kind of woman who was immune to Rick's particular brand of masculinity. Not that she had any intention of doing anything more than looking.

'There's something up here.'

That snapped her to. 'What is it?'

If only it'd give them another piece of the puzzle. Or, barring that, a clue as to how to solve that stupid coded message.

'I'm going up.'

With that, he disappeared completely into the ceiling space. Nell paced down below. 'What is it?' she called up again.

'Some kind of box.'

'Are there any photos in it? A family tree or birth certificates or—'

His face appeared at the hole and he laughed down at her. 'You really are the eternal optimist, aren't you?'

Her face fell.

'It's locked,' he said. 'Here—I'll pass it down to you.'

She had to stand on the chair to reach it. When she was on the ground again, he swung himself back down beside her. 'Don't worry, Princess. I'm a dab hand at picking a lock.'

She couldn't drag her gaze from the box.

'Nell?'

She swallowed and forced her gaze up to his. 'We won't need to pick the lock.' She handed him the box and reached up to open the locket at her throat. She removed the tiny key it contained.

His gaze narrowed. 'Where did you get that?'

She touched the locket. 'This was my grandmother's. And that—' she nodded at the box '—is her jewellery box.'

He stared at her and the lines around his mouth turned white. 'John Cox stole your grandmother's jewels?'

She laughed. It held little mirth, though it was better than sitting in the middle of the room and bawling her eyes out. 'I don't think he stole them. I think he probably saved them.'

Comprehension dawned in his eyes. 'From your father?'

'From my father.' Before she'd died, her grandmother had owned a couple of nice pieces. Nell had thought them long gone.

He slung an arm about her shoulders and led her back into the living room. He placed the box on the tiny kitchen table and pushed her into one of the two chairs. He sat in the other. Even though he'd removed his arm she could still feel the warm weight of it and the lean coiled power of his body as he'd walked beside her. He smelt like dust and something smoky and aromatic like paprika.

'Aren't you going to open it?'

Of course she was. It was just…she'd never expected to see this box again. She missed her grandmother. Seeing this only made her miss her more.

His face darkened. 'Or would you prefer to take it back to the big house and open it in private?'

Her spine stiffened. Her chin lifted. 'I never once thought you a thief, Rick Bradford!' A temptation, definitely, and one she fully intended to resist, but a thief? No.

For a moment his slouch lost some of its insolence. 'Goes to show what you know, Nell Smythe-Whittaker. My teenage shoplifting is on police record.'

'I'm not even going to dignify that with an answer.' She pulled the box towards her, unlocked it and lifted the lid.

Her breath caught. 'Oh, her rings! I remember her wearing these.' She had to swallow a lump. 'My grandfather gave her this one.' She touched a large diamond ring. 'And this emerald belonged to her grandmother. The gold signet belonged to her mother.' She lifted them out one by one and passed them to Rick.

'The diamond and the emerald might fetch you a bit.'

'I couldn't sell them!'

She knew he wouldn't understand her sentimentality, but…her grandmother was the only person in her life who'd loved her unconditionally.

'How old were you when she died?'

'Seventeen.'

'That must've been tough.'

Sure, but it was nothing compared to all Rick had been through in his life. 'Oh, look.' She lifted a shoulder in a wry shrug. 'John has left me a letter.'

He rolled his eyes. 'He's turning out to be the regular correspondent.'

Dear Miss Nell,
If you've found your grandma's box then I expect you
know why I hid it. I'm sorry I couldn't rescue it all be-
fore your daddy got a hold of the diamond necklace.

She stopped to glance into the box. 'Yep, gone,' she clarified.

'We only have John's word it was your father who took it.'

'And my knowledge of my father.'

Rick straightened. Unfortunately, it didn't make his shoulders any the less droolworthy. 'Hell, Nell.'

'Hell's bells, Nell, has an even better ring to it,' she told him, resisting the sympathy in his eyes and choosing flippancy instead.

Who are you really angry with?

She cleared her throat and smoothed out the sheet of paper.

I know the old lady meant these for you, and I know
you'd want to pass them on to your own daughters
when the time comes.
Regards, John.

She folded the letter and put it back in the box. Silently, Rick put the rings back on top. Nell locked it. She pulled in a breath and then met his gaze. 'Rick, would you please put this back where you found it?'

His head rocked back. 'Why? You should at least wear this stuff if you're not going to sell it. You should at least enjoy remembering your grandmother.'

In an ideal world...

She moistened her lips. 'The set of master keys for Whittaker House are nowhere to be found. Until I find them I can't...' She halted, swallowed. 'What I'm trying to say is that I can't think of a safer place to keep them than where we found them.'

'You're forgetting one thing.'

'What's that?'

'*I* know where they are.'

'I've already told you that I don't believe you're a thief.'

'No, but I do mean to make you a proposal, Princess, and that might change how you feel about things.'

CHAPTER FIVE

NELL'S HEART STUTTERED at the casual way Rick uttered the word *proposal*. It held such promise and she knew that promise was a lie.

Oh, not a lie on his behalf, but on hers. She wanted to invest it with more meaning than he could ever hope to give it—a carry-over from her childhood fantasies of making things right over the locket.

The childhood fantasy of having one true friend.

But Rick didn't know any of that. The man in front of her might look like the boy who'd starred in her fantasies, but inside she didn't doubt that her boy and the real Rick were very different people.

Life hadn't been kind to Rick Bradford.

And she needed to remember he had no reason to think kindly or act kindly towards her.

He stared at her with those dark eyes and she drew a long breath into her lungs. 'Proposal?' She was proud her voice didn't tremble.

'I was going to leave Sydney at the end of the week.'

That didn't give them much time to crack John's code.

'I've holidayed long enough and it's time to be doing something.'

She couldn't help herself. 'What do you do for work?' Did he have a regular job?

'I usually pick up some building labourer's work here and there.'

So, that'd be a no then.

He grinned—a lazy insolent thing, as if he'd read her mind. 'I don't like being tied down to one thing for too long.'

She knew then he was talking about women and relationships too.

'I like my freedom.'

Given how his freedom had been curtailed in prison, she could understand that.

A prison sentence he should never have had to serve, though. A prison sentence he had served because a woman had taken advantage of him.

'What are you thinking about?' he suddenly barked and she jumped.

'How awful jail must've been.' It didn't occur to her to lie, but when his face turned grey she wished she had. 'I'm sorry you were sent to jail for something you didn't do, Rick.'

'It's all in the past.'

The words came out icily from between uncompromising lips and Nell had to suppress a shiver. He'd carry the scars of jail with him forever. She glanced down at her hands before lifting her chin. She had no right picking the scabs off those wounds. 'You said you *were* planning to leave Sydney, as in past tense. Have you changed your mind?'

His eyes blazed. He stabbed a finger to the table and dust rose up in the air around him. His crisp white shirt, his hands and hair all sported streaks of dust and cobwebs. She guessed the skirt of her dress wasn't in much better shape. It was the kind of carelessness that as a child had earned her rebuke after rebuke from her mother.

She forced her chin up higher. Well, her mother was off somewhere with husband number four and Nell was old enough to do what she darn well pleased. She didn't have to answer to anyone.

But those dirty streaks on Rick's shirt reminded her that while he'd been convicted of a crime he hadn't committed, it didn't necessarily make him a law-abiding citizen.

It didn't mean he wasn't a heartbreaker who'd take advantage of weakness when he saw it in others.

And you're weak.

She swallowed. Correction. She had been weak. Past tense.

He continued to glare at her with those blazing eyes but he didn't say anything. She made her voice as impersonal as she could. 'You were saying?'

He pushed away from the table and paced to the other side of the room before striding back. 'I'm going to get to the bottom of this bloody mystery!'

He spat out his *bloody* with so much anger she couldn't help wincing.

He dragged a hand down his face, glancing back at her with hooded eyes. 'Sorry.'

She shook her head, cursing her own prissiness. 'You don't have to apologise. I understand your venom.'

'You know what, Princess?' He took his seat again. 'I believe you do.'

She didn't want to follow that conversational thread so she merely said, 'I think it wise to try and discover who your sibling might be.'

'Except I've overstayed my welcome at Tash's.'

She doubted that.

'Besides, she's in love. I'm cramping her style.' He grimaced. 'And I can't stomach much more of her and Mitch's lovey-dovey stuff.'

That sounded more like it.

For some reason, the skin on her arms started to chill.

'So what I was going to suggest is that you let me use this cottage rent-free for the next few weeks. I mean, it's just sitting here doing nothing.'

The chill spread up her neck and down her spine.

'And in return I'll do some work on the big house.'

The chill disappeared. He didn't mean to take advantage of her after all?

'What kind of work?'

He lifted one lazy shoulder. 'Whatever repairs I manage to get to and maybe even some painting.'

That would be brilliant! She opened her mouth to snap up his offer before he could retract it, but a glance in his direction had her closing it again. Rick had a look in his eyes that she recognised. A look she'd seen in her father's eyes—an *I'm going to get my own way and I don't care by what methods* look.

She wasn't a pushover any more. Her father had discovered that and now Rick could too. She pushed her grandmother's jewellery box towards him. 'Put that back where we found it.'

'Is that a yes or a no to my proposal?'

'It's negotiations are underway but, regardless of the outcome, it doesn't affect the fate of the jewellery box.'

He leaned back and folded his arms. For a moment she thought he was going to refuse. And then she started. 'Heavens, where are my manners? Would you *please* put the box back in the ceiling?'

One side of his mouth hooked up. 'I wasn't waiting for a please, Princess.'

'I know, but there's no excuse for bad manners. Have you seen enough of the cottage to satisfy your purposes?'

'Yes.'

'Then I propose we go back up to the house and see if we can come to some arrangement that will satisfy mine.'

He laughed at that. She wished he hadn't. He looked younger, nicer, when he laughed and it had the potential to turn her to jelly.

She didn't need jelly but steel.

Without another word, Rick rose and placed the box back in the ceiling. Nell locked the door behind them and pocketed the key. Rick watched her, but he didn't say anything. In fact, neither one of them spoke on the walk back to the house.

When they reached it, Nell cleared her throat. 'I'd prefer to nail you down to specifics, Rick. How long do you think you'll stay?'

He shrugged. 'Can we start with a month?'

'Absolutely.' She pulled her no-nonsense business voice out and dusted it off. 'We can agree to a week-by-week arrangement if need be after that.'

'Fine.'

Was he laughing at her? She glanced across but couldn't tell. 'So, included in your four weeks' worth of repairs...' she walked through to the front of the house to the grand hall with its staircase that curved up to the first floor and pointed to the front door '...can you fix that?'

'Check.'

She didn't care if he was laughing at her. She tossed her head and walked into the grand parlour with its enormous bay window. 'Can you fix the hole in the wall?'

He walked over to it, tested it with his fingers, bent over to examine it more closely and the denim of his jeans stretched across those powerful thighs and taut butt and Nell had to swallow as her saliva glands kicked into overdrive. *Oh, my word.* Rick Bradford filled out a pair of jeans to perfection. Her fingers fluttered about her throat. Her eyes widened in an effort to take in as much of the view as they could. A hunger, deep and gnawing, that no number of cupcakes would assuage, racked her.

Rick turned. 'This doesn't—'

He broke off, a grin bold and sure spreading across his face. Folding his arms, he leant a shoulder against the wall. 'See anything you like, Princess?'

Heat scalded her face. She wished the floor would open up and swallow her. 'Don't be ridiculous.' But her voice came out at a squeak, which only made his grin widen.

She gestured to the wall. 'You were saying?'

Very slowly, he sobered and straightened. 'I'm not on offer, Nell. I'm not part of the bargain.'

'I never for one moment considered you were.' How could he cheapen not only her but himself like that? And then she remembered his mother had been a prostitute.

She closed her eyes and swallowed. If she hadn't been weak fifteen years ago, if she'd stood up for Rick, she could walk away from all of this now and…

Oh, who was she kidding? It didn't erase her sense of responsibility towards John. The way he'd treated Rick was beyond the pale, but there had to be a reason for all of this—something they couldn't see yet.

She forced her eyes open. 'Can we please get back to the task at hand?'

His lips twisted. 'Gladly.' He gestured to the wall. 'This looks like damage caused by something hard or heavy being banged against it.'

That'd be the removal men her father had hired to pillage the house of its expensive antiques.

'I can replaster it and then paint the entire room.'

That was even worth putting up with Rick's mockery!

'Then you have yourself a deal.'

He laughed. 'You have no idea, do you?'

'What are you talking about?'

'So far we've nailed down about a week's worth of work.'

Was that all?

'I'll fix the guttering that's falling off the outside of the house—that's another day's work.'

Wow. Um… 'What about painting the outside of the house?' It was badly in need of it.

He shook his head. 'That's too big a job for one person. Given the style and heritage of this place, it'd be best left to the professionals. Besides, I'm not sure you could afford the materials at the moment if money is tight.'

Her mouth dried. 'How much would it cost?'

'For paint, scaffolding and labour? I wouldn't expect you to see any change from twenty grand.'

So much? She needed to sit down. Only there wasn't a

stick of furniture in the room. And yet if she were to put her plan into action it would need to be done.

'I can ring around and get some quotes for you if you like?'

She nodded. 'I'll need it for the business plan I mean to take to the bank.'

'I know this is none of my business...'

She glanced up at him.

'But is this place really worth going into so much debt for?'

'Yes.' She'd made a promise—a promise she had no intention of breaking. Her hands clenched. She could make this work!

Rick walked across to her with that indolent loose-hipped stride that could make her mouth dry in a milli-second. He stopped less than two feet away. His hands went to his hips—lean, sexy hips—and he leaned in towards her with narrowed eyes. 'What are your plans for this place?'

A husband and babies—a family. Lots of laughter. And love. But until then...

'I'm going to turn Whittaker House into the most in-demand venue for high tea parties that Sydney has ever seen.'

He blinked. She waited for him to laugh and tell her she was crazy. Instead, he turned back to survey the room. 'That's a nice idea for an old place like this. What rooms are you planning to use as public rooms?'

'These two front reception rooms—the parlour and the drawing room—the dining room as it opens onto the terrace, and the library. They're all large rooms. For more intimate gatherings, there's the morning room and the conservatory.'

She took him through each of the rooms. They ended the tour in the dining room—a grand room with French windows that led out to the terrace. Rick walked around the room's perimeter, checking skirting boards, picture rails and the windows and doors. 'Everything looks in pretty good nick, just the odd minor repair here and there—nothing that some putty and a screwdriver wouldn't fix.'

She let out a breath.

'It could do with some freshening up, though.' He pursed his lips. 'I could paint the two front rooms and this dining room in a month.'

Her heart didn't leap with the same unadulterated joy as it had earlier.

He shuffled his feet. 'Actually, throw the library in too—there's not much to do in there.'

She bit her lip. 'How much will the materials cost?'

'Depends on the kind of paint you want. You'll need something durable. What colours were you after?'

'The Victorians weren't afraid of colour and these rooms are big enough to bring it off. I thought a peacock-blue and a jade-green for the two front rooms, maybe coral in here. The library is lined with bookcases and there's not a whole lot of wall to paint so maybe just a cream to prevent it from becoming too dark in there.'

How much would it all cost, though?

'This room opens onto the terrace and lawn. You might want to consider making this the green room to fit in with the garden theme and have the coral room at the front.'

'Oh, that's a nice idea.' She pulled in another breath. 'But how much is this going to cost me?'

He tapped a finger against his jaw before straightening and naming a figure that made her wince. She nodded. 'Okay, I can manage that.' Just. 'Rick, it looks as if you have yourself a deal.'

He sent her a sly smile. 'Not so fast, Princess—negotiations aren't over yet.'

They weren't?

'You drive a hard bargain.'

He'd have had an easy one if he hadn't been so honest.

'In exchange for all of this slaving away on your house, I now have an additional demand.'

She folded her arms. 'Which is?'

Just for a moment his gaze lowered to her lips. Her breath stuttered. Oh, he couldn't mean...?

They both snapped away from each other at the same time.

'That you provide me with half a dozen cupcakes a day. A working man needs to keep up his strength.'

She planted her hands to her hips. 'Rick, you can't eat six cupcakes a day. You'll rot your teeth and make yourself sick.' She stuck out her jaw. 'How about two cupcakes a day and I'll throw in some sandwiches?'

'Four cupcakes and some sandwiches.'

Did he eat properly? Tash was probably taking care of that at the moment. How was he off for money? Not that she could talk, but she was making enough to cover the food bill and she still had some in her savings account, which would cover the cost of paint and materials. Sure, he might be getting rent-free accommodation, but he wouldn't be earning while he was here. She blew out a breath. 'And I'll throw in a Sunday roast.'

'Now you're talking.'

'C'mon.' She led him back into the kitchen. Taking a seat at the table, she dragged a notepad towards her and wrote out a brief contract outlining what they'd agreed to. She signed it and then pushed it across to him.

'You think this necessary?'

'I've learned not to take chances.'

His eyes darkened. 'You're prepared to trust me with your Gran's jewels, but not take my word about our deal?'

'I told you already—I don't believe you're a thief.' She glared because he made her feel self-conscious. 'It doesn't necessarily follow, though, that I trust you.'

Rick's heart burned for her, mourned that wide-eyed little girl who'd smiled at him with such open-heartedness it had made him believe there were better things in the world than he'd experienced up to that point.

'That sounds like hard-won wisdom, Princess.'

She didn't answer. He signed her contract because he wanted her to trust him. For good or ill.

'You've changed, Princess. A lot.'

She snorted. 'You mean I'm not fat any more?'

'Don't use that word!' His voice came out sharper than he intended, but he couldn't help it. Reverberating through his head, all he could hear were insults—*You're a fat piece of useless lard! How could anyone love you? You're fat and ugly!* Horrible things flung at women by men who'd meant to wound.

Nell eyed him warily. He glared at her. 'You were never fat!'

Her gaze slid sideways. She lifted a shoulder. 'I was plump, and I was awkward and almost chronically shy.'

Those things were true. 'I always thought you were kind of cute.'

That made her look back at him. She tried to hide it, but he could tell she wanted to believe him. 'If that's the case,' she said eventually, 'then you were in the minority.'

He still thought her cute, but he had no intention of acting on it. She was still trouble. And he avoided trouble wherever he could. And power games. And complications. He pushed his shoulders back. 'So how'd you go from shy and awkward to polished and sophisticated?'

She waved that away. 'It's too boring for words.'

Her reluctance intrigued him. 'I'd like to know.'

She blew out a breath before jumping up to put coffee on to percolate. He was about to tell her she drank too much caffeine but then she proceeded to set out some of her extraordinary cupcakes and he decided to keep his trap shut.

'Blueberry Delight and Tutti-Frutti,' she said, pointing. She made coffee and sat again.

He raised an eyebrow. 'Well?'

'As you've probably gathered, I wasn't precisely the kind of child my parents had been hoping for.' She blew on her coffee. 'They'd hoped for some pretty, delicate little thing who did ballet and uttered childish whimsies that charmed everyone.'

He winced. Nell hadn't fitted that picture.

'When I became a teenager, my mother hoped I'd become a fashion plate who'd be eager to accompany her on her many shopping expeditions.'

'And your father?'

'Who knows? He'd have probably been happy if his golf buddies made comments about me becoming a heartbreaker and that he'd have to beat the boys away with a big stick.'

Did she know that was exactly how she could be described now?

'When my grandmother found out how miserable I was she set about helping me.'

'How?'

'She took me to a therapist who helped me overcome my shyness. She took me to a stylist who trained me in what clothes and make-up best suited me, and she found me an up-and-coming young hairdresser who was an absolute whizz.' She sipped her coffee. 'Obviously, it didn't all happen overnight.'

Rick unclenched a hand to reach for a cupcake. 'You know your parents were wrong to have such expectations?' They should both be horsewhipped for making her feel like a failure, because she hadn't met their specific designer mould. People like that shouldn't have kids.

'I do now.'

He took a savage bite of cake and frosting. 'I mean, would you ever do that to a kid?'

Her eyes flashed. 'No!'

He set the cupcake back on his plate and eyed her for a long moment. 'Why all this determination to avoid self-pity?'

Something inside her eyes hardened. 'Because, regard-

less of my gripes about my parents, I never had it as tough
as you or Tash or even Crazy Cheryl who you went to
prison for.' She gave a half smile. 'Cheryl used to throw
stones at me whenever she saw me in the garden.'

It didn't surprise him. Cheryl's home life had been beyond shocking. But…there was more than one way to damage a kid.

'It's not a contest, Princess.' She was entitled to her pain
and disappointment.

'Tell that to my parents.'

Exhaustion hit him at the expression on her face. 'It
didn't work, did it?' He slumped back. 'Did they notice
at all?'

'They noticed. It just took me a long time to realise
that it didn't make any difference, that it didn't make them
love me more. It just meant they didn't mind parading me
around their friends so much.'

He wanted to swear, but he knew she wouldn't like it
so he didn't.

'And then I realised I was wasting all of this time going
to parties I didn't enjoy, buying clothes I didn't want and
doing coffee on a weekly basis with women who called me
their friend but who haven't had the decency to return my
phone calls since calamity came calling.'

He did swear this time.

She transferred her glare to her coffee. 'That was when
I decided to be done with all that and focus on something
more important.' Her lips lifted. 'Like cupcakes.'

He'd have laughed except he suddenly saw it all too
clearly, could see now why she'd done what she had.

'You handed your trust fund, your apartment, and your
car over to your father because you wanted to make a clean
break with your past.'

'Bingo, tough guy.' She might sound sophisticated and
self-assured, but she couldn't hide the vulnerability that flickered through her eyes. 'Do you think that's stupid of me?'

'I think it was smart and brave. You don't need to be beholden to people like that.'

'Thank you.'

She smiled and for a moment he swore he saw glitter flickering at the edge of his vision. He blinked it away. 'There's one thing I don't get.'

'What's that?'

'Why are you fighting to keep this old relic of a house? Why don't you rid yourself of the responsibility?' And rake in some much-needed moolah while she was at it?

'This house belonged to my grandmother. She's the only person who loved me unconditionally. And she loved this house.'

She wouldn't have wanted it to become an albatross around her granddaughter's neck, surely?

'My parents lived here once they were married, not because it was convenient for the factory but because they wanted to be seen living in the Big House, as you call it. They never loved the place. They look at it and all they see are dollar signs. I look at it and...'

She didn't finish the sentence.

'And you see a Victorian teahouse.'

'You think that's dumb?'

'I think it's an interesting business plan with definite potential.'

She leaned towards him, her face alive. It was the way she'd looked at him fifteen years ago when she'd given him her locket. Only she wasn't a little girl any more but a woman. And he was a grown man.

Heat circled in his veins to pool in his lap. He surreptitiously tried to adjust his jeans, reminding himself about trouble and complications and grief and misery. He was *not* going to travel down that road with Nell. This wasn't a fairy tale. It wouldn't end well. He gritted his teeth. Business—this was just business.

'I've done my homework. High teas have become big

business in Sydney. Lots of clients are looking for themed party venues—something a bit different. I think Whittaker House will fit the bill perfectly. I predict my Victorian teahouse will become a big hit, not only for birthday parties, but for hen parties, bridal showers, anniversaries and family reunions too.'

He didn't doubt her for a moment.

'I know Whittaker House isn't Downton Abbey, but it does have its own charm and I happen to think other people would enjoy the location too.'

'Absolutely, but…'

Her face fell. 'But?'

He hated being the voice of reason. 'It'll take a lot of start-up capital to get the business off the ground.' The house would need a lick of paint both inside and out. The grounds would need to be not only wrestled into shape but manicured to within an inch of its life. She'd need to kit out the entire operation with suitable tables and chairs, pretty linens and crockery. It wouldn't come cheap.

'Which is why I'm preparing a business plan to take to my bank manager with projected costs, profits et cetera in the hope I can secure a business loan.'

'Which, unless you have some other asset you've not told me about, will mean putting Whittaker House up as collateral.'

He watched the fire leach out of her eyes. 'How'd you know that?'

It wasn't an accusation but a genuine bid for knowledge. 'I did a business course when I was in prison.'

She chewed her lip and nodded. Her glance sharpened. 'Do you have your own business?'

He shook his head.

'If you're as handy as you say, then maybe you should start up your own building business.'

He choked. 'Me?'

'Why not?'

'There have to be at least a million reasons!'

'And probably just as many why you should,' she said in *that* tone of voice. 'Well, I'm still going to put my proposal together and make an appointment with my bank manager. If I get no joy there then I'll have to find investors.'

'Which means the business is no longer your own.'

'Which isn't ideal, but it's better than nothing.'

He could click his fingers and make the money appear for her. If he wanted. For a moment he was tempted. He cut the thought off. He hadn't told Nell he was rich for the simple reason that he didn't want the news getting about.

She tossed her head. 'I bet there must be some kind of government initiative to assist fledgling businesses. I'll check into that too.'

He had to give her credit. She wasn't sitting around waiting for Prince Charming to swing by and rescue her.

She lifted her chin. 'And if it takes longer to get off the ground than I want, so be it.'

In the meantime she'd be stuck with the upkeep of the place. 'You know your grandmother's rings would bring in the kind of money you need.'

'Out of the question.'

Stubborn. He respected that, but it wouldn't pay the power bills.

She dusted off her hands. 'In the meantime, you're going to do some work on the place in return for rent-free use of the cottage.'

'And cupcakes.'

Her lips twitched. 'And sandwiches and a Sunday roast or two.'

Her eyes narrowed and he recognised the calculation that suddenly flashed in their brilliant green depths. What amendment to their deal would she try and come up with now? He folded his arms and waited.

She moistened her lips. 'If I help you crack that code

of John's, would you consider glancing over my business plan once I've written it?'

He grinned. 'Princess, if you can crack that code I'll write the darn plan for you.'

Her hand shot across the table. 'You have yourself a deal.'

He closed his fingers around her hand. His hand completely encompassed hers, but her grip was firm. He didn't want to let go.

'When do you want to move into the cottage?'

He kept hold of it, even though he knew it was dangerous. 'Tomorrow.'

She glanced at the clock. 'Oh, dear Lord!' She pulled her hand from his. 'I'll need to get my skates on if I'm to get it into any fit state to live in.'

'It's fine the way it is, Princess.'

'It most certainly is not!'

'There's absolutely no need to drag your cleaning lady out at this late hour.'

Her head lifted, her chin jutted out—so unconsciously haughty that it couldn't be feigned—and for some reason it made him want to laugh. 'I'll leave the key in the same spot. Will you be able to find it?'

'I'm sure I'll manage.'

Amazingly, she bundled up the remaining cupcakes into brown paper bags. 'Take them home with you.'

'An early down payment?'

'It'll stop me snacking on them. Besides, Tash and Mitch might like one or two.'

He couldn't have said why, but his heart started to burn. He almost did something foolish like invite her to have dinner with him, Tash and Mitch that evening. A crazy, foolish impulse.

Why on earth would the Princess want to have dinner with him? He rose, thanked her for the cupcakes and left.

CHAPTER SIX

RICK HAD JUST finished his last cupcake and a mug of coffee when Nell walked through the back door. She stopped short when she saw him. 'Hey.' She swallowed. 'How's it going?'

Lines fanned out from her eyes and her *frock*—yellow with big purple polka dots—looked rumpled and tired. He wondered what she'd been up to all day. She dropped her handbag on the table, glancing at his plate and mug. Before her face could twist up with suspicion he said, 'You can start using the front door if you like.'

A smile lit through her, banishing the lines around her eyes. 'You fixed it?'

He swallowed. A woman like her could make a man like him feel like Superman if he wasn't careful. 'It was no big deal. The wood had swollen. I filed it back, rehung it and it's as good as new.'

He tried to pull himself back. She might be a damsel in distress…or not. But he was no hero. He knew that and so did she. 'I did promise to earn my keep,' he reminded her.

'Well, yes, but I didn't expect you to start working the moment you moved in. I thought you'd take a day or two to settle in.'

Settle in? It didn't take much 'settling in' to unpack a single suitcase.

'You left cupcakes and sandwiches for me at the cottage.' The cottage had been spotless too—not a speck of dust to be seen. He wondered who she'd had come in and clean it at such late notice.

'Oh, that was just a neighbourly gesture. If I'd thought you'd want to start work today I'd have left you a key.' She stuck out a hip. 'Which rather begs the question—how did you get in?'

His stomach burned acid and he waited for that soul-destroying suspicion to wash over her face, for her to rush off and count the family silver. Ever since he'd been released from jail it was how people treated him. They didn't believe a man could pay his debt to society and then move on and make something of himself.

If he'd known at eighteen what he knew now, would he have still taken the rap for Cheryl, claimed the drugs were his rather than hers? He stared at the Princess and had a feeling that answer would still be yes.

Which meant he hadn't learned a damn thing.

Which meant he was still as big a sucker as he'd ever been.

He'd gone to prison a boy but he'd come out a lot wiser and a whole lot harder. He couldn't draw comparisons between Cheryl and Nell—their lives were too different— but the same protective instincts rose up in him whenever he looked at Nell now.

Ice washed over his skin. He had no intention of getting that close to anyone again—no intention of taking the blame for anything that would land him back in jail. Ever. Regardless of who it was.

'Oh, get over yourself, you idiot!'

He blinked at Nell's rudeness.

'If I trust you with my grandmother's jewels I'm going to trust you with the contents of my house. For heaven's sake, there's nothing left worth stealing anyway. My father long made off with anything of value.'

Genuine irritation rather than suspicion chased across

her face and he jolted back into the present. He rolled his shoulders.

'Is my security that bad?'

'It's not brilliant. You should install an alarm system. I, uh, got in through the back door.'

'But I locked it.'

'You need to remember to use the deadbolt.'

She sighed. 'An alarm system? I'd better put it on the list.'

She bustled about making coffee. She eyed the jar of instant he'd bought with distaste. 'Would you like another?'

'No, thanks.'

'Why didn't you make yourself a proper coffee? It's worth the effort, you know.'

'That coffee is yours.'

Very slowly she turned. 'And I'm guessing there's milk in the fridge with your name on it too and sugar in the cupboard?'

He shifted. 'People can get funny about things like that.'

She pointed her teaspoon at him. 'Let's get one thing clear right now.' She raised her voice to be heard above the gurgling of the percolator. 'You're welcome to help yourself to tea, coffee, bread, biscuits and whatever else is in the pantry while you're working. And—' she thrust out her jaw '—if I feel like having instant coffee I mean to help myself to your jar. You have a problem with that?'

He grinned. 'None at all, Princess.'

'Hmph.' She made coffee, sipped it and closed her eyes as if it were the first chance she'd had to relax all day. He wondered again what she'd been up to—hobnobbing with society types hoping to find an investor or three?

'Oh, I meant to ask. Is that your car out front?'

'Yup.'

'There's room to park it in the garage if you want.'

'There's a garage?'

'Come with me.'

With coffee cup in hand, she led him out into the garden. About halfway between the house and the cottage she veered left. Hidden behind strategically placed trees and shrubs squatted a substantial wooden building with three large wooden doors. She walked across to the cast iron fence, fitted a key into the lock and slid the fence back. The fence slid along on a kind of roller. From the footpath it'd be impossible to see that this part of the fence also acted as a gate.

'I had no idea this was here.' And he must've walked past this section of fence a hundred times. He turned to survey the garage. 'What did that used to be?'

'The stables, once upon a time.' She slid the gate shut again. It barely made a sound. 'They were converted eons ago, which is why the gate and the garage doors aren't automatic. Maybe down the track. Mind you, these big old doors have a certain charm I'd be loath to trade in merely for the sake of convenience.'

She took a sip of coffee. 'This bay here is free.' She lifted a latch and walked backwards until the door stood wide open.

He entered. And then stopped dead. A van, a bit like the ice cream vans that had done the rounds of the neighbourhood during the summers of his childhood, stood in the next bay along. Only, instead of ice creams, the van's sides were decorated with cupcakes. 'Candy's Cupcakes' was written in swirly pastel lettering.

He turned back to her, folded his arms and leant against the doorframe. 'Your business is obviously bigger than I thought.'

She drained her coffee. 'Yes.'

'Why didn't you tell me?'

For a moment her gaze rested on his shoulders. She shook out her arms as if an itch had started up inside her. His heart started pounding to a beat as old as time then too.

He gritted his teeth. He and the Princess were not going to dance that particular tango. 'Nell?'

She jumped. 'Sorry, I—'

She averted her face, but that didn't hide the colour on her cheekbones. Rick gritted his teeth harder.

'Sorry.' She turned back. 'I'm tired. Concentration is shot.' She gestured to the van. 'Everyone expects me to fail. Some have said so outright. Some have laughed as if it's a joke. Others have smiled politely while raising sceptical eyebrows. I don't need that kind of negativity in my life.'

'And you thought I'd react that way.'

She met his gaze. 'You did.'

'I…'

'You thought my little cupcake business was limited to a few deliveries on the weekend and nothing more. You didn't even begin to entertain the idea that I might also work Monday to Friday. But I do. I have a weekly schedule and I head out in Candy for the CBD to take cupcakes and coffee to the masses.' She lifted a shoulder and let it drop. 'Or, at least, to office workers. You won't believe the number of people who now treat themselves to a weekly cupcake for morning or afternoon tea.'

Wow.

'I thought you'd know better than to pigeonhole me like you did.'

Everything inside him stilled.

'You've been in jail. I know what people say about you. They think once a criminal always a criminal. They think a man like you can't be trusted and is only out for whatever he can get. And they're still going to think that when your name's cleared because it doesn't change the fact that you were in prison.'

Each word was a knife to the sorest part of him.

'*I* haven't treated you like that.'

She hadn't, but he kept waiting for her to. His stomach

started to churn. That was hardly fair, though, was it? She'd shown him nothing but…friendship.

'I also happen to know what people think of me—the pampered society princess who has never had to lift a finger one day in her life.' She strode over and stabbed a finger to his shoulder. 'Well, I'm not useless and I'm not a failure and I'm not…I'm not useless!'

He grabbed the finger that kept jabbing at him and curled his hand around it. 'You're not useless, Princess. You're amazing. Completely amazing and I'm sorry I misjudged you.'

She tried to tug her hand free but he wouldn't let her. 'You really are skint?'

She stopped struggling to frown at him. 'Yes.'

'Yet amid all of your own troubles you've found the time to help me.'

'Help or hound?'

He chuckled and a warmth he'd never experienced washed over him. 'Thank you for cleaning my cottage.'

'You're welcome.'

God, such vulnerability in those wide green eyes, such softness and sweetness beckoned in those lips. She smelt like sugar and frosting and all the things he'd ever longed for. An ache gripped him so hard he had to drag in a breath. 'Princess…' The endearment scraped out of him, raw with need and longing.

She swayed towards him, those green eyes lowering to his lips. The pulse at the base of her throat fluttered faster and faster. Her hand tightened in his.

He gripped her chin and lifted it, needing to taste her so badly he thought he might fall to his knees from the force of it. Desire licked fire through his veins. He moved in close—so close he could taste her breath—but the expression in her eyes froze him.

They glittered. With tears.

'Don't you dare kiss me out of pity.'

She didn't move out of his hold and he knew then she was as caught up in the grip of desire as him.

'Please, Rick. Don't kiss me because you feel sorry for me.'

The tears trembled, but they didn't fall. Every muscle he had screamed a protest, but he released her and stepped back. He swallowed twice before he was sure his voice would work. 'Pity was the last thing on my mind, Princess. So was guilt and feeling apologetic.'

It was just…he'd allowed himself to see her properly for the first time and it had blown him away. He needed to get away from her, to find a sense of balance again. 'I just…' he dragged a hand back through his hair '…I just think it'd be a really bad idea to kiss you.'

'Definitely.'

He glanced at her sharply, but he couldn't see any irony or sarcasm in her face.

She tossed her head. 'Besides, I don't want you or anyone else to think I'm taking advantage of you.'

He almost laughed. 'Take advantage of me?' That'd be the day.

She waved an impatient hand in the air. 'You know what I mean—seducing you so you'll fix up my house all spick and span.' She glared. 'I can stand on my own two feet.'

He glanced at Candy. 'I don't doubt that for a moment.' Did she ever take a day off?

'Right.' She smoothed down her skirt. 'Good. I had some keys cut for you—the front and back doors and the gate here in the fence.'

There was an awkward moment where she held them out to him and he tried to take them and they danced around each other, trying not to touch. In the end she tossed them in the air and he caught them.

'Now, if you don't mind…' She collected her coffee mug from where she'd set it on the ground. 'I'm going to go have a much-needed shower.'

'There's something else we need to talk about, Princess.'

She turned back.

'Those jewels can't stay in the cottage while I'm living there.'

'But—'

'I've been to prison, Nell, and I'm not going back. If those jewels go missing the finger will be pointed at me.'

'Not by me!'

She said that now. 'You need to put them in a safety deposit box, because I'm not risking it.'

The shadows in Rick's eyes told Nell exactly what prison had been like. Oh, not in detail, perhaps, but in essence. She suppressed a shiver. 'I didn't think of that,' she finally said.

When really what she wanted to say was *kiss me, kiss me, kiss me*. Not that kissing would do either one of them any good.

She stroked her fingers down her throat. It might help iron out some kinks…scratch an itch or two.

Oh, stop it! Be sensible.

She cleared her throat. 'Is it okay if I collect them first thing in the morning? As soon as it opens I'll take them to the bank for safekeeping.'

For a moment she thought he might insist on her taking them now, but eventually he nodded. 'First thing.'

With a nod, she backed out of the garage and fled for the house, leaving him to close up, or to drive his car around, or whatever he pleased.

She sat, planted her elbows on the kitchen table and massaged her temples. Dear Lord, she had to fight this attraction to Rick because he was right—kissing would be a bad, *bad* idea. It'd end in tears—hers. The minute Rick discovered his sibling's identity he'd be out of town so fast she wouldn't see him for dust.

As a kid she'd dreamed of Rick riding up and rescuing her—like the prince rescuing Rapunzel from her tower.

That had all been immature fantasising mixed up with guilt, yearning and loneliness. It hadn't been based on any kind of reality.

It hadn't factored in Rick going to jail.

It hadn't factored in that she could, in fact, save herself.

She shot to her feet. 'I am a strong woman who can make her dreams come true.'

She kept repeating that all the way to the shower.

During the next week Nell marvelled at the progress Rick made on the house. He transformed the parlour from something tired and battered into a room gleaming with promise. He'd done something to the fireplace—blackened it, perhaps—that highlighted the fancy tile-work surrounding it. The mantelpiece shone.

It didn't mean they became cosy and buddy-buddy, though. They edged around as if the other were some kind of incendiary device that would explode at the slightest provocation.

When Nell returned home in the afternoons she and Rick would chat—carefully, briefly. Rick would either continue with whatever he was doing or retire to the cottage. She'd start watching one of the spy movies she'd borrowed from the video store or would investigate code breaking on the Internet. To no great effect.

'Oh, for heaven's sake! This is a waste of time.' She slammed down the lid of her laptop. Biting her lip, she reached out to pat it. The last thing she needed was to have to go out and buy a new computer.

'Not having any luck?'

She glanced up to find Rick in the doorway. Wearing a tool belt. Her knees went a bit wonky. She swallowed first to make sure her voice would work. 'I've trawled every website and watched every darn movie ever made about codes and code breaking and yet I'm still none the wiser.'

She pulled the piece of paper on which she'd scrawled the code towards her.

'*LCL 217, POAL 163, TSATF 8, AMND 64, ARWAV 33, TMOTF 102,*' she read, even though she'd memorised it.

'I don't get it, not one little bit, and I'm tired of feeling stupid!'

He didn't say anything.

She leapt up. It took an effort of will not to kick the table leg. 'Why on earth did he make it so hard?'

'Because he doesn't want me to find the answer.'

'Why tell you at all then?'

'To chase away his guilt? To feel as if he were doing the right thing and giving me some sort of chance at figuring it out?'

To chase away his guilt? In the same way he'd chased Rick away? Her stomach churned. And then she frowned. 'Rick, it's Saturday.'

'Yup.'

'You don't have to work weekends.'

'Why not? You do.'

She blinked.

'I want to attach the new locks I bought for the parlour windows. I've been trying to work that code out all morning and now I want to hammer something.'

She blew out a breath. John's code had evidently left him feeling as frustrated as it had her. 'You haven't given me the receipts for those locks yet.'

His gaze slid away. 'I can't find where I put them. I'll hunt them up tonight and give them to you on Monday.'

That was what he'd said on Wednesday.

'I might not be rolling in money, but I have enough to cover the work you quoted me.' Besides, he couldn't exactly be rolling in it himself. 'Fixing up this house is exactly what I choose to do with my money.' Well, that and eat.

'And I had some questions about the library,' he added as if she hadn't spoken. 'If you have the time…'

Something shifted in the darkness of his eyes, but she couldn't tell what, only that it made her pulse quicken. She scowled. 'Are they questions I'll be able to answer?'

He grinned. It was swift and sudden and slayed her where she stood. 'Colour schemes and stuff.'

She stuck her nose in the air. '*That* I can do. I've been trained by the best. Piece of cake.'

'Speaking of cake...' His gaze searched the table.

She rolled her eyes. 'Yes, yes, there're cupcakes in the cake tin. Help yourself.' It suddenly occurred to her... 'I didn't make you any sandwiches. Would you like me—?'

'Nope, not necessary. Sandwiches Monday to Friday was the deal.'

'Was it?' When he grinned at her like that she forgot her very name and which way was up. She had no hope of recalling anything more complicated. She swung away. 'Nell,' she murmured under her breath. She pointed to the ceiling. 'Up.'

'Talking to yourself, Princess.'

The warm laughter in his voice wrapped around the base of her spine, making her shiver. 'Library,' she muttered instead, pointing and then leading the way through the house.

'It's a nice room,' Rick said from the doorway.

She tried to stop her gaze from gobbling him up where he stood. 'I used to spend a lot of time in here as a child. It was my favourite room.' She hadn't disturbed anyone in here.

'You were a bookworm?'

The look he sent her had her rolling her shoulders. 'Uh-huh.'

He moved into the room. 'Do you mean to keep all of these books in here when you open for business?'

She hadn't thought that far ahead. 'All of the leather-bound collections will probably remain in here—the room wouldn't earn the term library if there were no books.' She trailed her fingers along one wall of glass-enclosed bookcases. 'But I'll take my old worn favourites upstairs. They're a bit tatty now. I suppose I could put some pretty ornaments on the shelves here and there for interest and—'

She stopped dead and just stared.

'What?' Rick spoke sharply and she suspected the blood had all but drained from her face.

'*POAL*,' she managed faintly.

'*POAL 163*,' he corrected.

She opened one of the bookcase doors and dropped to her knees in front of it. She ran a finger along the spines. 'I'd have never got it. Not in a million years.'

'What are you talking about?' He strode across to her, his voice rough and dark. 'Don't play games with me, Nell.'

She grabbed his arm and dragged him down to the floor beside her. 'Look.' She pointed to a book spine.

'*Lady Chatterley's Lover*,' he growled. 'So what?'

'*LCL*.' She pointed to the next spine along. '*Portrait of a Lady—POAL. The Sound and the Fury, A Midsummer Night's Dream, A Room with a View, The Mill on the Floss*. These are my first-year literature texts from university. She pulled out *Lady Chatterley's Lover* and handed it to him. 'Open it at page two hundred and seventeen.'

She had no idea if she were right or not, but...

He turned the pages over with strong, sure hands. They both caught their breath when the page revealed a single sheet of folded paper.

He handed her back the book and she could have sworn his hand trembled. 'It could just be some note or other you made.'

Her heart burned as the conflicting emotions of hope and pessimism warred in his dark eyes. 'It could be,' she agreed, though she didn't think it was. There'd only be one way to find out—if he unfolded it—but she didn't try to hurry him. She couldn't imagine what it must be like to suddenly discover you had a sibling you'd never heard about before.

He leapt to his feet and strode away. She swallowed back the ball of hurt that lodged in her throat. He wasn't obliged to share the contents of John's message with her. She stared instead at the book and waited for him to say something, her heart thumping and her temples pounding.

'A *T.*'

She turned to find him holding up the sheet of paper bearing the single letter. His lips twisted. 'He did say he wasn't going to make it easy, didn't he?'

She gathered up the other five books. 'Obviously it's going to spell something out. Maybe a name.' This room was devoid of any furniture so she took the books back through to the kitchen and set them on the table before walking away.

'Where are you going?'

He spoke sharply and she spun around. 'I thought you might like some privacy.'

He cocked an eyebrow, all tough-guy badness in a blink of his eye. 'Aren't you curious?'

She wished she could say no. 'Of course I am. I'm burning up with it.'

'Then stay. We'd have never got this far if it weren't for you.'

She didn't need any further encouragement. She moved back to the table and watched silently as he laid the six letters out. When he was done they both stood back and stared at it.

THE SUN

A growl left her throat. 'What the bloody hell is that supposed to be and what's all this nonsense of *X*, *C* and *M* on the last card?'

'Roman numerals,' Rick said, leaning over to look at them more closely. 'I think it's a date.'

He straightened. Nell stiffened. '*The Sun,*' they said at the same time, referring to a Sydney newspaper.

'I'm not good with Roman numerals.' Nell moved back around to her computer. 'But there's bound to be a site on the web that can tell us what that date might be.'

Rick didn't move. 'It's the twenty-sixth of May in the year of two thousand and thirteen.'

That was almost a year ago now. 'The paper is bound to archive its back issues online.' She went to the newspaper's homepage, flicked through several screens and found the paper issued for the twenty-sixth of May. All the while she was aware of Rick standing on the other side of the table, unmoving, and it started to worry her. 'Rick!'

He started and glanced her way. It hit her that inactivity wasn't good for him. 'Here, I found the right paper. I think. You do the search while I organise cake and coffee.'

Searching would keep him focused. Organising afternoon tea would give her something to do with her hands other than fidget.

He took her seat. 'What do you reckon—search the personal classifieds for some coded message?'

She growled. 'It better not be too coded.'

He laughed and turned his attention back to the computer screen.

She measured out coffee and set cupcakes on a plate— Citrus Burst, Pine Lime, Vanilla Cream and Café au Lait. She almost swiped a finger through the frosting of the coffee cupcake, but pulled back at the last minute. It had taken her a lot of work to lose her teenage puppy fat. As soon as she had her Victorian teahouse up and running she meant to enjoy the fruits of her labours to her heart's content and to hell with her waistline. But until then…

Her nose curled. It was a well-known fact that slender women received more chances and better opportunities than plump women. It wasn't fair. In her opinion it was downright scandalous, but she didn't have too many assets—a big house that was threatening to crumble down around her, her ability to cook the best cupcakes on the planet and a trim figure. She meant to make the most of all of them while she could.

Behind her, she sensed Rick's sudden stillness. She swung to him. 'Well?' Her voice came out choked, as if she had an entire cupcake lodged in her throat.

'There's a message here…for me.'

Her heart gave a giant kick. 'Does he tell you…?'

'No. The message reads: *Rick Bradford. Many Happy Returns.*'

The twenty-sixth of May was his birthday?

'*You've exceeded expectations. For she's a jolly good fellow.*'

'She?' That couldn't be right, surely?

'She,' he repeated.

'Do you think that's some oblique way of saying your unknown sibling is a sister?'

'I think he's referring to you.'

Her?

'*Return on the thirteenth of March.*'

She slammed the plate of cupcakes to the table. 'Return where?' she shouted.

'I think he means to the classifieds in the newspaper.' He leaned back. 'Which means he put some thought into all of this before he died—paid for these ads well in advance. I wonder how many years' worth he organised.'

The intricacy of John's scheme stunned her. 'The thirteenth of March is only a couple of weeks away.' She bared her teeth. 'That is if he's referring to this year. There's no guarantee of that, of course.'

'*All will be revealed then if you have the eyes to see it.*'

She opened a kitchen cupboard just so she could slam it shut again. 'That's what I think of that!'

'And it ends with *Hip Hip Hooray!*'

'Oh, and that's worth its weight,' she snarled.

He laughed. 'He was right about one thing. You are a

jolly good fellow. I'd never have got this far if it hadn't been for you.'

'Well, of course you wouldn't!' she exploded, pacing up and down. 'That's the whole stupid point, isn't it? How could you ever have possibly traced that stupid code to bits of paper in *my* books? How would you have ever known about *my* stupid marigold tin? How dare he risk everything on something so…so tenuous! How could he risk… All of it hangs on such a thin thread that could've broken at any time.' She slashed a hand through the air. 'How could he know I'd keep helping you? How could he know you'd even stick around? How could he know that I hadn't sold the house?'

'He couldn't.'

She stared at the plate of colourful cupcakes and made a fist. Rick dragged the plate towards him out of harm's way.

'Princess, it's not worth getting all hot under the collar about.'

'Not worth…' She started to shake.

'You're really furious at him, aren't you?'

She had a feeling they weren't talking about John any more. 'Yes,' she gritted out. Because whether they were talking about her father or his, it was true on both counts. 'How dare he drag me into his nasty little game!'

Again, that counted on both heads.

'What right did he have? What…'

The air went out of her and she sat with a thump.

Rick leaned towards her, his eyes wary. 'Uh, Nell… you okay?'

She swallowed. 'Earlier you said that he might be trying to make himself feel better…to make amends.'

'Yeah, so?'

'That's what this is about. He wants me to make amends too.'

CHAPTER SEVEN

RICK PULLED UP short when he strode into the kitchen to find Nell drinking coffee and eating cupcakes.

At ten on a Wednesday morning.

He counted two cupcake wrappers, which meant she was steadily making her way through a third. He frowned. That wasn't the way to eat one of those cupcakes! Every mouthful should be savoured to the full.

She didn't look up. He rubbed the back of his neck. 'Good morning.'

She continued to glare at the table. 'Morning.' Bite. Chew. Swallow.

Okay, take two. 'I ducked out to grab a few supplies. I ran out of sugar soap and sandpaper.'

'You don't need to justify your movements, Rick. I believe you'll keep your side of the bargain. The how and when is entirely up to you.'

He should leave her be and get back to sanding and painting, keep it all on a work footing. He hesitated and then pulled out a chair and sat. 'You don't need to justify your movements to me either, but what on earth are you doing at home—' eating cupcakes as if they were nothing more extraordinary than a digestive '—when peak morning tea time is about to hit Sydney's CBD?'

She ate more cupcake. Her shoulders hunched. 'Candy has broken down.'

He grimaced. 'She's at the garage being repaired?'

More cupcake and more shoulder hunching. 'No.'

'Why not?'

Finally she looked at him. He tried not to wince at the lines of strain that bracketed her mouth. 'Because of these.' She held up a pile of opened letters. 'Bills.' She then proceeded to set each one down onto the table, barking out the amount due. 'It adds up to more than half of what I have left in my account. At the moment I'm not sure I can afford to get Candy fixed.'

Yet without Candy on the road she wouldn't be able to earn the money to pay those bills.

If there was something he'd learned in the last fortnight—other than the fact he really wanted to kiss her—it was that Nell worked like a Trojan. If anyone deserved to cop a break, she did.

'How much money are you expecting to come in from your party orders and how much do you have outstanding?'

She blew out a breath, pushed her plate away and pulled her laptop towards her. 'Let's see…' Her fingers danced across the keyboard.

He came around the table to peer over her shoulder. What he saw made him frown. 'Princess, there're half a dozen orders here—' big orders too '—from over three months ago and the bills are still outstanding.'

If her shoulders drooped any further they'd be on a level with the table. He pointed to her spreadsheet. 'Look—here, here and here.' The movement brought him in close so her hair tickled his jaw and the sugar-drenched scent of her made his mouth water. He moved back a few inches to stop himself from doing something stupid. 'These three orders on their own would cover the cost of your bills.'

'I know, but…'

She leapt up and he shot back, dodging her chair before it could do him a serious injury. She paced to the end of the table and then spun back, flinging an arm in the air.

'How do you make people pay? I've sent each of them

at least three reminder letters. I've spoken to them on the phone and each time I've been assured the cheque is in the mail. Funny thing is, though, none of those cheques have yet materialised.'

'Do you know if any of these people are in financial difficulties?'

'No! That's the thing. I mean I have written off a couple of debts because I found out…'

She'd written those debts off because she knew what it was like, hadn't she? Because she had an amazing ability to empathise with others—something he'd have never expected in someone from her background. But then he'd misjudged her on so many levels.

It didn't change several salient facts. 'Do you think it's either reasonable or responsible to order a party load of cupcakes if you can't afford it?'

For a long moment she didn't say anything. 'I shudder to think how many bills my father didn't pay.'

'They weren't your responsibility, Princess.' And in the meantime people with the wherewithal to pay took advantage of her. He ground his teeth together.

She merely shrugged. 'You want to know something funny?'

From the tone of her voice he suspected he wasn't going to find whatever it was either amusing or humorous. 'What's that?'

'Each of those people—' she gestured to the computer '—with the outstanding debts; I thought they were my friends.'

It took an effort of will to keep his shoulders loose and relaxed. Two things were certain. Firstly, these people were not friends and secondly, she couldn't afford to write those debts off.

'What you need to do, Princess, is hire a money collector.'

She gazed at him blankly.

'And, as you currently have me at your disposal...'

She stilled. For a glorious moment her eyes gleamed that extraordinary emerald-green that made him want to kiss her all over again. 'Ooh, I couldn't...'

'You have no choice.'

He'd had experience of money collectors from the other side of the fence—they'd visited his mother and grand-mother on a too regular basis. But it meant he knew the grim and forbidding demeanour, and he knew how to come across as threatening without actually threatening someone illegally. He'd threaten this lot with exposure in the local paper if they didn't cough up.

She shifted from one foot to the other.

'You worked hard for that money.'

'I know, but...'

'Nell, if you don't have the stomach for this then maybe you need to rethink your plans for Whittaker House.'

She stiffened at that. Without another word she printed off those three bills and handed them to him. He glanced at them and nodded when he saw they contained all the information he needed—names, addresses and amounts outstanding.

'Please don't frighten them.'

'Of course not.' He crossed his fingers behind his back. After he was done they'd think twice before failing to pay a bill again.

'I mean...this will be seriously humiliating for them.'

He'd make sure of it. These people hadn't just humili-ated Nell—they'd hurt her, had tried to bully her. They were supposed to be her friends, for goodness' sake!

'And just so you know...' she moistened her lips '...the Fenimores have a Rottweiler.'

He tried not to focus on the shine of her lips. Or on the sweet curve of her lower lip and the way it seemed to swell under his gaze. He snapped away.

This attraction between him and Nell was crazy. It

couldn't go anywhere. Acting on it would be a stupid thing to do.

But glorious.

He ignored the insidious voice and tried to concentrate on the conversation. 'Is he vicious?'

'Not in the slightest. He's a big softie. Call their bluff if they…' She lifted a shoulder.

He almost laughed at that, but it wouldn't have been a pretty laugh. He didn't bother telling Nell that he didn't respond well to threats. He'd deal with the Fenimores.

Before he left, however… 'Nell, sit. We need to have a tough talk.'

She eyed him uncertainly, but did as he asked. He knew these bills were merely the tip of Nell's financial troubles. He'd been working on that darn business plan of hers and there wasn't a bank manager in Sydney who'd lend her a red cent unless she put Whittaker House up as collateral. He told her that now in plain unvarnished English.

'But—'

'I'm not telling you this because I want to make your life difficult, but you need to know the truth.' The panic that raced through her eyes clutched at his heart. 'Nell, I know you loved your grandmother.'

'Yes, of course, but…'

But what did that have to do with anything? He could see the question in her eyes even if she didn't ask it out loud. 'How badly do you want to save Whittaker House? How badly do you want to turn it into a Victorian teahouse?'

She shot to her feet and clenched her hands so hard she shook. 'It's the most important thing in the world to me.'

Because she wanted to honour the memory of the only person who'd shown her unconditional love? Because she wanted to prove she wasn't useless and that she could make a success of her life? Because she had nothing else in her life? *Oh, Princess, you deserve so much more.*

The last thought disturbed him. He shook it off. 'You really want it more than anything?'

'Yes.' Her chin lifted.

Stop thinking about kissing her! 'So you're prepared to make sacrifices?'

'Of course I am!'

His heart grew heavy in his chest. 'You have a source of income that will get you started and keep you out of trouble for a long while. Nell, you need to sell your grandmother's diamond ring.' And probably the emerald as well.

The last of the colour leached from her face. She sat.

He found himself crouching in front of her and clasping her hands. 'It's not a betrayal of your grandmother.'

'Then why does it feel that way?'

'If she were here now, what would she tell you to do?'

'I...'

'Did she place more value on things rather than people?'

'No! She...' She gave a half-laugh full of love...and loss. 'She'd just want me to be happy. If she'd ever had to choose between her diamond ring or this house she'd have sold the ring in an instant.'

He waited and eventually she lifted her chin and squeezed his hands. 'You're right. It's time to be practical. My grandmother's spirit doesn't reside in a few pieces of jewellery.'

He stood and moved back. Holding Nell's hand when she was upset was one thing. Holding it when she fired back to life was altogether different.

Different and compelling and bewitching.

'Besides, those jewels would've been more trouble than they're worth. I'd have had to be constantly looking over my shoulder waiting for my father to try and take them.'

Rick had grown up among people like that, but it made his gut clench that the Princess had experienced it too.

'For heaven's sake, look at me! Sitting around here comfort eating and feeling sorry for myself. How pathetic!'

She was a lot of things, but pathetic wasn't one of them.

He shifted his weight. 'If someone offered you a pot of gold to get you out of this fix…and it'd mean you'd get to keep your grandmother's rings, would you accept it?'

She bit her lip and then shook her head. 'No.'

He breathed easier.

'I want to do this under my own steam.'

Good.

'So while you go and play bailiff I'm going to get my grandmother's ring out of the safety deposit box and make an appointment with a jewellery evaluator. An antique piece like that…it might even be worth placing in an auction.'

A coil of tension in his chest loosened at the colour in her cheeks and the sparkle in her eyes. *Way to go, Princess.*

'I think it might be a good idea for me to attend that appointment with you.'

She stared at him and then a Cheshire cat grin slanted across her face. 'While I have absolutely no intention of being taken advantage of, I think that's an excellent plan. I dare anyone to even think of it while you have my back.'

Exactly. 'I'll see you back here in a couple of hours.'

'Won't you need more time?'

The addresses were all within twenty minutes of Nell's house. 'I don't think so.' He made for the door.

'Rick.' She bit her lip. 'Don't let any of them make you feel like a second-class citizen. You have more true honour in your pinkie finger than any of them have in their entire bodies.'

Something inside him expanded. He couldn't utter a word.

'And you—you who have every reason to bear me a grudge—have shown me more true friendship than just about anyone.'

As she spoke she moved towards him. All he could do was watch. Common sense told him to back up, but his feet refused to move. Reaching up on tiptoe, she kissed his cheek, drenching him in all of her sweetness. A groan rose in his throat, but he swallowed it back.

'Thank you.'

The sincerity of it shook him loose. 'No sweat, Princess.' He had to break the moment or something would happen—something earth-shattering that had the potential to break both of them.

It doesn't have to.

But it would. Guys like him didn't end up with girls like her.

He cleared his throat. 'I don't suppose you could spare a cupcake or two for a hardworking bailiff on his weary travels?'

She laughed at that, retrieved a large cardboard box of them and pushed it into his hands. 'Maybe you could leave one with each of them as a gesture of…goodwill.'

He grinned. 'Behind that pretty face you're evil, you know?'

She blinked.

'Because we both know one cupcake is never enough.'

That slow smile spread across her face again. 'Give them hell, Rick.'

He tipped an imaginary hat at her and left. He fully intended to.

Rick returned to find Nell waiting for him. She immediately leapt up to put the kettle on to boil. 'How did it go? Were they horrible to you? Did they say mean things to you?'

Not: *Did you get my money?* Not: *Was the mission successful?* But: *Were they horrible to you?* He stopped dead and just stared.

Her face darkened. 'They were.' He watched in a kind of bemusement as her hands clenched. 'I'm sorry! I shouldn't have asked that of you. I should've done my own dirty work and—'

'I had a ball.'

She eyed him warily. 'You did?' she finally ventured.

He could see she didn't believe him. 'Ever since I got out of jail, people like those clients of yours have made me feel like scum. I can't tell you how satisfying it was to turn the tables. Do you have any more outstanding debts I can deal with?'

That surprised a laugh out of her—as it was meant to. She pushed him into a chair, set a plate of sandwiches in front of him and grabbed him a beer. 'One thing's for sure. You've earned lunch.'

She stood over him then with arms folded. He glanced up, a sandwich halted halfway to his mouth. 'What?'

'I don't think you should let anyone make you feel like scum.'

That was easier said than done, but... It struck him then that Nell had only ever treated him as an equal—someone deserving of respect and consideration.

The realisation tightened his chest. He bit into the sandwich then took a swig of his beer. Neither loosened the tension growing inside him. He pulled three cheques from his pocket and handed them to her.

She flicked through them and her eyes widened. 'You managed to get them to sign cheques for the *entire* amounts outstanding?'

He wanted to puff out his chest at the delight bubbling up through her. 'What were you expecting?'

'More promises. Part payment at best.' She perched on a chair across the table from him and crossed a leg. 'It couldn't have been easy.'

'Princess, it was a piece of cake.'

Nell stared at him. It might've been simple for him, but there was no way on God's green she'd have been able to manage this same outcome. She checked the amount on the cheques again. 'This is amazing.'

He was amazing.

'This will keep the wolf from the door for a little while.' Enough to give her some breathing space at least.

'Were you really friends with those people?'

Some of the golden delight leached out of her. 'I thought we were.' If a single one of those people had found themselves in the same desperate financial straits that she had, she wouldn't have dropped them. She might not have been able to give them financial aid, but she'd have offered them moral support. She'd—

'Princess?'

She snapped to. Although she tried to keep her face composed she couldn't stop her lips from twisting. 'It seems my entire life has been a series of very poor judgement calls.' Letting her parents browbeat her into saying Rick had taken her locket; working so hard to earn her parents' love and approval to discover that they'd never been worth the effort, that they didn't know the meaning of the word love; spending her free time with people who only liked her when she was successful—shallow, callous people who enjoyed playing power games with those less fortunate than themselves.

It wasn't noble, but... 'I hope you gave them a seriously hard time.'

'I can assure you that they didn't enjoy the experience.'

The warmth in his eyes almost undid her. She leapt up to pour herself a glass of water. 'Oh, here.' She pulled a velvet pouch from her handbag. 'My grandmother's ring. You might like to keep a hold of it.'

'No.'

She frowned. 'I thought you were going to be my muscle, my brawn...my hard man.' It'd be safer with him than with her.

'You keep hold of the ring and I'll guard you.' There wasn't an ounce of compromise in his eyes. Slowly she pocketed it again, recalling his words when he'd demanded the jewels be removed from the cottage. *I've been to prison, Nell, and I'm not going back.*

Bile churned in her stomach. Jail must've been hell. Pure hell. She wished he'd been spared that.

'Did you make an appointment for a valuation?'

'Yes, we're to meet with the evaluator in an hour.'

He stopped eating to stare at her. It felt as if his gaze reached right down into her soul. She swallowed and wanted to look away, but she couldn't. 'You sure you're okay with this?' he said.

Was he afraid she'd become hysterical partway through negotiations?

'I wish things could be otherwise, but that's just not possible. So, yes, I'm okay with this.'

And because she didn't want him to read any of the other thoughts rising up through her, she backed towards the hallway. 'I'll just go powder my nose and get ready.'

He didn't call anything teasing after her and she wondered if he'd read her thoughts despite her best efforts. Thoughts of kissing him, of the need that pummelled her whenever he was near...of how close she'd come earlier to throwing herself at him.

Oh, that would've been another sterling example of her brilliant judgement. Rick might want her. She knew enough to know what the heat in his eyes meant when he looked at her a certain way. She knew that these days men found her attractive. And she knew she found Rick attractive, but where would it lead? To heartbreak, that was where.

Rick wasn't a criminal, but he was a heartbreaker. He'd made it clear that he had no intention of sticking around once he solved the mystery his father had set him. And she didn't fool herself that she'd be the woman to change his mind.

She was through with fairy tales. From here on she dealt in reality.

* * *

'I'm sorry, Ms Smythe-Whittaker, but this ring is a copy… a fake.'

The room spun, the ground beneath her feet bucked, and Nell had to reach out and grip the countertop in front of her.

'Mind you, it's a very good copy. It wouldn't have been cheap to have had this made.' The jeweller peered at the ring through his eyeglass again. 'But there's no doubt about it. The stone is just a very cleverly cut crystal and not a diamond.'

It was Rick's hand at her elbow that finally stopped the room from spinning. It took all her strength, but she gathered the shreds of her composure around her. 'How disappointing.'

'I am sorry, Ms Smythe-Whittaker.'

'I am too, but I do thank you for taking the time to look at it. I can't tell you how much I appreciate it.'

He handed her the ring. 'Any time. It's been a pleasure.'

Nell, with a silent Rick at her back, left the shop.

'Could he have been mistaken…or lying?'

She shook her head. 'The man has an impeccable reputation. He would never consider taking a bribe from my father to suggest the ring was a fake. He wouldn't risk his professional standing like that.'

'Nell—'

'Please, not here. Let's wait till we get home.' A home she might not be able to keep for much longer. A lump lodged in her throat. She swallowed, but that only shifted the heaviness to her chest.

Could she give up the idea of her gorgeous Victorian high teas and get a real job?

Doing what? Who would employ her? And even if she could get a job, the likelihood of making a wage that could manage the upkeep of Whittaker House was so slim as to be laughable.

She didn't realise they'd reached home until she found

herself pushed into a chair with a glass of something foul-smelling pressed into her hand. 'Drink,' Rick ordered.

Obeying was easier than arguing. She tipped the glass back and swallowed the contents whole.

'Omigod!' She gasped for air. She choked and coughed and struggled to breathe.

'That's better.'

'Better? What are you trying to do? Poison me!'

'You've at least some colour in your cheeks again.'

She bit her lip. *Dear Lord...* 'Have I gone pathetic again?'

'There's nothing pathetic about you, Princess. You've just had a nasty shock.'

She held her glass back out to him. 'May I have another one of those? It was very...bracing.'

He took the glass with a laugh and handed her a soda instead.

'I see we're being sensible now,' she grumbled.

'If you want to get roaring drunk we'll need to find you something better than cooking brandy.'

He had a point. Besides, she didn't want to get roaring drunk. Not really. She hunched over her can of soda, twirling it around and around on the spot.

'So...obviously my father ransacked the jewels before John hid the box.'

'But why have a copy made? Why go to that bother?'

She stared at him. 'That's true. He didn't go to the same trouble for the diamond necklace, did he?'

'Unless John moved the box before he had a chance to.'

She turned the question over in her mind. 'No,' she finally said. 'He wouldn't go to that effort just for me. He'd simply laugh as if he'd bettered me, got one up on me. He'd tell me to suck it up.'

On the table Rick's hand clenched. 'I'm fairly certain I don't like your father.'

Ditto.

She blew out a breath. 'He must've pawned that ring while my grandmother was still alive. He's not afraid of me, but he'd have been afraid of her retribution.' She twirled her can around a few more times, running a finger through the condensation that formed around it. 'Which means I'd better not pin my hopes on anything else in that box.'

'Nell…'

She glanced up at the tone of his voice. She immediately straightened at the expression on his face. 'What's wrong?'

'You're aware that I had both the means and the opportunity to take something from that jewellery box and to have had a copy made.'

'Oh, right, in all of your spare time in the what—one night it stayed there?'

'I knew about it for two nights.'

She folded her arms. All the better to resist the urge to pitch her soda at him. 'I've already told you more than once that I don't believe you're a thief. How many more times do I have to say it before you believe me?' If her glare could blister paint, the wall behind him should be peeling by now. 'Why are you so determined for me to think badly of you?'

He dragged a hand down his face and her chest cramped and started to ache. He *didn't* want her to think badly of him, but he kept expecting her to because that was how people treated him. She didn't blame him for this particular chip on his shoulder, but she wasn't 'people'.

He held up a hand to forestall her. 'If a complaint were made, I'd be a major suspect.'

'Oh, for heaven's sake, who's going to make a complaint? I can assure you that I won't.' Though it'd serve her father right if she did and the scandal was splashed all over the papers. But it wouldn't bring Grandma's ring back. 'And the only other interested party—my grandmother— is dead. I think you can rest easy on that head, don't you?'

He sat back as if she'd punched the air out of him. 'You really believe I'm not a thief.'

She pulled out her most supercilious shrug. 'I refuse to repeat myself on that head ever again.'

He laughed. 'You're an extraordinary woman, you know that?'

'Uh-huh, extraordinary and broke.'

He grinned, a sexy devil of a smile that made her heart lurch and her pulse beat like a crazy thing. She should look away, be sensible, but it seemed as if the fire from the brandy had seeped into her blood.

'Would you like a cupcake?' she offered.

'I'd love one, but I better not. You'd read me the riot act if I told you how many of those things I've eaten today.'

'With Candy breaking down, it's not like I didn't have plenty to spare,' she mumbled.

His grin only widened.

'Oh, okay!' she snapped. 'I'll take the bait. How come are you so darn happy when my life is imploding around me?'

He leaned towards her. 'Let me lend you the money, Nell.'

Her jaw dropped.

'I have the funds. Doing your business plan, I've calculated how much you need.' He named a sum. 'I've more than enough in the kitty to cover it.'

Her jaw dropped lower.

'And, believe me, if there's one person who can make a success out of a crazy Victorian teahouse, then, Princess, that person is you.'

CHAPTER EIGHT

NELL STARED AT RICK. For a moment she didn't know what to say. She moistened her lips. 'I can't let you risk your money like that.'

'Taking risks is how I've made my money. As far as I'm concerned, this is the safest risk I've taken with it so far.'

Did he mean that? For some reason his certainty only brought her insecurities rushing to the surface. 'You can't know that! You can't know that I'll pull this off. It may all end in disaster and—'

'I've yet to meet anyone who works as hard as you.'

His dark eyes fixed on her with an intensity that dried her mouth and sent her heart twirling and jumping with the kind of exuberance that made it impossible to catch her breath.

He rose, went to the sideboard and pulled the file containing all her clippings and notes from a drawer. 'I stumbled across this last week. I wasn't snooping. I was looking for string.'

She swallowed and pointed. 'Next drawer along.'

'I know that now.'

She stared at the folder and shrugged. 'That's just a whole bunch of pictures and ideas I've collected and...' She trailed off.

He reached across the table and took her hand. 'It's a whole lot more than that.'

Okay, there were recipes and menus and table settings

and names of businesses she might be able to use. There were colour schemes for Victorian houses, teapots, and anything else that had taken her fancy that she thought might prove inspirational for her own venture. She'd have to get a bigger folder soon because that one was bursting at the seams and she was adding to it all the time.

'This helped me visualise your dream.'

His hand on hers was warm and it seemed to be melting her from the inside out.

'Rick, I—'

'It made me see your Victorian teahouse wasn't some last-ditch plan to save your skin, but...'

She tried to pull her hand away, but his grip only tightened. 'Nell?'

She couldn't resist him. Not when he said her name like that. She lifted her gaze to his.

'This is a dream of long standing. It's something you've thought long and hard about. You have the drive and the work ethic to make a success of this business.'

His thumb stroked her wrist in lazy circles. She wanted to stretch and purr at his touch.

'I'm cynical enough to know that's not necessarily a recipe for success.'

'Well, of course not,' she said, because she had to say something and that slow circling of his thumb was addling her brain.

'But you have an X factor.'

His thumb stopped its stroking and the cessation added weight to his words.

'An X factor?' *What on earth...?* Had he had too much sun today?

'Talent.'

Everything inside her stilled.

'Your cupcakes could make grown men weep.'

'Oh, anyone can learn to do that.' She pulled her hand from his to wave it in the air. She'd reclaimed it deliberately.

Rick was treading on her dreams—admittedly very carefully—but if he suddenly became lead-footed she wasn't sure she could bear it.

He shook his head. 'Nobody makes cupcakes like you. Why are you determined to dismiss that as if it's of little value?'

Not holding his hand didn't help at all. She reached across the table to lace her fingers through his. 'The thing is, Rick, it doesn't actually seem like much. After twenty-five years of privileged living it seems the only talent I've acquired is to make cupcakes. I know they're pretty good, but...' She shrugged. As much as she tried to channel non-chalance, she'd never felt more naked in her life.

'They're not just good. They're spectacular. They're the kind of cupcakes people travel hundreds of kilometres for.'

She laughed. 'Now you're just being silly.'

'And you're wrong. You're good at lots of things. You're running your own small business, aren't you?'

'Not very successfully if today is anything to go by.'

'You troubleshot that.'

He'd troubleshot that.

'You have social poise and that's rarer than you know. It'll hold you in good stead as the face of the business when the teahouse is up and running—you'll need it. You also have vision and courage and you're not afraid of hard work or sacrifice.'

She opened her mouth, but he held up a hand to forestall her. 'Sorry, Princess, but you're not going to talk me out of believing in you.'

Unconsciously, her hand tightened in his. 'You believe in me?' she whispered.

'Heart and soul.'

Her heart leapt.

'I believe in you so much I'm willing to lay out the money you need to get your business off the ground.'

A lump the size of a teapot lodged in her throat. Nobody had ever told her they believed in her before.

'So will you accept my loan and make this dream of yours a reality?'

She really wanted to say yes, but the lump refused to dislodge. She stared at him and his face gentled as if he could read what was on her mind. He reached out his fingers as if to touch her cheek. She held her breath…

He snapped away.

They shook their hands free.

Bad idea. Touching of any kind. They both knew it was a bad idea.

'I'd best warn you, though, that there'll be some stipulations that come with the loan.'

Finally she was able to harness the strength to swallow deeply enough to clear her throat. 'Like?'

'It won't be interest free.'

'Of course not!'

Though she had a feeling that was just a sop thrown to her pride. Still… 'This can't be charity, Rick. It's business. I will be paying you back at business loan interest rates.'

'You bet it's business and I want it to succeed. It's in my best interests that it succeeds, which is why I want you to drop back to three days on the road with Candy.'

'But—'

'You need to start focusing some real energy on the new venture or call it quits right now.'

'I…'

'Between your weekend orders and three days out in Candy, you'll still be making enough to live on while you get Whittaker House ready. Your personal expenses are incredibly low…for a princess.'

They both knew her living expenses were incredibly low full stop. Circumstances demanded it. He might call her a princess but she lived like a pauper in her rundown castle.

'And you'll have the loan to cover the larger expenses like land rates and power bills.'

He was taking a risk and he was demanding that she take a risk too.

'Well?'

Her heart thumped. 'Yes, thank you, Rick. I would very much like to accept your offer.'

When Nell reached out a hand Rick shook it. He didn't keep hold of it like he wanted, though. The more time he spent in her company the more he wanted to touch her.

You only need to hold out for another couple of weeks. Once he found out the identity of his sibling he'd leave.

And go where?

Who cared? Just somewhere different where the people didn't know him, where they didn't whisper behind his back.

Nell's not like that.

Yeah, but Nell was one in a million. The fierce gladness that had gripped him when she'd accepted his offer of a loan, though, had taken him off guard.

But...

It was just...

The Princess deserved a break.

He leaned back in his chair, assumed his usual swagger. 'I'll organise to have the funds transferred into your account early next week.'

She peered down her nose at him. 'You need to have a contract drawn up.'

Whatever. He trusted her. His grin widened when she didn't ask the question he could see burning in her face. 'You're just dying of curiosity, aren't you?'

She lifted her chin. 'I have no idea what you're talking about.'

He laughed. 'You want to know how I came to have so much money.'

He watched her manners wrestle with her curiosity.

'Okay, you win. Yes, I do. I want to know how you came to have so much money that you can offer to help…' her lips twisted '…damsels.'

'You're no damsel, Princess. If you were some helpless woman looking for a man to make it all right I wouldn't still be here. Damsels are afraid of independence, hard work and taking risks. None of those things apply to you.'

She leaned back and folded her arms. 'It doesn't answer the question of how you made your money, though, does it? Or why you live even more cheaply than I do.' She frowned. 'Are you lending me all of your money?'

'No.'

Behind the glorious green of her eyes her mind raced. 'Have you left yourself enough money to cover emergencies and the like if they crop up?'

'Yes.'

She pursed her lips and he almost laughed out loud when he realised she didn't believe him. Did she really think he'd be as Sir Galahad as all that? The thought had him shifting on his chair.

'What percentage of your savings have you just lent me?'

And because he could see she was on the brink of pulling back he told her the truth. 'About five per cent.' And that was a conservative estimate. He had so much money he found it hard to keep specific figures in mind.

She stared. She seized a pen and piece of paper and did the maths. She held up the amount she came up with.

'That'd be about right.'

'You're a millionaire. Several times over.'

It wasn't a question so he didn't say anything.

She blew out a breath. 'That's a relief. I can stop worrying that I'll be leaving you short.'

Something muddied the green of her eyes. For reasons he couldn't begin to explain, a bad taste coated his tongue. Was she going to try to hit him up for more money? Would she—

'I'm glad you have money.' Those incredible eyes met his. 'How did you do it?'

Her surprise rankled. 'Shocked?' he taunted.

'To the soles of my feet,' she returned, evidently undaunted by his glare.

'Not to be expected of the jailbird?'

She maintained his gaze and it was so steady it made his heart thump. 'You're the one who keeps reminding everyone that you were in jail.'

Yeah, well, it was better to get in first than be taken by surprise when your guard was down.

'And you never qualify it with the fact your name has been cleared.' She frowned then glared. 'What is that about?'

Her question hit too closely to the sore spots inside him. 'When I was in prison a fellow inmate taught me how to count cards.'

Her eyes turned a murky green like a sea churned up by a storm. 'Was it horrible?' she whispered. 'Prison, I mean. Was it awful?'

Nobody had ever asked him that before. Nobody. And it ripped all his defences from him.

'Rick?'

The sympathy in her eyes, the care in her face, tore something in him. 'It was worse than awful.' The words burst from him before he could stop them. She reached out with both of her hands to grip one of his. 'There are men in there so terrifying they freeze your blood. I didn't think I would get out of that place alive.'

Memories, dark and powerful, pounded at him, one after the other. He rested his head on his free hand and gripped Nell's hands tightly, ordered himself to keep breathing. 'The things you have to do in there to survive... I thought anything in me that was good and kind would be gone for good.'

'But that didn't happen.'

That was when he realised her touch anchored him. He lifted his head and met her gaze. 'I'm not convinced about that, Princess.'

'I am.'

Her belief pushed back some of the darkness. 'How can you be so sure?'

'Tash is still friends with you. She wouldn't be if you'd changed that much. You've been kind to me. You want me to have the opportunity to follow my dream. Someone with no good left in them wouldn't care about that. And someone with nothing good or kind in them wouldn't care if they had ten unknown siblings who needed them or not.'

'I don't know if I do care about that yet.'

'You care enough to find out what their circumstances are like.'

His heart thumped.

Her gaze refused to release his. 'I'm sorry you went to prison. I'm sorry you had to suffer through all of the horror of it. But, whatever else you believe, know this. It didn't destroy who you are. It didn't destroy your honour and integrity. It didn't even destroy your sense of humour or your ability to appreciate the little things. I don't doubt that prison left you with scars, but you're a man in a million and don't let the naysayers convince you otherwise.'

He wanted to believe her with everything he had. He pulled in a breath, unable to deal with all of the confusion raging through him, the pain of remembering that time and all it had stolen from him. He pushed it all away to some deep inner depth where he hoped it'd never see the light of day again. 'I guess it did have its silver lining.'

She choked. 'I beg your pardon?'

'Like I said, I learned to count cards. When I was released from jail I was hired by a building firm. It was one of those parole programmes the powers that be are so gung-ho for. Anyway, I took my first pay packet to the casino and trebled it. Next fortnight I did the same. Within six months I'd made ten times my original winnings.'

'You made your money gambling?'

'I moved from one form of gambling to another. Once I had enough money I traded in blackjack for the stock market. I started making some decent investments, took some risks which paid off.'

'Where did you learn about the stock market?'

'One of the benefits of prison is access to education. I did a business course. Like I said, silver linings.'

Nell leapt up, poured herself a glass of water and drained it. 'You're saying that if it wasn't for prison you wouldn't be rich.'

'That's exactly what I'm saying.'

'What do you think your life would've been like if you hadn't gone to jail?'

He shrugged. 'I'd have ended up working in your father's glass factory or one of the auto parts factories. I'd probably have played on the local football team and I guess I'd have eventually settled down—got married and had a couple of kids.'

She stared down into her glass. 'That sounds kind of nice.'

Yeah, it did.

'But you speak as if none of that's possible now.'

It wasn't.

'You have all this money and yet this is how you choose to live—drifting around like a vagrant as if you don't have two dimes to rub together?'

'I'm not hurting anyone.'

She stared at him. Eventually she nodded. 'You're a good man, Rick—you're kind and you'd rather help than hinder—but prison did steal something from you.'

He stiffened. 'You want to explain that?'

'It stole your courage.'

His head snapped back.

'Before you went to jail you had dreams. Now...' She shrugged. 'Now you're too scared to dream.'

Her words sliced through him.

'Because if you did, you wouldn't choose to live your life the way you do.'

A film of ice covered him from head to foot. 'How I live my life is no concern of yours.' He stabbed a finger at her for added emphasis. 'It's no business of yours.'

Nell shrugged as if his coldness couldn't touch her. 'You're a hypocrite too.' She turned away to wash the dishes in the sink.

His jaw dropped, but he doubted she'd noticed. 'I'm lending you a ludicrous amount of money and all I get is abuse?'

She glanced over her shoulder and raised an eyebrow. 'You want me all doe-eyed and grateful?'

Actually, if he were honest, he wanted her hot and sweaty and horizontal.

'I don't think so,' she snorted. 'I have a feeling doe-eyed would have you running for the hills, tough guy.'

He ran a finger around the collar of his shirt.

'If you intend to concern yourself with my affairs then you can jolly well put up with me concerning myself with yours.'

He thrust out his jaw. 'I'll take back that offer of a loan.'

She turned and planted sudsy hands on her hips. They made damp patches on her dress and he found it hard to look away. 'Go on then,' she said.

He opened his mouth. He stared at those sudsy hands and swore. Nell merely laughed. 'You can't because you're too nice a man.'

Nobody called him nice.

'It's called friendship, Rick.'

He stilled. She went back to washing the last of the

dishes. Friendship. Had the Princess just offered him friendship?

Actually, he saw now that she'd offered it the moment he'd shared John's letter with her.

Back-alley guys like him didn't end up with uptown girls like the Princess, but... But it didn't mean they couldn't be friends, did it?

He rolled his shoulders. He stretched his neck first one way then the other. 'You never told me what was wrong with Candy.'

She pulled the plug and reached for a tea towel. 'The roadside assistance guy who got me started again said something about...points and plugs? Are they something that belong in a car?'

He bit back a grin. 'Yep.'

'Well, apparently they need replacing and so does my... alternator?'

She asked the last as if checking she had that word right too.

'Is that all?' His shoulders rolled suddenly free. 'I can fix that for you. I'll need to grab some parts, but all up it should cost less than two hundred dollars. Mind you, the shop would charge four times that to cover labour.'

She tossed the tea towel and slammed her hands to her hips again. 'Is there anything you can't do?'

He found himself laughing. Nell made him feel young— young and alive and free. 'You can deal with sleazy solicitors and smarmy estate agents and I can debt collect and fix cars.'

'You haven't seen under Candy's hood. What makes you so sure you can fix her?'

'I spent a ludicrous amount of time in my misspent youth with the guys in the neighbourhood trying to keep our rust-bucket cars on the road. I even helped restore a couple.'

She took a step towards him, her face alive. 'From scratch?' He nodded and her smile widened. 'What fun!'

The Princess was interested in cars? 'C'mon—' he hitched his head in the direction of the door '—let's go take a look.'

When they reached the garage, Rick popped Candy's bonnet. 'Tell me what you know about the engine.'

She wrinkled her nose. 'I'm afraid it's not much.'

She looked so pretty in her 1950s-style dress and heels peering into the workings of the old van it was all he could do not to kiss her. 'That doesn't matter.'

'I don't know what any of it does, but I know that's where I put in water if it's running low.' She touched the radiator cap. 'And that's where I put in the oil.'

'You put in your own oil?'

'A man at the garage showed me how. It's a cinch. Way easier than making cupcakes.'

All he could do was stare.

'So what are plugs and points and an alternator? What do they do?'

He pulled off the distributor cap and pointed to the plugs and points and explained how they worked. She asked questions—intelligent questions—and before he knew what they were about they'd dismantled the alternator from the van and had it spread on the floor of the garage.

'It's fascinating!'

She went to brush a strand of hair from her face, but he caught hold of her hand before she could. He turned it over and pointed. 'I'm thinking you don't want to smear grease all over your face or through your hair.'

She stared at both of her hands in astonishment. 'Heavens, this is messier than gardening...and just as much fun.'

The grin she shot him almost slayed him where he crouched.

'I think it'd be wonderful to be able to repair a car.'

'I can teach you how to change plugs and points. When we get a new alternator I'll show you how to install it. And if you want I'll even teach you how to do a grease and oil change. I warn you, though, it's a mucky business.'

Nell stared at Rick and was almost too afraid to breathe. 'You will? Really truly?'

'Sure I will.'

She'd get covered in grease, she'd break fingernails, and it'd be one more step towards becoming independent and not useless.

And it'd be fun!

It hit her then that she'd been so busy trying to plug all the holes in her life that she'd forgotten about fun.

She couldn't stop herself from beaming at Rick. 'Thank you!'

He grinned that slow grin that could turn a woman's world upside down. Her heart pounded up into her throat and back again to bam-bam in her chest and she couldn't have reached into her wardrobe of shrugs and pulled one on now for all the money in the Reserve Bank.

She didn't care about shrugs. She cared about learning new things and making a success of her life and…

And she cared about Rick.

As a friend.

Somewhere inside her a metaphorical eyebrow lifted. She swallowed and glanced back over at him. His smile had faded. Those dark eyes fixed on her with an intensity that froze everything—even the air—and then it all rushed back, wind roaring in her ears, and she swayed.

Rick reached out to steady her, but she shot to her feet and stumbled. He rose too—as if attached to her by some invisible string—and again he reached out a hand to steady her. 'You're a bit wobbly on your feet there, Princess.'

She didn't know if it were the touch on her arm or the way his teasing swagger didn't quite reach his eyes, but the ability to lie had deserted her. Either that or she'd flung it away recklessly. And she hadn't done anything reckless in fifteen years.

'I've been off balance ever since I saw you standing on my front veranda, Rick.'

All signs of teasing fled. 'Princess…'

One of his fingers slid up her arm. She glanced down at it. 'That's not helping.' But the finger didn't stop—it moved back down from her elbow to her wrist, tracing a path along the inside of her arm.

She wanted to dash herself against him like a wave against a rock and encompass him completely. And still that finger trailed paths of spiralling heat and delight across her skin.

'That makes both of us, Princess, because I find it hard to remember my own name when I'm around you.'

They'd cast pretence aside. She lifted her chin. 'I know you find me attractive sometimes.'

'All the time.'

'And I know there's a lot of reasons why I shouldn't kiss you and you shouldn't kiss me.'

'Uh-huh.'

'But I can't remember any of them at the moment so you better start reciting them to me, Rick, because…'

'Because?'

They moved an inch closer to each other. 'Because kissing you is the only thing I can think of.'

They reached for each other…and stopped at the same time. Nell glanced at her greasy hands. Rick glanced at his. She didn't want to ruin his shirt, but… 'I don't care about my dress,' she whispered.

His mouth hooked up in *that* way. 'But I like that dress. The things I dream of doing to you while you're wearing that dress would make you blush, Princess.'

She hadn't known her heart could beat any harder. She hadn't known her skin could flare with so much heat.

'I care about the dress…' But his words emerged on a

rough growl and they wrapped around the base of her spine until she trembled with the force of it.

His hand reached for hers, their fingers lacing. One tug brought them chest to chest. He glanced down at her and his eyes darkened. Very slowly she slid against him, relishing the feel of his hard chest against her softness.

His quick intake of breath curled her toes. 'It seems we don't need hands,' he murmured.

His thumb brushed against the sensitive pulse point of her wrist. Very slowly she turned her hands so his spooned them before dancing her fingers across the backs of his fingers and then lacing them through his again. 'I like hands.' The words came out on short, jerky breaths.

His hands tightened about hers. She tried to glance up at him, but her gaze caught on the pulse pounding at the base of his jaw. She ached to touch her lips to the spot. She wanted—

'Princess?'

She looked up at his hoarse rasp.

Very slowly his lips descended towards hers. She held his hands tightly as the world tilted and, leaning her weight against him, she reached up on tiptoe to help close the distance between them.

And finally their lips touched.

CHAPTER NINE

THEIR LIPS TOUCHED, their mouths opened, and the world spun away from Nell as the taste and feel of Rick filled her. The only thing that mattered was the way his mouth moved over hers—tender but firm, slow yet sure, practised but with a hint of tentativeness that spoke of his desire to please. It told her that the same stunned delirium that coursed through her veins coursed through his.

He nibbled her bottom lip and she moaned, arching against him, feeling anything might be possible in this moment, feeling she could be anything she wanted to be in this moment and that would be okay.

His lips slanted over hers again, less tentative, more urgent, and she met him kiss for kiss, deepening it at the same moment that he did—tongues dancing, teasing, awakening.

She'd thought he'd taste dark and dangerous…like the shadows she sometimes saw in his eyes, but he tasted like cupcakes—all vanilla and spice—and her sweet tooth sat up and begged. He tasted of every good thing she'd never had in her life before. He tasted of all the good things she wanted to be in her life—smart, capable, competent. He tasted like…life.

She wanted to crawl inside his skin or to pull him inside hers. He kissed her back as if he wanted that too. They kissed until they had no oxygen left and then very slowly they eased away from each other, fingers still entwined.

She touched her tongue to her bottom lip and sucked it

into her mouth. He watched with those dark eyes. 'Wow, that was something,' she said when she could finally speak.

He frowned. 'Yeah, it was.'

She frowned then too. 'There's a problem with that?'

'Kisses like that feel like promises and I can't make you any of those, Princess.'

Can't or won't? Reality slammed back into place. She shook her hands free of his and snatched up a clean rag to clench them in. 'I told you there were a lot of reasons we shouldn't kiss.'

She backed up to lean against Candy's side, needing the support for knees that threatened to give way. 'I don't do short-term flings.'

He adjusted his stance and blew out a breath. 'Yet they're the only kind of relationships I have.'

'Strike One.'

She stared down at the rag, shut her eyes for a moment before lifting her chin and tossing back her hair. 'Everyone thinks I'm going to solve my current financial difficulties by finding a rich husband or boyfriend. You're rich. Strike Two.'

He slammed his hands to his hips. She opened her mouth to remind him about the grease and oil, but it was too late. His glare made her mouth dry. 'You're counting me out because I'm rich?'

She pushed upright from the van. 'I'm counting you out because you're rich *and* you can't commit. I'm not going to let you try to buy me off to salve a guilty conscience.'

His jaw clenched so hard she thought he might snap teeth. She pulled in a breath, held it for the count of three and released it.

'It's three strikes before I'm out. What's Strike Three?' he demanded.

She reached for, and found, her most supercilious shrug. 'What? Do you want me to do all of the hard work? Can't

you possibly come up with a reason or ten of your own?'
She made her voice deliberately scornful.

His eyes narrowed. Very slowly he sauntered to where
she stood. Every instinct she had screamed for her to run.
Except for those rogue ones that told her to grab him and
kiss him again.

She squared her chin, forced herself to meet his gaze.

'You're confusing me with your lily-livered, pretty society boys, Princess. You won't get gallant manners from
me. I'm debating the benefits of simply taking what I
want—what, in fact, may be freely on offer—and to hell
with the consequences.'

He slanted a deliberately insolent gaze down the length
of her body and, to her horror, her nipples tightened and
her thighs softened. How could he be so ruthless?

'Taking it and enjoying it…over and over—and, believe
me, Princess, you'd enjoy it too—until I was sated.'

Her body responded to the smoky seduction of his voice.

'I know how to make a woman want…how to make her
respond and to yield.'

She didn't doubt that for a moment.

'And what I want right now is you writhing beneath me,
begging for release and calling my name as you come with
the kind of orgasm that would blow your mind.'

Her breath caught and her stomach clenched. 'Why?'
The word croaked out of her.

'The Princess submitting to the local bad-boy and begging for more—how satisfying would that be? What a triumph.'

She wanted him. His words set her body on fire. But
they chilled her too. She didn't doubt that, if he put his mind
to it, he could seduce her. She'd succumb. And it'd break
her heart.

She met his gaze. 'If you do that, I will put you through
as much hell as you do me. You might, in fact, be able to

seduce me, but don't doubt for a moment that I have the ability to make you pay.'

They stared at each other for long fraught moments. He lifted his hand as if to touch the backs of his fingers to her cheek, but he stepped back with a low laugh and let his hand drop. 'We're not all that different after all, are we, Princess?'

'No.' But she didn't know if that were a strike against them or not.

They didn't speak again. Nell headed for the door of the garage. Rick turned back to Candy's engine. It didn't stop the burn in her body. It didn't stop the burn in her mind. It didn't stop the insane urge she had to throw herself face first onto the nearest available garden bench to cry.

She didn't. She just kept walking towards the house.

The money Rick promised arrived in her bank account the following Monday. Her bank manager rang to tell her the good news—and to try and pump her for information. She didn't tell him anything, but she frowned as she snapped her cellphone shut. Her father and the bank manager were still as thick as thieves. It'd mean her father would now hear about the upswing in her fortunes.

She should've taken the time and trouble to switch banks, but with everything else going on…

She shook the thought off. She'd deal with her father when she needed to and not before.

She and Rick were careful not to spend too much time in each other's company. He fixed Candy. He painted the drawing room and the library. She baked and delivered orders and went out in Candy—on Monday, Tuesday and Wednesday.

She waited till Thursday before approaching him. 'You haven't given me a contract to sign yet,' she reminded him.

'Do we really need something that formal?' He didn't look at her as he painted the library wall a soft, lush cream.

'Yes.'

'I'll get onto it.'

She made a sceptical, 'Hmph.' No doubt he'd get onto it the same way he'd got onto those receipts for building materials. She'd yet to see a single one.

The problem with Rick was that he had all of this money, but he simply didn't care about it. He probably wouldn't even notice if she paid him back or not. What he needed was a reason to care.

Her feet slowed. *Maybe...*

She came to a complete stop. *Well, why not?*

She made a beeline for the telephone to call her lawyer.

Rick started at the knock on his door on Friday evening. He glanced at his watch. It'd just gone six. *Who on earth...?*

Nell.

For a moment he was tempted to pretend he wasn't in. *Prison stole your courage.*

With a muttered oath, he stormed over to the door and flung it open. Nell stood on the other side. Holding a bottle of champagne. Holy Mother of God! She wasn't going to try and seduce him, was she? Damn it, he wouldn't stand a chance and—

'Hello, Rick.'

It took all his strength not to shut the door in her face. 'What are you doing here, Nell?' He didn't have to work hard at making his voice unwelcoming. It came out that way. His only other option was to drag her into his arms and kiss her until neither one of them could think straight.

It'd taken all of his strength not to seduce her last week—every single ounce of it. He hadn't been able to re-call anything he'd wanted more than to lose himself in her sweetness, to forget himself, to let himself believe in fairy tales if only for a few brief moments, to see if she could help heal the dark places inside him. He still wanted that with a fierceness that shocked him. And a man had only so much strength.

He hadn't seduced her then and he couldn't seduce her now. Nell deserved better from him. She deserved better from the world.

'Aren't you going to invite me in?'

'Do you think that wise?'

'I don't mean to stay long.'

He glanced at the champagne bottle and raised an eyebrow.

She laughed. 'I don't have shenanigans in mind. I just wanted to deliver this.' She held up an official-looking A4 business-size envelope.

Biting back a sigh, he moved to let her in, careful to keep his distance. 'What is it?'

She handed it to him. 'Open it and see.'

She sauntered across to the kitchen as if she owned the place. Which, technically speaking, she did. She reached up into the cupboard for two glasses. She didn't seem to mind that they were old food jars rather than champagne flutes. The cork of the champagne left the bottle with a pop. She didn't send it flying across the room, nor did she let a single drop of champagne fizz out of the bottle and onto the floor. She poured the bubbly, lifted both glasses and turned back to him.

'Well, open it.' She nodded at the envelope he still held. 'It's not an evil omen or bad news. I promise.'

God give him patience. He lifted the flap and slid out the single sheet of paper inside. He read it.

His heart stopped. The edges of his vision darkened. He blinked and read it again. His throat started to ache. She pushed one of the glasses into his hands, clinked it with hers and took a sip. He couldn't move.

'I wanted to say thank you, Rick.'

But...

'You've lent me the money that will allow me to follow

my dream. I doubt there's anything I can do or say to tell you what that means to me. But I want you to know my gratitude is real, that I don't take your financial assistance for granted and that if, in the future, I can ever do you a good turn then I'll do my absolute best to deliver on that.'

He couldn't move and he couldn't speak. The ache in his throat travelled to his arms, his chest, his temples.

She set her glass on the tiny kitchen table, wiped her hands down the skirt of her Hawaiian frock. 'Well, that's all I wanted to say. I'll be off now. Enjoy your evening.'

'Nell…' He managed to croak out her name before she reached the door.

She turned.

'You've…you've…' She'd given him a thirty per cent share of her business! 'You can't do this.'

She frowned. 'Yes, I can.' Her frown deepened. 'Why not?'

'It's too much.'

Her face cleared. 'No, it's not. I talked it over with a lawyer. He assures me that's fair.'

'But I don't care about the money I'm lending you!'

She gave a little laugh, but there was more sadness in it than joy. 'I know, but I do. I care about it hugely. It means so much to me and I…I want to try and show you how much.'

She'd managed that, but…

'And I wanted…' her fingers clutched at the air as if trying to find the words to explain '…I wanted to give you something back that might mean something to you. That's all.'

He rustled the paper entitling him to thirty per cent of her business under her nose. Was she crazy? 'You're giving me power over your dream!'

'Yes.'

She said that simply, as if it were no big thing, when it was the biggest thing he knew.

'I could destroy it!'

'Without you, my business had no chance of getting off the ground in the first place.'

'You shouldn't give anyone this kind of power over you.'

She moved forward and clasped his face in her hands and bizarrely it felt as if she held his heart instead. Those amazing green eyes blazed at him. 'I keep telling you that I trust you. Maybe now I've shown you how much.'

She pulled her hands away slowly, as if she'd have rather left them there. He stamped on the primal, savage impulses pounding through him. Impulses that ordered him to grab her and kiss her and to make her his.

She backed up a step as if she sensed the fight taking place inside him. Her eyes spoke of her own primal battle. He bit back a groan. She shot him a brave little smile. 'Enjoy the champagne.' And then she was gone.

Rick stumbled over to the sofa and collapsed onto it. He knocked back a generous slug of champagne, coughing when the bubbles hit the back of his throat. He stared at the paper in his hands entitling him to thirty per cent of her business.

I trust you.

Thirty per cent!

Maybe now I've shown you how much.

Oh, she'd done that all right. Nobody had shown this much faith in him. Not ever. And he didn't know what to do with it. Just as he didn't know what to do with the conflicting emotions coursing through him—a mixture of dread and elation, fear and satisfaction.

Enjoy the champagne.

With a laugh, he took another sip. It was good stuff. The Princess didn't skimp at the big moments.

He paused halfway through his third sip. Maybe she had some ulterior motive, maybe…

His shoulders sank back into the softness of the sofa. She didn't have an ulterior motive. She wasn't playing some deep game. Nell had a heart as big as Sydney Harbour.

Something around his heart loosened then and some dark thing slipped away. Nell wanted to give him something important because she believed he deserved it, because she didn't believe he was a no-hoper or a loose cannon, but because she saw something in him that no one else saw.

And it gave him hope.

Not that he knew what he was hoping for.

The next morning—the thirteenth of March—Rick knocked on Nell's back door where before he'd have just strolled in. Before—as in before that kiss. His groin tightened at the memory.

Nell glanced over her shoulder and gestured him in. 'The paper's arrived.'

It sat on her table, still rolled up. She hadn't even had a peek, though he knew her curiosity must be eating her alive. She finished packing up a box of the most mouth-watering-looking cupcakes and set it on the end of the table with a host of other boxes. Pouring mugs of steaming hot coffee, she pushed one into his hand and sat at her usual spot at the table. She rolled the paper across to his usual spot.

A bad taste rose up in his mouth. He gulped coffee to chase it away. Nell stared at the paper and her nose curled. 'C'mon, then, there's no point in putting it off. We may as well find out what wild goose chase John means to send us on next.'

Us? He tried to resist the warmth the word threaded through him. 'Nell, you know you don't have to—'

'Yeah, right. Blah-blah fishcakes. You'd have never got this far without me, and you're not cutting me out of the game now.'

How was it this woman could make him grin at the most unlikely moments?

'And, look, I know it's not a game. I'm not trying to trivialise it.'

He knew that. He raised an eyebrow. 'Blah-blah fish-cakes?'

'It's a wonderful phrase, don't you think? I mean to do my bit to bring it back into the common vernacular.'

She'd donned her prim and proper, hoity-toity princess manners, but he knew her well enough by now to know it for a sign of nerves.

'I'm not going to push you out of this, Princess. Rest easy. I just wanted to give you the chance to back out if that's what you'd prefer.'

She snorted in a very un-princess-like way. 'Get over yourself, tough guy. Sit. Turn to the classifieds.'

She was right. Putting it off was pointless. With a sigh, he did as she bid.

He pushed his coffee to one side. He didn't want it. He'd had one earlier. The Princess drank far too much of the stuff. He opened his mouth, only to shut it again. Now mightn't be the time for that particular lecture. Instead, he ran his fingers down the line of classifieds. On a Saturday morning the paper was full of birthday and anniversary announcements, of births, deaths and marriages, and personal ads.

His finger stopped. '*Rick*,' he read.

'What is it?' Nell demanded.

'*Freemont Park. Two p.m. Wear your party clothes.*'

'What on earth...?' She leapt out of her chair and came to stand behind him to read over his shoulder, her hand resting lightly against his back. His heart rate kicked up at the warm feel of her. She read John's message, harrumphed and went back to sit in her chair. Rick closed his eyes and pulled in a breath. 'He's proving just as chatty in death as he was in life.'

Rick laughed. Nell flipped open her laptop. 'Okay,

Freemont Park. It's in the south-eastern suburbs. It'll take us the best part of forty minutes to get there.'

Rick thrust out his jaw. 'I'm not wearing party clothes.'

Nell leapt to her feet. 'I'm off to do my deliveries. I'll meet you in the garage at one o'clock sharp. Right?'

He scowled. 'Right.'

Nell and Rick stood on the edge of the park and glanced around at the assorted picnickers and walkers.

'Where in the hell are we supposed to start?'

Rick's face had gone as tight as his shoulders. She clutched a box of cupcakes and pulled air into her lungs. 'It's not a ridiculously large park.'

'It's big enough!'

'We'll just amble for a while.'

She hooked her hand through his elbow and propelled them forward, setting them on a path that led diagonally through the park. They must look an odd couple. She wore her cherry print dress with a red patent leather belt and heels. Rick wore his oldest jeans—torn at the knee—and a tight black T-shirt. He hadn't shaved.

In defiance of John's strictures?

She didn't mind. That T-shirt showed off the breadth of his shoulders to perfection and did rather nice things for his biceps. If he'd stop scowling at their surroundings he'd be downright hot and handsome.

Oh, who was she kidding? He was devastatingly and dangerously delicious, regardless of what expression he wore. And that day-old growth...

She had a vision of being stretched out beside him and running her tongue across his jaw and...

'Any particular reason you're pinching me, Princess?'

Oh! She relaxed her grip and swallowed. 'Sorry.'

She forced her gaze and mind from Rick's, uh, finer points, to focus on their surroundings until her breathing returned to within the realms of normal. The park was lush and green, with distant views of the harbour. Gum trees and Norfolk Island pines swayed in the breeze, providing shade for picnic blankets and camp chairs. Oleanders in lush blooms of pink, white and red added a riot of colour. At one end stood a rotunda amid a rose garden.

The bright sunshine, blue sky and chatter from a flock of nearby rainbow lorikeets spoke of summer, holiday fun and relaxation and something inside her yearned towards it all.

A rowdy and boisterous happy birthday chorus had them both turning to their right. They moved off the path and onto the grass, stopping by an oleander in full pink flower to watch.

'Happy birthday, dear Poppy…'

She couldn't help smiling. There had to be a crowd of at least twenty people—of varying ages—and everyone was smiling and jolly. An ache started up inside her chest. 'I always wanted a family like this,' she whispered. People who loved each other—enjoyed each other's company—and wanted to spend time together.

'Me too.'

Of course he had. She had no right to moan when one compared her childhood to his.

They continued to watch. Small children danced around, elderly folk sat in chairs, and everyone else stood as they hip-hip-hoorayed. What must it be like to be the focus of all that love? The birthday girl cut the cake, but her back was mostly to them. She mightn't be able to see it, but Nell could imagine the breadth of the girl's smile.

Oh, if only this could be Rick's new family!

'Poppy is a botanical name,' she offered.

'Grasping at straws, aren't you?'

Probably. With a shrug, she turned back to survey the party. And then the birthday girl swung around and Nell's breath jammed in her throat.

Oh, my God!

Oh! My! God!

When she was able to tear her gaze away she glanced up at Rick. Had he seen it? The family resemblance was unmistakable.

Rick's eyes had fixed on the girl's face. His jaw clenched tight and his chest rose and fell as if he'd been running. 'How old do you think she is?'

The words growled out of him and Nell had to swallow before she could speak. 'Eighteen or nineteen.' She had no idea what to do.

A woman, probably in her late forties, turned at that moment and saw them. With a smile, she set off towards them. With a curse, Rick turned and strode away, his long legs eating up the distance.

'Oh, Rick, wait! I—'

'Hello?'

Nell turned and hoped her smile didn't appear as sick and green as she felt. 'Um, hello. I… Well, we…I…kind of received an invitation.' It wasn't precisely a lie.

'You must be one of Poppy's friends. I'm her mother, Marigold Somers.'

Marigold! She reached out to steady herself against the oleander.

'Is everything okay with your friend?'

Oh, dear Lord. 'He…he had to take an urgent phone call.'

'Never mind, come and join the party.'

'Oh, I don't think I can.'

The woman stared at her.

Um...what to do? 'You see, my invitation came from a rather unusual source and…' She bit her lip. 'My name is Nell Smythe-Whittaker and I don't know Poppy, but I believe you knew my late gardener and…'

The woman blanched. 'Oh, please, no!'

The distress in Marigold's face tore at her. She reached out to clasp the other woman's hand. 'Oh, please, I haven't come to cause you any trouble, but…'

'But?'

'Did you know John died?'

She swallowed and nodded. 'Yes.'

'Did you know he left behind another child?'

Her jaw slackened. 'You?'

'Not me.'

'Your friend?'

'I…'

Others in the group were starting to glance in their direction. Nell didn't want to create a scene. It wasn't her scene to create. She wanted to find Rick. That was what she really wanted to do. She pushed the box of cupcakes into Marigold's hands. 'Say they're from a secret admirer. My card is taped to the lid. Please call me?'

The other woman nodded and, before anyone else from the party could approach, Nell turned and made her way back the way she'd come—as quickly as she could on grass in heels.

So…

They'd found Rick's sibling. Finally. She didn't blame him for his shock, but… *Oh, my word.* To be a part of such a family! Her heart pounded against her ribcage, the blood raced through her veins. Still, there were so many variables. Did Poppy know she was John's child? And how would she react to discovering she had a brother?

And, of course, there was Rick.

He was waiting for her in the car. She slid into the passenger seat, turned to him and opened her mouth.

'Don't.'

She winced at the darkness in his eyes.

'Put your seat belt on.'

Once she had he pulled the car onto the road and roared away from the park. She glanced once more at him before keeping her eyes fixed to the front. Swallowing, she tried to put herself in his shoes. It had to be a shock to come face to face with someone who looked so much like you.

The shock she understood, but the anger…?

After a moment she shook her head. No, she understood that too and Rick was entitled to it. How dared John and Marigold keep such secrets? How dared John taunt Rick with a vision of a life that had been closed to him his entire childhood?

And how dared John father children he'd had no intention of nurturing!

When they arrived home, Nell leapt out of the car to open the gate to the garage. Rick drove in, just as silent as he'd been for the entire trip back.

She folded her arms and leant against the doorway as he emerged from the car.

He barely met her gaze. 'I'm leaving. Today.'

What the…? She didn't move. 'The hell you are.'

He swung to her with a glare that should've reduced her to ash, but she rushed on before he could blast her with a barrage of abuse. 'You promised me until the end of next week. We signed an agreement. You *will* keep your word.'

He stabbed a finger at her. 'That agreement is not some binding contract! And—'

'Regardless of any of this other nonsense, you owe me.'

'I owe you nothing!'

She agreed with that but had no intention of telling him so. 'I've kept my word to you. In fact, I've more than kept it. You can jolly well do the same.'

'What the hell for?' he shouted at her.

She gripped her hands in front of her. 'Because we're friends and that's what friends do.'

He stilled

'And because none of this situation is of my making.'

He dragged a hand down his face. 'You're right. You don't deserve this from me.'

'The situation isn't of your making either, Rick. You're entitled to your anger.'

He fixed her with that hard gaze. He stalked over to her,

intent outlined in every muscle. 'You promise me right now that you won't interfere any further in this godforsaken mess.'

'What are you going to do about this godforsaken mess?'

'Nothing.'

Her jaw dropped.

'That girl's life is perfect.'

'You can't know that after five minutes of spying from the bushes!'

'And she sure as hell doesn't need someone like me coming in and ruining things.'

'Ruining?' Her jaw worked. 'You're her *brother*.'

'We're strangers.' He fixed her with a glare. 'And you either butt out or I leave now.'

She held up her hands. 'Fine, whatever.' But if he thought this situation had finished playing out he was seriously mistaken.

'And, Nell, I will be leaving at the end of next week.'

She didn't bother trying to disguise the way her face fell. 'I'm sorry about that. I'll miss you, Rick.'

He froze for a moment, closed his eyes and dragged a hand down his face. Nell turned and left. She didn't wait to hear what sop he meant to throw her. It wouldn't help to soften the blow.

Blinking hard, she made her way across the garden…to find the kitchen door open. She had locked it, hadn't she?

She went to call for Rick when a figure appeared in the doorway. 'Good afternoon, Nell.'

Her heart slithered to its knees. She forced her legs forward. 'Hello, Father.'

CHAPTER TEN

NELL MADE COFFEE out of habit. She set a mug in front of her father. She was too tired for games. 'I expect this isn't a social call?'

'I want the money you made from pawning your grandmother's diamond ring.'

It took all of her strength not to throw her coffee at him. She pulled in a breath, held it and then slowly let it out. 'I know you already pawned it and replaced it with a copy, a fake. Why are you playing this game with me?'

He leapt out of his chair so fast it fell to the floor, his face twisting in purple fury. 'It's a what?'

She stilled. For a moment she almost believed him and then she remembered what he was like. 'You're afraid I'll go to the police and that the theft of the jewels will be traced back to you.'

'Those jewels should've been mine!'

'But they were left to me. What a scandal it'd be if it was known you'd hocked your mother's jewels—jewels that rightfully belonged to your daughter. It'd serve you right if I did go to the police.'

He stared at her. Very slowly the ugly colour faded from his cheeks, replaced with a calculating gleam in his eyes that was twice as ugly and had acid burning in her stomach.

She set her coffee down, folded her arms and leaned back against the sink. 'Who told you I'd found the ring?'

'I know you found more than just the ring.'

It took an effort not to sneer. 'I'm getting a new bank manager.'

'I know who you have living here.'

'What business is it of yours?'

'Rick Bradford's a thief, a drug addict and a jailbird.'

Her composure vaporised. Coffee sloshed over the sides of her mug. 'He's a hundred times the man you are!'

He laughed. He actually laughed. He righted his chair, sat and sipped his coffee. 'Daughter, here's how it's going to be. You're putting this house on the market.'

It was her turn to laugh. Oh, this should be good. 'How do you propose to convince me of that?'

'If you don't, I'm going to lodge a complaint with the police. I'm going to tell them your grandmother's jewels were stolen and replaced with copies and where do you think suspicion will fall?'

'You!'

'I'll make sure it falls on your little friend, Rick Bradford.'

Her heart flew up into her throat. She fought for breath. 'It'll never stick. He's innocent!'

He laughed again, and too late she realised her mistake. She'd shown weakness, had bared her Achilles heel.

'I know when he started living here. I know when you placed those jewels in the safety deposit box. I know he had the opportunity.'

No!

'And, given his background, he'd have had the means.'

Rick was innocent!

'He'll be hauled in for questioning. I will bribe men to say he took the rings to them for copies to be made. I will make sure he goes down for it.'

Her heart pounded. She couldn't speak. Would her father really stoop so low? He knew people. He still had connections, but would he really…?

He shook his head, his eyes hard. 'I wasn't born to be a

poor man, Nell, and I have no intention of remaining poor. The sale of this house will get me out of trouble and give me a chance to rebuild my business.'

'And you really don't care who you hurt in the process?'

'It's a dog eat dog world.'

'You really don't care that if you do this I will disown you? That I will never speak to you again?'

He laughed. It was an ugly sound that made her stomach churn. 'You'll come crawling back when you see the money come rolling in, demanding your share. Just like your mother. Yes, you're your mother's daughter. Mind you, I'll be generous.'

She stared at him. Had she ever really known him? 'What a sad life you must have.'

He stiffened.

'You judge your value by the amount of money you have rather than anything more substantial like how good you are at certain things or the good you do or the friends you have. I...I wouldn't want to be like you for all the jewels in Grandma's jewellery box.'

'Excellent.' He rose. 'Then you won't mind handing them over when I return tomorrow with the estate agent. There'll be a sale contract for you to sign.'

Her heart pounded. Sell the house? The house counted for nothing beside Rick's freedom, but... *Oh, Grandma, I'm sorry.*

'You can make all the pretty little moral speeches you want, daughter...'

He said that word as if he owned her. Her chin snapped up. He didn't own her. Nobody owned her. She was her own woman.

'But I don't see you making a success of yourself from whatever it is you're good at. I don't see you doing any good in the world. I don't see you surrounded by loving and loyal friends.'

She forced herself to meet his gaze. 'Maybe not, but

I'm a hundred times the person you are.' And she knew that now, deep down in her bones. 'At least I can sleep at night.'

He blinked.

'You might regain your riches, but you're going to be a very lonely man if you insist on this course.' She gestured to the house. 'If you have any feeling for me whatsoever turn back now and there may still be a chance we could forge some kind of relationship. If you don't...' she pulled in a breath, all the while maintaining eye contact with him '...when I marry, you won't be invited to my wedding. When I have children, you will not be allowed to meet them. And don't bother calling for me when you're on your deathbed because I will not come.'

His gaze hardened. 'You always were a stupid and useless girl.'

The old taunt had her shoulders inching up to her ears. She forced them back down. She wasn't useless.

'I'll bring the estate agent around at eleven on the dot. Be here.'

'It's a Sunday!'

The smile he sent her was pure smug self-satisfaction. 'There are buyers interested, and some people who still jump when I ask it of them.'

Unlike an ungrateful, useless daughter?

He left. Nell limped over to a chair and lowered herself into it. If she didn't do as he ordered, he would send Rick to prison. She didn't doubt his ruthlessness...or how much he wanted the money the sale of Whittaker House would bring. And it wasn't just ruthlessness, but spite. Spite directed at her for not jumping when he demanded it, for not marrying money when he'd ordered it, for not getting him out of his financial straits.

Signing over her apartment and sports car and her trust fund—none of that counted as far as he was concerned. Apparently she was still useless!

She ground her teeth together. She wasn't useless. In fact, that had been a darn fine ultimatum she'd given him. And she'd meant it. Every word. Not that it had done any good. She swallowed, battling nausea. She rubbed her temples. What guarantee did she have that her father wouldn't go after Rick once the house was sold anyway, just to punish her? She might not be useless, but she needed advice.

But who could she turn to?

She tapped her fingers against the wooden table top. Who wouldn't go tattling to her father the minute her back was turned—the sleazy solicitor? Not likely.

The thing was, her father had been right on that head. She wasn't surrounded by an army of loving and loyal friends. She had one friend in the world—Rick—and she wasn't telling him about this. She wasn't giving him the chance to be noble. She didn't need noble.

One friend… She pushed a hand back through her hair. *Useless…*

A moment later she straightened. She mightn't have any friends, but Rick did.

She reached for the phone book, searched and then punched a number into the phone. 'Tash? Hello, it's Nell Smythe-Whittaker. I was wondering if I could possibly trouble Mr King—uh, Mitch—for a quick word?'

'He's not here at the moment. Would you like me to have him drop by some time?'

'Oh, no, not here.' She didn't want Rick to see.

'Would you like to make an appointment at the station?'

'God, no!'

Tash didn't say anything for a moment. 'Nell, are you in some kind of trouble?'

'I…I don't know. And please don't mention this to Rick. I don't need a white knight—I just need some advice.'

'Okay.'

But she drew the word out and Nell knew Tash would

talk to Rick eventually. Her loyalty did reside with him, after all.

She swallowed. 'Would it be possible…I mean would you mind if I came over to your place at a time convenient to both you and Mitch?'

'Sure, why not? Mitch should be here within the next half an hour if you're free this afternoon.'

'Thanks, Tash.'

She knew the other woman didn't think much of her, and she didn't blame her. But at that moment she could've hugged her.

Nell sat opposite Tash and Mitch at Tash's kitchen table and her mouth went dry. What if they accused her of ruining Rick's life? She'd have no answer for that.

'Would you like me to leave the two of you alone?' Tash eventually said.

Nell shook her head. Tash should know what was in the works in case Rick needed her. Besides, it didn't take a genius to work out that Tash and Mitch were besotted with each other. And not just besotted but a team. If Tash left now, Mitch would only fill her in later.

She was the outsider here. And as long as she made sure nothing bad happened to Rick because of her father then it didn't much matter what either Tash or Mitch thought of her.

She lifted her chin. 'I guess I better start at the very beginning so you get the full picture.'

'Sounds like a plan.' Mitch nodded his encouragement and his calm sense helped ease the racing of her pulse and frightened leaps of her heart. She could see why Tash had fallen for him.

She told them how she and Rick had searched John's cottage. She didn't tell them about John's letter, though. That was Rick's secret to tell. She told them about finding the jewellery box and how she'd asked Rick to put it back, thinking it'd be safe there. She told them about the deal she and Rick had come to—rent-free accommodation in return for maintenance work on Whittaker House—and how after one night in the cottage he'd refused to keep the jewels there and how she'd put them in a safety deposit box at the bank.

As she spoke, Tash's face grew darker. Mitch merely listened, his eyes intent, his face revealing nothing of his thoughts.

And then she told them about her father's threats and demands. Tash's face darkened further. She leaned across the table towards Nell, but Nell held up a hand. 'I know, okay, I know. My father is a nasty piece of work. I'll do what he demands...I'll sell my grandmother's house.' Her voice cracked. She swallowed and cleared her throat. 'But none of that will ensure Rick's safety. I mean, once the house is sold and my father has the money, what's to stop him from attempting to press charges against Rick anyway?'

Hell, if her father found out how much money Rick had... The thought made her temples throb.

Tash slumped back. 'You believe Rick is innocent then?'

'Of course he's innocent!' Surely Tash hadn't thought—

'Who do you think is responsible?' Mitch broke in.

'My father, of course.'

Mitch frowned. 'But you said he demanded the money you made from the sale of the ring.'

'No doubt to cover his tracks. He has no right to that jewellery. It was left to me. I could press charges against him if I chose to.' Not that she would.

'The rest of the jewellery is still in the bank?'

'Yes.' First thing on Monday she was changing banks.

'Would you trust me with it?'

She gazed at Mitch. 'Of course I would, but, Mitch, I don't want to make any of this official.'

Tash straightened. 'What do you want?'

'I want to ensure Rick is free from any of this. I want to make sure my father can't go after him.'

Mitch nodded. 'You said you're signing a contract with some estate agent tomorrow?'

'Yes.' She could barely get the word out.

'You're not doing that on your own. I'm sending my solicitor along.'

'I'll pay.'

Tash shook her head. 'We'll sort all of that out later.'

Nell swallowed and fished the diamond ring—the fake diamond ring—from her pocket and set it in front of Mitch. 'I'll retrieve the rest of the jewellery first thing Monday— I expect they'll all be fakes.'

Mitch surveyed the ring. 'Whittaker House is in your name, right? That means, even if a buyer is found immediately, we have six weeks before the property officially changes hands and the bulk of the money is transferred into your account.'

Which she'd then have to transfer to her father.

'That means for at least the next six weeks, Rick is safe.'

A sigh eased out of her. Six weeks of knowing Rick couldn't be hauled in and charged with a crime he hadn't committed. But what then…? All the tension shot back into her.

'If we have to,' Mitch said, 'we'll force your father to sign a clause to the effect that he won't press charges against Rick.'

That could be done? Nell sagged in relief. 'Thank you.'

There didn't seem to be anything else to say after that, so Nell left.

'Damn!' Tash muttered as she and Mitch watched Nell drive away.

Mitch rested an arm across her shoulders. 'What?'

'She's in love with him.'

'Lucky man.'

Tash snorted. 'As soon as he realises he'll bolt.'

'Why?'

She shook her head. 'He just will. It's what he does.'

'She's prepared to make a hell of a sacrifice for him.'

Tash glanced up. 'Will we be able to get him off the hook *and* save her house?'

'We'll give it our best shot.'

She reached up on her tiptoes to kiss him. 'Have I mentioned lately how much I love you?'

Nell wasn't sure what to do when she returned home. Start packing boxes in preparation for her imminent eviction?

She fell into a chair, pulled a box of cupcakes towards her, opened the lid, stared at them for a few moments before pushing them away again. Eating cupcakes wouldn't make her feel better.

She could hear Rick hammering something in the dining room, even though it was past six o'clock on a Saturday evening. She should tell him not to bother. She should tell him...

She dropped her head to the table. How was she going to explain selling Whittaker House to him? She'd have to give him his money back too, of course. The dream of a Victorian teahouse wasn't going to come to fruition any time soon.

She frowned. Had her bank manager traced where that money had come from? If so, had he informed her father? She lifted her head...

To find herself staring at a woman in the doorway.

Marigold.

Marigold shifted her weight from one foot to the other. 'Have I come at a bad time?'

Nell stared and then shot to her feet. 'Of course not. I... Please! Come in.'

She thought about Rick thumping away in the dining

room and swallowed. Dear Lord, all of this could end in tears. Lots of tears.

Mostly hers, probably.

She swallowed, but the uncertainty in the other woman's face caught at her. 'Please, sit down. Can I get you a coffee or a soda?'

Marigold perched on a chair, twisting her hands together, her eyes wide in a pale face and Nell shrugged—nothing practised or elegant, but simply a shrug. 'To heck with that, let's have some wine.'

She pulled a bottle from the fridge, grabbed two glasses and poured. 'You'll have to excuse this—' she handed Marigold a glass '—but it's cheap and cheerful rather than elegant and expensive.'

'If it's alcohol, bring it on.'

'Amen, sister.'

They clinked and drank. Rather deeply. Nell topped up the glasses and then wondered what to do...what to say.

'I remember when you were a little girl.'

Nell's glass halted halfway to her mouth. 'You do?'

'I went to school with your mother. I came to a few parties and afternoon teas here over the years. You'd have not been more than six or seven when I fell pregnant with Poppy.'

'And that's when you stopped coming round?'

Marigold took a gulp of her wine and nodded. 'I met John at one of those parties.'

'And you had an affair?'

Marigold stared down into her wine and a tiny smile touched her lips. 'We did, yes. It was rather short-lived, but intense. We were very careful to keep it secret. If we'd been discovered John would've lost his job and my friends would've...well, they wouldn't have understood.'

Wow! 'And you fell pregnant?'

She nodded and they both gulped wine. 'That's when things turned bad. John wanted nothing to do with a baby.'

Nell swallowed. *Double wow.* 'Do you know why?'

'Not really. I glimpsed something extraordinary in him, but there was a hardness there too. Maybe it's because he grew up in a boys' home and from what I understand it was a rather brutal place. He never said as much, but I don't believe he trusted himself around children. Or maybe he didn't want to be reminded of the childhood he'd had.'

'Does Poppy know he was her father?'

Marigold nodded. 'I told her when she turned fifteen. You see, she knew the man who she calls Dad—my husband Neville, who she adores and who adores her back—wasn't her biological father; we met when she was two. But she really wanted to know who her biological father was… and it only seemed fair to tell her.

'She sent him a letter that he never answered, and she insisted on sending him an invitation to her birthday party every year—the party in the park is an annual tradition. But he never did turn up.'

Nell stared into her glass of cheap wine and recalled the way he hadn't let her plant marigolds. Was it because they'd have reminded him of this woman and a vision of a different life, a different path he could've taken? None of them would ever know now.

A sigh escaped the other woman. 'But if Poppy has a brother…'

Nell glanced up.

'Well, of course, she has every right to know him. I can't prevent that and I wouldn't want to. All I ask is that you give me a chance to tell her about him first, that's all.'

'But of course!'

'I'm sorry I panicked earlier and—'

'Nell!'

Rick's voice boomed down the hallway, his footsteps growing louder. 'Where the hell have you put the masking tape?'

He stopped dead in the doorway. Across the table from

her, Marigold gasped. 'Dear heaven, you're the spitting image.'

Those dark eyes fixed on Nell with an accusation that cut her to her very marrow. Very softly he said, 'Deal's off.' He walked through the kitchen, out of the back door, and she knew he headed for John's cottage to pack. To leave. For good.

'What just happened?' Marigold whispered.

Nell blinked hard. She reached for her wine and tried to force a sip past the lump in her throat. 'Rick is... I don't think he means to make himself known to Poppy. He thinks it'll complicate her life.' *And he thinks I betrayed him.*

Marigold rose. 'I mean to tell Poppy about him. She has a right to know and I don't want there to be any lies between us.'

Nell rose too. Marigold pushed a card into her hands. 'I sincerely hope you can convince that young man to reconsider his decision. Perhaps you'll be kind enough to give him this?'

Nell stared down at the card—a business card with Marigold's phone number and address. 'Yes, of course.'

Marigold left. Nell grabbed her glass of wine and drained it. Then she headed outside for the cottage. She knocked twice—a quick rat-tat—and then opened the door and walked in.

Rick whirled around from throwing things into a hold-all. 'I didn't say you could come in,' he snarled.

'Oh, for heaven's sake, shut up and listen for once, will you?'

He glared. She merely thrust her chin up a little higher. 'You need to know some things.'

'If it's anything to do with Poppy or John-bloody-Cox then no, I don't.'

'Back at the park after you raced off,' she said as if he hadn't spoken, 'I told Marigold that John Cox had another child.'

MICHELLE DOUGLAS   163

'You had no right!'

She snapped herself to her full height. 'If you'd hung around I'd have let you deal with it, but you'd raced off! You left me to improvise the best I could.'

His glare didn't lower by a single degree.

'Marigold—that's Poppy's mother—went pale at the news. So I pushed the box of cupcakes at her, told her my business card was taped to the lid and asked her to contact me. And then I left. That's what happened in the park and that's why Marigold was in the kitchen this afternoon. She didn't ring or give me any warning.'

'You were drinking wine together!'

'I wasn't going to turn her away! Besides, she was nervous…and so was I. Wine seemed like a good idea.' She thrust her chin out, daring him to challenge her. 'And it still does.'

Rick dragged a hand down his face.

'And now you can jolly well listen to what she had to say.' And then she outlined the conversation she and Marigold had just shared, leaving nothing out.

'I don't care,' he said when she finished.

Her heart stuttered. 'But—'

'I'm leaving.'

Just as she'd known he would, but it didn't stop the blow from nearly cutting her in half. Given her father's threats, it'd probably be better if he did leave. If he left Sydney and went far, far away, but…

But it didn't mean he had to turn his back on his family!

'Do whatever you damn well please!' she hollered at him. She strode forward to poke him in the shoulder. 'We can't choose our families. You and me, we're perfect proof of that except…'

She whirled away from him. 'Except in this case you can choose—you can decide to choose your sister!' She swung back. His face had gone pale and wooden. 'Poppy seems lovely. Marigold seems lovely. Her husband Neville sounds lovely. They all seem lovely, but you're not going to choose them—you're going to reject them instead. Just like John did!'

Rick's jaw worked for a moment, but no words came out. 'Reject?' he finally spat out. 'Their lives are perfect!' He wasn't going to waltz in there and ruin it for them.

He'd met people like that before—good, decent people who wouldn't turn him away. But their lives would be that bit worse for knowing him, their happiness diminished. They didn't deserve that. That lovely girl—his sister! She didn't deserve that.

Nell glared at him. 'Who's to say their lives wouldn't be more perfect with you in it?'

He stepped in close to her, pushed his face close to hers and tried to ignore the sweet scent of cake and sugar and spice. 'Fairy tales don't come true.'

'You have a sister. *That's* a reality. This *isn't* a fairy tale.'

Her belief in happy ever afters was a fiction, though, and he had to take a step back before some of that magic took hold of him. 'This is my decision to make.'

Her head snapped up. 'You're going to walk away?'

He glanced heavenward. 'Finally she gets the message.'

'Fine!'

He glanced back down.

'Marigold asked me to give you this.' She took his hand and slapped a business card into it and then dropped his hand as if she couldn't bear to touch him. 'Now get the hell off my property.'

Rick scowled and pounded on Tash's door. Tash opened it. 'Is it okay if I bunk here tonight?' he asked without preamble.

'Sure.' She pushed the door wide. 'I take it you and Nell have had words.'

'What?' He rounded on her.

Tash didn't even blink at his growl. She gestured for him to dump his stuff in the spare bedroom and then continued through to the living room. Mitch sat at the table. He and Rick nodded their greetings to each other. Tash turned. 'You ought to know she was here earlier.'

He slammed his hands to his hips 'So she told you about John Cox and Poppy and the whole mess of it, I suppose, and tried to enlist your help?'

Mitch opened his mouth but Tash took the seat beside him, elbowing him in the ribs, and he shut it again. 'Something like that. She made a good case.'

'Can it, Tash.' He couldn't believe she'd be on Nell's side. 'I don't care if that girl is my sister.' And it didn't matter what Nell or Tash or Mitch had to say about the matter. 'There's no law that says I have to meet her.'

'Holy crap!' Tash's jaw dropped. 'John Cox, the gardener, is your father?'

He stilled and then swore. She'd played him to perfection. If Nell hadn't riled him up so much he'd have never fallen for one of Tash's tricks.

'*And* he fathered more than one child?'

He closed his eyes.

'That wasn't the mess she told us about.'

Obviously. He waited for Tash to grill him further, but she didn't. A wave of affection washed over him then. Tash knew how to give a guy the space and privacy he needed. His face darkened. Unlike some others he could name. He glanced up, but the expression on Tash's face made his blood chill. He straightened. 'What the hell was she here for then?'

Tash and Mitch shared a glance. 'You might want to sit down to hear this, Rick,' Mitch said.

CHAPTER ELEVEN

RICK LISTENED TO the tale Tash and Mitch recounted with
growing disbelief. 'You have to be joking? You're telling
me she's going to sell her house—the house she's done everything in her power to hang onto—in an attempt to keep
me out of jail?'

'That's exactly what we're saying.'

Oh, Princess. 'She knows that's crazy, right?'

'No,' Tash said, as if it were obvious it wasn't crazy. Or
as if it should've been obvious to him that Nell wouldn't
think it crazy. She had a point.

'And she'd be right,' Mitch said. 'It's not crazy.'

Ice filtered through his gut. He wasn't going to prison
again for anyone. Ever. Again.

Except…

Except he wasn't letting the Princess sell out on his
behalf.

'She picked a fight with me on purpose. She kicked me
out to get me out of the way.' Because Nell could twist him
around her little finger and if she'd wanted him to stay, if
she'd argued with him to stay, if she'd promised no more
interference on the Poppy and Marigold front, he'd have
stayed.

'That's my best guess,' Tash said. 'It's what I'd have
done in her shoes.'

Rick's mouth opened but no words came out.

'She has a point, Rick. It might be best if you do disappear.'

And leave Nell to bumble along as best she could? 'No way, I'm not going anywhere.'

Tash fixed him with a look that made him fidget. He rolled his shoulders. 'I'll buy the bloody house.'

'No you won't!'

Tash and Mitch both said that at the same time. He scowled at them. Mitch leaned towards him. 'It wouldn't be a good idea at this point in time for Roland Smythe-Whittaker to know you have money.'

Rick slumped back in his chair, silently acknowledging the truth of that.

Mitch glanced at his watch. 'I've gotta go.' He rose, kissed Tash and left.

'Do you have enough money to buy Whittaker House?'

He nodded.

'How?'

He lifted a shoulder. 'It's amazing how much money you can make playing poker, Tash.'

She closed her eyes. 'Oh, Rick.'

He didn't know why, but her words burned through him. He shifted on his chair. 'I could buy the house anonymously.'

Tash grabbed two beers from the fridge and tossed him one. 'No.'

His hand tightened around the can. 'This is not your decision to make!'

She snorted at him. 'What would you be doing tomorrow if we hadn't told you about the situation?'

He didn't answer.

'You'd jump in your car and head up the coast without a backward glance, right?'

She was spot on. As usual. The thing was, she had told him about the mess Nell was in and—

'She came to us for help—me and Mitch—not you. It's not even help but advice she asked for. All Mitch and I plan to do is arm her with the information she needs to make her next move.'

He opened his mouth, but she cut him off. 'She said she doesn't want some white knight riding in and saving the day.' Tash took a long slug of her beer. 'She's not some helpless woman you can ride in and rescue to ease your damn guilt, Rick.'

'What guilt?'

'The guilt at leaving.'

He stared at her. He could barely breathe, let alone speak.

'She can save herself. What's more, I think she needs to do this on her own so she can prove exactly that.'

The Princess was resilient—strong. It was just...

He wanted to be her white knight.

Why? To ease his guilt, as Tash said? His stomach churned. 'She thinks you don't like her, you know?' It would've taken a lot of courage for her to approach Tash.

'I don't really know her, but I like her just fine. I *really* like what she's prepared to do for you.'

That only made his stomach churn harder. 'It harks back to when you made it clear she should leave the Royal Oak after one drink and kept such a close eye on her the entire time.'

Tash stared at her beer. 'I didn't want any trouble. I didn't want anyone hassling her. Her father wasn't a popular man at the time.'

'I knew it'd be something like that.'

'She's in love with you, Rick.'

His beer halted halfway to his mouth. His heart pounded.

'Don't play games with her.'

He wanted to jump up and run.

'You have two choices as far as I can see. You either get up in the morning, get in your car and drive off into the sunset.'

He thrust out his jaw. He wasn't leaving. Not until he knew Nell and her dreams were safe.

'Or if you're so hell-bent on sticking around you better start doing something to deserve her.'

Tash rose then and left the room. He realised his beer was still stranded at that crazy angle and he lowered it to the table, his heart pounding. Why wasn't he already in his car, tearing away from Sydney as if the hounds of hell were at his heels?

Because Nell was about to sacrifice everything that most mattered to her for him.

For him!

He couldn't let her do that, because…

He stared at the wall opposite as it all fell into place. He loved Nell. He was in love with the Princess.

Somewhere along the line her dreams had become his dreams. She'd given meaning to his hobo existence and he didn't want to go back to drifting aimlessly through life.

He wanted…

He swallowed and tapped a finger against his beer. He wanted the dream he'd had before he'd gone to prison. He wanted the wife and kids and a regular job. He wanted a place in the world and he wanted that place right by Nell's side.

You better start doing something to deserve her.

On Sunday her father and Byron Withers, the estate agent, arrived promptly at eleven a.m.

Byron smirked at her with so much I-told-you-so satisfaction it was all Nell could do not to seize him by the ear and toss him back out of the front door. It took an effort to pull all of her haughty superiority around her, but she did. She wasn't giving these two men the satisfaction of knowing how much she cried inside.

Besides, she was doing this for Rick. He didn't deserve

what her father had planned for him and that gave her strength too.

Both men, though, faltered when they found the solicitor Mitch had organised for her already ensconced at the kitchen table.

'This isn't necessary,' her father boomed.

'Nevertheless, I am having Mr Browne read over the contract before I sign it. That's non-negotiable.' She wasn't afraid her father would walk away in a huff. She knew how much he wanted the sale of Whittaker House to go through. 'So the sooner Mr Withers hands the contract over the sooner my solicitor can read it and the sooner you can both be on your way.'

With a curt nod from her father, Byron Withers did as she'd suggested. She'd provided Mr Browne with coffee and cupcakes when he'd arrived. Her father eyed the cupcakes hungrily. 'Coffee, daughter?'

'No, Roland, I'm afraid there's none on offer.' She'd never called him by his Christian name before and the shock in his eyes gave her little pleasure. But she wanted him to know that she'd meant what she'd said to him the previous day. If he insisted she sell Whittaker House, if he persisted in his threats against Rick, she would never acknowledge him as her father again.

The solicitor glanced up. 'We are not signing this clause, this clause or this clause. Mr Withers, these are not only immoral but they're bordering on illegal.'

Her father's cheeks reddened and his face darkened.

The solicitor turned to her. 'If it's okay with you, I'd like to take this to the authority that is, in effect, the Estate Agents' watchdog. This kind of thing shouldn't be allowed.'

Thank you, Mitch.

Byron came bustling up between them. 'I'm sure there's no need for that! It'll have merely been some innocent oversight by the contract department.'

'But—' Her father broke off at Byron's shake of his head. He took to glowering at her instead.

She folded her arms and glared back while her solicitor forced Byron to initial the changes and insert clauses that had apparently gone inadvertently 'missing'. 'I've had a lifetime of that look,' she informed him. 'But I find I'm impervious to it now.'

His jaw dropped.

They both glanced back to the table when Byron groaned. 'But that means she can pull out of the sale at any time without making any financial recompense to the agency for advertising or...or...anything!'

Nell lifted her chin. 'As my father claims he already has a buyer for the property, pray tell me what advertising you'll actually be doing? I mean, of course, if you'd prefer we took this to the authority Mr Browne mentioned earlier then by all means...'

'There's no need to be so hasty,' Byron muttered, scrawling his signature at the bottom of the newly formed contract. He pushed it across to her.

She almost laughed when Mr Browne winked at her. 'This is now a document I'm prepared to let you sign.'

She signed it.

She turned to her father and Byron. 'The two of you can leave now. I'm busy. And I don't see any point in the two of you lingering.'

'I'll need to contact you when I have clients to show through the property,' Byron said.

'Yes, of course, but you'll do that without Roland present if you please.'

Her father's head came up. He stared at her as if he'd never seen her before.

'I'm afraid I don't trust him not to steal from me any further.' Something flickered behind his eyes and if she hadn't known better she'd have almost called it regret. 'Now, good day to you both.'

They left. She walked back to kitchen and to Mr Browne. 'Thank you for your advice. I have a feeling it was invaluable.'

'They were trying to rob you blind.'

No surprises there, but… 'You helped me gain back a little of my power. I'm very grateful.'

'It's all part of the service,' he said, gathering up his things. 'Besides, I haven't had that much fun bringing someone to their knees in a long time.'

She grinned and handed him half a dozen cupcakes. 'Make sure to send me your bill.'

He merely winked at her again and left.

Nell sat at the kitchen table with burning eyes and rested her head against the wooden table top. She gripped her hands in her lap. She pulled in a deep breath and then another. She kept deep breathing until she was able to swallow the lump lodged in her throat. When she'd done that she forced herself to her feet. There was work to be done—another two orders to fill. And then boxes that she would need to start packing.

Mitch turned up on her doorstep on Tuesday morning, just before she was about to set off in Candy. Candy who was now running like a dream thanks to Rick.

Rick.

A burn started up in her chest, at her temples and the backs of her eyes. He'd be hundreds if not thousands of kilometres away by now. She hoped so—she dearly hoped so. She wanted him well and truly beyond her father's reach.

Oh, but how she ached to see him, hungered to hold him, yearned to know he was safe.

'You okay?' Mitch asked.

Nell shook herself. 'Yes, sorry. Please come in. Can I get you a coffee or a—'

'No, thanks, Nell, I only have a few minutes before I have to get to work.'

Right. 'I want to thank you for sending Mr Browne on Sunday. He was superb.'

'I heard. I've also spoken to him about your father's threats against Rick and he assures me that he can draw up a clause that prohibits your father from bringing any action against Rick.'

She fell into a seat and closed her eyes. 'Thank God,' she whispered. They flew open again. 'Is it watertight?'

'As watertight as these things can ever be.'

Right.

'I've also hunted up some other information that might be of interest to you.'

She gestured for him to take a seat. He did and then pulled her grandmother's ring from his pocket and laid it on the table in front of her. 'I've found out who really had this copy made.'

Her lips twisted. 'I know—my father—but he'll bribe people to lie for him and I'm not putting Rick through a trial. He's suffered enough grief due to my family.'

'It wasn't your father.'

She stared at him. 'Not...' She swallowed. 'Then who?'

Mitch glanced down at his hands and she stiffened. 'If you tell me it's Rick I won't believe you. He's not now nor has he ever been a thief. If that's what your informers have led you to believe it's because they're on my father's payroll.'

Mitch smiled then. 'You think a lot of him, don't you?'

She nodded. She loved him.

'It wasn't your father and it wasn't Rick. This fake was made almost thirty years ago.'

Her eyes felt as if they were starting out of her head. Mitch pulled several receipts from his pocket and handed them to her. She read them, blinked and then she started to laugh. 'These are signed by my grandmother.'

'During the recession in the eighties, your grandfather's business took a bit of a beating.'

'So my grandmother sold her jewels to help him out?'

'That'd be my guess.'

She stared at the receipts, she stared at the ring and then she stared at Mitch. 'This is proof.' The import of that suddenly struck her. Her shoulders went back. 'I…I don't know how to thank you.'

'No thanks necessary. It only took a little digging to find the truth. I was glad to be able to do Rick a good turn.'

She nodded.

'And it means, as far as all this goes, the ball's now in your court.'

She could now ensure Rick didn't go to jail. She could save Whittaker House. She could make her dream of a Victorian teahouse a reality. And she could make sure Rick's investment paid him back fourfold.

She straightened. She lifted her chin and pushed back her shoulders. 'I feel dangerously powerful.' And very far from *useless*.

'If you want me here when you confront your father or if you want me to haul him in on blackmail and attempted extortion charges, just say the word.'

'No, thank you, Mitch. I'd like to deal with this on my own now.'

The moment Mitch left, Nell rang Byron Withers and took her house off the market.

'But,' he blustered, 'it's only—'

'It's non-negotiable, I'm afraid, Byron.'

'Your father will be most displeased!'

She smiled. 'Yes, he will.'

Then she rang her father. 'I've just taken the house off the market,' she said without preamble. 'If you wish to discuss this any further then you're welcome to drop over at five this afternoon.'

She hung up. She switched off her phone. And then she went out in Candy to sell cupcakes and coffee.

* * *

Her father was waiting for her when she returned home that afternoon. 'You changed the locks!'

'Yes, I did.'

'I've been waiting over half an hour!'

'I told you what time I'd be here,' she returned, not in the least perturbed, unlocking the door and leading the way through the house. *Her house.* She'd become immune to her father's demands and anger. Her body swung with the freedom of it.

'Would you like coffee and cake?'

'No, I wouldn't! I want to know the meaning of this!'

'Would you like to take a seat?'

'No!'

Fine. She shrugged. 'I found out it wasn't you who had the copy made of the ring after all.'

'I told you it wasn't.'

'I didn't believe you. I also discovered it wasn't Rick Bradford who had it made either.'

The skin around Roland's eyes sagged, making him look a lot older than his fifty-seven years.

'It was Grandma herself. It seems she did it to help Granddad out of some financial difficulty at the factory.'

Roland closed his eyes, but she refused to let pity weaken her. This man had bullied and harangued her all her life, had made her feel she'd never measure up. He'd threatened the man she loved.

She lifted her chin. 'I have the receipts to prove it. So now I'm going to tell you for the last time that I am *not* selling Whittaker House. I promised Grandma I would cherish it and that's exactly what I mean to do. You can demand and yell all you like.' She shrugged—a straight from the heart *I am not useless* shrug. 'But none of that will have any effect on me.'

'I'll be ruined!'

'Maybe so, but I'm not the one who ruined you.'

He sagged, looking older and more helpless than she'd ever seen him.

'When you demanded it, I gave you my trust fund, my apartment, my sports car and I didn't even say a word when you took the majority of my designer wardrobe, but not once did you ever say thank you. You just wanted more and more. Nothing I have ever done has been good enough for you. I'm through with that. I'm not giving you anything else.'

His face turned purple. 'This house should be mine!'

'But it's not. It's mine. And I'd like you to leave now.'

He called her names, but none of them hurt. He threatened her, but it merely washed over her like so much noise. And then he left and a weight lifted from her shoulders. She would never have to deal with his demands, his threats and his ugliness again.

At nine o'clock on Thursday morning a registered package arrived; Nell had to sign for it. It was from the solicitor, Clinton Garside.

Clinton's enclosed note merely said: *Following the instructions of the late Mr John Cox.* Inside was a letter from John. Her heart picked up pace as she read it.

Dear Miss Nell,
I left instructions with my solicitor to have this sent to you if Rick should ever turn up to claim his letter. I know you won't understand my attitude to my children or why I've spoken now after so long keeping the secret. You were about my only friend and you added the only sunshine I had in my life, so I'll try to explain it to you.
The truth is, when I was a young man, I killed someone. I was charged with manslaughter and went to jail for eight years. I've always had a temper. I was never afraid you'd be in any danger of it because

you were too well supervised, but I couldn't inflict it on my children. I didn't dare. That's why I stayed away from them.

Her jaw dropped. The words blurred. Nell had to swallow hard and blink before the page came back into focus.

I could've loved the woman who had my other child, but I would've had to tell her the truth about my past and I couldn't do that.

'Oh, John,' she whispered, wiping her eyes.

So why haven't I told Rick who his sibling is outright? I stayed away in the hope it'd protect him, but he turned out too much like me anyway. He needs to prove himself and that's why I set him the test. I involved you because... Well, you were such a shy, quiet little thing but I saw the way you two connected when you were just little tykes. You'll know now why I chased him away. Maybe you'll become friends after all.

'In my dreams, John.'

I wish you well and very happy and I hope you don't think too badly of me.
Your friend, John.

She folded the letter and stared at the wall opposite for a long time, wishing she could share its contents with Rick.

Standing, she moved to the door and picked her way through the overgrown lawn and wild garden down to John's cottage. Rick's cottage. A path had been worn through the undergrowth to it during the last few weeks.

With her heart in her throat, she reached beneath the

step and her fingers curled around the key. She rose and inserted it into the lock. She pushed open the door and...

Her eyes filled with hot tears. Her throat burned. Rick was gone. As she'd known he would be, but...

Some crazy thread of hope had remained alive inside her, hoping to still find him here, hoping he'd ignored her demand that he leave.

She halted on the threshold for a few seconds before forcing herself inside the room. She immediately pressed her hands to her eyes and pulled in a breath. If she inhaled deeply enough, concentrated hard enough, she could still catch the faintest trace of him in the air—a scent she couldn't begin to describe, but it had his teasing dark eyes and wicked grin rising up in front of her.

A breeze wafted through the door behind her, disturbing the scent and amalgamating it with the perfume of warm grass and native frangipani instead.

No! She leapt to slam the door, but it was too late. All that registered now were smells from the garden.

She wanted to drop to the floor and pound her fists against it. She didn't. She forced herself to inspect the entire cottage—all of it neat and clean. She didn't even have the garbage to take out. Rick had done it before he'd left.

Nothing.

Not even a note.

'What on earth did you expect?' she whispered.

This was always how it was going to end—with Rick riding off into the sunset.

Without her.

With stinging eyes, she walked back through the cottage and locked the door behind her. She didn't replace the key beneath the veranda. There didn't seem to be any point.

Rick paced through Tash's currently deserted house and tried to make sense of the conflicting impulses raging through him—the urge to run and the urge to stay. The urge to jump into his car and drive until he was too tired to drive any more. Or the urge to race over to Nell's house, take her into his arms and kiss her until she swore she'd never send him away again.

His chin lifted. He started for the door.

What can a guy like you offer a girl like Nell Smythe-Whittaker?

He slid to a halt with a curse and went back to pacing.

Do something to deserve her.

Like what? He planted his hands on his hips and glared about the room. How on earth could he do that? How the hell could he prove to her that he meant to stick around? How—

For a moment everything stilled and then he slapped a hand to his forehead and planted himself in front of Tash's computer. He typed 'How to start a business' into the search engine.

And he started making notes.

It took Rick two days to register Bradford's Restorations with the business bureau, to obtain an Australian Business Number and to have business cards printed. He bought a van and organised for a sign writer. He bought tools. He hired someone to design him a website. He barely slept three hours a night.

Surely a business would convince Nell he meant to stay, would prove to her he was serious about making something of himself?

She'd believe it more if you had family ties in the area.

He swallowed and turned to the phone. Family? Poppy? What if Poppy rejected him? He swung away to throw himself down on the sofa and drag both hands back through his hair, his lungs cramping.

What if she doesn't?

The voice that whispered through him sounded suspiciously like Nell's. He stared at the phone again. Swallowing, he pulled Marigold's business card from his wallet and dialled the number.

'Hello?'

The voice was female and he had to fight the urge to slam the phone down. 'I, uh…' He cleared his throat. 'May I speak with Marigold Somers please?'

'Yes, speaking.'

He swallowed again. 'Mrs Somers, my name is Rick Bradford and I…' How did one say it—*I'm your daughter's brother*? 'You met my friend Nell Smythe-Whittaker at the park the other day.'

'Rick!' He heard the catch in her voice. 'I'm so glad you called. I've told Poppy all about you and we're dying to meet you.'

His throat tightened at the warmth in her voice. 'I'd like that.'

'Come for dinner, please? We'd love you to.'

Her eagerness and sincerity made his heart thump.

'Promise you'll come. Tomorrow night?'

His eyes burned. He stared up at the ceiling and blinked hard. 'I…you're sure?'

'Positive.'

They made a time. He rang off and then he didn't know what to do. He knew what he wanted to do. He wanted to go and find Nell and tell her what he'd done and have her assure him it was the right thing to do.

You haven't earned her yet.

He pulled a receipt from his pocket—a copy of the one Mitch had retrieved for Nell. It was time to see a jeweller about a ring.

CHAPTER TWELVE

NELL GLANCED THROUGH her dream folder, sipped a glass of wine and tried to find the tiniest hint of excitement.

And failed.

Closing the folder, she rubbed her fingers across her brow. Her zest for life would return. Other people recovered from broken hearts, didn't they?

She glanced at the kitchen clock. Was six o'clock on a Saturday evening too early to go to bed?

A knock sounded on the front door. She glanced towards the hallway without the tiniest flicker of interest. Maybe whoever it was would go away if she ignored it.

Another knock.

Ignoring it won't help you get over a broken heart.

She pulled a face, but all the same she forced herself to her feet to answer it.

Smile.

She pasted one on before opening the door.

The smile slid straight off again. Her heart gave such a big kick she had to reach out and cling to the door to remain upright. 'Rick?' she whispered.

'Hey, Princess.'

Those dark eyes smiled down at her, the mouth hooked up, and all she wanted to do was throw herself into his arms.

Now there was a sure-fire way to embarrass herself.

'I… I…' She swallowed. 'I thought you'd left Sydney.' Why had he come back?

For her?

Oh, don't be deluded and pathetic. Nonetheless her pulse raced and her palms grew slick. Very carefully she released her grip on the door and wiped them down the sides of her yoga pants.

Her rattiest yoga pants. Why couldn't she be wearing one of her fifties-inspired dresses?

He shifted his weight. 'I never left. I've been staying with Tash.'

'Oh.'

Oh!

So he knew then? She swallowed and gestured him inside. 'Come on in. I was just having a glass of wine. Would you care for one?'

It took a superhuman effort, but she found her manners and managed not to sound stilted. Well done her!

'That sounds great.'

Now, if only she could pour him a glass without her hand shaking.

She didn't believe she could pull that off so she poured it with her back to him while managing a breezy, 'Take a seat.' She turned. 'Oh, and help yourself to a cupcake.' And she gestured to the tin on the table, which averted his gaze from the way her hand shook when she set his wine in front of him.

She sat. She twisted her hands in her lap. She didn't want to talk about her father. She didn't want to find out that Rick felt beholden to her in some way. 'How long are you planning to stay in Sydney?' she asked instead, determined that her stupidly optimistic heart should know the truth asap.

His grin lost its cockiness. He swallowed. It made her swallow too. 'I'm, um…planning on sticking around.'

Her fingernails dug into her palms. *He's not hanging around for you!*

'Why?' The word croaked out of her. She didn't want it to. She'd do anything to recall it, but she couldn't.

His eyes darkened. 'Damn, this is awkward.'

He could say that again.

He drew in a breath. He stood. He came around the table to where she sat and dropped to one knee in front of her. She almost fell off her chair. 'Nell, I love you and I want to spend the rest of my life with you.'

He pulled a small velvet box from his pocket and opened it. Her grandmother's diamond ring winked back at her and some instinct told her this was no copy.

'Will you do me the great honour of marrying me?'

He was offering her everything she wanted!

She closed her eyes, counted to three and opened them again. The ring still hovered there, winking at her with all of its promise. Her throat and chest burned. Her eyes stung. 'No,' she whispered. 'No, Rick, I won't marry you.'

Rick stumbled to his feet, a darkness he'd never experienced before threatening to descend around him. He stumbled around the table and back into his chair because he didn't have the strength to make it all the way to the front door.

'Tash was wrong.'

He couldn't believe his voice could emerge so normally while everything inside him crumbled.

'Tash?'

Nell's voice didn't come out normally at all, but strangled and full of tears. *Damn it all to hell!* He wished he could rewind the last five minutes and erase them. But he couldn't and he was too tired to lie. Nell might not love him, but she'd never be cruel. 'She told me you were in love with me.'

'She wasn't wrong.'

It took a moment for him to make any sense of that.

When he did a shaft of light pushed the darkness back. He straightened. 'What did you just say?'

Her green eyes suddenly flashed. She leapt up and slashed both hands through the air. She paced to the sink, gripped it till her knuckles turned white and then swung back to stab a finger at him. Her hand shook and he wanted to capture it in his and never let it go.

'If you've been staying with Tash then you know what my father threatened.' Her hands slammed to her hips, the long line of her leg clearly defined in those stretchy pants, and his mouth dried. He tried to keep his mind on what she said rather than how she looked…and how much he wanted to ravish her.

'Which means you know I put Whittaker House on the market.'

'To save my skin!'

'Which means you also know,' she went on as if he hadn't spoken, 'that Mitch provided me with information to finally, once and for all, defeat my father.'

He didn't know where she was going with this—just that the pain in her eyes tore at him. He gave a wary nod.

'Damn it, Rick! I don't want a husband who marries me because he feels beholden to me.'

His jaw dropped. 'I don't feel beholden to you.' He loved her!

She gave a laugh. 'Oh, right.'

He opened his mouth.

'You've been playing white knight all your life. As a boy you tried to protect all the kids in the neighbourhood, you took the blame and went to prison for one of those friends. Heaven only knows how many women you've rescued from untenable situations since then. You specialise in damsels.'

He swallowed. Everything she said was true, but…

'I'm just the latest in a long line. Well, I don't want to be a defenceless female. I want to be strong enough to deal with my own problems.'

'You are. You have!' He didn't see her as someone who needed rescuing.

'And I don't want a white knight!' she shouted. 'When I marry I want it to be an equal partnership.'

'Damn it, Nell.' He leapt to his feet. 'Can't you see that I'm not the white knight here? You are!'

Her jaw dropped. He passed a hand across his eyes. 'You are,' he muttered, falling back into his chair.

Her mouth opened and closed but no sound came out. She stood there, staring at him as if she didn't know what to do, what to say or if to believe him.

'I've spent the last week trying to do things to earn you—to prove to you that I'm worthy of you.'

She plonked down on her chair as if the air had left her body. She reached for her glass of wine, but she didn't drink from it.

'I'm in the process of establishing my own restoration building company. I'm hoping to interview potential employees next week.'

She blinked. 'I… Congratulations.'

'Thank you.' He nodded. 'I rang Marigold and I've met Poppy. In fact I've met the whole family.'

Her glass slammed to the table. She leaned towards him. 'How did it go?'

It almost made him smile. 'Pretty well. She's great. In fact her whole family is great.' His gaze captured hers. 'She's not a damsel either.'

Nell sat back. 'No, she's not.'

Steel stiffened his backbone. 'And neither are you. You're a lot of things—maddening, stubborn, generous to a fault and optimistic in the face of all evidence to the contrary—but the one thing you're not is useless.'

Her eyes filled with tears and he ached to go to her, to pull her into his arms, but then she smiled and it was like a rainbow. 'I know.'

Something inside him unclenched.

She frowned. 'You aren't either.'

He rested his elbows on the table and dropped his head to his hands. 'Princess, I've always been able to save other people, but I've never been able to save myself.'

'Oh, Rick!'

And then she was on his lap and in his arms. He pressed his face into her neck and breathed her in. 'You saved me, Princess.' She ran a hand back through his hair and then her arms went about his shoulders and she held him so tight he could feel the broken bits of himself start to come back together.

He drew back to touch a hand to her face. 'You believed in me so strongly that you made me believe in myself again.'

She pressed a kiss to the corner of his mouth. 'You're wonderful! You *should* believe in yourself.'

'Nobody has ever been so completely on my side before you came along.'

'There are lots of people on your side.' Her eyes flashed. 'Tash and Mitch and all your friends, and now Poppy and her family. You just won't let yourself see it. You're afraid of not being the strong one everyone else can rely on.'

Was that true?

'I went to Tash and Mitch for advice about the fake ring. Do you think that makes me weaker or less strong?'

'Hell, no! It shows how smart you are to approach the people who have the expertise you need.'

She raised an eyebrow.

His heart thumped. Slowly he nodded. 'There can be strength in reaching out and asking for the help you need.'

'Precisely.'

In that moment a spark of light lit him up from the inside, so bright it almost blinded him. He ran his hands slowly up her back and she shivered. 'Princess, you're in my lap.'

She grinned at him. 'Would you like me to get up?'

'Not a chance.'

She laughed and then gasped when he shifted her a fraction so she could feel what she did to him. 'Oh.' Her eyes widened. She wriggled against him. 'Ooh.'

He bit back a groan. 'Steady, Princess. Not yet.'

Her face fell. 'Why not?'

He tried for mock stern but probably failed. 'There's another couple of things we need to clear up.'

She bit her lip and then nodded. 'Okay.'

'You gave me the courage to reach for my dream again.'

'It only seems fair. You're giving me the chance to chase mine.'

'I want to have a family that's the polar opposite from the one I had growing up. I want to do that with you, Nell. Not because I feel I owe you or because I think you need a man in your life to look after you, but because I love you.' A tear hovered on one of her eyelashes. He wanted to kiss it away. 'I need to know if you believe me.'

She took his face in her hands and stared into his eyes. He felt exposed in a way he never had before, but he didn't look away. 'Yes,' she said. 'I do believe you. I never thought I'd be the kind of girl who could convince you to settle down. You kept telling me how different we were and—'

He touched a finger to her lips. 'I was fighting what I felt for you.'

She nodded. 'I know that now, but when you proposed I was too afraid to believe it was for real.' She brushed his hair back from his forehead. 'But I'm not afraid any more, Rick.' And then she leaned forward and touched her lips to his and they kissed so fiercely and with all of their hearts that they were both breathing hard when they finally broke apart.

He tried to get the racing of his blood under control. 'So you'll marry me?'

'Yes.'

He slipped her grandmother's ring onto her finger. She

stared at it and then covered it with her other hand and pressed it to her heart. 'How did you find it?'

'I approached the jeweller who'd sold it on behalf of your grandparents and tracked down the buyer. I made an offer to buy it back and he accepted.'

'I bet you paid twice what it was worth.'

More or less. 'I wanted to give you a ring that meant something special to you.'

She twisted around to face him more fully. 'I don't need fancy rings or fast cars or pretty clothes.'

She mightn't need them, but he meant to lavish her with all that and more.

'I don't even need this house.'

He had every intention that it remained in the family.

'I love you, Rick. All I need is you.'

'Princess, you have me for as long as you want me.'

'Forever,' she breathed.

'And beyond,' he agreed. 'Now, can I have a cupcake to keep up my strength before I take you upstairs to ravish you?'

She laughed and the sound of it filled him. 'I can see we're going to have to find ourselves a good dentist.' She reached over and lifted the lid on the tin and offered them to him.

'On second thoughts…' He replaced the lid, lifted her in his arms and headed upstairs instead. There'd be time for cake later.

EPILOGUE

MITCH RUSHED UP and clapped Rick on the shoulder. 'I have it on good authority that the show's about to start. Ready?'

'I've been ready for eight months!' Rick shot to his feet and glanced down the red carpet that led from the ornate wooden rotunda to the terrace of Whittaker House. Rows of red and white roses created an avenue for Nell to walk down. Once she appeared, that was.

Mitch took his place beside Rick, tugging at the jacket of his tux. 'I can't believe how much you guys have transformed this place.'

It'd taken a lot of hard work, but he and Nell had relished every second of it. And it had paid off. Whittaker House gleamed, apricot and cream in the warm November sunshine, the deep red accents providing a perfect contrast. His chest swelled. He'd done that. *Him!* His gaze moved to the garden—a riot of spring colour—and his pulse quickened. This was the real triumph, though, and all Nell's doing.

Nell.

He glanced at his watch and then back towards the house, his fingers drumming against his thighs. The wedding guests murmured quietly among themselves on chairs arranged beneath a red and white striped awning whose bunting danced joyfully in the breeze. A group of less than thirty people that included Poppy and her family, some of his old school friends, Nell's employees and his, as well as friends they'd made in the course of setting up their businesses—an intimate and generous-minded group. On nearby trestle tables covered in fine white linen was a wedding tea fit for a princess. In pride of place was the cupcake tower—the wedding cake—that Nell had baked and assembled herself.

It was all ready.

He touched unsteady fingers to his bow tie and then swung to Mitch. 'I thought you said it was about to—'

The band kicked up with *'Here Comes the Bride'*.

Rick turned to find Nell standing at the other end of the red carpet. His breath jammed. A fist squeezed his chest. *She was beautiful.*

She started down the avenue towards him in a magnificent 1950s frock in white silk. A scarlet sash circled her waist. Her white satin heels sported scarlet bows. In her hands she held a bouquet of marigolds. He stared and stared and his heart hammered.

She was walking down the aisle to him. *To him!*

Everything blurred. He had to blink hard. Swallow hard. 'I'm marrying a diamond of a woman,' he croaked to Mitch.

'Me too,' Mitch choked back.

Tash, Nell's bridesmaid, looked pretty in scarlet. She and Mitch had booked a date here in February for a garden wedding of their own.

Nell was setting a trend—high tea weddings.

When she finally reached him he took her hand, kissed it and held it fast. 'You look beautiful, Princess.'

'So do you,' she whispered back, her green eyes sparkling, her lips soft and her grip as tight as his.

He wanted to kiss her, but the wedding celebrant cleared her throat and he and Nell turned to her. They made the vows that would bind them together for life. They kissed— a solemn, almost chaste kiss. They signed the register. His heart grew so big he thought he might burst.

Nell leaned in against him, drenching him in the scent

of sugar and spice. 'Once upon a time a girl met a boy and fell in love, but she lost the boy.'

He touched a finger to her cheek. 'Many years later the boy met the girl again and fell in love.'

Nell turned to face him, her hand resting against his chest. 'And they lived happily ever after.'

'I'm counting on it, Princess.' His throat thickened and his breath bottled in his chest. 'You've made me believe fairy tales can come true.'

'I'm going to spend the rest of my life proving it to you,' she whispered before reaching up on tiptoe to kiss him.

Warmth washed through him. She didn't need to prove anything. His arm snaked around her waist and he pulled her closer. She'd made a believer out of him. He believed in her. Most of all he believed in them. And he made sure his kiss said as much—he and Nell, together forever.

* * * * *

FALLING FOR
FORTUNE

**NANCY ROBARDS
THOMPSON**

This book is dedicated to the memory of my
sweet mother-in-law, Juanita Eitreim.
I miss you every day.

Chapter One

"I'm sorry, sir, I've checked the directory three times. There's nobody by that name listed."

Strains of the new receptionist's voice carried in through Christopher Fortune's partially open door. He looked up from his in-office putting green.

What was her name again? He couldn't remember. It was only the start of her second week. Jeez, but she was shrill. He'd have to talk to her about her tone. Not good for community relations. But first…

He realigned his stance as the golf pro had taught him, making sure that his toes were parallel to the pin at the end of the fourteen-foot portable green. He set the putter in the hollow part of his left hand and placed the right hand so that his right thumb rested on the left side of the shaft. He pulled back to take his shot—

"Sir, I don't know what else to tell you." Now her

voice was teetering on exasperation. He couldn't hear what the other person was saying, but she was giving him a headache. "We have a Christopher Fortune, but nobody by the name of *Chris Jones* works here. Could he be the one you're looking for?"

The words made Christopher hit the ball a little too hard. It rolled off the end of the green and under the coffee table that was part of the furniture grouping at the end of the room.

Who was asking for Chris Jones?

Two months ago, Chris Jones had adopted his mother's Fortune family name and moved to Red Rock from Horseback Hollow, Texas. He'd dropped the Jones portion of his name when he'd accepted the new job. Now, he was Christopher Fortune, vice president in charge of community relations for the Fortune Foundation.

Christopher set down his putter, walked over and fully opened his office door to see what the ruckus was about.

What the hell—

"Toby?" Christopher said flatly when he saw his brother and his new sister-in-law, Angie, standing there. "What are you doing here, man?"

The receptionist, a slight woman with close-cropped black hair, looked so young that she could've easily been mistaken for a sixteen-year-old. She turned and froze, all wide dark eyes and pale skin, when she saw Christopher.

"Oh! I'm sorry, Mr. Fortune. I didn't understand that they were looking for you. They asked for Chris Jones."

Now she was blushing.

Christopher glanced at the name plate that was front and center on the reception desk.

"Don't worry about it, Beverly. It's fine."

"Hey, little brother," Toby said, extending a hand. "Good to see you."

Christopher shook Toby's hand. His brother immediately pulled him into an awkward hold that their sister, Stacey, was fond of calling a *man hug*: a greeting that started as a handshake and ended with the guys leaning in and stiffly slapping each other on the back a couple of times.

When they broke apart, Christopher stepped back, reclaiming his dignity just in time to see both elevator doors open and Kinsley Aaron, the Foundation's outreach coordinator, step into the reception area.

Her long, straight blond hair hung loose around her shoulders, framing her pretty face. God, she was gorgeous, even if she was a little too uptight for his taste. He straightened his tie and raked his fingers through his hair, trying to right what Toby's enthusiastic bear hug had mussed.

Kinsley had the bluest eyes he'd ever seen. Those eyes were two of the reasons he always remembered her name. Although, the dowdy way she dressed wasn't much of an enticement. He couldn't figure out why such a beauty chose to dress like a schoolmarm. She always covered up as much of herself as possible. Didn't she know her modesty only made him daydream about the gifts that were undoubtedly hidden beneath all that wrapping?

As Kinsley approached Beverly's desk, she arched a brow at him. For a split second he could've sworn she'd read his mind. But he knew it was a ridiculous thought. She was probably just curious about Toby and Angie, since she tended to take her job so seriously. After all, this was an office where visitors generally came seeking help, something that typically fell into her community outreach division.

Before Kinsley could start asking questions, Christopher turned to his brother and sister-in-law. "Why don't we go into my office? We can talk in there."

He made quick work of ushering them out of the reception area. This sure as hell wasn't the most ideal time or place for a family reunion. Especially when he was determined to keep his life in Horseback Hollow worlds apart from the new life he'd created for himself in Red Rock.

Before he shut the door, he cast one last glance back at Kinsley, who was still lingering by Bev's desk. They locked gazes, and Christopher felt that old familiar *zing* that always happened when he looked into those eyes. The virtual vibration lasted even after she looked away.

And she was always the first one to look away.

He was pondering that when Toby said, "Since you were too darned busy to come home for the wedding, I decided I'd bring my beautiful bride to see you. Angie, you've met Chris before. Chris, this is my wife. Can you believe it?" he said, grinning. "I have a wife."

"Good to see you again, Angie," Christopher said, keeping his tone all business and shaking Angie's hand.

"So, they call you *Mr. Fortune* around here?" Toby asked, a note of good-natured ribbing in his voice. But before Christopher could answer, Toby let loose a low whistle as he glanced around Christopher's new digs. "Would you look at this fancy place? I guess you're doing all right for yourself, little brother."

"It's a pretty sweet gig," Christopher said. "Actually, I wanted to work directly for Uncle James at JMF Financial, but how could I argue after I found out that he'd created a position just for me? I'm sure he could do something for you if you want. All you have to do is ask."

What Christopher didn't say was that the work was a little boring and "do-gooder" for his taste. But the salary they were paying him, which was commensurate with the Fortune name rather than his experience, more than made up for the lack of excitement.

If Christopher had learned one thing over the past two months it was that he had to create his own excitement, ensure his own future. It wasn't as if he'd been blazing trails in Horseback Hollow. Nope, back home, he'd been bored and broke.

And a nobody.

Now he had a job that people respected and the bank account to go with it. So he figured why not go for the trifecta and take on the Fortune name? It was his birthright, after all, even if his old man would be mad as hell when he found out.

But those were the breaks, weren't they? His father Deke's attitude was one of the things that had driven Christopher to Red Rock in the first place. Once he was settled, he'd gone to court and filed a petition to change his name. Once the judge had signed the order, Christopher Fortune said *Hasta la vista, baby* to Chris Jones and Horseback Hollow and claimed what was rightfully his.

Christopher glanced around his office, trying to see it through Toby's eyes. The Fortune Foundation had been founded in memory of Lily Cassidy Fortune's late husband, Ryan Fortune, who had died of a brain tumor nine years ago. The Foundation had started out in a small storefront on Main Street in downtown Red Rock but had since expanded and was now located in a stately three-story brick building just outside of town. Christopher had one of the corner offices with rich polished mahogany architectural wall paneling on the walls—or at least the ones that didn't have floor-to-ceiling windows with a to-die-for view of the local landscape. His traditional executive's desk and credenza still left enough room for the putting green, two chairs and a couch that were grouped conversation-style around a coffee table.

Hell, his office was bigger than his old studio apartment back in Horseback Hollow.

He directed Toby and Angie over to the couch. Until now, he hadn't even tried out the office's living room furniture.

"I just can't get over the change in you," Toby said.

Christopher turned to Angie, who was still as pretty as she had been in high school with her light brown hair, blue eyes and delicate features. His brother had done well catching her. He'd tell him so later if they had a private moment. But just as the thought crossed his mind, it was overshadowed by the hope that the newlyweds weren't planning an extended visit in Red Rock. Christopher had work to do.

He hoped this visit wasn't because Deke had sent Toby to do his dirty work. If any of his family got him it was Toby. But it would be just like Deke to send one of Christopher's brothers to hassle him.

But right now, Toby was talking to Angie. "The Chris I knew never wore anything but jeans and boots. I don't know who this suit is standing in front of me with those shiny pointy-toed shoes. How many crocodiles had to die to make those shoes?"

Christopher laughed, but it was a dry, humorless sound. "They're not made out of crocodile," Christopher said.

"It was a joke, Chris." Toby frowned. "No offense, but you're even acting differently. Just remember, I know where you came from."

Awkward silence the likes of which he had never known with Toby hung in the air. He didn't want to fight with him, and it seemed every time he opened his mouth he said the wrong thing.

That was the story of his life when it came to family. But Christopher wasn't about to sit here in his own office and let family drag him down to feeling bad.

"How was the wedding?" Christopher asked, hoping for neutral ground. He directed the question to Angie, who had been remarkably quiet.

"I would say it was the happiest day of my life, but each day I wake up seems to take that title," she said. "We wish you could've been there."

"Yeah, well, it's better that I didn't come. That way the focus was on the two of you. All sunshine and happiness. No dark clouds, you know?"

Angie looked at him with big blue eyes.

"Well, we certainly did appreciate your generous gift. A thousand dollars was…" Angie shook her head as if at a loss for words.

"It was too much," said Toby as he leaned forward and plucked a business card out of a brass holder sitting on the coffee table. "Ten crisp $100 bills. Leave it to my little brother not to miss an opportunity to show off— Wait. Christopher *Fortune?*" he read aloud from the business card. "Did they forget to print your entire last name on here?"

"No," said Christopher.

Toby held up the card. "Where's the *Jones?*"

Christopher shrugged, but didn't feel the need to explain himself.

"So, that's why the receptionist was having a hard time helping us." Toby gestured with his thumb toward the reception area. "It's true, then? They don't even know who Chris Jones is?"

"Don't take it personally, Toby," Christopher said. "I just needed to make a fresh start."

"How can I not take it personally? I mean, I get that you and Dad don't see eye to eye on your moving to Red Rock and working here at the Foundation, but come on, Chris. What the hell? Aren't you taking this a little too far?"

"Is that a question or an accusation?" Christopher challenged, holding his brother's gaze until Toby leaned forward again and put the card back where he'd found it.

This life was exactly what he wanted.

He wanted what the Fortunes had: money, power, respect. He had gotten none of that back in Horseback Hollow. What was wrong with claiming it now?

"I figure the family can't be any more disappointed in me now than they've always been. I never was any good to anyone around the ranch, anyway. Don't you think they'd consider the new and improved Christopher Fortune a vast improvement over Chris Jones, the son who couldn't do anything right?"

Toby looked down at his hands, then back up at Christopher. A somber expression crept into his eyes. "I don't even know what to say to that, except that Mom asked me to tell you she loves you."

Touché.

That was just about the only thing that Toby could've said to hit Christopher where he'd feel it.

The thing was, he didn't even sound mad. Just... disappointed. A look that said, *remember where you came from and don't let the Fortunes change you into something you're not.*

He hadn't forgotten and the Fortunes hadn't changed him. He would be the first to admit that embracing the Fortunes' world and starting on a desk job had taken some getting used to. He was surprised by how he sometimes missed not getting outside between the hours of nine and five. This indoor, sedentary job has been a challenge, but every time he looked at the view outside the windows of his executive's office or at his bank account balance, it got easier and easier.

"Y'all must be hungry," Christopher said. "Come on, let's go get a bite to eat. I'll treat you to lunch."

"Excuse me, darlin'." Kinsley Aaron frowned as she looked up from the notes she was taking while manning the third-floor reception desk for Bev. Christopher Fortune stood outside his office door, smiling broadly, no doubt thinking he was God's gift to women.

Darlin'? Excuse me?

Had they somehow time traveled back to the 1960s?

"My name is Kinsley," she said, doing her best to keep the bristle out of her voice. He may have been young and good-looking and a Fortune, but how dare he call her that?

"I know what your name is," Christopher said.

"Then why did you call me *darlin'*?" She didn't smile.

The man and woman who were with him looked a bit sheepish, perhaps a little embarrassed for him, before they ducked back inside his office. Actually, Christopher should've been embarrassed for himself. But did the guy do anything for himself?

The only reason he worked at the Foundation was because his uncle was James Marshall Fortune.

"Where is Betsy?" he asked

"Who is Betsy?" she returned.

"The new receptionist?" he answered with a tone better suited for talking to a small child.

Well, Mr. Man, two could play that game. "No-body by the name of *Betsy* works here. Do you mean *Beverly?*"

Christopher shrugged. "Yes, the one who was here earlier." He motioned to the desk where Kinsley was sitting. "Where is she?"

If Bev was smart, she'd handed in her resignation and left.

Kinsley blinked away the snotty thought. She hadn't meant it. The Fortune Foundation was a fabulous place to work. Even though Christopher Fortune was full of himself, other members of the Fortune family had been very good to her. Not only did they pay her a decent salary to work as an outreach coordinator, a position she considered her life's work, but also she would be forever grateful that they had taken a chance on her.

She'd come to them with little experience, having not yet earned her degree. She was working on it, but with a full-time job and going to school part-time at night, it was going to take her a while before she completed her coursework.

"I'm covering for Beverly while she's on her break," Kinsley said. "She should be back in about fifteen minutes. In the meantime, is there something I can help you with?"

Christopher smiled and looked at her in that wolfish way he had that made her want to squirm. But she didn't. No way. She wouldn't give him the satisfaction.

What was with this guy? Better question, what was with her? Kinsley had always subscribed to the Eleanor Roosevelt philosophy: nobody could make you feel *anything* unless you gave them permission. Actually, the quote was nobody could make you feel inferior, but this adaptation felt just as authentic.

"Yes, will you please call and make a lunch reservation for three at Red for 1:15?"

At first Kinsley thought he was kidding. But as she squinted at him, it became quite clear that he was indeed serious.

News flash! She had not been hired as Christopher Fortune's personal secretary! And why did he want to eat at Red, of all places, today? She rarely went out to lunch, but today she had a 12:45 business lunch at the restaurant. She was meeting Meg Tyler, the Red Rock High School PTA president, to discuss the school's Cornerstone Club, an extracurricular student leadership organization, and to talk about the role the kids could play in implementing an anti-bullying program.

For a split second, Kinsley thought about calling Meg and asking if they could change restaurants, but then quickly decided against it. She'd been looking forward to lunch at Red. Why should she deny herself her favorite Mexican place just because he was going to be there?

Yeah, what was up with that? Why was she still feeling so shy around him? He'd started working with the Foundation about two months ago. They hadn't had much contact until recently, when Emmett Jamison had asked them to work together to establish a stronger online presence for the Foundation's community outreach program.

Why did she allow him to make her feel twelve years old? Worse yet, why did she shrink every time Christopher walked into the room? She didn't need his approval. So what if he was charismatic and good-looking? He skated through life on his looks and charm, much like her father had done when he was sober. At least she did her job better than he did.

Fighting the riptide of emotions that threatened to sweep her under, Kinsley stared unseeing at the notes she'd been writing before Christopher had come out of his office. She wasn't going to allow herself to be drowned by the past. Her father had been dead for six years, and she certainly wasn't twelve anymore. In all fairness, despite Christopher's bravado, he really didn't have the mean streak that had possessed her father when he had been drunk. That was when her dad had drummed it into her soul that she would never amount to anything. That she wouldn't be good enough, strong enough, smart enough, pretty enough. No man in his right mind would ever want her.

But that was then and this was now. She was well on her way to proving him wrong. She had a good job, and she was making her own way in the world. No matter how the scarred memories of her bastard of a father tried to convince her that she would never be enough, she needed to muster the strength to exorcise his ghost and set herself free. She needed to quit projecting her father and his twisted ways onto Christopher, who, like so many other men, had a way of making her feel overlooked, dismissed.

She knew her value and what she was capable of. That was all that mattered.

Because she was sitting at the reception desk filling in for Bev, she swallowed her pride and placed the call to Red. A few minutes later, Christopher and his posse emerged from his office and made their way to the elevator. But Christopher hung back. "Thanks for taking care of my family and me, Kinsley."

He looked her square in the eyes in that brazen way of his and flashed a smile. For a short, stupid moment part of her went soft and breathless.

"Mmm" was all she managed to say before she tore her gaze from his and he walked away to join his party.

Mmm. Not even a real word. Just an embarrassing monosyllabic grunt.

Kinsley sat at the reception desk waiting for Bev to return, pondering the shyness that always seemed to get the better of her whenever he was around.

Why?

Why did he have this effect on her?

It was because this job meant so much to her.

And maybe she found his good looks a little intimidating. But good grief.

So the guy was attractive with his perfectly chiseled features and those mile-wide broad shoulders. He had probably played football in college. One of those cocky jock types who had a harem clamoring to serve him. Not that Christopher Fortune's personal life—past or present—was any of her business.

Kinsley blinked and mentally backed away from thoughts of her coworker. Instead, she reminded herself that she had done the right thing by taking the high road and making his darned lunch reservation rather than trying to make a point.

Looks didn't matter. Not in her world, anyway. She had Christopher Fortune's number. He was a handsome opportunist who was riding his family's coattails. In the two months he'd been in the office he hadn't done much to prove that he had high regard for the actual work they were trying to do at the Foundation.

Obviously, he didn't *get it.* Guys like him never did.

But one thing she was going to make sure he understood in no uncertain terms—he'd better never call her *darlin'* again or there would be hell to pay.

Chapter Two

"Oh, look at the flowers." Angie sighed as Christopher guided her and Toby up the bougainvillea-lined path to Red.

"Just wait until you see the courtyard inside," Christopher said with as much pride as if he were showing off his own home. "Red is built around it. There's a fountain I think you'll love."

Angie stopped. "Red?"

"Yes, that's the name of the restaurant." Christopher gestured to the tile nameplate attached to the wall just outside the door, which he held open as he tried to usher them inside, but Angie stopped.

"Is this the same Red that's owned by the Mendozas?" Angie asked.

"One and the same," Christopher said.

"Wendy and Marcos Mendoza catered our wedding

reception." Angie sighed again as she looked around, taking it all in. "They have to be two of the nicest people I've ever met." She turned to Toby. "I can't believe we're here. Chris, did you plan this?"

He wished he could take credit for it, but until now, he'd had no idea what had taken place at their wedding. He'd been so intent on staying away to avoid clouding their day with bad vibes that he hadn't realized he didn't know the first thing about the event other than the fact that his brother had taken himself a bride.

Regret knotted in his gut.

"The Mendozas catered your wedding?" Christopher asked.

"Yes, they did a beautiful job," Angie said. "Everything was delicious. Oh, I hope that chicken mole they served at the reception is on the menu. I've been dreaming of it ever since."

A twinge of disappointment wove itself around the regret. Christopher knew it was totally irrational, but he had brought them here because he'd wanted to introduce them to something new, something from his world that he had discovered. Yet by a strange twist of small-world fate, Red was old news to them.

"This place is so beautiful," Angie cooed. "I could live here quite comfortably."

"I'll bet we could." Toby beamed at his wife. His love for her was written all over his face. Watching the two of them so deeply in love blunted the edges of Christopher's disappointment. He wasn't surprised that Toby had settled down. Of all of his siblings, Toby had been the one who was the most family oriented, especially after taking in the three Hemings kids. He was happy for his brother and Angie. He hoped things worked out and that they would be able to adopt the kids. But although Christopher looked forward to being an uncle, he couldn't imagine any other kind of life than the one he was living now.

On their way to lunch Christopher had seized the opportunity to show off his new town and lifestyle. He'd loaded the newlyweds into his spankin' new BMW and given them the fifty cent tour of downtown Red Rock.

Although there were certainly fancier restaurants in town, none spoke to Christopher quite the way Red did. Obviously the Mendoza appeal wasn't restricted to Red Rock, since Toby and Angie seemed to love their food as much as he did.

Christopher held open the door as Angie and Toby stepped inside. He breathed in deeply as he followed them. It smelled damn good…of fresh corn tortillas, chilies and spices. There was something about the mix of old and new that appealed to him. The restaurant was housed in a converted hacienda that had once been owned by a Spanish family rumored to have been related to Mexican dignitary Antonio López de Santa Ana. Santa Ana was known as the Napoleon of the West. Christopher had recently learned that the current owners of the property, Jose and Maria Mendoza, had been fortunate to purchase the house and land at an affordable price before anyone realized its historical significance. The place couldn't have been in better hands because the Mendozas had given the place its due reverence. That was especially true after the restaurant had been largely destroyed by an arson fire in 2009. Luckily, the family rebuilt and reopened after several months and had been going strong ever since.

Inside, the restaurant was decorated with antiques, paintings and memorabilia that dated all the way back to 1845 when President James Polk named Texas the twenty-eighth state of the Union.

In college, Christopher had complemented his business major with a history minor. So it was only natural that he liked the place for its history.

But the food…he *loved* the place for its food.

Red offered a mouthwatering selection of nouveau Mexican cuisine. The chef had a talent for taking traditional dishes such as huevos rancheros, the chicken mole that Angie was so crazy about and tamales, and sending them to new heights using fresh twists on old classics. The menu was bright and vibrant, familiar yet new and exciting.

Christopher had experienced nothing like it in Horseback Hollow. His mother, Jeanne Marie, was a great cook, but her repertoire was more of the meat and potatoes/comfort food variety. The food at Red was an exotic and surprising twist on traditional Mexican.

The chef was always coming up with new specials of the day and anytime Christopher was in, he asked him to taste test and share his opinion. Christopher loved being able to offer his input.

"Good afternoon, Mr. Fortune," said the hostess. "We're so glad you chose to join us for lunch today. Come right this way. Your favorite table is ready."

The shapely brunette shot Christopher a sexy smile before she turned, hips swaying, as she led the three of them to an aged pine table next to a large window where they could enjoy the comfort of the air-conditioning, but still look out at the well-landscaped courtyard. As far as Christopher was concerned, it was the best seat in the house.

After they were settled, the hostess handed each of them a menu. "Enjoy your lunch, and please let me know if you need *anything.*"

She winked at Christopher before she turned to make her way back to the hostess station.

That was quite obvious of her, Christopher thought as he watched her walk away on her high-high heels with the grace and assurance of a tightrope walker. Her skirt was just short enough to draw the eye down to her firm, tanned calves. Now, that was a woman who knew how to dress. Unlike Kinsley, who hid herself under all that heavy tweed fabric that left her looking buttoned-up and shapeless. What a shame.

Suddenly, seeing Kinsley in a skirt and heels like that became his new fantasy.

"I see you come here for the good service," Toby said, a knowing glint in his eye.

"Of course." As Christopher turned back to his brother and Angie, a blonde caught his eye. She was was seated at a table to their left—and he couldn't help noticing that she resembled Kinsley—

Wait, that is *Kinsley.*

She was dining with a woman he didn't recognize. He had a view of Kinsley's profile. If she just turned her head ever so slightly to the right she would see him, but she seemed engrossed in her conversation. Just as he was contemplating getting up and going over to say hello, her server brought their food.

She must have gotten here before him and ordered already. Besides, he, Toby and Angie had just sat down. They hadn't even placed their drink order. He would wait.

When she'd made his reservation she hadn't mentioned that she'd be dining here herself, even though she knew he was going to be here right around the same time. Maybe she was afraid that he would think she was angling for an invite to join them. Most of the women he knew wouldn't have been shy about doing that. But Kinsley was different. Quiet, understated, more conservative.

She was a refreshing change from all the other women he'd met since he'd been in Red Rock. And there had been more than a few. Most of them were sassy and assertive, not at all afraid to reach out and let him know exactly what they wanted and how they wanted it. None of them was a keeper, either. They were all nice and fun, of course, but they left him wanting.

Kinsley, on the other hand, was a puzzle, and most definitely, he realized as he was sitting there, one he was interested in trying to solve.

Hmm. Why had he never thought about her like that before? He'd always thought she was pretty, and on occasion he'd tried to flirt with her, but until right now, he'd never really thought about what made her tick.

As if she felt him watching her, she glanced his way, and their gazes snared. He waved and she lifted a finger before turning her attention back to her lunch companion.

Despite this strange new Kinsley-awareness coursing through him, Christopher decided he should do the same and turned his focus to his brother and Angie.

But pushing her from his mind was harder than he had expected.

The view of the courtyard helped. It was spectacular, with colorful Talavera tiles scattered here and there on the stucco walls, Mexican fan trees and more thriving bougainvillea that seemed to be blooming overtime today in a riot of hot pink, purple and gold. But even the crowning glory of the stately, large fountain in the center of the courtyard couldn't keep Christopher's gaze from wandering over Kinsley's way.

"Too bad we couldn't sit outside," Toby said.

If the temperature wasn't pushing ninety, Christopher would've insisted that they sit out by the fountain. Even though the outside tables were shaded by colorful umbrellas, the humidity was a killer. He didn't want to sweat through his suit and then go back to work.

Not the image he wanted to portray, he thought, glancing at Kinsley.

"Is this okay?" he asked Toby and Angie. "We could move, but it's a killer out there."

"No, this is so lovely," said Angie. "I want to stay right here."

Before she could say more, Marcos Mendoza, the manager of Red, appeared at their table.

"Christopher Fortune, my man." Marcos and Christopher shook hands. "It's great to see you."

"You, too," said Christopher. "My brother Toby and his wife, Angie, are visiting. I couldn't let them leave Red Rock without dining at Red."

"Well, if it isn't the newlyweds." Marcos leaned in and kissed Angie on the cheek then shook Toby's hand. He hooked a thumb in Christopher's direction. "This guy is your brother?"

"Yep, I'll claim him," Toby said without a second's hesitation. His brother's conviction caused Christopher's heart to squeeze ever so slightly, but he did a mental two-step away from the emotion and everything else it implied: the problems between him and Deke; the way he'd left home; the fact that he'd allowed all the ugliness to cause him to miss his own brother's wedding.

"Christopher here is one of our best customers," Marcos said. "I can't believe I didn't put two and two together and figure out that the two of you were related. But different last names?"

"I go by Fortune. Toby goes by Fortune Jones." Angie flinched. Christopher hadn't meant to bite out the words. There was a beat of awkward silence before Toby changed the subject.

"Did you know that Marcos and Wendy are opening a new restaurant in Horseback Hollow?" he asked Christopher.

"Seriously?" Christopher said. He'd only been away a couple of months and he felt like a stranger.

"We're opening The Hollows Cantina next month. In fact, my wife, Wendy, and I are in the process of packing up and moving there with our daughter, Mary-Anne." Marcos paused, a thoughtful look washing over his face. He turned to Christopher. "So if you and Toby are brothers, that means Liam Fortune Jones is your brother, too?"

Christopher nodded.

Marcos smiled. "I've hired his fiancée, Julia Tierney, to be the assistant manager at the restaurant."

Christopher forced a smile.

"I had no idea that you were leaving Red Rock, or that Julia would be working for you," Christopher said.

"I kept it on the down low until I was sure that everything would pan out," said Marcos. "This is a great opportunity for my family, and having my own restaurant will be a dream come true. Really, we owe this happy decision to Julia. She is the one who talked us into opening a place in Horseback Hollow. Your future sister-in-law should work for the Horseback Hollow Chamber of Commerce—she can't say enough good about the place."

"Congratulations," said Angie. "We will be sure to come in after the Cantina opens."

"I have your contact information," said Marcos, "and I will make sure that the two of you are invited to the grand opening. The Fortunes are like family, and family always sticks together."

Toby shot Christopher a knowing look. "Yes, they do."

"In fact, Fortune," Marcos said to Christopher, "I'd better see you at the grand opening celebration, too. Especially now that I know that you're a native son of Horseback Hollow."

Christopher gave a wry smile. "Yeah, well, don't go spreading that around."

Everybody laughed, unaware or ignoring the fact that Christopher wasn't kidding.

"I need to get back to work," Marcos said. "So please excuse me and enjoy your lunch."

The men shook hands again and Marcos planted another kiss on Angie's cheek before he moved on to greet the next table of guests.

"When are Julia and Liam getting married?" asked Christopher.

"That remains to be seen," said Toby. "It's a big step that he's committed to one woman. Julia is good for him. She gets him, but doesn't let him get away with squat. I think she's about the only woman who could make an honest man out of him."

Nodding, Christopher gave the menu a cursory glance. He wanted to hear the day's specials, but it would take something extra appealing to sway him away from his favorite beef brisket enchiladas.

Toby looked up from his menu. "It looks like the marriage bug is infesting our family. I just heard that our cousin Amelia Chesterfield Fortune has gotten engaged to some British aristocrat."

"That just seems so odd," mused Angie. "She was dancing with Quinn Drummond at our wedding. It was the way they were looking at each other... The two of them seemed so happy. In fact, I would've wagered that something was blossoming between them. I just can't imagine that there's another man in the picture."

"Yeah, but I heard the news from Mama and she usually gets things right." Toby shook his head as if trying to reconcile the idea.

Their server was a woman named DeeDee. Christopher had seen her socially one time, but he hadn't called her again. He hadn't realized that she worked at Red. Within the first hour of their date, he'd realized DeeDee was after a whole lot more relationship than he was able to give. No sense in stringing her along, even if she was nice. The world was full of nice women and he needed to get to know a lot more of them before he settled down. He found his gaze sliding over to Kinsley's table yet again. It looked as if they were finishing up with their meals. "Well, if it isn't Christopher Fortune as I live and breathe," DeeDee said, a teasing note in her voice. She twisted a strand of her long red hair around her finger as she talked. "It's been so long since I heard from you, I thought maybe you'd fallen off the face of the earth or maybe you moved to some exotic, faraway land."

Christopher laughed, keeping things light. "It's good to see you, DeeDee. How long have you been working here?"

"It's only my second day."

"Which explains why I've never seen you here," said Christopher.

After a little more playful banter, DeeDee flipped her hair off her shoulder with a swift swipe of her hand and took their drink orders. Next, she described the day's specials, which didn't tempt Christopher's taste buds away from his usual order. After she left to get their drinks, Christopher recommended some of his favorites from the menu to Toby and Angie.

A few minutes later DeeDee returned with a bottle of champagne and three flutes. "This is for the newlyweds, compliments of Mr. Mendoza and the staff at Red."

"Oh, my goodness," said Angie. "Champagne in the middle of the day. How decadent. And how absolutely lovely. Thank you."

"Well, the way I see it," said Toby, "I'm only getting married once, and it's an occasion to celebrate. Right, little brother?"

Toby didn't wait for Christopher to answer. He put his arm around his bride and leaned in, placing a sound kiss on Angie's lips. If DeeDee hadn't been standing there, Christopher might have joked and told them to get a room. But really, it was nice to see Toby and Angie so happy.

"So this is your brother and sister-in-law?" asked DeeDee after she popped the cork and filled the glasses with the bubbly.

Christopher didn't want to be rude, but he didn't want to get too personal. "Yes," he said. "They're visiting, but I'm on my lunch hour so we should place our orders now."

"Of course," said DeeDee, snapping into professional mode. She wrote down their selections and headed toward the kitchen.

After she left, Christopher said, "I just can't get over the fact that you're *married*. But it suits you. It really does."

Toby gave Angie a little squeeze.

"Where do the adoption proceedings stand?" Christopher asked. Seven months ago, Toby had taken in the Hemings children: eleven-year-old Brian, eight-year-old Justin and seven-year-old Kylie. The kids had had nowhere to turn and faced possible separation when their aunt was ordered into rehab for a drinking problem and child neglect. Both Christopher and Toby had known the kids from the Vicker's Corners YMCA where they had worked as coaches. Most people would've run from that kind of responsibility— Christopher knew he certainly couldn't have handled it—but Toby hadn't thought twice before agreeing to take them in.

Unfortunately, the kids' aunt, who obviously didn't have the children's best interests at heart, had decided to try and take the kids from Toby and send them into another unstable situation in California. Her reasoning was the kids should be with relatives. Never mind that the relative she'd chosen was out of work and on parole.

That's all it took for Toby to decide he needed to legally adopt the children.

"Everything is still pending," said Toby. "Frankly, it's taking so long I'm starting to get worried."

"I just don't understand what the holdup is," said Angie. "They not only have a loving home with us, but they also have become part of the family. They call Jeanne Marie and Deke Grandma and Grandpa. They're calling your sisters and brothers Aunt and Uncle. How anyone could think that uprooting these poor kids is what's best for them is beyond me. It breaks my heart."

Toby caressed Angie's shoulder. "We are going to do everything in our power to make sure they stay with us."

"What can I do to help?" asked Christopher.

Toby shrugged. "At this point I don't know what else anyone could do."

"The Fortune name carries a lot of clout," said Christopher. "Maybe we can use its influence to get things going in the right direction."

Toby peered at him. "What exactly are you suggesting?"

Christopher gave a one-shoulder shrug as he rubbed the fingers of his left hand together in the international gesture for *money.* "Money talks, bro."

Toby frowned and shook his head. "Please don't even suggest anything like that. I don't want to be accused of doing anything unethical. That might hurt the situation more than it helps."

"Nonsense," said Christopher. "I think you're being very shortsighted if you don't take full advantage of your birthright."

Christopher saw Toby take in a slow deep breath, as he always did when faced with conflict. It was as if he were framing his response so that he didn't lose his cool.

"I appreciate your concern, Chris," said Toby evenly. "But the caseworker told me she's worried that the Fortunes themselves may be part of the problem. Since the Fortunes invaded Horseback Hollow so many strange things have happened. The authorities still think Orlando Mendoza's accident might have been directed at the family."

"Don't be ridiculous," said Christopher. "Why would anyone want to hurt the Fortunes? I mean, look at me. I'm living proof. Since I changed my name nothing bad has happened to me."

Christopher turned his palms up to punctuate his point.

"That is, if you don't count your running away from home and shunning your entire family as something bad."

Toby cocked an eyebrow at Christopher.

Christopher locked gazes with his brother and crossed his arms.

"Look, I know this Fortune Foundation gig is still new and exciting to you," said Toby, "so don't take this wrong. But someday you're going to learn that some things are more important than money."

Christopher glanced over at Kinsley, but she and

her friend were gone. His gaze swept the restaurant, but she was nowhere to be seen. How had he not seen her leave?

He picked up his champagne glass and knocked back the contents.

"Come on, Chris," said Toby. "When are you coming home? No one has seen you in months. They certainly have no idea that you've completely disowned Daddy's name."

Toby was usually the only one who could see Christopher's side in times when he and Deke disagreed, which was more often than not. Awkward silence hung in the air and, for once, Christopher didn't know how to fill it. He didn't want to fight with Toby, but he wasn't going back to Horseback Hollow. His life was here now, and he would prefer to keep his old and new lives separate. The contrast between the Joneses and the Fortunes was stark. Christopher couldn't take the chance of losing the respect he'd earned at the Foundation.

"Man up, Chris," Toby urged. "Take the high road and be the one who extends the olive branch to Deke."

"Yeah, well that high road has two lanes. Deke can bring that olive branch to me easier than I can bring it to him. I'm a little too busy right now to coddle a grown man."

Toby made a *tsk* sound. "An *old* man. Don't wait too long. You may be sorry if you do."

"Don't pull that guilt trip crap on me," said Christopher. "Just don't. But please do tell me why it's okay for Deke to resent me for making an honest living in a career I love. For making my own way. For not having dirt under my fingernails. No offense to you, but why should I have to grovel to him because the ranch life is not the kind of life I want? Until Deke understands that, I don't think we're going to meet anywhere, much less with an olive branch."

Truth be told, he would rather be known as James Marshall Fortune's nephew than as the son of Deke Jones, crusty old cattle rancher. Christopher hoped that Toby wouldn't make him come out and say that.

Toby stared at Christopher, looking thin-lipped and angry.

"So you've got the fancy suits, the brand-new car and a parade of women who think you're a big shot," said Toby, virtually rolling his eyes at what he obviously perceived as self-importance. "Looks like you've finally achieved your dream, haven't you?"

"You shouldn't knock it since you've never tried it," said Christopher. "No offense to you, Angie. I'm just saying."

Toby took his wife's hand and laced his fingers through hers. "No loss. Believe me, I wouldn't trade my life for yours. I couldn't possibly be any happier than I am with Angie and the kids. On that note, I think we'd better start heading toward home."

Toby pulled out his wallet and tossed a crisp $100 bill onto the table in payment for the food they hadn't managed to stay long enough to have delivered to their table. It was probably one of the ten that Christopher had given him as a wedding gift.

Christopher slid the bill back toward his brother. "Here, Toby. I've got this."

Toby stood. "No, you don't. If you *got this,* you would stop acting like such a pretentious jackass and come home and make amends with Dad. You may have given up on us, Chris, but we'll never give up on you. Take care of yourself and call me when you're ready to talk."

Chapter Three

With his long lunches and daily putting practice, was it any wonder Christopher Fortune didn't get much done? Kinsley mused after fielding a call from Emmett Jamison, the head of the Foundation. Even so, she'd covered for Christopher when Mr. Jamison had asked if she'd seen him. She'd explained that he'd taken a late lunch with family visiting from out of town. She didn't mention that he'd been gone nearly two-and-a-half hours.

She may not have agreed with the way Christopher conducted himself, but she wasn't about to throw him under the bus. That would just make her look bad in the eyes of Mr. Jamison.

She wanted him to see her as a problem solver, not the type of person who pointed fingers and ratted people out. Besides, with the Fortunes, blood was definitely thicker than water. If she wasn't careful the situation might get turned around and come back to bite her. She was sure if it came down to her or Christopher Fortune, Emmett Jamison would side with the man whose last name was on his paycheck.

Kinsley drummed her fingers on the desk. The Fortunes were all about family. She knew Mr. Jamison would excuse him for that. She couldn't deny that she envied Christopher and his huge support system. What was it like to come from such a large, protective family that would circle the wagons at a moment's notice?

Kinsley had no idea. Growing up the only child of an alcoholic father and a mother who couldn't stand up for herself didn't give her much experience to draw from.

She and her mother only had each other to intervene when her father was on a drunken bender. When they did stand up to him, there was always hell to pay.

Her grandmother—her mom's mom—had passed away when Kinsley was about eight, but Grandma hadn't had the wherewithal to extract her daughter from what Kinsley would later look back on and realize was a situation that had robbed her mother of her life.

But wasn't hindsight always perfect?

From the moment Kinsley was old enough to realize she could take care of herself, she vowed she would never personally depend on a man. For that matter, she preferred to not depend on anyone, because didn't people always let you down?

She'd only had two boyfriends, and both of them had proven that to be true. They were hard lessons, but she'd learned. And she prided herself on not repeating the same mistakes.

Family ranks or not, Emmett had said he was concerned because he had received a call from a woman named Judy Davis who was perplexed because she'd emailed the community relations office three times about a donation she wanted to make and still hadn't heard back. She was beginning to think the Foundation didn't want her money.

Kinsley made an excuse that there had been technical difficulties with the email account and had assured Mr. Jamison that she and Christopher would make sure everything was working as it should as soon as he got back...which should be any minute.

Technically, Christopher was being *difficult.* Right? Did that count as technical difficulties? She hoped so. Because it was all she had.

She would cover for Christopher this time, but they were definitely going to have a little heart to heart.

She wrote down Judy Davis's information and assured Mr. Jamison that they would follow up with her today and make sure she knew how much her donation was needed and appreciated.

Kinsley's cheeks burned.

She didn't appreciate being left holding the bag for matters like this, especially when it was something Christopher had insisted on handling. The new Foundation Community Relations email address had been her idea, but they had decided to split the work: as she went out into the community, Kinsley would get the word out about the new way to contact the Foundation; as vice president of community relations, Christopher had insisted on being the one to respond to the emails.

Thank goodness Kinsley had insisted on knowing the password. Christopher had agreed that it was a good idea for more than one person to have access to the account, but he had assured her that he would check it regularly. She had taken him at his word. Kinsley mentally kicked herself for trusting so blindly. People might have been reaching out for help or there could be more potential funding for the Foundation in these unread messages. Yet Christopher was too busy perfecting his putt…and she'd covered for him.

Feeling like a fool, Kinsley gritted her teeth as she typed in the URL to bring up the login page so she could sign into the account.

As a Fortune, Christopher was set for life. Unlike the other family members who worked at the Foundation, he didn't seem grounded in the realities of what mere mortals had to face in the world.

No, Christopher Fortune was fat, spoiled and smug—

Well, maybe not fat. Kinsley hated herself for it, but somehow her gaze always managed to find its way to Christopher's abs. The way his expensive, tailored dress shirts tapered in at his trim waist, she could plainly see that the guy didn't have an ounce of fat on his body.

No, he was all broad shoulders and six-pack abs— or at least she imagined he was sporting a six-pack under his buttoned up exterior. Who wouldn't be if they had time to work out daily? Actually, it didn't matter what Christopher Fortune was packing under his crisp cotton shirt. Mr. Vice President was still spoiled and smug. And completely irresponsible when it came to doing his job.

When the login page came up, she was relieved to see that it hadn't been that long since Christopher had checked the account. In fact, it had only been two days. She scrolled through the ten emails in search of Judy Davis's three messages. When she found them, she realized the three emails had arrived within a span of 36 hours.

Mr. Jamison had been under the impression that she'd been waiting a long time to hear back. Though it really hadn't been an excessively long time since Christopher had checked the account, it did need to be monitored regularly. Several times a day, in fact, to keep something like this from happening.

If that was too much for Christopher to handle, he needed to hand it over to someone who could keep a closer eye on it, Kinsley thought as she started to click on one of the unopened message.

But then she stopped. Instead, she had a better idea.

She took a screenshot of the emails that still needed attention and printed it out. Then she took a fluorescent yellow highlighter and marked each one that he needed to check.

She'd already covered for him. If she did his work for him, too, she would simply be fostering his habit of letting someone else pick up the pieces.

The thought took her back to another place and time that made her unspeakably sad. Maybe if she'd intervened a little more on behalf of her mother things would've turned out differently. She stared at the computer screen as the memory threatened to cut into her heart. But she shrugged off the feelings before they could take root. What had happened to her mother was entirely different from what was happening now.

No amount of wishing or dwelling would change the way things had played out. That's why Kinsley's job at the Foundation was so important. She couldn't change the past, but maybe, if she did her job well, she could make a difference for someone else.

Christopher Fortune didn't need saving. He needed a good swift kick in the rear.

Kinsley had her own workload to worry about. The last thing she needed was to try and reform Mr. Silver Spoon. He was a big boy; he could take care of himself. He needed to start pulling his load. She fully intended to tell him as much when he got back.

Well…in so many words.

She wasn't going to do anything to jeopardize her job. But she could still stand up for herself.

This would be a good time to make sure Christopher knew that, although she didn't mind helping him out with things like checking the Foundation's Community Relations email account and making his lunch reservations, she wasn't his secretary. She didn't intend to mince words about that.

She paper clipped Judy Davis's contact information on top of the highlighted list of unanswered emails and set the papers on the corner of her desk.

She knew it wasn't her place to call him out; she intended to do it tactfully. She'd make him think it was all his idea. But yes. They were going to have a little reality check when he got back. She glanced at the clock on her cell phone—was he even coming back to the office today?

She picked up the phone and dialed. "Hi, Bev, would you please let me know when Mr. Fortune gets back into the office? I want to schedule a meeting with him."

"Speak of the devil," Bev whispered. "He just walked in from lunch. Want me to see if he's available?"

"No, that's okay," Kinsley said. "I'll just walk down the hall and stick my head in his office."

Christopher swiveled his office chair so that it faced the window. He leaned back, stretching his legs out in front of him and resting his hands on his middle.

The more he thought about what had happened at lunch, the more he was sure Deke had sent Toby to do his bidding. It made him so angry he wanted to wrap his putter around the trunk of the magnolia tree out in front of the building.

It could've been a good visit with his brother. A chance to get to know his new sister-in-law a little better. But Deke had to insert himself, even if it was virtually, and mess things up.

His father was so good at messing things up.

But then Christopher had to wonder if his brother would've come to Red Rock if it hadn't been to prod him to go home. Well, it hadn't done any good. If anything it had given him more incentive to stay away. The Joneses couldn't stand anything that varied from their idea of normal. But Christopher had news for them all—this was his new normal.

He looked up at the sound of a knock on his door. He straightened up in his chair and turned back to his desk, moving the mouse to wake up his computer screen.

"Come in," he said.

He was delighted when he saw Kinsley standing in the threshold. Suddenly the afternoon was looking a lot brighter.

"Do you have a moment?" she asked.

"For you, I would clear my schedule."

She rolled her eyes. Not exactly the response he was hoping for, but he would've been surprised if he'd gotten a more enthused reaction.

"I'm just kidding," he said. Actually, he wasn't. "Come in. I'm not the big bad wolf. How was your lunch?"

She shut the door and walked over to stand in front of his desk. "It was fine."

"I saw you at Red," he said. "I was going to come over and say hello, but by the time we ordered you were gone."

"I only had an hour for lunch. I had to get back."

Since he'd seen her at the restaurant she'd pulled her hair back away from her face. And what a face it was; she had a perfect complexion that didn't require much makeup. In fact, he wasn't even sure if she was wearing any makeup. His mind wandered for a moment, imagining the curves that hid beneath the conservative clothes she wore. He smiled at the thought. But then he realized she wasn't smiling at him.

God, if he didn't know better, he might be afraid she'd read his mind.

"Is something wrong?" he asked.

"Since you asked," she said, "actually, yes, there is something wrong."

She held out a piece of paper. He reached across the desk and took it from her.

"What's this?"

She was standing there with her arms crossed—
defensive body language. Her sensible blue blouse was
buttoned all the way up to the top and was tucked into
a plain lighter blue skirt that didn't show nearly enough
leg. Legs, he thought, that would look killer in a pair of
shiny black stilettos, ones like the hostess at Red had
worn, rather than those low-heeled church lady shoes
that looked like something out of his mama's closet.

"It's a message from a woman who has been trying
to get a hold of you to make a donation to the Foundation," she said.

Christopher read the name and number scrawled on
the paper. Judy Davis? He didn't know a Judy Davis.

"Who is she and when did she call?"

Kinsley crossed one ankle over the other, keeping
her arms firmly across her middle. Good grief. If she
twisted herself any tighter she was going to turn herself inside out.

"After she emailed you three times, unsuccessfully,
she called Mr. Jamison to voice her displeasure. He
called me while you were at lunch, none too pleased."

What the hell?

Christopher lifted up the paper with the message
and saw a photocopy of what looked like a list of
emails. Someone had taken a highlighter to it.

"Did Emmett do this?" he asked, gesturing at her
with the paper.

Her cheeks flushed the slightest hue of pink, which
made her look even prettier, if that was possible.

She cleared her throat. "No, I did. Christopher, you
haven't checked the community relations email account in two days. She emailed us three times—"

"Three times over the course of what, 48 hours?"

he asked looking at the paper to check the time the emails came through.

"Actually, it's closer to 36 hours," she said. "I know she was a little impatient, but she wants to give us money and nobody contacted her in a reasonable amount of time. I can understand why she was a little upset."

Christopher watched Kinsley as she stood there, obviously irritated with him. The funny thing was, usually when people nagged him it made him mad, but he found her completely disarming. His gaze dropped to her full bottom lip.

He'd be willing to wager that those lips would taste better than that expensive champagne that Marcos had given them at lunch, and he was getting a little hot and bothered at the realization that he hadn't yet had a taste of Kinsley's lips.

He smiled as he added that task to his mental to-do list.

"I'll be happy to call her now," Christopher said, offering his best smile.

"That's a good idea. The sooner the better. I don't mean to tell you what to do, but you really should check that email account several times a day."

"I checked it three days in a row and there was absolutely no email," he said. "I've been busy. I know this is your brainchild, but people aren't exactly lining up to leave us messages."

Her brows knit. "Christopher, do you see that piece of paper I gave you? There are ten unanswered messages on there. Well, seven if you don't count the three from Judy Davis."

Her face was so expressive. Those lips were so full.

It was mesmerizing to watch her mouth as she talked. He realized he was sitting there grinning stupidly as she reprimanded him. Still, he wanted to laugh. Not at her, but at the situation—at the way the woman had somehow gotten under his skin, but in a good way. A sexy way. A way that made him want to walk over and unbutton the top button of her blouse to loosen her up a bit. Hell, he didn't want to stop there—

"Are you listening to me?" she asked.

"Every single word." He pursed his lips to remove the grin from his face.

Now her hands were on her hips. The stance drew her blouse tight across her breasts. The fabric between the middle buttons gaped a little bit. He forced his eyes back to her face. And she wasn't smiling.

Uh-oh. Busted.

"Then would you please tell me what I just said to you?" she said.

"You were talking about the messages from Susan Davis."

"Judy," she enunciated. "It's *Judy* Davis. For goodness' sake don't make matters worse by calling her the wrong name."

He looked down at the papers he was still holding in his hand. He shuffled the two sheets and saw that yes, indeed, the message said *Judy* Davis.

He smiled to mask his embarrassment. He never had been good with names. "I know her name is Judy. Says so right here." He waved the paper at her. "I was just seeing if you were paying attention."

She rolled her eyes again.

"You don't like me very much, do you?" he asked, eager to hear what she would say. Of course, he was daring her, and he got exactly the reaction he was hoping for.

She blanched. Her eyes flew open wide, and a look of innocence overtook her formerly contemptuous expression.

"I have no idea why you would say that," she said. "You're my coworker and I respect you."

Respect, huh?

But then she surprised him.

"And while we're on the topic of respect," she said, "I need to make sure that we understand each other in a couple of areas."

"Of course," he said. He gestured toward the chair in front of his desk. "Kinsley, please sit down."

She shook her head. "No, I'd rather stand, thank you."

Christopher shrugged. "Okay, suit yourself, but if you're going to stand I guess that means I will, too."

He stood and the slightly panicked and perplexed look clouded her face again. "You don't have to do that. Really, you don't."

"Of course I do. It makes me uncomfortable to have you towering over me."

"What? You're not going to tell me that you're one of those people who believes his head should always be higher than the heads of his subordinates?"

What was this? A dry sense of humor?

He walked around to the other side of the desk, careful to respect her personal space.

"No, but that's not a bad theory."

This time she looked at him as if he had just grown another head on his shoulder.

"You do know I'm kidding, right?"

"I wasn't sure."

"Kinsley. We've been working together for what—two months now? I would *hope* that you would know me better than that by now. You're great at what you do. But you need to loosen up just a little bit. This isn't brain surgery."

"It may not be brain surgery, but I take what I do seriously and I would like for you to take *me* seriously."

What?

Was that what she thought? That he didn't take her seriously? She was one of the most competent, capable people he'd ever worked with. He liked her poise, he liked the way she related to their clients and of course, he loved the way she looked. But maybe that was the problem....

The Fortune mystique didn't seem to work on this woman who was all business, all the time.

Why not?

Why was she immune when most of the women in Red Rock practically bowed down when a Fortune entered the room?

He liked that about her.

All she wanted was to be taken seriously. He understood. That's all he'd wanted from Deke. To be respected for what he did and how he did it.

"Point taken," he said.

She took a deep breath, held it for a moment and then silently released it. He saw her shoulders rise and fall as she did so.

"There's one more thing," she said.

Christopher gestured with both hands. "Please. Anything. You can talk to me."

"First—"

"I thought you said there was only *one* more thing?"

She gave him that look again, as if she were saying *really?*

"I'm sorry," he said. "I do respect you, Kinsley. But could you please unfurrow your brow for just a moment? Unfurrow your brow and smile. Will you do that for me?"

She stood there for a moment looking at him as if she still wasn't sure whether or not he was joking. He held his ground, looking at her expectantly. Finally, she forced a smile. It was the most pathetic and amusing attempt at one he'd ever seen.

"I mean a real smile."

She put her palms in the air, finally uncrossing her arms. "I don't understand what you want from me. But I'm going to tell you what I expect from you—I'm not your Girl Friday. I don't mind helping you, but I'm not your secretary. Secretaries make lunch reservations. Outreach coordinators, which is what I was hired to do for the Foundation, will check the email account if it's something you don't want to do. But you have to communicate with me, Christopher. I'm the one who had to deal with Mr. Jamison when he called wondering why we had dropped the ball. I told him we were experiencing technical difficulties with the new email account. But I don't want to lie, and I can't continue to cover for you."

Her voice was serious but surprisingly not accusatory. What amazed him even more was his reaction to what she was saying. He simply nodded and said, "You're right. We do need to communicate better. If you have suggestions on how we could do that, I'm happy to listen to what you have to say."

"Maybe we could have regular meetings and discuss where we're going with new venture...er, the Foundation's community relations and community outreach efforts?"

"I think that sounds like a wonderful idea," he said, trying not to acknowledge the voice inside his head detailing exactly how he would like to *communicate* with Kinsley.

The woman had asked for respect. He understood that and revered her even more for telling him that was important to her.

"I'm sorry if I gave you the wrong impression. Because you're a very important part of this team and I don't want you to ever feel uncomfortable."

There it was. An almost imperceptible shift in her demeanor, but he saw it. She had re-crossed her arms and was still standing there with her closed-off posture, but her brow was slightly less furrowed and her shoulders were somewhat more relaxed.

"I appreciate that," she said.

He resisted the urge to tell her that he knew there was a lot more to Kinsley Aaron than a pretty face and a potentially great pair of legs. There was something guarded and a little troubled about her and he wanted to know who or what had made her that way because she was way too young and pretty to be that uptight.

He silently vowed that he was going to find out. He was going to be the one to teach Kinsley Aaron how to loosen up.

Chapter Four

Two days later, Kinsley got a call from Emmett Jamison's assistant, Valerie, asking her to meet with Mr. Jamison at two o'clock. Apprehension knotted in her stomach.

Christopher had called Judy Davis right after their discussion. Kinsley had followed up and made sure that Christopher had placed the call. Christopher could be all wit and charm, so Kinsley had been certain that he would win the woman over. She hadn't given it a second thought.

Until now.

Now, Kinsley was nervous that maybe Judy Davis had called back with more complaints and, once again, she would take the fall. Well, she wasn't going to lie and she wouldn't go down without a fight. As she made her way to Mr. Jamison's office, she racked her brain for the words to defend herself if he was calling her in to level the boom.

She loved this job. She was good at it. She'd made great strides with the community outreach program. Really, her work should speak for itself.

When her heartbeat kicked into an irrational staccato, she took a deep breath and reminded herself not to jump to conclusions. Just because Mr. Jamison has never called her to his office before in the year and a half she'd worked there didn't mean the first visit spelled doom.

Valerie looked up and smiled at Kinsley as she approached.

"Hi, Kinsley," she said. "Have a seat. I'll let Mr. Jamison know you're here."

Kinsley had no more than settled herself on the edge of the maroon wingback chair when Valerie hung up the phone and said, "He said to come right in. He's ready to see you."

Kinsley dug deep to offer her most self-assured smile. "Thank you."

When she opened the door, Christopher was the first person she saw. What was he doing here?

He wasn't her boss. Yet he was her superior if you went strictly by job title. When he had started at the Foundation, his place in the chain of command hadn't been officially defined.

But here he was, sitting on the sofa in Emmett Jamison's office. Mr. Jamison occupied the chair across from Christopher. Notes of their laughter still hung in the air. They stood up and smiled at Kinsley as she walked in.

She hoped the convivial air was a good sign. Usually, people didn't sit and joke when they were planning on letting an employee go. She was eager to know what this was all about.

"Hello, Kinsley," said Mr. Jamison. "Thanks for taking time out of your day to meet with us."

That was a good sign.

"No problem at all," she said.

He gestured to the empty space on the couch next to Christopher. For a moment Kinsley silently debated whether she should sit in the chair next to her boss, but she walked over and took the seat he'd indicated.

After their talk the other day, Kinsley had forgiven the flirtation. Maybe it was because despite how incredibly maddening—and flirty—the guy could be, he seemed to have taken seriously her requests to be treated professionally. She couldn't ask for more than that.

She felt him watching her as she settled herself next to him. Okay, so maybe the old dog hadn't completely changed his ways. Or maybe she just needed to relax and own up to the fact that maybe she was the one with the problem. That maybe she found Christopher just a little bit more attractive than she would like to admit. *There.* She'd said it. And immediately blinked away the thought, wondering where it had come from.

"I want to thank both of you for the way you handled Judy Davis," said Emmett. "She called back to say she was delighted with the response she received. I think you charmed her, Christopher."

No doubt.

"But, Kinsley," said Emmett, "Christopher tells me you're the one who alerted him to the fact that there was a problem, allowing him to correct the situation.

That's great teamwork. It started me thinking that the two of you should collaborate on another community relations project."

Christopher had admitted that there had been a problem?

Kinsley checked herself to ensure that her expression didn't expose her surprise.

So he'd fessed up... Hmm... Maybe I need to give him more credit.

"Do you have something in mind?" Christopher asked.

"As a matter of fact I do," said Emmett. "Jed Cramer, principal over at Red Rock High School, told me that you, Kinsley, had lunch with his Cornerstone Club president the other day. He was telling me that there has been an increase in bullying among the students, and he's very concerned. He believes the Foundation can help since we've been successful in reaching teens through our community outreach program. Kinsley, you're really doing a wonderful job with that. I think this is a project that the two of you could really sink your teeth into. Together you could do some real good and put a stop to this bullying problem."

Emmett's eyes darted back and forth between Christopher and Kinsley. "Does this sound like something you would like to handle?"

Kinsley and Christopher both looked at each other and started to speak at the same time. Then they stopped talking and started again at the exact same time.

Finally, Christopher smiled and gestured to Kinsley. "You go first."

She felt her stomach flutter a little, but she ignored

it and simply said, "Thank you. Meg was telling me this is an unfortunate reality that's happening more and more these days. The challenge is getting the kids to speak up—not only the ones who are being bullied, but the ones who witness the bullying. A lot is going on here—self-esteem issues, cliques and a general feeling of wanting—no, needing—to be accepted."

Christopher was nodding his head. Kinsley paused to let him put in his two cents, but he remained quiet. So she continued.

"To reach the kids, we have to not only go where they are, but we also have to reach them on a more personal level. What would you think about the Foundation having a booth at the annual Red Rock Spring Fling?"

"I think it's a wonderful idea," said Emmett.

"I agree," said Christopher. "But we will have to move fast because it's happening toward the end of the month. How about if I check into the logistics of securing the booth?"

"That sounds like a plan," said Emmett. "The two of you can work together to plan the approach you'll take and the material you'll use. Here's more good news. We have about $20,000 in the unspecified reserve account. We had a board meeting yesterday and the board of directors approved your using some of that money to implement an anti-bullying program. How about if we make the Spring Fling our target launch date? Does that sound doable?"

Again, Christopher and Kinsley's gazes met. Maybe it was her imagination, but Kinsley could've sworn that something vaguely electric passed between them. For some reason, despite everything that had already happened, it didn't bother her like it would've before she and Christopher had talked. And that felt a little reckless. She refocused her attention on Emmett.

It was probably just the residual adrenaline rush she'd felt at Mr. Jamison's praise. He'd noticed her hard work. She was having a hard time keeping herself from smiling.

"It sounds doable to me," she said. "We will have our work cut out for us, though, with this timeline. But we can do it."

"Sounds like a very worthy project," said Christopher. "I'm definitely up for the challenge."

His words made Kinsley's breath catch in her throat, which was ridiculous. She needed to stop this nonsense. After her big declaration the other day, if she knew what was good for her she would just keep her mind on the job and stop thinking about how blue Christopher Fortune's eyes were and relishing the times when those eyes lingered and seemed to only see her.

What was wrong with her? Two days ago she had all but read him the riot act about treating her with respect, and here she was in her boss's office contemplating Christopher Fortune's eyes. She needed to get her head on straight. She would do this project and do it right without allowing inappropriate thoughts to get in the way. The last thing she wanted was to let a fickle man come between her and the only stability she'd ever really known.

If her mom had been strong enough to do the same, things would be so different today for both of them.

Well, she would just have to be strong…in memory of her mother.

"Fantastic," said Emmett. "I know the two of you will make a fabulous team. You complement each other. Christopher, you bring the charm, and Kinsley, I know you will keep Christopher on task. I have a very strong feeling I will be calling the two of you my dream team."

Dream team, Kinsley mused.

Why did that seem to work on so many different levels?

Over the next few days, Christopher realized just how many members of the Fortune family worked at the Foundation. The organization was run by Emmett and his wife, Linda Faraday, but working here had given him so many opportunities to meet his cousins: Susan Fortune Eldridge and Julie Osterman Fortune, who were doing great work with troubled teens; Nicholas Fortune, a financial analyst who monitored the Foundation's investments; and Jeremy Fortune, who was a doctor for the Foundation's medical clinic. Yet they always seem to have room for one more. He didn't want to be the slacker amid the bunch. He wanted to make sure that Emmett and Linda didn't regret hiring him. He vowed to be his most professional self.

Christopher had taken to heart Kinsley's request for him to treat her with respect. The anti-bullying project Emmett had assigned was the opportunity for him to prove himself—to Emmett, to his family and, of course, to Kinsley.

If he wasn't able to woo her with the Fortune name and charm that seemed to work on every other woman in Red Rock, he would win her over with his new-

and-improved work ethic. She was an inspiration. She made him want to be a better man.

He would show her that he wasn't just hired because he was a Fortune. Though she hadn't come right out and said it, he knew she must be thinking it.

The anti-bullying project was a worthwhile venture. It was an opportunity to do some good for the community. After two months of feeling as if he was spinning his wheels, he finally felt as if he had a foothold. Plus, it offered the bonus of extra time with Kinsley. It would be a chance for him to get closer to her, a chance for him to woo her and win her over.

Because they didn't have much time to put the display together, the two of them had been spending a lot of time together. They had agreed to a standing hour and a half meeting every afternoon so they could plan their approach.

He should've known by now that Kinsley would throw herself wholeheartedly into anything she committed to. Even so, he hadn't planned on her practically transporting her office to his. But for their first meeting, there she'd been with reams of files and at least a dozen three-ring binders that detailed the different branches of the Foundation's outreach program.

She'd brought so much stuff it required several trips to transport it all. Christopher had helped her carry the bulk of it. Now, the two of them sat across from each other in his office—since it was the larger space— with the information spread out across the coffee table.

"First, I think we should figure out what sort of printed material we need," Kinsley suggested. "I was thinking we could put together a brochure that offers tips about bullying prevention. Like what to do if you find yourself the victim of a bully, and what to do if you see someone else being bullied. We'll need to have these finished first because we'll need some lead time for the printing. What do you think?"

What did he think?

He thought she was one of the most beautiful women he had ever laid eyes on. With her long blond hair and complicated blue eyes, the saying *still waters run deep* came to mind. Kinsley might seem quiet and unassuming, but from what Christopher had experienced, there was a whole lot more going on beneath the surface.

"I think that sounds great," he said. "Do you want to write the copy for that? Somehow I have a feeling you would be a lot better at it than I would."

She had gorgeous skin. He just knew it would feel like silk… He balled his fists to keep from reaching across the table and running a finger along her jawline. She was a natural beauty, and he was willing to bet she didn't even know it.

"I'm happy to do it," she said. "In fact, I already have a couple of ideas for themes. Would you like to hear them?"

Smart. Beautiful. She just needed to know that she didn't have to be all business, all the time. He could help her with that. He felt himself smiling.

"I would love to hear them."

She surprised him by smiling back at him. "Well, the first one I thought of was *Take a stand. Lend a hand.*"

She paused and watched him. Though he knew she would never admit it, he could see in her eyes that she was looking for approval.

"That's great. It's catchy and concise."

Her blue eyes shone. "I'm glad you like it. I thought it served two good purposes. We're encouraging people to take a stand—that could mean standing up for yourself or stepping in when someone else is being bullied. And of course, the *lend a hand* part is all about helping those who are in distress. My research shows that one of the reasons people bully is because they're allowed to get away with it. When people speak up and then get together the bully loses his or her power."

He nodded. "That makes a lot of sense. It's important that we let people know it's okay to intervene."

"Exactly." Her eyes sparkled, and she spoke with such conviction he wondered if she was speaking from personal experience.

"I'm blown away by how much you know about this subject. Did you research it, or is this personal?"

In the seconds it had taken him to ask the question, the glint had disappeared from her eyes and her arms were crossed over her chest like body armor.

"It's just…" She shrugged. "It's really just common sense. But, hey, I have another idea. Are you familiar with the quote, 'Be the change you wish to see in the world'?"

"I am," he said.

"I thought it would be appropriate for something like this."

Christopher cocked his head to the side. "Why does that sound like something that would be your life's motto?"

Kinsley blushed a pretty shade of pink. "Oh, no, I can't take credit for that. It's a famous saying…."

As her voice trailed off, she looked down at her hands, which were tightly clasped in her lap now.

"I know you didn't invent it," Christopher said. "I was just saying it sounds like a good theory to subscribe to. I didn't mean to embarrass you."

Her head snapped up, and she looked at him with intense eyes. "I'm not embarrassed."

He was tempted to razz her about blushing, but he held back. "Kinsley, you've got to loosen up."

She stiffened. Her back was ramrod straight. Suddenly he wished he would've taken the teasing route.

"I don't know what you mean," she said.

She was fidgeting with the top button on her blouse. It wasn't the first time that Christopher had thought about reaching out and unbuttoning it. But that was a surefire way to get himself into a heap of trouble. He finally decided it was best just to move on.

"Either of those slogans would be good," he said. "Frankly, I'm partial to the first one. I think the kids might relate to it better."

She nodded, obviously just as relieved as he was to move away from his thoughtless comment about her needing to loosen up.

"I saw some rubber bracelets and pencils that we could have personalized with the slogan and the Foundation's phone number. We could have them sign an anti-bullying pledge card. And each kid who signs gets a bracelet and pencil as a sign of his or her commitment."

Christopher nodded.

"That's a great idea," he said. "I was doing some homework, too. How do you feel about some pricier giveaways?"

"What did you have in mind?"

"I was searching online and found a place that offers T-shirts, water bottles and dog tag necklaces. We could put the slogan on them and offer them to kids who stop by the booth."

Her brow was knitted again.

"What are you thinking?" he asked.

"That's a great idea, but it might get a little expensive if we gave something like that to everyone who stops by."

Christopher laughed. "I hope we get that much traffic at our booth. That would show a lot of community interest. But I do see what you mean. Plus, I don't want to giveaway throw-away swag."

"What is throw-away swag?" she asked.

"If it's free, the kids will grab it, but once they get home it won't have any value to them. We want the freebies we're offering to be worth something. So if we invest in higher-quality giveaways, purchase fewer of them and offer them as prizes, they will have more sticking power. See what I mean?"

"I do," she said. He followed her gaze and saw she was staring at his putting green. "Maybe we can use that as the game. Anyone who gets a hole in one wins one of the big-ticket items. We could offer less expensive prizes to those who take longer to putt the golf balls into the holes."

His putting green? Did she know how much that cost? Obviously not if she was expecting him to take it to the Spring Fling.

She laughed. "Now I have to ask you what you're thinking."

"I was contemplating one hundred teenagers with

muddy sneakers running up and down my putting green."

"And judging from your expression, am I right in guessing you didn't like the idea?"

He shook his head. "No, not really."

"Oh, right. Anything for the kids, huh?"

"Well, within reason. I was thinking we could have a price. You know, one of those things that they spin, like on Wheel of Fortune. Have different sections with prizes written in each. The kids can spin the wheel and wherever it lands, that's what they get."

"Or they could putt for a prize."

He laughed. "I see what you're doing there. What is it that you have against my putting green?"

"Me? I don't have a thing against your putting green. I just think you should share it."

"Do you golf?" he asked.

"No. I work."

His jaw dropped. *Touché.* The woman had a quick wit.

"Hey, my putting green helps me think."

She shrugged, but the mischievous gleam was back in her eyes. "Lounging by the pool helps me think. But you don't see me doing that during work hours."

"Are you suggesting that I'm a slacker?"

"I didn't say anything of the kind."

"No, but you insinuated it. My putting green and I, you see, we're really close. It's not the kind of thing I just indiscriminately lend out. I'm kind of monogamous when it comes to my green."

"Christopher Fortune monogamous? I'm not buying it. I'll bet I could make a hole in one before you could be monogamous."

"Is that a challenge?"

She looked at him, the amusement apparent on her face.

"I'd love to say yes, but I have no idea how to quantify that challenge. Besides, out of all the women you date, who would you choose? On second thought, don't answer that. I'm changing the subject into safer territory. I don't completely understand the fascination with golf. Can you enlighten me?"

"Come on." He stood and grabbed her hand, pulling her to her feet. "I'll show you."

"Christopher, I was just joking."

As he picked up the putter, he gave her his most wicked smile. He took her hand and led her to the putting green.

"Have you ever putted before?"

"When would I have time to do that?"

Their gazes snared, held. "Don't answer my question with a question."

He handed her the putter. "Go on. Let me see what you've got."

She laughed. "I'm afraid I might put someone's eye out."

His mouth twitched a bit, but he took care not to laugh outright. He was trying to be careful, going with the flow of the chemistry, afraid he might scare her off if he moved too fast or made the wrong move.

He positioned the golf ball on the tee. "Come here." He motioned to her, and she stood where he indicated. He stood behind her and hesitated for a moment, wanting to wrap his arms around her but instead he explained how she should position herself and hold the club.

When she was in place, she looked over her shoulder at him. "Like this?"

"Not exactly."

"Will you show me?"

Her gaze held his and he was sure she knew what she was asking. So he moved in closer, put his arms around her and positioned his hands over hers, holding very loosely and hesitating a moment to give her a chance to pull away. They were so close he could smell her shampoo...or maybe it was her perfume. Whatever it was, it smelled clean and fresh and edible...fruity with a hint of floral.

He breathed in as he drew her arms and the club back. His body completely engulfed her slender frame, making him feel big and broad as he leaned into her with his chest pressing into her back. He liked holding her so close, feeling her body next to his. For a moment, he pushed aside work and the Fortunes and proper decorum and allowed himself to imagine what it would be like to be Kinsley's lover.

Only for a moment. Then he had intended to dial it back to a safe emotional distance that added up to the respect and decency that she deserved. But after she let him pull back her arm and push it forward in a quick flick of motion, he felt her relax.

He didn't move. Neither did she. They stood there together, him engulfing her and her allowing herself to be engulfed, and the ball sank into the cup at the end of the green.

"Look at that." His voice was low and raspy in her ear.

She turned her head ever so slightly to the left. Her cheek brushed his. He turned to meet her, his lips brushing hers. It was a whisper of a kiss that made his blood surge and his need for her spike. Her lips tasted like peppermint and something indefinable—sweet and female. He didn't stop, despite good sense warning him that he should even if she wasn't showing any signs of objection.

It was a leisurely, slow kiss that started with lips and hints of tongue. Until he turned her around to face him so that he could deepen the kiss. She slid her arms around his neck and opened her mouth, fisting her hands into his hair.

Christopher responded by pulling her in closer. He couldn't remember the last time he'd felt so alive, felt so much need, so much want.

When they finally pulled away, they stood there blinking, both a little dazed and disoriented. Christopher was searching for his words. But Kinsley found her voice first.

"That was unexpected," she said. "Now that we've gotten it out of our systems, let's pretend like it never happened and get back to work."

Chapter Five

That kiss.

She couldn't forget that kiss. Even if she had insisted that they put it behind them and pretend like it had never happened.

She could still taste him. Still feel his lips on hers.

What was she supposed to do now?

Focus on the bullying prevention project that Mr. Jamison had assigned her to do, that's what.

Christopher had been out of town for the past two days. They had managed to maintain their cool and continue with their last planning meeting as if nothing had happened. It was both weird and a relief. They'd kissed. And then they'd acted as if nothing had happened. But that's how Kinsley had wanted it.

Or at least, she'd thought it was what she wanted.

After the emotional dust had settled, she was no

longer sure. If she didn't know herself better, she might let herself believe that she was hoping this chemistry brewing between them could morph into a good thing.

Right now, it was a dangerous thing.

Dangerous, seductive and reckless.

Growing up, Kinsley had witnessed firsthand the havoc a dangerous, reckless man could wreak on the life of a vulnerable woman.

If she knew what was best for her, she would get her mind off Christopher Fortune and get her head back into work.

Especially because he was back and they were meeting this morning at Red Rock High School to talk to the kids the principal had identified as leaders and potential candidates for an anti-bullying advisory board. Kinsley had thought it would be a good idea to ask some students to join forces with the Foundation's initiative to help kick-start the program.

Focus on the kids.

That's what she needed to do. If she did that, she would be just fine.

All that positive self-help talk went right out the window when Kinsley pulled into the parking lot and saw Christopher's car. Her stomach flip-flopped like crazy.

Glancing around the lot, she realized the only available spot was the one next to his car. She steeled herself and steered her old Toyota Camry into place.

For a split second, she grappled with the idea of parking across the street or driving around back to see if there was anything back there—away from Christopher's pristine new car.

But she let go of that thought as fast as it had floated into her mind.

She was who she was.

She had worked hard for everything she owned, including this seventeen-year-old sedan. It wasn't flashy, but it was clean and it ran well. As she eyed Christopher's shiny red BMW, she reminded herself that she had never been embarrassed of her station in life. No one had ever handed her anything. She'd never competed against anyone other than herself or pretended to be anyone other than who she was.

And she sure as shooting wasn't about to start now.

Killing the car's engine, she sat for a minute, thinking about the situation. She had enough on her plate with work and school. She didn't have time to worry about things that were beyond her control, such as whether she wanted to be Christopher Fortune's conquest du jour. And if the sad reality—that the only reason he was probably interested in her was because he couldn't have her—wasn't enough proof that this game was a very bad idea, then she deserved to crash and burn.

And possibly lose everything.

With that reality check firmly reframing her perspective, she got out of the car and made her way up the path toward the front doors of the old brick building that had housed Red Rock High School for more than fifty years.

A plaque next to the entrance proudly proclaimed that the building was considered a historical landmark and was registered with the Red Rock Historical Preservation Society. Over the course of the years, the building's interior had been renovated to serve modern needs, but the facade still exuded an ageless charm and held true to the history that this town celebrated so steadfastly. Ancient laurel oaks dripping with Spanish moss shaded the rolling front yard, as if they were standing sentry over the school and all the children inside. The sense of history, place and peace was one of the things that made Kinsley feel so at home in this town.

She pulled back the heavy glass-and-brass front doors and stepped into the cool air-conditioned space. Straight ahead, a long hall of polished hardwood lined by lockers on either side stretched before her. The reception desk was to her immediate right.

"Hello," said a smiling middle-aged woman. Kinsley figured she must be the receptionist, Carol. She'd spoken to her when she'd called to set up the meeting with the principal. "Are you by any chance Kinsley Aaron?"

"I am," Kinsley answered. "And you must be Carol."

"That's right." Carol offered a hand. Kinsley accepted it, appreciating the warmth she felt radiating from the woman.

"Come right this way. Principal Cramer and Mr. Fortune are in his office. They asked me to bring you back as soon as you arrived."

As Kinsley followed Carol past the desk and through a set of doors, she fished her cell out of her purse and checked the time, suddenly fearing she was late. But no, she was actually a few minutes early. That meant that Christopher had been even earlier. He might have had a lot of quirks, but habitual lateness wasn't one of them. In fact, punctuality was one of the things they had in common.

Thank goodness Carol stopped in front of a closed door and knocked before Kinsley's mind could continue too far on the journey of the other things she found attractive about Christopher.

Stop that. She silently reprimanded herself as a deep voice issued the message for them to "Come in."

As Carol pushed open the door, Kinsley realized she was frowning and quickly checked herself to make sure that she not only had her most pleasant business face on, but also that all errant, inappropriate and unbusinesslike thoughts were firmly contained.

There would be no more kissing Christopher.

Not even to get what remained out of their systems.

What a ridiculous thought. How had she ever thought something like that would help? Why had she allowed it to happen?

When she stepped into the principal's office, the first person she saw was Christopher. Her tummy flip-flopped again like crazy, throwing off her equilibrium. Each of her unwavering keep-it-businesslike resolutions flew out the window.

After the meeting with Jed Cramer, Christopher admitted to himself that he wasn't making much headway with Kinsley. Not on the romantic front, anyway.

When Kinsley had walked into the meeting at the high school, she might as well have been on another planet she was so distant.

Christopher was finally admitting to himself that what had started out as a game had turned into something more. He was trying to catch something unattainable.

This wasn't just about physical attraction. It was about not being able to get her out of his head.

This woman was special. She was different from anyone else he'd met. It wasn't like him to be so preoccupied over a woman.

The kiss that they'd shared...and her subsequent parting words about them getting it out of their systems and moving on had plagued him since she'd walked out of his office that day. He'd thought about calling her while he was gone, but he wanted to give her some room. And, truth be told, he needed some space to sort out his own feelings, too.

He kept coming back to the fact that even though he couldn't explain why, he couldn't keep away from Kinsley Aaron the way he had from other women who had gotten too close. Not even after reminding himself of all the problems that could arise if they started something and things ended badly.

He was not ready to settle down. He'd worked too hard to gain his freedom from the ranch in Horseback Hollow to think of tying himself down now that things were just starting to work for him.

But even reminding himself that he and Kinsley would still have to work together if things went south didn't dull this driving need that had him careening toward her.

Since he'd come to Red Rock and started the job at the Fortune Foundation, he'd struggled to keep his professional and personal lives separate. Was he really willing to rethink his personal code for one woman who had somehow managed to get under his skin?

He scrubbed his hands over his eyes as if trying to erase the undeniable answer: yes.

They'd gone their separate ways after the meeting at the high school but had agreed to meet again in his office—the site of that amazing kiss—for their standing meeting.

Christopher glanced at the Waterford crystal clock on his desk. That meeting was set to start in ten minutes.

He had to hand it to her; Kinsley had a way with the kids. The way she'd dealt with the students Jed Cramer had gathered in his office had been amazing. She seemed to have this ability to reach teenagers, especially the girls, on their own level. By the time they left the high school, she had commitments from all seven students to serve on the Fortune Foundation Community Outreach Teen Advisory Board.

During their meeting today, he and Kinsley would work out a game plan for the teen advisory board, outlining exactly what role they wanted the kids to play.

This had come up so fast, and he had a million things to do after being out of town for two days, but he wanted to come into their meeting today with some suggestions. It seemed as if showing her that their project was a priority might be the best way to break through the wall of ice that had formed since the last time they met…. The day of the kiss seemed to have changed the way he looked at everything.

Christopher spent the next five minutes jotting down some ideas that came to mind. The next thing he knew, Kinsley was knocking on his door.

"Come in." He straightened his tie and raked his hand through his hair.

She walked in with her leather folio tucked under

her arm. The knotted tangle of emotions inside him
threw him a little off balance.

I'll be damned.

For the first time in his life, Christopher was a little unnerved by the presence of a beautiful woman.

How had this happened to him?

Really, it didn't matter. She was here. He was here.
They were going to break through this wall of ice even
if he had to turn up the heat again.

"Good afternoon, Christopher," she said.

He rolled his hand in front of his body and made
a show of bowing formally. "Good afternoon, Miss
Aaron."

It worked.

She knit her brows. "Miss Aaron? My, my, are we
a little formal today?"

Christopher smiled at her. "I thought that was the
mood that we were going for here. You with your *Good
afternoon, Christopher.*"

She hugged her leather folio to her chest and
frowned at him. Okay, maybe glib humor wasn't such
a good choice.

"Kinsley—"

She held up her hand. "If you're going to tell me to
lighten up, just save it. We have a lot of work to do and
not much time to do it. We better get busy."

Her voice was neutral. At least she wasn't annoyed
or didn't seem to be.

Why was it that none of his usual methods of flirtation seemed to work on her?

Since they didn't, in an effort to keep things light,
he decided to quit with the clowning and get down to
business.

He gestured toward the coffee table, which was still cluttered from end to end with their previous notes and samples of collateral material. "We've been so prolific, it looks like we are running out of room."

He caught her eyeing the putting green. The thing that had started it all. "Yes, why don't we go into the conference room where we will have more space?" She tore her gaze away from the green and looked him in the eyes. "Plus, maybe we can use the whiteboard in there for outlining our ideas."

Christopher wasn't about to argue with her. He just wanted things to get back on even footing. He couldn't help but wonder if she felt safer with a conference table separating them.

"Sounds good to me," he said. "The whiteboard might come in handy."

With that she seemed to relax a little bit. He had to consciously keep his mouth shut as he forced his mind away from offering her a massage because her shoulders still looked so tense.

Instead, he held his office door for her as they exited and made their way toward the conference room. He was careful to give her enough personal space so that she didn't feel crowded or compromised.

Really, he wanted to make sure he understood the new rules they were playing by.

As he passed Bev's desk in the center of the reception area, she said, "Mr. Fortune, a package just arrived for you. Would you like me to put it on your desk?"

He paused and picked up the homespun-looking package, which was wrapped in plain brown craft paper and tied with twine, glancing first at the return address. Just as he feared, it had a Horseback Hollow postmark. The return address indicated that it was from Jeanne Marie Fortune Jones.

His mother.

A pang of guilt twisted Christopher's heart. He and his father may have had a hard time seeing eye to eye, but his mother was one of the sweetest, kindest women he'd ever known. Christopher new that his move to Red Rock had been hard on her, but he also knew in her heart of hearts she wanted what was best for him.

Unlike his father, who only valued Christopher as another set of hands to help out on the ranch. As he ran his thumb over the paper's rough-hewn surface, he knew that thought wasn't entirely true, even if it did make it easier to justify the way he left.

Christopher felt Kinsley's gaze on him. He looked up to see that she had paused in the hallway that led to the conference room. She was watching him expectantly.

"Thank you, Bev. I'll take this into my office so you don't have to get up. Kinsley, go ahead and start laying things out in the conference room. I'll meet up with you in a second."

Once he was behind closed office doors, he took a pair of scissors from the top drawer of his desk and cut the twine. He used the scissors to loosen the tape and cut away the excess paper, revealing a sturdy cardboard box. He lifted the lid and was a little disappointed when he saw that the package contained what looked like a photo album rather than the cookies he'd been so sure his mother had sent.

He opened the first page and saw a handwritten letter slid into a page protector that his mother had included at the start of the album. The letter said:

My Dear Sweet Chris,
Words can't even begin to express how much I miss you every day. Our family just isn't complete without you here. While I know it's important for you to set out and make your mark in the world, I just want you to know that you will always be welcome to come home when you're ready.
    In the meantime, I wanted to send you some pictures to catch you up on everything that has been going on since you moved to Red Rock.
With all the love in my heart,
Mama

Christopher paged through the album and saw photos of various family members—Stacey and her baby girl, Piper; Toby and Angie's wedding portrait. He lingered over that picture, breathing through a stab of regret for not being there to support his brother on his big day.

The next picture he came to was a snapshot of the Hemings kids hugging his father, Deke. The crusty old jackass was dressed up in a plaid shirt with a bolo tie, that damn cowboy hat that he never went anywhere without perched on the crown of his head. He smiled broadly and regarded the kids with such a look of true adoration. Christopher remembered Toby and Angie mentioning that the kids had started calling his parents

Grandma and Grandpa. Sometimes a man didn't know how to be a father but by the mercy of God became an exemplary grandfather. Funny thing was, even though he resented the hell out of Deke for being such a lousy dad to him, he was glad to see the old man showing the kids some benevolence. Lord knew they had been through enough in their short lives; a little compassion would go a long way with them.

An odd feeling squeezed Christopher's chest. He tried to cough, to dislodge the emotion that was blocking his windpipe, but he couldn't manage to make a sound.

He closed the album and set it down on the corner of his desk. Kinsley was waiting for him in the conference room. He'd look at the photos later.

Much later.

Christopher's grumbling stomach was the first clue that it had gotten late. He glanced at his watch and was surprised to see that it was almost nine o'clock. He and Kinsley had been hashing out the copy for the bully prevention brochure since four-thirty that afternoon. He hadn't noticed how much time had passed until his stomach started to complain.

"I don't know about you, but I'm starving," he said. "We've made some good progress here. What do you say we take a break and go get a bite to eat?"

Kinsley swiped the hair out of her eyes and shot him a weary look. "No, thanks. I'm okay, but you go ahead. We're running up against a tight deadline here and I want to make sure this gets done."

Christopher propped his elbows on the table and watched her as she continued to jot down notes.

"Come on," he said. "You have to eat. I don't want you passing out on me."

Actually, the thought of her *on him* was more appetizing than food. But he kept his thoughts to himself. They had been working for nearly five hours and neither had said a word about what had happened between them the last time they were alone.

"I'll eat after this brochure is finished."

"Even if we get this to the printer by the end of the week we'll still be ahead of schedule. Don't you think there comes a point of diminishing returns after you've been at something so long? Especially if you're hungry."

Her lips puckered with annoyance.

"I'm not hungry. I want to finish my work."

He stood.

"Everyone around here knows how hard you work, Kinsley," he said. "You don't have to prove yourself."

She leveled him with a glare. "That's easy for you to say. But other people around here do have to work hard to get noticed. We don't have everything handed to us."

Ouch. Her words cut to the bone.

"Is that what you think?" he asked. "That just because I'm related to the Fortunes I've had everything handed to me, that life's been one big easy ride?"

She gave him a one-shoulder shrug that was more sexy than it was irritating.

"That just shows how much you don't know. You don't know me at all. So I would suggest that you not judge me until you know me better."

"Is that so?"

"Yes."

"So the guy in the expensive suit who drives the

fancy car and has the $3,500 putting green in his of-
fice and a different date every night is different from
the Christopher Fortune who is standing in front of
me now?"

Christopher cleared his throat. "You have no idea
who I am on the inside or where I've come from to
get where I am now."

"All I know is what I see," she said.

"Well, you've obviously formed your own conclusions," he said. "If you want to go on thinking the
way you're thinking, then that's your right to do so.
But if you are really as compassionate as you seem
to be when you work with those teenagers, then have
dinner with me tonight and get to know the real me."

She put her pen down and stared up at him with an
unreadable expression.

"So what's it going to be?" he asked. "Are you going
to stick to your preconceived notions? Or will you give
me a chance to redeem myself?"

Chapter Six

She should be taking her own car, Kinsley thought as Christopher held open the passenger-side door of his pristine status mobile.

Actually, she should've maintained her *no, thank you* to dinner with him and kept working. But here she was, feeling an awful lot like the Country Mouse who had been ensnared in the City Mouse's grand trappings.

Oh, well, it had been her choice to come. It wasn't as if Christopher had kidnapped her.

Before he got in, he opened the back door on the driver's side and tossed what looked like a photo album onto the backseat. After he had settled himself behind the wheel, Kinsley gestured to the album and asked, "What's that?"

He glanced over his shoulder and stiffened as he looked where she pointed. His blue eyes looked pensive.

"It's nothing. Just a photo album."

"I love photos," she said, leaving the door open for him to say *take a look*.

But he didn't answer, just put the key in the ignition, started the car and backed out.

They drove in silence to Red Brick Bistro, but the place was dark and the parking lot was empty.

"What time is it?" Christopher asked. "Are they closed?"

The clock on the dashboard glowed *nine-twenty-five*.

"It looks like it," said Kinsley. "Maybe they're not open today."

Christopher shook his head. "That's one of the things that I just can't get used to. The restaurants close in Red Rock so early on weeknights. I would expect that from Horseback Hollow, but I thought Red Rock was a little more cosmopolitan."

"Why would you expect that in Horseback Hollow?" she asked.

His left wrist was draped casually over the steering wheel and his right elbow was propped on the center console. The stance caused him to pitch toward her ever so slightly. Despite everything, she was tempted to lean in so she could smell his cologne.

A lot of challenges came with working with Christopher Fortune, but his smell was not one of them. It wasn't just the cologne he wore; it was *him*. His own personal scent that had Kinsley breathing a little deeper and leaning in a little closer—even though she desperately wanted her personal space. The dichotomy

was hard to reconcile. But he smelled of leather—
probably from his car—soap and something else she
couldn't define. It all added up to an alluring essence
that made it difficult to stop everything female inside
of her from roaring to life.

"That's where I'm from," he said. "It's a sleepy
little town less than half the size of Red Rock. The
sidewalks roll up at sundown and there's absolutely
nothing to do. Well, okay, there's The Two Moon Sa-
loon and The Grill, but I wouldn't take you to either
of those places."

She blinked. "Why not?"

"Are you kidding? Neither is known for its am-
bience. They're just not the type of place you take a
woman."

It vaguely occurred to her to remind him this was
not a date. They were two colleagues who had worked
late and were in search of a quick bite. But despite her
better judgment, she liked the cozy feel of sitting there
with him in the car, with him leaning in slightly, the
amber glow of the streetlight casting shadows on his
features. Cars passed on the road that ran alongside
the parking lot, but in a way it felt as if they were the
only two people in the world.

Strange that she would feel so safe and contented
sitting in the confines of a car with a man she'd vowed
to keep at a distance.

"Where is Horseback Hollow?" she asked, angling
her body toward him.

Her peripheral vision caught sight of the photo
album in the backseat. It reminded her that Christopher was an anomaly. In so many ways, he was all
about flash and being a Fortune, but in other ways he

was extremely guarded. That was evident when his brother and sister-in-law had arrived unexpectedly and he'd whisked them out in short order.

It almost seemed as if he had something to hide. Maybe he was embarrassed. Or maybe he was simply trying to keep the Horseback Hollow part of his life private.

"It's outside of Lubbock," he said. "It's about 400 miles from here. Believe me, it's worlds apart from what you're used to."

From what I'm used to?

What did he think her background was? She was born and raised in a small town about fifty miles away from Red Rock. It was a speck on the map. No one had heard of it and she was doing her best to forget it. She'd moved out as soon as she'd graduated high school. Growing up with a verbally abusive father who sometimes physically took his frustrations out on her mother wasn't exactly the life of royalty.

Both of her parents were gone now. A pang of regret swelled inside her that she hadn't done more to help her mother. The worst fights between her parents had always seemed to be centered around her. Sometimes her mother would put herself in between her father and her, and that's when her mother always got the worst of his wrath.

In her naïveté, Kinsley thought she was doing her mother the biggest favor by leaving since she had always seemed to be at the heart of some of her parents' worst fights. But little did she know she was actually leaving her mother even more in harm's way.

Kinsley was a levelheaded woman. She knew darn good and well that all the wishing in the world wouldn't change the past. So she did what she'd always done when the past crept up behind her and threatened to take her down—she pushed it out of her mind and looked forward.

That was her motto: look forward, not back.

But right now she was looking into Christopher's eyes, and she knew that wouldn't lead to anything good.

She shifted her weight so that she was leaning against the passenger door. As if picking up on her nonverbal cue, he shifted away, too.

The pang of regret surprised her.

"I have a feeling everything else around here is probably closed or close to closing," he said. "How about we go to Mendoza's and get a bite there?"

Kinsley didn't get out much. If she wasn't working, she was studying. If she wasn't doing either of those things, she was probably sleeping or attending classes to be a Lamaze coach for a teenage girl who she had met through the Foundation.

Work, school and volunteering didn't give her much time for frequenting places like Mendoza's nightclub. This was only the second time she'd been there. The other occasion was for the grand opening celebration nearly a year ago. Miguel Mendoza, the club's owner, had invited the entire staff of the Fortune Foundation, in addition to what seemed like the entire population of Red Rock, to the club's opening night celebration. Kinsley had considered it more of a work obligation than a night on the town. She had stayed long enough to put in a good showing but had left at the first opportunity.

She looked around, taking in the place, as she and Christopher claimed two places at the long, old-style cowboy bar.

It was hard to believe that just a year and a half ago the place had been an abandoned building. After Miguel, who was a former New York record company executive, had worked his magic, the club was all flash and neon.

A pink neon sign behind the bar that spelled out *Wet Your Whistle* in flowing cursive letters. Neon boot signs illuminated the raised wooden dance floor, where couples danced to music that was accompanied by videos playing on oversize screens located around the room.

At the back a doorway with a neon arrow pointed down over a sign that read *Play Time*. Kinsley wondered if the Play Time room still had the pool tables, dart boards, Skee-Ball and old-model video games that had gotten everyone so excited about the place at the grand opening. If she remembered correctly, there was even an old-fashioned fortune teller machine back there, too. It reminded her of one she had seen once when her grandmother had taken her to an arcade, on one of those nights when her mother had sent her out of the house because her father had been in one of his *bad places*.

That seemed like a lifetime ago. She filed the thought where she kept most of her childhood memories, in a very dark corner in the back of her mind where they wouldn't get in the way. She preferred to live in the here and now rather than dwelling on the past.

And right now, she recognized Miguel Mendoza, who was manning the bar himself tonight.

"Good evening," Miguel said over the music as he placed two cardboard coasters with beer logos in front of them. "What can I get for you?"

After they placed their orders—a glass of white wine for Kinsley and a beer for Christopher—Miguel poured the wine and set it in front of Kinsley, then pulled a frosty mug out of the small freezer and served up Christopher's beer from a tap right in front of them.

"Do I know you?" Miguel asked Christopher. "Maybe I've just seen you here, but I have a feeling we've met before. I'm Miguel Mendoza."

He set the beer in front of Christopher and offered a hand, which Christopher shook.

"Christopher Fortune," he said. "I don't know that we've ever been formally introduced, but I'm in here a lot."

Figures. Kinsley did her best not to roll her eyes, but then made herself step back and reframe her thoughts. He was a young, good-looking, wealthy, single guy. Of course he would want to blow off a little steam after hours at a place like this. That's what people with normal social lives did.

She supposed he could turn the tables on her and wonder why she never made time for fun. Sometimes she wondered that herself. But once she finished her degree and had saved a little money…

Then she would start her life.

However, at the rate she was going, she'd cross that bridge in the very distant future. The truth was she'd never been much of a barfly. That just wasn't her idea of fun. After she graduated she probably wouldn't feel the burning desire to go out and tear up the town any more than she wanted to now.

To each his or her own, she thought as she sipped her white wine. But she suddenly realized that both Christopher and Miguel were looking at her expectantly. She'd obviously missed something.

Christopher leaned in, much too close for her comfort. He placed a hand on her shoulder and whispered in her ear, "I just introduced you to the owner. You might want to say hello or something." He punctuated the suggestion with a quick raise and lower of his brows. It was one of those looks that wasn't cocky enough to be annoying. Cheeky was more apropos. In fact, it was almost endearing. She hated herself for thinking so.

"Hello," she said. "I'm Kinsley Aaron. I work with Christopher at the Fortune Foundation."

Miguel shook her hand and smiled. "That's what he tells me."

"I'm sorry," she said. "The music is a little loud. I didn't hear you the first time."

"I understand," said Miguel. "It's an occupational hazard. So since you both work at the Foundation, would you happen to know Sierra Mendoza Calloway? She's my cousin and she works there."

Kinsley and Christopher answered at the same time. She said yes; Christopher hedged as Kinsley did a double-take, but she did her best to keep her expression neutral. Inside, she was aghast. Sierra had just helped them secure some stock photos for the brochures they were putting together for the Spring Fling. He really didn't remember her? He probably did, he just didn't know her name.

Well, she wasn't about to embarrass him in front of Miguel.

"I adore Sierra," she said. "In fact, just the other day she helped me find a photograph that Christopher and I desperately needed for a brochure we're putting together for a project." She glanced at Christopher and saw a flicker of recognition register on his face.

"I'll be sure and tell her we met you," Kinsley said, turning back to Miguel.

"Please do," Miguel answered. "She's a sweetheart. It's too bad. We have so much family right here in town, yet we don't get to see each other as often as we should."

He looked to Christopher. "As a Fortune, I'll bet you understand how that is."

Christopher gave a quick shrug. "Actually, I've only been in Red Rock a couple of months, and I work with so many of my relatives we get to see each other plenty."

Miguel leaned on the bar. "Oh, yeah, where are you from?"

Kinsley saw the look of hesitation flash across Christopher's face. It was only there for a moment before he stiffened and said, "I'm from a small town outside of Lubbock. I doubt you've heard of it. I moved up here to take the job at the Foundation."

"Lubbock, huh?" said Miguel. "I'm familiar with the area. Try me."

"It's a little dot on the map called Horseback Hollow."

Miguel slapped his hand on the counter. "Get out! Are you serious? I have family there. My brother, Miguel, and his wife are getting ready to open a restaurant there, and my cousin Orlando Mendoza works at the Redmond Flight School."

"I was so sorry to hear about his accident," said Christopher. "It was good of his daughter Gabi to come and care for him."

Miguel looked a little embarrassed. "I haven't seen him since the accident. But I am glad to hear he's doing better."

"You know Gabi is engaged to my brother, Jude, right? She's going to be my sister-in-law. So, doesn't that make us related in some distant way?"

"What a small world. The Fortunes and the Mendozas have always considered each other family. So tonight, your drinks are on me."

"It is a small world," said Christopher. "It's great to meet you. Thank you for the drinks, my friend. But what we really came for was a bite to eat, which, of course, I will pay for. Could we see some menus, please?"

"Of course." Miguel pulled two menus out from behind the bar. "But just so we understand each other, your money is no good here. Money does not change hands among family."

Christopher shook his head and smiled. "I appreciate the generous offer, but really I would be happy to pay. We'll sort it out at the end of the evening."

"Please let me know when you're ready to order," said Miguel. His confident smile seemed to say that he'd already made up his mind. The bill was settled, and nothing Christopher Fortune could say would make a bit of difference.

After they placed their orders for burgers and fries, Miguel set another round of drinks in front of them and went to deliver their dinner request to the kitchen.

Christopher raked his hand through his blond hair. Kinsley was beginning to recognize that habit as a nervous tic.

"What the hell? Is everyone in this town related to someone?"

She couldn't help laughing at him a little. "Pretty much. If they're not a Fortune, they're a Mendoza and a lot of the Fortunes are married to Mendozas.

"May I give you a little bit of unsolicited advice?" Kinsley offered. The beer had loosened him up, and right about now he was longing to hear anything Kinsley had to say. He could be quite content listening to her read a dictionary out loud because it would give him license to drink her in. He could watch her lips move as she formed the words, study the graceful way her delicate jawline curved into her neck and imagine kissing her at that sweet spot where they intersected....

"Sure." Even if he was in for a Kinsley-style reprimand, he didn't mind. She had a firm but gentle way about her. She didn't grate on him the way Deke did when he spouted off with his holier-than-thou statements and rubbed Christopher's nose in I-told-you-sos.

He could tell Kinsley didn't suffer nonsense lightly, but she was also sensitive enough to temper what she said so that it didn't feel like a personal attack.

He appreciated that.

"You would do yourself a world of good to start remembering names. People around here get kind of funny about that. It's off-putting."

She wrinkled her nose and something inside him went soft...and then another part of him, farther south, felt as if it was about to go rock-hard. He held his breath for a moment to get a handle on his libido.

This wasn't college. She deserved his respect, especially after she'd made it perfectly clear where they stood.

He focused on the point she'd made. Remembering names was his weakness, and if he was going to succeed, he needed to fix that.

He still hadn't gotten used to the pop quizzes that jumped out at him just when he thought he had everything under control. All the more reason that he needed to be on the ball.

Sierra Mendoza Calloway was a perfect example. Even if they did call her Sierra Calloway around the office, he should've remembered her. He should've put two and two together. If he really wanted to make his mark in Red Rock, he knew he'd better pay attention and learn the players. He had to know everyone, by sight, right away—especially because so many of them were apparently family, or practically family.

Because wasn't that all anyone wanted—to be valued and respected?

"Thanks for covering for me with Miguel. It would've been embarrassing if he'd known that I spent a good half hour with his cousin and didn't connect the dots."

She nodded. "Well, giving you the benefit of the doubt, I guess there's no way you could've known she's a Mendoza. But don't worry, as long as you pull your weight, I've got your back. And I know that you've got mine, too."

A strangely protective feeling swept through him. "Of course I do. We're a team."

Somehow he didn't think she needed his help as much as he could benefit from hers. Beauty aside—

and she didn't seem to realize how stunning she was—
he was in awe of her strength and people skills. She
was young to be so self-possessed, so stalwartly sure
of herself, yet it was all tempered with a vulnerability that made him want to gather her in his arms and
promise her the world.

They sat in amiable silence for a moment, sipping
their drinks and watching the people on the dance
floor.

"So, Kinsley Aaron, tell me about yourself," he
said.

She shook her head. "I seem to recall that we had
a deal. You promised if I would have dinner with you
tonight, you would tell me *your* story. So don't try to
turn the tables, Mr. Fortune."

"There you go with the formalities again." He
smiled so that she knew he was kidding.

"What's wrong? Does it make you feel like your
father when someone calls you Mr. Fortune?"

He almost laughed. "Absolutely not. As a matter of
fact, it has pretty much the opposite effect."

"Really? Do tell."

He took a long swallow of his beer, trying to think
about where to begin.

"Obviously, you have a misconception that I'm
someone that I'm not."

"Are you not a Fortune, or have you been imper-
sonating one for the past two months?"

If she only knew how close to the truth that really
was....

"Not exactly."

Thank goodness Miguel chose that moment to bring

the food. He set the plates and another round of drinks in front of them.

"Can I get you anything else?"

The food smelled delicious and the company was perfect.

Christopher looked at Kinsley. "I think we're all set," she said. "Thanks for everything, Miguel."

Miguel gave them a salute and hurried off to attend to other customers.

For a weeknight, the place was really rocking. It was great to see it doing such a healthy business.

As they ate their burgers, Christopher told Kinsley about growing up in Horseback Hollow with his mom and dad and six siblings. She was surprised to learn that they had little money and none of the advantages of the Fortune family she knew.

"Are you kidding?" Her wide blue eyes reflected sincere surprise.

"No, I'm not kidding. I had a very humble upbringing. When you have that many kids to feed and clothe, a rancher's income doesn't go very far."

She put down her burger and looked at him with true concern.

"Was your childhood difficult?"

"That depends on how you define *difficult,*" Christopher said. "I mean, we never went hungry or wanted for the necessities. But do you know what it's like to be lost in a crowd of strong-willed siblings, always having to fight for attention and approval, even the last piece of fried chicken?"

She shook her head. "I was an only child. So, no, I don't."

"Being an only child sounds like a little piece of

heaven," he said. "But I guess the grass is always greener when you're looking over the picket fence at someone else's life."

He shrugged. "To be fair, I guess I wouldn't trade my siblings. In fact, that was my brother Toby and his new wife, Angie, who stopped by the office the other day. They were on their way back from their honeymoon and stopped in to see me before they headed back to Horseback Hollow."

And he'd screwed that up, too. He and Toby hadn't spoken since that day. His brother had left the ball in Christopher's court, and Chris hadn't moved on it. What was he supposed to do? Toby had clearly come to do Deke's bidding. His sole purpose was to talk him into coming home. It wasn't going to happen. Not anytime soon.

Christopher laughed a humorless laugh. "My siblings are great at making life more challenging."

"How?" Kinsley asked.

"Compared to them, I guess you'd say I'm the black sheep of the family. My little sisters are sweethearts, but my brothers are hard acts to follow. We're just different. I'm the youngest of the boys. They all seem to be cut from the same cloth. They're right at home on the ranch, exactly where Deke wants us all to be."

"Deke is your father?"

Christopher nodded. "Good old Deke just can't understand how I could want more than spending my entire life in Horseback Hollow and working on the ranch. He clings to that broken-down place like it's life support. And he won't take a word of advice from me on how to make it more profitable."

Kinsley sat there with attentive wide eyes, but remained mostly silent. So, Christopher continued.

"Then my mom, who grew up thinking she was an only child—" he gave Kinsley a knowing look "—discovered not only did she have siblings, but she was one of a set of triplets who had been put up for adoption when they were very young. So then my uncle James, who is one of the triplets along with my aunt Josephine, who lives in England, felt bad that he had so much and my mom had grown up with so little, and he gifted her with a bunch of money."

Kinsley's jaw dropped.

Christopher shrugged. "It seemed like our lives would finally get a whole lot easier. But then, as fast as Uncle James had given Mom the money, she decided she couldn't accept it. She gave it back.

"Every stinking penny of it," he said.

Kinsley was leaning in, rapt. "Oh, my god, this sounds like a movie."

"I know, right?"

"Why?" Kinsley asked. "Why did she give it back if he wanted her to have it?"

"She didn't want to be the cause of any tension between Uncle James and his children. She said discovering that she had this huge family she never knew about was a big enough gift."

Christopher forced himself to leave it at that, because suddenly revealing his ill feelings over getting and then losing the money felt...selfish and narcissistic.

"But on the bright side, between my mom and her three siblings there are twenty-four cousins."

"Wait, you were just complaining about being lost

in a family of nine. How could adding eighteen cousins to the mix make it better?"

"My cousins—most of whom are the Fortunes that you know, or at least resemble what you think a Fortune should be, are a bit more... How do I put this tactfully... They're a bit more worldly than my humble family."

Christopher held off telling her about the fight he'd had with Deke the night he left Horseback Hollow for good.

Equal parts shame and regret washed over him as he thought about the harsh words he'd exchanged with his father that night. But what the hell was he supposed to do? If he'd listened to Deke, he wouldn't be sitting here with this incredible woman right now. If that in itself wasn't proof that he'd made the right decision to come to Red Rock, then he didn't know what was.

Kinsley shook her head. "I can't imagine having that many relatives. That would just be... I mean it would be cool, but no wonder you have a hard time remembering names. What's your mom like?"

"She is the sweetest person you could ever imagine meeting," he said. "She's all about her family and kids. But I wish she would be stronger when it comes to standing up to Deke. He can be the worst kind of bully," Christopher snorted. "Talk about someone who could benefit from a bully prevention program."

Empathy colored Kinsley's beautiful blue eyes.

"I understand what it's like to have father conflict," Kinsley said. "I was close to my mom, too. Your mom must be a good soul if she is content to build Fortune family relations with none of its monetary perks."

Christopher shrugged. "Are you saying I'm wrong

for wanting a different life than the ranch has to offer? As far as Deke is concerned, my birthright is in Horseback Hollow."

"Why don't you go visit your dad and talk things out?"

Chapter Seven

Why was she trying to give Christopher advice on family relations? Kinsley knew she was certainly in no position to do that. She'd run away from problems with her own father, and in the process had left her mother high and dry. Obviously, she was no expert on making things right.

"I'm not ready to go home yet," Christopher said, answering her question after a long pause.

"Why not?" Kinsley asked.

"It's complicated."

Kinsley shrugged. "Yeah, life gets that way sometimes."

She was speechless, listening to this man who was turning out to be nothing like the shallow, glad-handing guy who on his best days had irritated her... and on her worst days had tempted her.

She didn't want to think about that right now. In fact, she felt a little guilty about the preconceived notions she'd formed.

She wanted to know more about his life at the Horseback Hollow ranch, more about what he'd been like before he'd discovered his Fortune relatives. Even though she only knew a few things about his life before he'd moved to Red Rock, she sensed she knew his heart better now.

Everyone struggles with something, even if they hide behind a smile. Or in Christopher's case, expensive clothes and a fancy car.

Her mask was work and school.

She knew that, but she wasn't ready to do anything to change. If she wasn't willing to amend herself, why should she expect Christopher to present a different face than the one he showed?

She had to give the guy credit. At least he seemed to understand how fortunate he was to have been, given a leg up to starting his new life.

His upbringing explained a lot: his need for attention, his tendency to show off and his penchant for the ladies.

Yes, there was that, she reminded herself. If she knew what was good for her, she would keep that firmly in mind.

Christopher was charming and charismatic. Kinsley was willing to bet that this revolving door of women was as new to him as his red BMW.

Even if he'd always been popular with the ladies, if Horseback Hollow was as small as he'd made it sound, he'd probably never had the smorgasbord available to him now.

Despite that, her esteem for Christopher had risen. She could tell that he had genuine affection for his mother, brothers and sisters. She had to admit that she was just a little bit envious of his big, boisterous family. When she was little, she used to long for a big brother to watch out for her. Maybe if she'd had one, things would've been different. Maybe her mother would still be alive today.

"It sounds like Toby was trying to entice you to come home when he dropped by the other day."

He shifted in his seat and his face closed. "I wish it were that easy."

"I know it's a big trip," she said. "But maybe you could take a long weekend. I'm sure Mr. Jamison would understand."

As Christopher looked at her, she could see him choosing his words. "It's not the distance. I could fly there and back in less time than it would take to get to the airport. I'm just not in a very good place with my father right now."

"I know there's more going on between you and your father than what you've told me, and I understand if it's a private thing. You don't have to tell me. But logic does dictate that he must be a pretty good man to have raised such great kids."

Again Christopher shifted in his seat. This time he moved away from her and turned his attention to his beer.

"Christopher, nobody's perfect. But please take my advice. Sometimes it seems like the people who have taken care of us will be around forever, but the truth is life is short."

Her mother had been just forty-six years old when

she'd died. Way too young. It sounded ridiculous to say—she couldn't even say the words out loud, and she could barely admit them to herself—but it never occurred to her that her mother could die. Her mother, the one who had always looked out for her, the one who had thrown herself between Kinsley and that horrible man who just happened to be related to her by genetics.

Kinsley had been far too wrapped up in her own life, in getting out of the abysmal, abusive situation she was born into and starting the life she knew she was meant to have.

What she wouldn't give to go back and do everything differently. She would've insisted that her mom come with her. The man who had abused them both and cheated on her mother could've rotted in hell for all she cared.

Surely he was burning there now.

But there were no do-overs. She could only look forward and hope that she might be able to honor her mother's memory by helping some other unlucky woman who was caught in an unfortunate situation. More immediately, maybe she could help teenage girls realize that they didn't have to settle for someone who treated them poorly. That by the virtue of being born they were princesses—even if they never had a father to tell them so.

"Hey," said Christopher. "Where'd you go?"

She blinked at him, unsure what she had missed.

"You were somewhere far, far away," he said. "Would you care to share?"

This was one instance when she was glad she had never been able to cry about her mother and the whole sorry situation. She had always worried that if she let down the floodgates she might never stop crying. At that very moment, she vowed that she would never put her theory to the test.

The way Christopher was watching her she had a feeling that because he had shared his story, he was going to expect reciprocation from her. That was something else that wasn't going to happen.

The music changed to a medium-tempo Blake Shelton tune.

"I love this song," she said. "Dance with me."

She was on her feet and headed toward the dance floor before Christopher could refuse and before she could change her own mind.

By the time she'd wedged her way into a spot on the dance floor, Christopher was right there next to her. Only then did it dawn on her that he would probably hate this song that talked about red dirt roads and doing manual labor.

Oh, well.

The dance floor was small, hot and crowded, forcing them into close proximity even though it wasn't a slow dance. But that was okay because the music was even louder over here, and it seemed to keep Christopher from asking questions. Some couples tried to do a slow two-step around the perimeter of the close confines, but Christopher kept his hands to himself and didn't try to pull her into that kind of dance.

Given the kiss they'd shared, he'd proved himself unpredictable enough that she wouldn't have been shocked if he had pulled her close, but this was fine.

Really, it was.

After three glasses of wine, she would probably melt in his arms. She wasn't drunk, just nicely loosened up. Once they had established their dance M.O., she let herself be swept away by the pounding rhythm of the music. It felt good to let her hair down and lose herself.

Christopher looked as if he was enjoying himself, too, moving unselfconsciously to the beat. Maybe it was the wine talking, but suddenly she wondered why she didn't go out more often. Christopher smiled that endearingly cheeky smile as he moved next to her. It struck her that it was a pretty darn attractive quality for a guy to be willing to dance. So many of the guys she'd known had refused to let go like this.

As she took in Christopher's subtle moves, she couldn't help but wonder what he would be like in bed. She hadn't had that much experience, and really none of it was notable, but she'd always heard that the way the guy danced gave a lot of clues as to how he would make love.

If that was the case, Christopher seemed to be proving himself *quite* capable.

Lord have mercy.

She was glad the music was so loud because she felt a giggle bubble up and escape. It must have come across as a smile because Christopher beamed at her.

The two of them got into the spirit, communicating with only their eyes and expressions.

Again, this guy, who she'd been so quick to dismiss, was showing her another side. Here he was in his white dress shirt with the sleeves pushed up past the elbows getting down as well as any of the cowboys in the place. She was tempted to tease him about his ranch upbringing coming out on the dance floor, but that was for later.

This was now.

This was fun.

This was a high she wished would last...and last...and—

An overzealous couple two-stepped right into Kinsley, knocking her into Christopher. He caught her, holding her close in his strong arms. The two of them stood breast to chest, staring into each other's eyes, vaguely swaying to the song's refrain.

Then, right there in the middle of the dance floor, he didn't ask permission; he simply lowered his head and kissed her unapologetically, ravenously. And she kissed him back shamelessly, completely taken by their mutual hunger.

The kiss bypassed slow and soft, immediately igniting into a voracious fire that had her parting her lips and deepening the kiss. Her arms found their way around his neck and her hands fisted into the cotton of his shirt. They leaned into each other as if they depended on this intimate contact for their life's breath.

The whole world disappeared—Mendoza's, the dance floor, the music. She didn't care who was there or who might be watching them. The only thing that mattered was the way he was holding her so tightly against him, staking his claim, in this wordless confession of desire.

The taste of his beer mingled with her wine and merged with hints of the truffle salt from the fries. And then there was that familiar hint of *him* that she had tasted when they'd kissed in his office. But that was then. Now, she tasted a hint of the forbidden mixed with the temptation of right now.

A moment ago she had convinced herself that this

was taboo, and now he was kissing her so thoroughly that she didn't want to stop. Feelings inside her that had awakened when he'd kissed her the first time were now laced with a passion that threatened to consume her.

She'd forgotten the once logical rationale for protecting her heart. Or maybe she no longer cared. The reasons had shifted and transformed *why not* into *oh, yes* were promising to be so worth the risk.

Kinsley had no idea how much time had passed as they held each other and kissed as people whirled around them on the dance floor.

As they slowly came up for air, Christopher held her face in his palms, his forehead resting on hers. Maybe it was the liquid courage talking, but this kiss felt right, and the way he was holding her seemed to say he felt it, too.

"Oh, my God, Christopher, what are we going to do now?"

No matter what Kinsley said today, he wasn't going to let this go. They couldn't go back to being purely platonic, not after last night's kiss. They were definitely in a different place now. And he liked it.

Christopher smiled to himself as he picked up the phone.

His gut told him that after he'd dropped her off at her apartment last night she'd probably overthought everything.

He dialed Red and made a lunch reservation for two at his favorite table, then sat back in his leather chair, glancing at the putting green. One kiss might have been a mistake. But two? There was no denying the fire that blazed between them last night.

Even if she resisted, he was going to prove to her that there was something special between them. Something worth fighting for.

He hadn't seen Kinsley yet today, but when he did, he wanted her to know beyond a doubt that last night meant something to him. What better way than to go back to when everything seemed to start—that day that Toby and Angie had arrived and he'd asked Kinsley to make a lunch reservation at Red. He hoped she'd see the meaning behind this lunch date.

He started to pick up the phone again to call her and ask her to lunch, but then he thought better of it. He got up and walked to her office.

The door was open, so he rapped lightly on the door frame.

"Good morning," he said when she looked up from her computer.

"Good morning." Her tone was neutral. She finished typing whatever it was he had interrupted before she said, "Come in."

He walked in and sat down in the chair across from her desk.

"I'm glad you're here," she said.

He smiled and quirked a brow, but she carried on business as usual.

"I realized this morning that we need to come up with a calendar of deadlines so that we make sure we get everything done in time for the Spring Fling. Do you realize it's less than two weeks away?"

What?

"That's not what I came in here to talk to you about, but sure. We can do that."

Her expression remained neutral, but her voice held

the faintest notes of exasperation. "Would you please close the door?"

Christopher complied. When they were safe behind closed doors, he said, "I enjoyed last night."

She tensed and closed her eyes a blink that was a few beats too long before she opened them again. "About that.... Listen, I appreciate you being so nice about it, but I think we both had a little bit to drink last night."

"We did and it was a great time. I hope we can do it again. In fact, I made reservations for us to have lunch at Red today at twelve-thirty. Of course, it might not be a good idea for us to drink as much as we did last night, since we have to come back and work on these things that you're putting on the calendar." She was sitting there staring at him blankly. "And I had hoped you might catch the meaning in me making the lunch reservation instead of asking you, but..."

He thought he saw her wince ever so slightly as she continued to regard him with that neutral expression. He reminded himself that he had expected her to react this way. *See, he knew her.* And he had also been prepared for the possibility of having to take things slowly as she came to terms with the fact that this was right—and good.

And very real.

"Okay, so why don't we discuss this calendar and everything we need to put on it at lunch today? At Red."

He winked at her. Then promptly realized that was probably not a good move.

"Or if you have a few minutes now," she said, "we can talk about it and get everything all squared away."

He saw what she was doing.

He stood. "Sorry, I don't have time right now. I'll pick you up at 12:15 and we can discuss everything over lunch."

He flashed his most charismatic smile and was pleased to note that some of her bravado seemed to wither away in front of him.

"Okay. Fine. We can have a working lunch."

He opened the door. "See you soon." He left it open, exactly the way he had found it.

As he walked back to his office, he was more determined than ever to make Kinsley see just how good they could be together.

"Hello, Mr. Fortune. It's nice to see you," said the tall, thin, pretty hostess at Red. "A table for two for you and...your girlfriend?"

"Oh, no. I'm not his girlfriend. We're not... We just work together."

The hostess regarded Kinsley with a subtle air that suggested she was just being polite and hadn't been convinced they were even a couple to begin with.

"Well, that's very good to know." The hostess smiled and boldly looked Christopher up and down.

Kinsley's cheeks burned.

How rude and unprofessional.

A little voice in the back of Kinsley's mind reminded her that it was a lot more professional than she had been when she'd made out with Christopher on the dance floor at Mendoza's. Anybody in town could have seen them acting like a couple of hormone-driven teenagers who couldn't keep their hands off each other.

Even though common sense told her that nobody

was looking at them as she and Christopher followed the hostess to their table, it felt as if every eye in the place was on watching them.

Once they were settled and the hostess had managed to tear herself away, Christopher looked her squarely in the eyes and said, "Kinsley, we make such a good team, in and out of the office—"

"That's why we need to pretend like nothing happened last night," she said.

"That's what we said after our first kiss," he countered. "And we see where that got us. Why are we fighting this? I think we could be very good together if you would just give us a chance."

Kinsley's heart pounded an insistent staccato in her chest. It was almost like a finger tapping her chest urging her to do the right thing—to set the record straight with Christopher, to make sure he understood exactly where they stood.

As long as they both worked at the Foundation, all they would be were platonic coworkers. Since she didn't plan on leaving her job anytime soon, apparently that was all that fate had in store for them.

Christopher would be free to fully enjoy all the perks of being a young, good-looking guy with too much money and a tendency to flash it to get whatever and whomever he wanted—like the hostess who had given Kinsley the stink eye when they'd arrived.

Women like that might throw themselves at him, but Kinsley would not be his conquest, and that was at the heart of why they would never work. The two of them came from different worlds. He might think he'd had it bad off being lost in the chaos of a large family where money had once been tight, but he had no idea what it was like to have lost the only person in the world who had ever shown unconditional love.

Kinsley had witnessed firsthand the pain her mother had suffered at the hands of her womanizing father, who couldn't or wouldn't stop himself when it came to the ladies. No matter how her mother had cried and threatened to leave him, he would simply turn the tables on her and somehow manage to blame her mother for his own philandering. Even after her front-row seat for this cautionary tale, in college Kinsley had still been stupid enough to put her faith in a man who ended up proving himself as verbally abusive and faithless as her own father. In her studies she had learned that victims of abuse often unwittingly fell into the trap of falling for abusive partners.

She wasn't convinced that Christopher had abusive tendencies, but he sure did have an eye for ladies. That was enough to make Kinsley put on the breaks. It was clear that Christopher still had oats to sow. She wasn't going to fall into the same trap that her mother had suffered or repeat the same mistake she'd already made....

Last night was her last dance with Christopher Fortune.

Chapter Eight

Thursday night was ladies' night at Mendoza's. That's why Christopher was surprised his cousin Sawyer Fortune who was in town for the day, suggested that they meet there to discuss a fund-raising opportunity for the Foundation over a beer and a quick bite to eat.

Ladies' night didn't officially start until nine o'clock, so even though it was nearly eight o'clock, Mendoza's still had the air of a restaurant. The lights were a little brighter than they would be later on, and the music was much softer and less honky-tonk than it would be when the clock struck nine. So they had time to wrap up their business before the party overtook the place. Sawyer would be long gone before then, anyway, because he had to fly to Horseback Hollow before it got too late.

Sawyer was happily married to Laurel Redmond, had been since New Year's Eve. After the wedding, they had moved to Horseback Hollow to open a branch of Redmond Flight School and Charter Service. The operation was headquartered out of Red Rock, so Sawyer still came to town occasionally. Today, Sawyer had been involved in nonstop meetings all day and had suggested that the two of them grab a couple of Mendoza's famous tacos before he flew home that evening.

Whether they were talking business or not, Christopher was always glad for a chance to visit with his cousin because he hadn't really had the opportunity to get to know him very well before his own move to Red Rock. This was not only a good chance to spend time with him, but also a chance to discuss a way for the flight school to make a charitable contribution to the Foundation.

Christopher had asked Kinsley to join them, but she had her statistics class tonight and after that, she was attending a Lamaze class with a teenage girl she had agreed to help.

Kinsley had so much on her plate that Christopher didn't know how she handled it all. But working all day, going to class and then finding the energy to help this girl were just a few of the many reasons Christopher found her so amazing.

She had said she would text him when she was free so that he could fill her in on the details of what he and Sawyer had come up with. She had mentioned that she should be finished shortly after eight o'clock. Christopher found himself glancing at his phone, alternately checking the time and making sure he hadn't missed a text from her.

Nothing yet.

"Are you expecting a hot date?" Sawyer kidded.

"Nope. Not tonight," Christopher said as he clicked off his phone yet again.

Sawyer gestured to the phone. "You keep checking that thing. I thought maybe you were waiting for someone to call you."

"Actually, I'm waiting for Kinsley Aaron, my colleague, to text me so I can fill her in on how you're going to help us raise all kinds of money."

Christopher and Sawyer had discussed the possibility of having an air-show fund-raiser to benefit the Foundation's bully prevention program. Unfortunately, the date of the Spring Fling was too close for them to get something together, but the event was definitely a possibility for the future. In fact, it was probably best to do it as a separate experience, anyway, because it would be another opportunity to raise awareness for the cause.

"Just tell Kinsley not to get too excited yet," said Sawyer. "I need to run all this by Tanner and Jordana before we can give it the official green light. But I have a feeling they will be just as thrilled as I am about having the chance to help with this worthy cause."

Tanner Redmond and his wife, Jordana Fortune Redmond, owned and operated the Red Rock branch of Redmond Flight School and Charter Service.

"I'm sorry Tanner and Jordana couldn't be here tonight to discuss this," Christopher said.

The Redmonds were out of town. That was one of the reasons Sawyer had flown up for the day, to cover some meetings, check on the Red Rock office and make sure everything was running smoothly.

"I am, too," said Sawyer. "Later on, after they give me the thumbs up, we'll all get together and discuss everything. Maybe your Kinsley will be able to join us then, too."

Your Kinsley. If Christopher had anything to say about it, next time Sawyer was in town, she *would* be his. Something intense flared inside him at the thought, and the sensation made him double his determination to make that so.

But the feeling was interrupted by a shapely brunette who slid into the seat next to Christopher.

"Hello?" Christopher said. "May I help you?"

The young woman looked familiar, but he couldn't place her.

"You don't remember me, do you?" she said, smiling as she twisted a strand of long dark hair around her finger.

Christopher darted a glance at Sawyer, who was watching them, in the off chance that the woman might be a friend of his. Christopher knew it was highly unlikely, though.

"I'm Crystal?" she said. "I seated you at Red for lunch the other day? And the time before that when you were in with the newlyweds?"

Crystal was pretty enough, but she seemed to have an annoying habit of turning every sentence into a question. Still, he didn't want to be rude.

"Right, I remember. Hello, Crystal. I'm Christopher Fortune. This is Sawyer Fortune, my cousin."

"Ooh," she said. This time it wasn't a question as much as an exclamation. She looked Sawyer up and down, her gaze lighting on his wedding ring. She turned back to Christopher.

"It's your lucky night. I'm going to let you buy me a drink."

Her question-phrasing was strike one. Strike two was calling him Chris. No one in Red Rock called him Chris.

Still, he played along. "Oh, you are, are you?"

Crystal nodded. "Yeah. And if you play your cards right tonight? I will make it very worth your while."

Christopher had gotten used to bold women, but this was the first time he had encountered someone who was downright carnivorous. He glanced at Sawyer, who looked as befuddled as Christopher felt, then he turned back to Crystal.

"Well, you're a very beautiful woman...and that sounds like an offer that would be hard for most men to refuse. But I'm right in the middle of a business meeting here."

At least he didn't have to ask her to leave. She scooted out of the booth. "Well, you come find me after you're done here, okay?" She blew him a kiss and tottered away in high heels and a short miniskirt that didn't look as alluring tonight as they had that first time he'd seen her.

Sawyer whistled under his breath. But it wasn't an appreciative sound; it was more the sound somebody made when they had witnessed a train wreck.

"Looks like someone's celebrating ladies' night a little early," said Christopher.

As he watched the woman walk away, he realized he wasn't interested. Not the least bit. Maybe he had finally had his fill of the pretty-girl smorgasbord. Or maybe he really did have standards when it came to women. How many other men had found it *worth their while* to buy her drinks? He really didn't want to know.

What he did know is that he wanted a woman with more substance.

As if right on cue a message from Kinsley flashed on his phone.

Just got home. How was the meeting?

Christopher picked up his phone and typed, Still with Sawyer. It's going well. A lot to tell you.

She returned, Good to hear. Fill me in when you're done?

He typed back, You bet!

"So, is your *colleague* back?" Sawyer asked.

"She is."

Sawyer took a long sip of his iced tea, then set the glass down on the table. "You seem pretty happy to hear from her."

Sawyer laced the words with insinuation. Christopher shrugged but couldn't hide his smile.

"Yeah, well…" He shrugged again.

Sawyer nodded. "Are you two dating?"

Christopher glanced at his phone again to see if Kinsley had responded. She hadn't.

"Why do you ask?"

"Well, I was just about ready to get on my way to Horseback Hollow so you could *make the night worth your while.* But I'm sensing you're not into that." Sawyer nodded toward the general area where Crystal waited.

Christopher didn't dare look over there for fear of sending her the wrong message. He really wasn't interested.

"It's complicated," he answered.

"It doesn't have to be," Sawyer said. "When it's right, it's the most uncomplicated feeling in the world. That doesn't mean things are always easy, or that in the beginning you don't have to fight the good fight. But when it's right you'll know."

Christopher weighed his words. He really didn't need to explain. In fact, there really wasn't anything to explain. He and Kinsley were in limbo right now, but something told him to stay quiet.

"Okay, then, let's just say, I'm fighting the good fight right now."

Sawyer nodded, a knowing look in his eyes. "Good luck, man. I hope she's worth it. Not to say she's not."

Another text flashed on Christopher's phone. His gut contracted but then released when he saw it was from his buddy Joe.

Art and I are headed over to Mendoza's for ladies' night. See you there.

Christopher considered typing, *Already here,* but Sawyer said, "Are you concerned at all about dating someone you work with? I know a lot of people caution against it, but Laurel and I work together and Tanner and Jordana do, too. We might be the exception to the rule, but at least we're proof that it can work. If you have feelings for this woman, don't let being colleagues scare you off."

Christopher pushed his phone away. "I have to admit I've wondered how Uncle James would feel about workplace dating. She's important to me, but I don't want to rock any boats at work."

Sawyer made a *pffff* sound. "If you only knew

how many Fortunes met their spouses on the job, you wouldn't be worried. The only thing you might need to keep in mind is if things don't work out, you can't let it get in the way of anything."

Christopher crossed his arms in front of him. "Of course not."

"Well, since you said Kinsley is important to you, I say go for it. You seem to have your priorities straight and a level head on your shoulders. Just use good common sense."

Sawyer looked at his watch. "It's getting late. I'd better get out of here so I can get home at a decent hour. I'm not going to lie. It's pretty nice to have someone to come home to."

Sawyer reached for his wallet, but Christopher held out a hand. "You came all this way. I've got the tab."

He was relieved that he hadn't seen Miguel tonight. Although it was generous of the guy to cover the bill the night he was there with Kinsley, Miguel's comment about Christopher's money not being any good there made him uncomfortable. He was perfectly prepared to pay his own way. He didn't want to seem like a moocher. In fact, even though he greatly appreciated Miguel's hospitality, he had to admit the thought of Miguel doing so in the future made him uneasy about hanging out at Mendoza's. Christopher's eyes darted back to the phone. Still no response from Kinsley. Then again, his response had been sort of closed-ended. He'd told her he would text her after Sawyer left, which was happening now.

Sawyer stood and so did Christopher. The two shook hands.

"It was great seeing you," said Sawyer. "And thanks for dinner. Next time it's on me."

Christopher clapped him on the back as he walked with him toward the entrance. "Next time, you bring me good news about the air-show fund-raiser and I'll not only buy you dinner, but I'll also throw in a bottle of champagne."

Sawyer laughed. "You better start chilling that bubbly because I'm pretty confident I'll have good news for you soon. Good luck with the girl."

As they were walking out to the parking lot, Christopher ran into Art and Joe, who were on their way inside.

Christopher introduced his cousin to his buddies and after quick small talk Sawyer said good night and excused himself.

"Should've known you'd already be here," said Joe. "You get an early start on the night? So what are we waiting for? Bring on the ladies."

Funny thing, for the first time ever, Christopher wasn't in the mood to party. He was more eager to get to a quiet spot where he could write down all of the ideas that he and Sawyer had come up with and text Kinsley.

"Actually, I was here for a business meeting," he said. "It's been a long day. I'm beat so I think I'm just going to hit it." He gestured toward the exit.

"Oh, come on, man," said Art. "Just one drink."

Joe elbowed Art. "If we can get a drink down him, he'll start talking to the ladies and end up closing down the place. What do you bet?"

Christopher usually had a good time with these guys he'd met them through a local men's pick-up basketball league and they'd hit it off straightaway. Maybe it was just his mood, but he really wasn't feeling it tonight. And he didn't like being pressured into staying.

Across the room, he saw Crystal. She looked up, saw him and waved. Then she got up and started walking toward him. Even stranger than not being in the mood to stay, he wasn't in the mood to deal with her tonight, either.

The thought actually made him do a mental doubletake. What the hell was wrong with him? His buddies were ready to have a good time. And here was a woman who, for all intents and purposes, was a sure thing.

And he wasn't in the mood for any of it.

"Hey," said Crystal. "I see you finished with your business meeting. Come dance with me."

Joe and Art were standing there pretending to be cool, like they weren't watching him interact with Crystal. And Christopher was willing to wager that if he didn't go home with Crystal tonight, one of them would.

"Normally, I'd love to dance with you," he said to Crystal. "But I have more business I need to take care of. These are my friends Art and Joe. Joe, Art, this is Crystal. I'm sure one of these guys would love to buy you a drink." He dug his car keys out of his pocket and handed his friends a fifty-dollar bill. "Enjoy yourselves, everyone. First round is on me."

Kinsley had just finished washing up her dinner dishes when her cell phone rang at about 8:45 p.m. She knew it would be Christopher before she even looked. Still, her heart leaped a little bit when she saw his name on her phone's display screen. She didn't even bother to dry her hands before she picked up the phone and accepted the call.

"Hello?" she said, taking care to keep her voice as level as possible.

"I hope I'm not calling too late." His deep voice was like sex. The thought made her blush. Where the heck had *that* come from?

Well, she knew where it came from; she just wished she could put it back in its box so that she could put the lid on tighter and ensure that thoughts like that never got out again.

Remember, last dance. Over. Done. Finito.

Good luck, said an impudent little voice that was probably responsible for unleashing the thought in the first place. *You know you want him.*

"Of course not," she said. "How did the meeting with Sawyer go?"

"The only way it could've gone better is if you would have been there."

"What? And miss all the fun of my statistics class and being a Lamaze coach? Actually, the Lamaze coaching is pretty cool. I'm glad I can be there for Tonya. She doesn't have anybody."

"You've got a really great way with kids, you know?"

She found herself smiling in spite of herself. "Thanks." She didn't quite know what else to say to that. She heard what sounded like a car horn in the distance.

"Are you in your car?" she asked.

"I'm sitting in Mendoza's parking lot."

She hated herself for it, but her heart sank. "Oh, that's right. It's Thursday—ladies' night at Mendoza's."

She did her best to put a smile in her voice. "Listen, I won't keep you. Why don't we talk about this tomorrow at the office? Oh, wait, I'm going to be out most of the day. I'm going over to the high school to work with the advisory board and the kids in the Cornerstone Club to finalize the plan for their part at the Spring Fling. I really want them to take ownership of this program. If they do, it will stand a much better chance of taking hold. But listen to me blabbing on. I'm sure you want to get inside. I'll talk to you tomorrow."

"Kinsley, wait. I'm actually leaving Mendoza's. I'm not staying for ladies' night. Sawyer wanted to go there for the tacos. I figured I'd let him choose where we ate since he doesn't get to town very often."

Why was she so relieved to hear this? "Is ladies' night canceled?"

"Canceled? No, why?"

"Well, I can't imagine it going on without you there. I thought you always closed the place down."

He laughed. "No reason to since you're not there."

Against everything she knew was prudent and good for her, she melted a little bit inside.

"Contrary to your etched-in-stone thoughts of me, I'm really not a player," he said. "I don't know what I have to do to make you believe that."

She walked over to the couch and sat down, curling her bare feet beneath her. She was still in the gray skirt and white blouse she'd worn to work. Her apartment suddenly felt stuffy. She reached up and unbuttoned the top two buttons on her blouse.

"I'm not quite sure what I'm supposed to say to that," she said.

"What you can say is that you had as good a time

dancing with me at Mendoza's as I had dancing with you."

Her hand fluttered to her throat, lingered there.

"You could say that maybe we could try it again. Say, maybe Saturday night?"

Her fingers pushed aside her blouse's cotton fabric and traced the line of her collarbone. She wasn't sure if it was his voice or his words that made her shiver a little…in a good way…with an anticipation that made her feel naked and vulnerable, that had her rethinking every reason why it was a bad idea to get involved with him.

"Christopher…"

"Yes, I'm here. And since you didn't say no, I'll consider it a yes."

Even though it was after four o'clock, Kinsley headed back to the office after finishing up with the kids at the high school. She could've gone home. She'd already put in an eight-hour day, but… Okay, if she was going to do this, she at least had to be truthful with herself.

She was going back with the hopes of running into Christopher. After all, if he had been serious about taking her out on Saturday night—tomorrow night— she needed to know where they were going and what they were doing, what time he would pick her up, all the details so that she could get ready. She played a crazy little game with herself when she found herself in a situation and was unsure of what she should do— and she still wasn't quite sure going out with him was such a good idea. After all, what happened at Mendoza's had happened by chance. If he picked her up on

Saturday night and took her someplace purely social, it would be a date. Even though their date wasn't until tomorrow, she decided to toss everything up to fate: if it was a good idea to see Christopher socially—to go out with him tomorrow—he would still be at the office. If he wasn't there, well that meant it was not a good idea. If he wasn't there she would cancel the date and explain to him that they needed to keep things platonic. She was usually such a practical person that she only used the toss-it-up-to-fate method of decision-making on the rarest occasions. It was like flipping a coin to help her decide what to do on occasions like this, when her head was telling her one thing and her heart was insisting on another. On one hand, if she got involved with him, it could end in disaster. On the other hand, what if this could be the start of something good. He sure had been trying hard, and she needed to give credit where credit was due.

And there was the fact that she just couldn't stop thinking about him.

When she turned into the Foundation parking lot and saw his car in his reserved parking space, she couldn't breathe for a moment.

There was her answer. She should keep the date. And she was so relieved that she almost shook with joy. Before she got out of the car, she took her compact and lipstick out of her purse and touched up her makeup, then ran her fingers through her hair, gave herself a once-over in the rearview mirror and decided that was as good as it was going to get.

She let herself out of the car, feeling as giddy as a girl who had just been asked to the prom by the captain of the football team. As she walked toward the entrance, she contemplated her strategy—she would go to his office under the guise of discussing what she had accomplished at the high school today and ask him about the fund-raising idea that he and Sawyer had come up with last night.

She actually had a spring in her step as she emerged from the elevator into the third-floor reception area.

"Hi, Bev," she said to the young woman who looked as if she was already starting to pack up and head home for the weekend. But Bev was young and she would learn that when you got a job you really cared about sometimes you had to put in longer hours to get where you wanted to go.

Or you had to come back to the office to find out whether or not you were going to go anywhere that weekend, said the snarky voice in her head.

In the movie in her mind, she reached up and stuffed a sock in her doubting mouth.

"Oh, hey," Bev said. "What are you doing back here? It's nearly five o'clock."

"I know. I need to talk to Christopher. Is he available?"

Kinsley started walking toward his office before Bev had the chance to answer.

"I don't think you should go in there," she said. She looked around the office as if confirming nobody else was within earshot. Still, she lowered her voice to a stage whisper. "He has a woman in there. And she's really, really pretty. She just got here about fifteen minutes ago. I don't know that it's a business thing. But don't you dare say that I said that."

Kinsley's whole body tingled. And not in a good way. It was more like a pang of regret that was trying to undermine her confidence. She took a moment to put things in perspective. Sure it was Friday evening, but why would Christopher have a date meet him at the office? The woman could be a donor. She could be his sister. He had told her he had a sister. Two, in fact. If she stayed out here when the two of them came out of his office he would probably introduce her.

No, that would look contrived and desperate. A little stalker-ish. Instead, she would wait in her office and when she heard them come out she would grab her things and just happen to meet them at the elevator.

Yes, that plan would work.

"Hey, Kins," Bev said. "Could I ask a huge favor? It's like ten minutes to five and I have a date tonight. Is there any way you could cover the phones for me? Since you're gonna be here, anyway…?"

"Sure," Kinsley said. "Just forward the main line back to my office. But answer a question for me. What did she look like?"

Bev pressed some buttons on the phone, then stood there with her purse on her arm, her cell phone in her hand and a baffled look on her face. "I don't know… really pretty…really classy…like she has a lot of money…like somebody he'd take to the symphony or ballet with on a Saturday night. You know, that kind of woman."

"Do you think she's here to donate to the Foundation?"

Bev was already edging toward the elevator. "I don't know…. She seemed to be kind of into him."

Bev pushed the elevator button and the door opened immediately. She backed into it. "I've got to go," she said. "Let me know what you find out. Maybe she's his new girlfriend?"

As the elevator doors closed and carried Bev away, Kinsley replayed in her head the conversation she'd had with Christopher last night. He had said that he wasn't staying at the night club because she wasn't there. He'd said that he wanted them to go out again. When she hadn't answered he'd said he would take that as a yes.

Given all that, why would he bring another woman he was interested in to the office? It just didn't make sense.

Kinsley went into her office, left the door open, settled herself at her desk and waited.

About fifteen minutes later, she heard laughter coming from the reception area. She stood and started to grab her purse so that she could go out and make the *accidental* meeting at the elevator happen, but something stopped her—something in the tone of their voices. Something in the way they seemed to be laughing intimately at a private joke...

She dropped her purse on her desk chair and edged her way to the door. She peeked out, hoping Christopher wouldn't see her. If he did she would just say she thought that she was the only one left in the office and... She looked just in time to see Christopher with his hand on the small of a very beautiful woman's back.

"Our dinner reservation is at seven," he said. "We should have time for a drink before they seat us."

As the elevator doors opened, his hand stayed there as he ushered her in. Kinsley ducked back inside her office so that they wouldn't see her when they turned around to face the front.

Standing there alone in the empty office on a Friday night, Kinsley suddenly felt like the biggest fool in the world. So she'd gone against her better judgment and had agreed to go out with Christopher tomorrow night. Here was proof positive that she was simply one of a string of women.

Her rational mind reminded her she had no right to be upset or jealous. She had known all along that this was his M.O. But she couldn't help the way her heart objected. Tomorrow night obviously meant something completely different to her than it did to him.

If she let herself fall for Christopher Fortune any more than she already had, she was setting herself up for a world of heartbreak. She'd grown up with a mother who had been so desperately in love with a man who treated her wrong. Her mom's love for her dad ended up killing her.

Even though Christopher had certainly given no signs of being physically abusive, his fickle ways, his seeming to want only the things that were out of his reach—and then abandoning them when he was finished toying with them—did not make Kinsley feel good.

If she invested any more emotion in him, she would be mentally abusing herself. That wasn't going to happen.

She forwarded the office phones to the answering service, gathered her purse and turned off the office lights, realizing that fate had given her the answer she'd been looking for earlier that evening.

Christopher Fortune had been in the building, but he was emotionally unavailable.

Chapter Nine

Okay, she was avoiding him.

She had been most of the week.

It was Thursday morning and she hadn't seen him in the office since she'd watched him leave with that woman on Friday. She admitted it was a little childish. But she felt a little burned and very foolish for letting her heart control her usually clear head. She needed to put space between them.

When he'd called her, she'd responded by text—except for Saturday and Sunday. She carefully avoided personal topics of conversation—such as *What happened to our date on Saturday? Didn't we have plans, tentative as they were?*

She hadn't bothered to explain that if he wanted to take her out he needed to firm up plans sooner than the day of—and not parade his Friday night date through the office.

Even if their relationship was casual, that was simply bad taste.

Oh, who was she kidding? If she hadn't seen him with that woman she probably would have overlooked his lax planning. But it didn't matter now. It was better that reality, the inconvenient interloper it was, crashed the party sooner rather than later. Now, she was intent on locating the silver lining in the gray cloud that she refused to let rain on her career.

This near miss had been fair warning that dating someone she worked with was simply a bad idea.

It wasn't that every man who took her out had to commit to exclusivity before the first date. But she realized—too late—that what she felt for Christopher was different. She should've known better than to let herself lose control. Playing with Christopher Fortune was like playing with fire. She knew who he was and what he was all about. She knew that she couldn't play by his rules.

It was best to keep their relationship strictly business. That way, no one misunderstood and no one got hurt.

Monday and Tuesday she had conveniently scheduled herself to be out of the office. With a little investigating, Kinsley learned through Bev that Christopher would be out of the office on Wednesday and today. That should be enough time to clear her head and regain her equilibrium. She was professional and she knew she couldn't avoid him forever. After all, the Spring Fling was on Saturday. But everything was in place. She had done her tasks and had discreetly followed up to ensure that he had taken care of everything on his list.

She wasn't surprised to discover that he had.

That's why she chose to focus on the good, the professional side of their relationship, the part that worked. She just needed to remember to not let herself get snared in Christopher's charismatic web.

She had the rest of the day to collect herself. Because he was supposed to be back tomorrow, she planned on emailing him later today and asking if he had time to meet at the fairgrounds Friday afternoon to do a walk-through and preliminary set up for the event. They would be so busy with their booth preparations there would be no time for personal talk. Plus, Christopher was a smart guy—he seemed to catch on quickly. Surely by now he understood that their relationship had been relegated to the "professional zone."

She printed out her to-do list and had just begun checking off items and making notes when she sensed someone standing in the doorway of her office.

Christopher.

Her stomach did a full-fledged triple gainer, and as much as she hated it she audibly inhaled. She bit the insides of her cheeks hard to get her emotions in check.

Act like a professional.

"Hey, stranger," said Christopher. "Just wondering if there's room for the putting green under the tent?"

Kinsley couldn't look him in the eyes. It wasn't very professional, and she knew it. But neither was the way his gaze seemed to be burning into her. She straightened a stack of paper on her desk. She put a few loose pens into her desk drawer. Aligned her coffee mug on the coaster on the edge of her desk.

"The putting green?" Good. Her voice was neutral. "Christopher, you know I was only joking when I suggested you bring it to the Spring Fling. You don't have to do that if you don't want to."

"I know I don't have to," he said.

She picked up her pen and circled an item on her list.

"I figured we could just have a raffle. The kids can put their name into a drawing for prizes when they sign the bullying prevention pledge card—"

"The raffle sounds great. But let's bring the putting green, too. It will be an active visual. We can use it to draw people in. Oh, hey, and I wanted to tell you that I got word earlier this week that not only is Redmond Flight School offering a couple of prizes for us to give away—a couple of glider flights, which the kids should really love—but also everyone over there is behind doing an air-show fund-raiser in the fall. And Susan Eldridge and Julie Fortune were able to snag some gift cards from some of the local restaurants and merchants for us to use as prizes. I'm just blown away by how great and helpful everyone has been. It's a great team, don't you think?"

"Of course. I've always found everyone here to be exceptionally helpful."

"I know. But good teams are hard to find." Something in his voice changed. "When you have one, you should hang on to it."

Oh, no. Here it came.

She decided to head it off before he could shift things into the personal.

"Yes, we are lucky to have such great coworkers, aren't we? And if you'll excuse me, I'm going to go talk to Hank in maintenance about getting some extra chairs for the tent."

She stood, but Christopher closed her office door.

"I called you on Saturday and Sunday, Kinsley. Did you get my messages?"

"I had to go out of town."

"If I didn't know better, I might think you've been avoiding me. We had plans over the weekend. Or so I thought."

"Well, you should have thought about that before you brought your Friday night date to the office. Christopher, you shouldn't have kissed me if you were involved with someone else." The words slipped out before she could stop them. Now she had no choice but to look him square in the eyes.

The sight of him completely upended her equilibrium. She fisted her hands at her side, digging her nails into her palms. It was supposed to distract her from how she always seemed to get drawn in simply by looking at him. Even now, as he stood there looking baffled.

Wow, not only was he a player, but he was a good actor too.

"I don't know what you're talking about," he said. "I'm not involved with anyone else."

Maybe *involved* was overstating it. "Well, you shouldn't have kissed me if you were even dating other people."

"Kinsley, I really have no idea what you're talking about. I mean, sure, I've dated other women in the past, but nobody seriously. You are the first woman I've even considered dating exclusively."

She suddenly felt claustrophobic. Hearing him say the words but knowing they were encased in a lie made her want to run. How could he stand here, look her in the eye and tell her she didn't see what she knew she saw? At that moment, she realized just how different she and this man who was playing with her heart really were.

"Please don't, Christopher. Don't insult me. I saw you with that woman here at the office on Friday."

Confusion contorted his face. "Nora?"

And now he was going to try and change his tune, try to explain it away, but she wasn't going to have it.

"I have no idea what her name is, but she is beautiful. You have great taste in women—at least outward appearances. But what you don't seem to understand is that *Nora* and I are obviously cut from different material. Women like her might be fine with kissing and keeping it casual, but I'm not. I don't *give myself away*. Not even a kiss. Kisses are intimate, and I don't take intimacy casually."

She seemed to have struck him dumb because all he could do was stand there and stare at her, his lips pressed into a thin line.

"Since we have to work together," she said, "we have to keep things strictly professional, Christopher. Unlike you, I don't have family who can come to my rescue. My contacts aren't unlimited. I need this job."

Christopher looked taken aback, but there was a new light in his eyes.

"Kinsley, Nora Brandt is an etiquette coach. I hired her because I took your advice to heart. I was thinking about how I needed to get better at learning people's names, and that made me wonder about my other social and professional deficiencies. Nora and I went out to dinner Friday night so she could see me in action."

For the love of God, she wanted to believe him.

"But I saw you with your hand on the small of her back. That's pretty intimate."

"Apparently so. She told me as much when we were in the elevator. Honestly, the entire night was pretty humiliating. I'm not good at this...this." He gestured with both hands, at her, around the office. "I was raised on a ranch. My role models were my buddies and my brothers. We hung out at The Grill and flirted with the same handful of girls who didn't know any better than we did. I have no idea what I'm doing. Sometimes I feel so far out of my element I feel like a total buffoon. So, I hired an etiquette coach to help me. You are so smooth and polished. You deserve to be with someone who is your equal. Someone who doesn't embarrass you like I would."

Kinsley was so stunned that her mouth actually hung open.

Christopher held up a finger.

"Wait just a moment. I can prove it to you."

He pulled a business card from his wallet and handed it to Kinsley. The card had Nora Brandt's photo on it. Sure enough she was the woman Kinsley had seen him with on Friday.

"You can call her if you want. She'll confirm everything."

Now Kinsley was the one who felt like the total buffoon.

"And just so you know, she's married. And even if she wasn't, *she's* not my type at all. There's no other woman in the world I'm interested in right now besides you."

* * *

Kinsley had been jealous.

The thought made Christopher smile as he filled the last helium balloon and tied a knot in the stem. Because if she was jealous, that meant she had feelings for him. Even though she was still keeping him at arm's length, the chill had thawed.

There was still a chance, he thought as he tied a ribbon to the balloon and added it to the bunch that would join its twin at the entrance to the tent.

He fully intended to seize that chance and make things work between them.

Today was the day of the Spring Fling. He and Kinsley had met at the fairgrounds early to get everything in place inside the white tents. Hank from maintenance had generously agreed to transport the putting green in his pickup truck. The guy had even taken it upon himself to build a wooden platform to keep the green out of the dirt.

Christopher made a mental note to get Hank a gift card to Red or something else he would enjoy. He had gone out of his way transporting the putting green on his day off. Building the platform was above and beyond.

But Christopher was beginning to learn that was how everything worked at the Foundation. They were all one big family. They helped and supported each other.

After he finished getting the balloons in place, Kinsley introduced him to a young pregnant woman named Tonya Harris who had agreed to help them today. He realized she was the teenager Kinsley was coaching through Lamaze.

Along with their anti-bullying message, the Foundation was also teaching self-esteem. The two went hand-in-hand. If a teen had low self-esteem, he or she might be more apt to fall prey to bullies. Bullies didn't all come in the same package. Sometimes the bully was the enemy. Other times the bully might be the boyfriend who pressured his girlfriend to have sex against her better judgment.

If they could save even one young woman from ending up pregnant and alone like Tonya, then he would consider this program a success.

He admired the way Kinsley spoke to the teenager like a friend, asking her advice on the placement of chairs and even entrusting her with manning the table where kids would pick up information and sign the anti-bullying pledge cards.

By the time the Spring Fling was open and running at nine o'clock, they actually looked as if they knew what they were doing. Music was playing from a sound system he had secured through one of his contacts. The putting green, which he was in charge of, looked pretty cool on its custom-made, green-painted plywood perch. Kinsley had wrapped a large rectangular box, where the kids would enter the drawing for the various prizes they were offering.

He thought back to Thursday when he'd been talking about what a great team they made. It was the truth. Look at everything that they had accomplished working together in such a short time. They seemed to have the same vision. There was a synergy between them, and if he had to spend an entire year proving himself to her, he would.

She was worth it.

As Christopher was demonstrating proper putting technique to a young boy who was frustrated because he couldn't seem to sink a hole in one, Lily Cassidy Fortune, who had created the Foundation in memory of her late husband, Ryan, who had succumbed to a brain tumor nine years ago, walked up and beamed at him, just as the boy sank his first putt. The kid let out a cheer and Lily clapped for him. After Christopher handed him his prize of two movie tickets and directed him to the table where Tonya could help him with the pledge card, Lily greeted Christopher as warmly as if he were part of her own family. It dawned on him that they actually were related somewhere down the line.

"I came over here purposely to shake the hand of the person who has been doing such a great job getting the word out to the community about the Foundation," she said. She gestured around the tent. "This is just magnificent. It's exactly the direction that I am proud to see the Foundation going. I know my Ryan would've been proud of this, too."

A pang of guilt spurred on by her genuine affection and appreciation stabbed Christopher. He glanced over at Kinsley and saw her helping a kid fill out an entry form for the drawing. There was no way he could stand here and take all the credit, especially when she was over there doing all the work.

"I appreciate you coming by, Mrs. Fortune," he said.

She put a hand on his arm. "Oh, please, do call me Lily. All my family does."

Christopher smiled at her generosity. "I would be honored to, thank you. If you have a moment, I want you to meet somebody who has been instrumental in putting together what you see here, and, I suspect,

everything you've heard about the community outreach program."

"I absolutely have time."

Christopher motioned her over to the table where
Kinsley sat with Tonya. Kinsley looked up and smiled
at the two of them, genuine warmth radiating from
her eyes.

"Lily Cassidy Fortune," he said, giving Kinsley a
significant look. "I would like for you to meet Kinsley
Aaron. She is an outreach coordinator for the Foundation and has tirelessly worked to put together everything you see today and more."

Christopher saw a faint hint of pink color Kinsley's
cheeks as she stood and offered her hand to Lily.

"It is such an honor to meet you, Mrs. Fortune,"
she said. "I'm proud to work for such an incredible
organization. The Foundation took a chance on me
when I had very little experience—I'm still going to
school. Their faith in me has made me want to work
even harder to connect the Foundation with the Red
Rock community. However, you need to know that this
guy right here is doing incredible work. He is making
a real difference. He has a great vision and nice way
about him that everybody seems to love."

Kinsley's eyes sparkled good-naturedly, but the real
meaning of what she said wasn't lost on Christopher.
He smiled back at her and quirked a brow, sending a
message that she was the only person he wanted to
love.

Chapter Ten

Christopher was right—they had been working hard. The turnout at the booth had been better than Kinsley had ever dreamed it would be.

When they started, she was afraid they were going to have prizes to spare. But because of the fabulous response, they were having to tell the kids that they would do the drawings on the hour and that they had to be present to win. At the start of each hour, kids of all ages would cluster around the tent to hear the name of the lucky person whose name had been drawn from the box.

Each time a name was announced the crowd would cheer wildly. It struck Kinsley that even this was bringing the kids together. There seemed to be no rivalry or resentment from those who didn't win. Of course, Kinsley always made sure to announce that

they could win prizes, like T-shirts, rubber bracelets and water bottles, instantaneously by signing the
pledge card. Maybe these kids just needed a common
meeting ground.

The crowd was dispersing after the most recent
drawing, and for the first time since they had arrived
Kinsley had a chance to step back and look around.
Every single volunteer who had signed up to work the
booth had shown up. Most of them were even hanging around after their shift was over. In fact, right now
they had a plethora of help.

So when Christopher suggested that they take a
break, she only hesitated for a moment. She was thirsty
and what she wouldn't give for a bite of the cotton
candy that she had seen the kids enjoying.

"Okay, but only if you promise we can go get some
cotton candy," she said.

"Ahh, cotton candy. The way to Kinsley's heart."

She tried to ignore the butterflies that swarmed
when he said that. She was beginning to realize he
was an insufferable flirt. He couldn't help it any more
than he could help the fact that his hair was blond and
his eyes were a shade of blue that matched the clear
spring sky.

She couldn't seem to help the fact that she noticed
things like that about him. But what she had also noticed, she thought as they walked away from the Foundation tent, was that he had a much bigger heart than
she had initially given him credit for. A lot of his bravado was to cover the insecurities of his upbringing.

She silently vowed to never judge another person
until she learned their story. After all, who would've
known that slick-dressing, fancy-car-driving Chris-

topher Fortune had actually come from very humble roots? He may have been a Fortune by name, but his modest upbringing really was at the heart of everything he did.

After they grabbed some cotton candy to share, Christopher won her a giant teddy bear at the arcade shooting gallery.

"You surprise me every day," she said. "I never imagined that you'd ever even held a gun, much less that you knew how to use one. You're a pretty sharp shot."

"And that's just the start of my good qualities," he said, wiggling his eyebrows comically. "If you don't believe me, just give me a chance to prove myself."

His free arm, the one that wasn't holding the teddy bear, lightly brushed against hers as they walked side by side through the fair. The skin-on-skin contact made her shudder with a strange anticipation and an emotion that she couldn't remember ever feeling.

"You know what I've always wanted to do?" Christopher said.

"What's that?"

"Ride on the Ferris wheel with a beautiful woman," he said.

Kinsley rolled her eyes at him. "You are too cheesy for words sometimes," she said.

He laughed and and nudged her with his arm. This time the contact was on purpose. She couldn't help but wonder if he'd felt the same electricity the last time their arms brushed.

They made small talk as they made their way over to the Ferris wheel. By a stroke of luck the line was negligible. They were seated and the ride was in motion in less than five minutes.

With the giant teddy bear at her feet, the warm sun on her face and Christopher sitting next to her, Kinsley couldn't remember ever feeling so content or so free. When their car stopped at the top of the wheel, she felt as if she could see all the way to San Antonio. It was magical up there.

The car rocked a little and Kinsley gripped the safety bar that stretched across their legs.

"Don't worry," he said, stretching an arm around her and pulling her to him. "I'll keep you safe."

It was as if they were alone in their own little world. Kinsley leaned into Christopher, relishing how they seemed to fit so perfectly together. And when Christopher lowered his head to taste her lips, she didn't resist. In fact, she met him halfway.

All too soon, the car was moving again, breaking the spell and propelling them back into the real world. The only thing different was that Christopher did not remove his arm from around her shoulder until they stepped off the ride.

She wished that they could continue strolling around the fair hand in hand, stealing kisses and sharing cotton candy. But work called. They strolled back to the booth, not touching, looking as platonic as two coworkers ever looked walking with a giant teddy bear between them.

"You're an only child, right?" Christopher asked.

"Yes."

"How did you get to be so good with kids? You really are a natural. I thought only children were supposed to have a hard time empathizing with others. And that was supposed to be a joke but it didn't come out very well."

She smiled as he pretended to knock himself up the side of his head with the palm of his hand. "Just because I was an only child doesn't mean I can't relate to people, Christopher."

"What I'm trying so ineloquently to say is that I love watching you with the kids. They really listen to you and respect you. I think kids have a natural B.S. meter. They can tell when someone is sincere and when they're not. You're really good at what you do."

Her natural inclination was to make a joke out of his compliment or to spit out some snarky retort. But the words got caught in her throat. All she could manage was a choked "Thank you."

She cleared her throat. "I feel so lucky to do what I do, to have a job where I have an opportunity to make a real difference."

Christopher smiled. "Only-child anomaly number two—you're not selfish, either."

She felt her cheeks warming. "Would you stop with the compliments, already?" She shot him a smile so that he knew she was kidding. "Thank you. But good grief, if you keep this up my head is going to swell as big as the bouncy castle over in the kids' area."

"If it does, you'll have good reason."

"Christopher…"

"How did you meet Tonya?"

She smiled at the mention of the sweet teenage girl. "I met her at the high school a few months ago when I was there doing a presentation for Principal Cramer. She had just found out she was pregnant. Her parents had kicked her out of the house, and she really didn't have anywhere else to go. The boyfriend lives over in San Antonio and dumped her as soon as he found out they were going to be parents. She had slept at the bus station the night before and had almost gotten on a bus to San Antonio to try to talk to the boyfriend. The only thing that stopped her was that she didn't have enough money for a ticket. She went to school the next day because she didn't have any place else to go. I feel like it was divine intervention that I was there for her."

Christopher raked his hand through his hair. It wasn't a gesture of vanity as much as what seemed to be an expression of disbelief. The astonishment in his eyes spoke volumes.

"She broke down that day and cried and cried, right in my arms. I cried with her. And then I told her that she was allowed to have a twenty-four-hour pity party, but after that she needed to be strong for both her sake and the baby's. She stayed at my apartment that night and I went with her to talk to her parents the next day. They let her come back and that's where she is now. Her grades are good and she'll miss a little school when she has the baby in about three months, but I've already talked to the principal and we've arranged for her to do schoolwork while she's out. Her mother is going to watch the baby during the day, and she might have to get an after-school job to afford diapers, but she should be okay. I just keep telling her the most important thing is that she can't get behind on her schoolwork and she can't just give up. If she doesn't, everything will be fine."

Kinsley shrugged at a loss for what else to say.

"Isn't that what everybody needs sometimes?" Christopher said. "For somebody to tell them that they can do it? That the road ahead may be hard, but if they're persistent everything will be fine. Kinsley, you may have saved that girl's life. You helped her smooth things over with her family so that she has the support she needs until she graduates and gets a full-time job."

She didn't know what to say. So she didn't say anything for a long while as they walked. Then she identified one of the feelings knotted in her belly. It was shame.

"I meant what I said to Lily Fortune earlier. You really have done a good job. I didn't give you enough credit when you first started. I thought you were just trading on your name and your good looks."

"Oh, well, you've got to cut a guy a break in the trading-on-his-looks department." He shrugged and did a Justin Bieber-ish shake of his head, despite the fact that his close-cropped hair didn't move.

She knew he was kidding, but she couldn't resist egging him on. "And here I thought you were the humble Fortune—"

Her words were eclipsed by a commotion coming from the Foundation tent. She and Christopher exchanged a concerned glance and jogged over to the tent to see what was happening.

A sluggish-looking teenage boy was standing in an aggressive pose over Tonya, who was still seated at the table. The two were exchanging heated words. When Tonya stood and backed away from the guy, he reached out a hand, grabbed the back of her T-shirt and pulled hard. Tonya stumbled and immediately put her hands up, as if to shield herself from a blow. That's all it took for Kinsley to break into a sprint and put herself between Tonya and the boy.

"What the heck do you think you're doing?" she said to the guy. She got right in his face, determined to prove that she wasn't afraid of him. She looked the thug square in the eyes but kept her voice level and low as she spoke with authority. "You need to leave now. *Now*. Or I am going to call the police and have them escort you out of here."

A cocky sneer spread slowly over the guy's face. He was tall, but he was skinny. And although she didn't want to lay a hand on him, she was perfectly prepared to practice a few self-defense moves that she had learned over the years.

"I'm just here to talk to my baby mama," he said.

"It didn't look like you were talking to her. It looked like you were upsetting her."

"I don't need you interfering with me and my family," the thug said.

Kinsley sneered right back at him. "Oh, then you must be Jared. I've heard about you, Jared."

The kid seemed to flinch at the revelation that Kinsley knew him. "I think Tonya's dad would like to have a conversation with you. In fact, he's supposed to be stopping by any minute. Why don't you have a seat over there and wait for them?"

Kinsley could honestly say it was the first time she had seen all the blood drain from a person's face. Jared didn't say another word. He turned and sprinted away. It was only then that Kinsley realized that Christopher was standing right next to her, looking as if he was ready to spring into action if Jared had made one false move.

He squeezed her arm. "Why don't you see to Tonya? I'll deal with the crowd." He motioned with his head to the knot of onlookers that had gathered to watch the confrontation.

"Thank you," she said, giving him a squeeze back.

Tonya was huddled in the far corner of the tent, sobbing.

"Honey, I'm so sorry. Did he hurt you?"

Tonya shook her head as tears streamed down her face.

"What did he want?" Kinsley asked this question only to find out if Jared had been coming around other times or if this happened to be a chance encounter.

"Nothing," Tonya said. "He was just being disgusting. He's here at the Spring Fling with his buddies and he just wanted to act like a jerk."

And nobody had stepped in to help her.

"How long had you been standing there before I got back?"

Tonya shrugged as she swiped at her tears. Kinsley reached into her pocket and handed the girl a tissue. The girl blew her nose.

"He first saw me about ten minutes after you'd gone on break. He and his friends came up to me. I thought he wanted to say hi, but he called me a whore, asked me why I was here. He said they didn't allow whores at the Spring Fling. Then he walked away laughing with his friends. He came back just before you did."

Kinsley's mouth went dry.

"I'm so sorry this happened. But I don't think he's going to bother you anymore. If he does, you need to tell someone."

A dozen questions darted through her mind—at the top of the list was whether this was the first time she'd seen him since she told him about the baby and whether he had ever hit her in the past. His aggressive posture and Tonya's reaction made Kinsley wonder, but now wasn't the time to ask her. She gathered Tonya in her arms and let her cry on her shoulder, gently patting her on the back the same way she had the first day they'd met.

When Tonya's father arrived, she would let him know that Jared had been hassling her.

The girl needed to know she didn't have to put up with that kind of treatment. She needed to know she deserved better. Once she had calmed down, they would talk about that.

But there was one thing she needed to know right now. "Sweetie, did anyone try to help you? Did anyone tell him to go away?"

"No."

That was the crux of the matter. That's why they needed to educate people about taking a stand to help others. Kinsley focused on the clinical side of it because if she thought about all those people standing there looking on and no one caring enough to get involved, she would be sobbing as hard as Tonya was. How could people be so heartless? To stand there while an innocent girl was being verbally attacked. Who knows what might have happened if she and Christopher hadn't come back when they did.

She squeezed her eyes shut to dam the tears that were welling and to try and erase the image of her father swinging and hitting her mother when she had jumped between them, just as she had jumped between Tonya and Jared.

A few hours later, it was time for the Spring Fling to close. The booth was empty except for Christopher and Kinsley. Tonya's father had come to get her as soon as Kinsley had called him. She had sent home all of her volunteers after they had put in such a long day's work. There wasn't much to break down now, only the chairs and the tables, which they just needed to fold up and set aside so that Hank could come by tomorrow morning and load it along with the tent into his truck.

"What did Tonya's father say?" Christopher asked.

Christopher kept a respectable distance when Mr. Harris had come by to collect his daughter.

"He said he was going to talk to the sheriff about a restraining order," Kinsley said. "I think that's a good idea."

Her voice cracked on the last words. It was probably the combination of fatigue and the letdown after the adrenaline rush, but suddenly all the tears that she'd been able to contain while she was comforting Tonya threatened to break through. If they did, she was afraid she might not stop crying.

"You were the epitome of grace under pressure," Christopher said.

Kinsley opened her mouth to say, "No," but the words lodged in her throat as tears broke free and rolled down her cheek. She turned her head, hoping that Christopher wouldn't see.

"Hey—" he said, putting a gentle hand on her shoulder. "Everything is going to be okay."

She wished she could believe him, but for girls like Tonya and for women like her mother, nothing ever turned out okay. The tears crested and streamed. The harder she tried to stop them, the harder she cried.

The tables and chairs could wait.

Kinsley could not.

Christopher had to get her out of there and to a place where she felt safe enough to let out whatever it was that had her so tied up in knots. The episode with Tonya and Jared was upsetting, but she'd handled it well. However, it had obviously brought up something else.

He hoped she would let down her walls and trust him enough to let him help her.

He saw two boys who had been helping at the Foundation tent that afternoon. Now they were just hanging around. He offered to pay them twenty dollars each if they would stack the chairs and break down the tables and leave them over by the tree. The two jumped at the chance to make an easy buck, freeing Kinsley and him to leave.

She seemed much too upset to drive, so Christopher was relieved when she allowed him to take her home. He told her he would pick her up in the morning and they would come and get her car then. Just to ease her mind, he phoned the fairgrounds security office and informed them they would be back to get the car tomorrow.

By the time they had gotten to her apartment, Kinsley had composed herself. Even so, he tenderly helped her upstairs, but just as he expected, once they were inside, she tried to downplay what happened.

The walls were firmly back in place.

"Kinsley, you don't have to do this with me," Christopher insisted. "You're not an island. You don't have to go this alone—whatever it is that is torturing you. Haven't we gone beyond that?"

He reached out and tucked a strand of hair behind her ear.

"Talk to me," he said.

She was silent for a moment as they sat together on the couch. Christopher was determined to not fill the silence. It worked.

"I told you that both of my parents are dead," Kinsley said in a small voice.

Christopher nodded.

"It was my father's doing. Well, mostly. He drank himself to death, and my mother never recovered. It's as if she died from a broken heart. Not because she loved him. Her heart broke because of the way he had treated her. He was the quintessential bully, made her believe that she was worthless. No one should have to live that way."

Listening to the words, Christopher felt all the blood drain from his face. He reached out and took Kinsley's hand in silent support.

"I couldn't do anything to help her," she said. "I guess I thought she would heal, that her life would get better after he was gone. But she didn't, she just wasted away. And died. As I was growing up, as far back as I can remember my father always belittled my mother, and she was defenseless against his words— and sometimes his fists. He had such an anger problem. He thought I had a smart mouth when I would stand up for her, so he'd come at me, and my mother would put herself between us and bear the brunt of his anger so that I could get away. She just let him treat her that way."

He squeezed her hand and shut his eyes for a moment. When he opened them, he said, "Kinsley, I am so sorry."

She shook her head. "Please don't feel sorry for me.

I don't want anyone's pity. Sure I wish I could've done things differently. I wish I could go back and force my mom to move out, to get away from him, but I can't and I know that. I made a decision long ago, Christopher, not to let my past define me. But it does inform my choices."

"Is that why you were so quick to put yourself in between Tonya and Jared?"

And why you tend to keep people at arm's length.

She nodded.

He pulled her into his arms and held her, just held her, for the longest time.

"I am so sorry for what you went through," he whispered in her ear. "But I'm not sorry for who you've become. You are one of the strongest, most amazing people I have ever met in my entire life."

He leaned his head in so that his cheek was on hers. The next thing he knew her mouth, soft, warm and inviting, had found his.

It vaguely registered that he shouldn't be doing this—she was vulnerable right now. But he was kissing her and she was kissing him back.

Her lips tortured and tempted him more than they satisfied his craving for her. As he sat there with his arms around her, the feel of her lips on his urged him to lean in closer. Raw need swirled inside him, as if taking possession of her might bind them and fix everything that was broken.

A moan deep in his throat escaped as desire coursed through him, a yearning only intensified by the feel of her lips. His one lucid thought as Kinsley melted into him was the taste of her: sweet as spun sugar and candy apples and something warm…like cinnamon and sunshine.

It made him reel.

For a few glorious seconds he never wanted to breathe on his own again. He could be perfectly content right here with her in his arms for the rest of his life.

His hands slid down to her waist and held her firmly against him as his need for her grew and pulsed.

He slowly released her, staying forehead to forehead while the heat between them lingered, drawing him to her almost magnetically. He reached out and ran the pad of his thumb over her bottom lip.

"I'd better go," he whispered. "If I don't…you know what's bound to happen."

"I know," she said. "And I want you to stay."

Caught in the twilight between craving and clarity, he claimed one more kiss of her lips but knew this was as far as they should go. As much as he wanted her, it wouldn't be right.

"I don't want to force things," he said, his lips still a breath away from hers.

"You and I both know we've been moving toward this moment for weeks—for months," she said. "Probably since the first moment we saw each other."

Her words, the nearness of her, sent heat rippling through his body. As she gently nipped at his bottom lip, he had to fight the desire to take her right there, right now, but in a way that would reach back through space and time and make right all the wrongs and ugliness that had ever darkened her world.

Tonight felt different.

This *thing* between them felt deeper and undeniably

right. For the first time in a long time—maybe ever—his heart was no longer his own. Her essence had infused his senses. All the Fortunes' money couldn't buy what he'd found in her.

Then those lips that had been driving him crazy took possession of his once again, and he knew there was no turning back from what was about to happen.

They were inevitable.

Chapter Eleven

Kinsley got to her feet and took Christopher's hand. If this was going to happen, she was going to have to prove to him she wasn't simply seeking sanctuary in his body. She needed to show him that she was truly ready.

She led him to the bedroom.

It had been a long time since she'd allowed herself to fully want, to fully trust, but all that mattered was how she needed this man. His evident need for her made her feel powerful and desirable. Strong and beautiful. No one had ever made her feel like this before.

Piece by piece their clothes fell away until they stood naked in front of each other in the dim light of the bedroom lit by moonlight filtering in through the sheer curtains. His gaze searched her face as if he were giving her one last chance to protest.

Not a chance.

As if reading her mind, he walked her backward to the bed and lowered her onto it. Climbing in beside her, he stretched out, propping his head on his free hand to look into her eyes.

She rolled over to face him so that their lips were a whisper away. She wanted him to see that this was exactly what she wanted. He reached out and smoothed her hair away from her face, then traced a finger down to her breasts. He smoothed his palm over the sensitive skin, making her inhale sharply.

"You are so beautiful," he said. "I can't tell you how long I've wanted this…wanted us."

He closed the distance between them, allowing no room for doubt. Her lips were still swollen and tender from kissing him earlier, but still she opened her mouth to let him all the way in.

He responded by rolling her onto her back and gently nudging her legs apart. He covered her with his body as she ran her hands down his arms, then up his back as he settled himself on her, positioning himself so that his hips were square to hers. The feel of him on top of her released all the desire and longing that had been bottling up in her since the day she'd first realized that she wanted him.

She tried to stifle a groan that bubbled up in her throat as she savored the heat that coursed between them. She reveled in the feel of him, in the anticipation of the imminent joining of their bodies.

It had been such a long time since she'd felt this way about anyone, since she'd allowed herself to lose control and trust someone like she trusted him.

It was good that they'd talked tonight, that she'd

opened up to him. It was cathartic, as if trusting him with her past had cleared a path to the future.

She wasn't sure what was going to happen after tonight, but she wasn't going to think about that now. All she cared about was the tender way he was kissing her neck as she lolled her head to the side to give him easier access. Now, his lips were trailing a path over her collarbones, then dipping down into the valley between her breasts.

One thing she had learned from Christopher was that you had to seize every moment, every opportunity and live. Until now, she hadn't been able to do that. But tonight she was in the here and now. Tonight, she intended to make love to him as if there would never be another moment like this one.

His kisses had found their way to her abdomen and were circling her belly button. Then he took a detour and kissed the insides of her thighs. She inhaled sharply and her eyes widened.

"Why did we wait so long for this?" Her voice was soft and breathless in the darkness.

"I don't know, but I can promise you it will be worth the wait." He flashed a wicked smile at her as he climbed back toward her. With a firm, quick move he pulled her on top of him. She could feel the hard length of him and she had to fight the urge to slide her body down and take him inside of her.

She drew in a jagged breath, determined to not rush things. Determined to savor every last delicious second of their first time together.

"But if you've changed your mind, I can stop," he said. "Are you sure about this?"

She nodded, then kissed him lightly on the mouth.

"I want you so badly, I can't think of anything else. So, if you're sure, then—"

"Shhh..." She pressed her finger to his lips. "I'm sure. Kiss me. Make love to me. Let's let what's in the past stay in the past. We can worry about tomorrow...tomorrow. Because tonight, I'm really glad we're right here."

He kissed her softly, then he slowly spread his hands over her breasts before gently cupping them. She was beautiful, all curves and legs and porcelain skin. He marveled at the ivory breasts in his hands and reverently closed his mouth over a nipple.

The sound of her sigh made him want her all the more.

He stretched out on top of her, gently nudging her legs apart with his knee. But then he felt her stiffen. She bit her lip and looked at him as if there was something she needed to say but couldn't find the words.

Had she changed her mind?

"What's wrong?" he asked, smoothing the back of his hand over her cheek.

She bit her bottom lip. "It's been a long time since I've been with anyone. So I'm not on birth control."

He bit back a curse. How could he have been so damn stupid? He was always cautious. He never had unprotected sex. It was a chance he wouldn't take for so many different reasons. Reasons that could justify a whole new division at the Foundation. Yet, tonight, being here with her so unexpectedly...wanting her as badly as he did, he'd pushed toward this coupling without thinking things through. Mainly because he hadn't been so presumptuous to think that he'd find himself in her bed.

"Oh...well...wow." He pulled himself off her and shifted onto his side so that he could look at her. He definitely needed some space, some room to cool off. "I don't have anything, either."

He cursed silently for not being prepared because he wanted her so much it almost caused him physical pain. He hoped it didn't show on his face as he stared into her beautiful, tormented blue eyes.

As she lay there illuminated by the moonlight filtering in through the slats in the plantation shutters, he realized he'd probably never seen her look quite so beautiful. That's when he knew...being here with her like this...holding her, feeling the warmth of her against him was all he needed.

"We don't have to make love tonight. We can just hold each other...or do other things. I can pick up some condoms tomorrow."

Never in her life had she experienced the perfect blend of euphoria and disappointment.

Euphoria because Christopher didn't have protection ready and waiting in his wallet or wherever grown men kept them these days. It meant that he wasn't prepared for a spur of the moment encounter, which put her mind at ease, and it showed that he cared about her and about his own health. He wasn't willing to have unprotected sex.

But she was also disappointed because she wanted him so badly that she... Okay, now she was blushing.

"So, here we are," he said, drawing in a deep breath.

Clearly, this sudden one hundred miles per hour to zero stop was just as jarring for him as it was for her.

He made a pained noise as he adjusted his position on the bed.

"So, here we are," she said.

He raked his hand through his hair. "Not to bring up a sore subject, but does this prove to you that I'm not as big a player as you think I am?"

She ran her fingers over the hair on his chest. His perfectly natural chest was almost as sexy as his broad shoulders, which she touched appreciatively.

"Honey, if I still believed you were a player, you wouldn't be here naked in my bed."

"Touché."

He looked almost edible lying there propped up on his side, watching her with his sexy eyes. She didn't feel the need to cover up or hide from him. In fact, she loved the fact that, judging by his body language, he obviously liked what he saw.

"So I gather you must not have been a Boy Scout," she said.

He grinned. "Ahh, because I'm not prepared." He laughed. "Actually, I *was* a Scout, way back when. I guess I'm a bit rusty in the preparedness department these days. But don't tell anyone because I may have to give back my merit badge."

"You can always earn that badge back."

"Oh, yeah? Exactly what did you have in mind?"

She ran her hand down the length of his body until she found his manhood. She touched him, happy to see that he was still every bit as ready to go as he had been before they'd been forced to stop.

"How do you feel about going and getting something for us? There's a twenty-four-hour drugstore two blocks from here. Will you do it? Please?"

He pursed his lips, and at first he seemed uncertain. For a moment she thought he might say no. But then he leaned in and feathered a kiss onto her lips before he lifted himself off the bed and got dressed.

He was back within ten minutes.

While he was gone, Kinsley opened a bottle of wine and lit some candles.

She handed him a glass when he came into the bedroom. "I was going to say that this deed deserved another kind of merit badge," he said as he sat on the edge of the bed, "but I see that you're way ahead of me."

She smiled. "So kiss me."

He complied, kissing her for a long time. Leisurely and thorough kisses that had her wondering, once again, if he had changed his mind while he was out and decided to take things slowly. He was still dressed even though he was stretched out beside her on the bed.

She ran her hand along the waistband of his blue jeans, tearing at the fabric of his shirt until her fingers struck gold…bare skin. He helped her by drawing it up and over his head.

She sighed as she drank in the raw beauty of him. When she straddled him, she could feel his erection through his pants. The thought of his body—so sexy and large—moving inside her ignited a slow burn in her belly. She wanted him more now than when he'd first touched her.

She ran both hands over his abs, up his chest and out onto his well-defined biceps. And, hello, there were those shoulders. They were broad and ropy, making his torso taper into a manly vee that disappeared beneath the waistband of his jeans. Those jeans.

They were the only thing that still stood between them.

She inhaled sharply.

Pace yourself.

She steadied herself by allowing her hands to travel back down over his abs, memorizing his form and the feel of the muscles under her hands.

She was so caught up in the beauty and feel of him, of his skin on her skin, that she was a little startled when he rolled her over and his hands did the exploring. They glided over her hips, down to her thighs and dipped between them.

This was really going to happen. She was ready and hyperaware of every breath, every kiss, every touch. When his hand found her most vulnerable spot, she shivered with anticipation. She noticed that his body seemed to tremble, too.

She put a little space between them and slowly unzipped his jeans. Together they got him out of his pants and his underwear. Finally, when nothing stood between them, she reached out and brushed her fingertips over his manhood. His body shuddered. He inhaled a sharp breath and his body arched slightly. Even though she'd already gotten a good look at him, she devoured his male glory with her eyes, from his flat, muscled stomach…up farther to his biceps and his shoulders…to his throat and the chiseled planes of his face. She stroked him and learned every inch of him, committing his body to memory, but he didn't let her linger for long. He pulled away and picked up the condom packet, ripping it open. As she watched him put the condom on the generous length of his maleness, she thought she would go over the edge before they'd even began. Once everything was in place, he settled himself between her legs. She welcomed him by opening her thighs so that their bodies could join.

The physical sensations of what was happening made her shudder with excitement. He entered her with a tender, unhurried push. The heat that radiated from him seeped into her. His body was stiff as he gently inched forward, going so very slowly and being so careful. As her body adjusted to welcome him, she joined him in a slow rocking rhythm.

"Christopher," she whispered. "Oh...Christopher..."

Her sighs were lost in his kiss. He touched her with such care and seemed to instinctively know what her body wanted.

Pleasure began to rise and she angled her hips up to intensify the sensation. Their union seemed so very right that she cried out from the sheer pleasure of it.

She wanted him to feel good, too. She needed to touch him, to give him the same pleasure he was giving her. So she slid her hand between their bodies, reaching for him, wanting to heighten his pleasure. But he grabbed her wrist and held her hand firmly.

"Not yet," he said.

"Why?" she asked.

"Because. Just...not...yet." His breathlessness matched her own. "When you touch me, you make me...crazy. And this...this time is for you."

He stretched her arms up over her head and held them there as he rocked her toward her first release.

As spasms of ecstasy overtook her body, his lips reclaimed hers.

The gentle, almost reverent way he touched her proved that he had been worth waiting for…but his hunger for her was never so evident as when he came up for air and devoured her with voracious eyes.

She couldn't get enough of his touch. As if he read her mind, he drove into her with such intensity she fisted her hands into the bed sheets and gasped, arching against him, propelled by the pulsing heat that was growing and throbbing inside her.

"Let yourself go," he said, his voice hoarse and husky. "Just let go, Kinsley."

Maybe it was the heat of his voice in her ear; more likely it was the way he made her body sing with his touch, but the next thing she knew he had driven her over the edge for the second time that night.

Again, he wrapped his arms around her, holding her tightly, protectively, until she had ridden out the wave.

She buried her face in his chest, breathing in the scent of him, of their joining, needing to get as close to him as possible. He continued to hold her tight. She lost herself again in his broad shoulders and the warmth of his strong arms.

"How was that?" His voice was a throaty rasp.

When she lifted her head and looked at him, his eyes searched her face.

"It was great. Really, breathtakingly great."

He smiled. "And I'm not finished yet."

The feel of his bare skin against hers almost put her into sensory overload.

She was so aware of him, of the two of them fused so closely that it seemed they were joined body and soul.

Christopher buried his head in the curve of her neck and let out a deep moan.

She eased her palms down his back, kissed him hard and fast and then things got a little crazy as she wrapped her legs around his waist and dug her nails into his shoulders. He didn't seem to mind how tightly she was clinging to him. So she held him in place by the shoulders and shifted under him. The way he groaned was so delicious that she arched beneath him again, drawing him deeper inside.

At that moment, staring down into her clear eyes, his body joined with hers, Christopher felt the mantle of his life shift. All of a sudden, without explanation, everything was different.

How could that happen now when it had never happened before?

Because he'd never been in love before now.

He was in love with Kinsley's laugh and her mind and the way she was able to set him straight without making him feel as if he'd been lambasted. He loved the way she felt in his arms right now, the smell of her smooth skin and the way she gazed up at him with a certain look in her eyes that was equal parts courage and vulnerability. It was everything he already knew about her and all the things he had yet to discover. He wanted to be the first face she saw in the morning and the last face she saw before she closed her eyes and drifted off to sleep at night. He wanted to be the shoulder she cried on and the lips she kissed.

He wanted to prove to her that all men weren't like

her father, and she deserved someone who was crazy about her, someone who adored her the way she deserved to be loved.

He wanted to show her that love didn't have to hurt. The only problem was the prospect of doing that, rendering his heart that vulnerable, leaving it in someone else's hands, scared him to death.

But it was too late now. Judging by the way he felt, he had a feeling he'd already passed the point of no return.

"Christopher?" Kinsley's eyes searched his face. "Are you...okay?"

"I am absolutely better than okay." He kissed her deeply, pulling her to him so tightly that every inch of their bodies were merged. He hadn't particularly cared how close he'd felt to other women he'd been intimate with. But as he built up to the pace that would simultaneously transport Kinsley and him to nirvana, he wanted to see her face. He needed a one hundred percent connection. Not just body to body, but eye to eye and soul to soul.

It didn't take long before their bond, coupled with the rhythmic motion of their bodies, carried them over the edge together. As he lay with her, sweaty and spent, he cradled her against him.

As they'd made love, three words had been darting around inside his head. Now they'd somehow found their way to the tip of his tongue.

Oh, man.... Don't do that, he thought. *You're caught up in the moment. Don't say things you don't mean.*

The problem was, he did mean it. With all his soul.

Even so, meaning it and following through with the implications of *I love you* were two very different things.

Kinsley rolled over onto her stomach and looked up at him. "Are you really okay?"

He wanted to tell her exactly how he felt. Except when he opened his mouth all that came out was, "I've never been better."

Christopher wasn't used to being in this position of vulnerability. Since he'd been in Red Rock, he'd been used to being in command. But this woman lying in his arms had changed everything.

Frankly, it scared him to death.

Chapter Twelve

Christopher didn't find his way home until late Sunday night. And that was only because he didn't have any suitable work clothes over at her place.

Once he was at home, with a little space to digest what had happened between them, he realized two very important things about himself: that he was in love with Kinsley, even if he didn't know how to tell her, and that he needed to be the one to reach out to his father and set their relationship on the road to right.

Funny, last week if someone had told him that falling in love would change him so much that he'd be willing to extend the olive branch to Deke, he would've told them to go to hell.

But here he was, at nine o'clock on Sunday night, staring at his cell phone as he dialed his parents' number.

He had to do it now before he changed his mind or the spell that Kinsley had cast on him wore off.

Somehow, he didn't believe that this call would do any good. His old man was as stubborn as a bulldog that had clamped down on a stick. Once Deke sank his teeth into something there was no prying it loose. Everything in his world was black-and-white. He wasn't about to change his mind about his son.

How his sweet mother had put up with him all these years was a mystery. As he listened to the phone ring two-three-four times, the realization washed over Christopher that the reason he had decided to be the one to reach out and try to make amends was so he could know in his heart that he had done everything in his power to not be like his father.

Good, bad or indifferent, it had taken him a while to realize that. And it had taken the childhood experiences of a great woman to help him reframe his situation and see his family with a new appreciation. Kinsley was right, the family you took for granted wasn't going to be there forever. Having lost both of her parents within a one-year period, Kinsley was living proof of this.

Her father sounded like a monster. While Deke could be difficult, the old coot had never emotionally or physically abused his family. Sure he was hard on them. You could say a lot of things about Deke Jones, but he always did right by his family. Or at least, his version of right.

Wasn't that something to hold on to? Something to focus on? Because when he put it all into perspective, Christopher knew his upbringing could've been a whole lot worse.

It was probably too late to call the house on a Sunday night, anyway. Deke, the creature of habit he was, had probably been in bed for a good half hour.

Maybe, subconsciously, he'd known that and that was the reason he'd decided to call...or maybe he shouldn't overthink it. He could try again tomorrow.

Christopher had just pulled the phone away from his ear, when he heard a craggy voice grunt and gruff, "Hello?"

Hesitating, Christopher drew in a breath as he brought the phone to his ear.

"Hello?" the man repeated, the irritation in his voice mounting.

Deke and Jeanne Marie didn't have caller ID so there was no way he would've known it was his son. In his mind's eye Christopher could see Deke giving the phone a dirty look before he slammed the receiver back into the cradle.

"Pops? It's Chris."

Silence answered him. For a moment he wondered if Deke had already hung up. But then the old man said, "Son?" His voice was so soft, it was barely audible and most un-Deke-like.

"Yeah, Pops, it's me. Is this a good time? I hope I'm not calling too late."

Christopher waited for Deke to cut him off at the knees as he was so fond of doing. The old man had had two months to stew on his anger at Chris for abandoning the ranch to take a desk job pushing papers, for disassociating himself from the Jones name, moving to Red Rock and surely a plethora of other sins real or imagined of which he had found Christopher guilty.

"You can ring this house at midnight and I would take your call, son. It's good to hear your voice."

As Deke's positive response registered, Christopher exhaled a breath he didn't realize he'd been holding. On the other end of the line, he heard his father call to his mom. "Jeanne, it's Chris on the phone. Get in here."

"Chris, it's ladies first. Talk to your mama and then she'll give me the phone."

His mother was her usual, sweet, unconditional self, saying how much she and the family had missed him but that they all understood that he was making a nice life for himself in Red Rock.

"I do wish you would come home to visit soon," she said, her voice a little wistful. "You don't know what I'd give to hug you."

Christopher made noises about being busy at work but promised that he would see what he could do about arranging some time off for a visit. He thought about telling her that she and Deke were always welcome in Red Rock but decided against it. Deke would never hear of making the trip. Not even if it was his wife's dying wish— Christopher stopped himself from tumbling down the path of negativity that he usually traveled when he conversed with his father. Old Deke had started the conversation off nicely enough. Even though it raised his hackles, Christopher forced himself to take the high road and not instigate an argument...and to refuse the invitation if Deke invited him to one.

"I got the photo album you made for me, Mama. I really appreciate it."

"I wanted you to have some pictures from Toby and Angie's wedding. We all missed you. It was a beautiful day, but it would've been even better if you had stood up with your brother."

A pang of guilt stabbed Christopher right in the heart. He grabbed the album off the end table where it had been hidden under a stack of magazines and financial newspapers since he'd brought it home from the office.

He opened it to a page featuring a five-by-seven photo of the smiling bride and groom. He flipped the page and saw another of the entire family—minus him, of course—gathered around his brother and his new sister-in-law.

It really had been ridiculous and selfish to miss such an important occasion. But with the frame of mind he'd been in then and as mad as Deke had been at him, there was no way he was going to cast a dark shadow over his brother's big day.

He heard Kinsley's voice in the back of his head saying, *Don't dwell on things you can't change. Look forward and spend that energy on things that matter.*

Toby understood why he'd stayed away and that was all that mattered. Still, a funny feeling circled in his gut like a shark poised to attack.

"It was great to see Toby when he and Angie were here in town. Will you please be sure and tell him I called?"

"I sure will, honey. But I'm going to hand the phone over to your dad now. He's getting a little antsy waiting to talk to you."

Right. That would be the day the sky fell when Deke stood antsy with anticipation waiting to talk to his black-sheep son. Christopher wanted to snort, but he didn't. Instead, he told his mother he loved her and

promised her one more time that he would do his best
to make it home for a visit as soon as he could manage.

Then he put on his emotional armor and prepared
for Deke to shoot him like a sniper poised and ready
high atop a building.

"Well, now it's my turn," Deke said.

Christopher held his tongue, unsure if that was sarcasm or sincerity in his dad's tone.

"You made your mama really happy by calling tonight, son."

Oh. Okay. Could it have been sincerity? Or was it
a verbal trap designed to lure Christopher into a false
sense of security so that Deke could turn around and
sucker punch?

He closed the photo album and set it on the coffee
table, scooting forward so that he was sitting on the
edge of the couch.

"It was good to hear her voice," Christopher said.
In a split second he decided to stick to his original
plan and play nice. "It's good to hear yours, too, Pops."

The words hung out there for a few beats before
Deke answered, "I'm glad to talk to you, too. Son, I
have a confession to make. I regret the way we parted
when you took off for Red Rock. You and I have had
our differences over the years, but we've never left
things so badly between us."

The old Christopher would have quipped, "You regretted it so much that you waited for me to call so
you could tell me." But from his view on the high
road, he could see that this was a hard confession for
Deke to make.

"I've regretted it, too, Pops. I'm...I'm sorry."

As soon as the words escaped Christopher clamped

his mouth shut, gritting his teeth so hard he could feel it all the way up to his temples.

"That's right big of you to say that, boy. To be the first one to apologize." Deke's voice sounded small and...humble? So much so that Christopher wasn't even sure it really was his father on the other end of the line.

"How's that job of yours going?" Deke asked.

So in the end his father couldn't bring himself to say the two little words that would have gone such a long way toward healing them...reuniting their family. Then again, maybe this was Deke's version of an apology. Christopher swallowed his pride and decided it was.

"It's great. I'm really enjoying it. Working for the Foundation is giving me a lot of opportunities to do some good in the community."

And that was as far as he was going to justify what he did for a living.

"That's what I hear. James has been in touch with your mama and he's had a lot of good things to say about you. He bragged about you, saying that you have a great work ethic and a real creative head for business. He says you've been such an asset to the Foundation, he would've hired you even if you weren't a blood relative. I'm really proud of you, son."

Proud of you, son.

Christopher fell back against the couch cushions so hard it knocked some of the air out of his lungs in a *whoosh*.

For the first time in his life, his father had told him he was *proud* of him. Christopher had a hard time hearing the rest of what his father said because of the blood rushing in his ears.

Family could be the most amazing people in your life while simultaneously being the most exasperating.

If an apology was gold, the words that had just passed from Deke's lips and traveled four hundred miles through the phone line were platinum.

No, they were priceless.

What was the Foundation's policy about fraternizing with a superior?

As Kinsley flipped through the employee handbook, she silently chastised herself. *Now was a heck of a time to worry about that.*

Still, for her own peace of mind she needed to know. After Christopher left her on Sunday evening, Kinsley had fallen back to earth with a terrifying awareness of her vulnerability.

She'd decided when she saw Christopher again, it should be business as usual. If they were going to work together, they had to keep their emotions (and libidos) in check.

Or at least *she* had to.

That sounded like common sense, but it was easier said than done. Now she was having a hard time keeping her mind on work when she knew Christopher was right across the hall.

That was the problem. He sat right. Across. The hall. And that's where he'd been, holed up in his office, for the better part of the day Monday.

Now it was midday Tuesday and he hadn't come into the office yet, which was no big deal. Before things had *changed* between them, she hadn't felt it necessary to know his schedule. They had never checked in with each other. Why should they do that now? It was a ridiculous thought.

Yet every time she heard a deep voice in the reception area she looked up, hoping to catch a glimpse of him.

To no avail.

He was acting as if nothing had happened between them. He wasn't exactly avoiding her. Or maybe he was…she wouldn't know because she hadn't seen him except for late yesterday afternoon, when she'd run into him as she was on her way out and he was on his way in. He'd held the elevator door for her, and he had acted like the same old Christopher—the "before sex" Christopher. After the initial exchange of hi-how-are-yous, he'd mentioned that he had the germ of a wonderful idea for educating people on how to intervene when they saw someone being bullied. He had been saddened and inspired by what had happened to Tonya at the Spring Fling.

"Maybe we can talk about it soon?"

"Absolutely," she'd said, trying to figure out if he had run with the idea because he knew how important the cause was to her. Then again, adding another leg to the bullying prevention campaign would reflect well on him, too.

Although she hadn't expected him to kiss her at the elevator, she had wished for a little more. A whispered *Saturday night rocked my world;* a *Let's do it again soon;* or even better, *What are you doing for dinner tonight?*

He looked as if he was about to say something, but the elevator had buzzed, scolding them for holding the doors open too long.

He'd simply said, "Don't let me keep you," and she'd answered, "Good night," and had gotten into the elevator...alone with her pride.

She wasn't about to let herself appear needy because at that point, weren't his feelings pretty clear?

Today, after paging through the handbook no fewer than five times, she still couldn't find the answer to her question about superior/subordinate relationships. Did that mean there was no policy? And why wasn't there one? Probably because not sleeping with your superior/subordinate was common sense—something every savvy professional knew.

Instead of driving herself crazy dwelling on it, she busied herself doing something more productive: polishing the recap of the Spring Fling event for the staff meeting next week.

As she was reading through her draft, her mind drifted. Maybe she should call him and ask him where they stood?

And maybe she should just stamp the word NEEDY on her forehead.

Stop it.

She had two choices. She could talk to Christopher about it, or be confident that things would turn out the way they were meant to be.

She had always prided herself on being confident. She had never obsessed over things she couldn't control, and she wasn't going to start now.

Realizing that her eyes had been scanning the recap but her mind had been thinking about Christopher and nothing of what she had just read had registered, she started back at the top of the page and forced herself to focus.

Bev buzzed her phone.

"Hey, Kinsley," she said. "Sawyer Fortune is on line one for you."

Sawyer Fortune?

"Thank you, Bev."

She pressed Line One.

"This is Kinsley Aaron."

"Hi, Kinsley, it's Sawyer Fortune. Am I catching you at a good time?"

"Absolutely, Sawyer," she said. "How can I help you?"

"I've been trying to reach Christopher today, but he seems to be unavailable. When I met with him the last time I was in town, he mentioned that the two of you worked closely in the community relations department, so I thought I would run it by you."

Sawyer went on to tell her about possible dates for the air-show fund-raiser that would benefit the Foundation. She assured him that she would talk to Christopher today and make sure he got back with Sawyer as soon as possible to reserve the date.

So, Christopher had even been unavailable to Sawyer.

That shed a new light on things. Something was up. Maybe that meant he wasn't avoiding her.

She was about to hang up with Sawyer when he said, "Oh, and, Kinsley, thanks for talking Christopher into calling his father. When I last spoke to Christopher, he said he had talked to Deke and that you were the one who had urged him to do so."

A knot of emotions formed in Kinsley's stomach as she mumbled something to Sawyer, then hung up the phone. He had called his father. That was great, a true breakthrough for him. He had told Sawyer that he had done so at her urging. That was tremendous, especially because he had mentioned her to Sawyer yesterday. She could let her mind go in all sorts of directions, imagining what he had said about her to his cousin.

But why did there always have to be a qualifier? If she had been the one who convinced him to take such an important step, why hadn't he shared the news with her? It was pretty important. He could've said something when they were standing at the elevator.

A cold, prickling realization settled around Kinsley. Maybe he hadn't shared this personal news with her because it was *personal*.

Maybe she needed to take a hint from his lack of communication over the past day and a half.

A bubble of laughter escaped, but the sound was dry and devoid of humor. Despite Christopher's claims to the contrary, he had a love-'em-and-leave-'em reputation. Facts were facts. She had put too much stock into their night together. Their...liaison.

Oh, God. That was all it had been.

Icy hot humiliation settled around her. She bit her lip until it throbbed in time with her pulse. She sat there—just sat there—for several long minutes, letting reality seep into her pores, flogging herself with I-told-you-sos.

You knew this was a very plausible outcome. Whenever she violated her gut instinct, she always lived to regret it.

Now, if she knew what was good for her, she'd get herself together. No moping. No sniping at Christopher. No looking back with regret.

She would not let this interfere with her work.

Because in her work, she would find the solidity that would distract her and camouflage the despair that colored everything in sight.

For what must've been the hundredth time, Kinsley reminded herself that the Fortunes considered blood thicker than water. She didn't want to chance losing her job should someone disapprove of her affair with Christopher. Or worse yet, if talk started around the office that Kinsley was attempting to sleep her way to the top, Christopher might see her as a burden and decide the office would be better off without her.

If she had learned one thing growing up in an abusive home, it was that the less attention you drew to yourself, the better off—the safer—you were in the long run. That meant no more jealous outbursts like the time she thought he was dating his etiquette coach.

From this moment forward, she would put a smile on her face and it would be business as usual.

Good thing, too, because when she looked up, Christopher was standing in her doorway smiling and holding a big presentation board.

Christopher was simply flat-out scared to fall in love. He recognized that but had no idea what to do, besides stop hiding and acting like a child. Kinsley deserved better than that.

He knew he had been distant, using the excuse that he had been immersed in work, busy coming up with a plan for them to use as a follow-up to the initiative that they'd started at the Spring Fling.

But if he were completely honest with himself, he had been avoiding Kinsley. By doing so, he didn't have to face his feelings.

Why could he analyze so easily, but he had no idea what to do with it?

He had been heartened by his father's newfound respect and bolstered by his uncle's good report.

With this newfound support system, in a day and a half he had managed to outline the basics of the follow-up program. His initial reaction had him wanting to involve Kinsley, but fear caused him to back away. He simply needed a cooling-off period, time to put things into perspective and remember how to be her colleague without wanting to undress her and lay her flat across his desk.

But seeing her at the elevator yesterday, he knew that his silence was hurting her. Hell, it was hurting *him*. But last night he'd decided that in a similar way that he'd reached out to Deke, he needed to break the ice with Kinsley.

He thought the best way to do that—at least, for starters—was to ask her opinion on the new idea.

As he stood in her office doorway, gripping the presentation board, he felt the same pull of attraction that he felt every time he looked at her.

"May I come in?" he asked.

Her blue eyes looked wary as she smiled at him. Her professional smile. He recognized it.

"Sure," she said.

He left the door open on purpose, to discourage the conversation from veering off on a personal path.

"Remember how I told you yesterday that I had come up with a new plan for us to use in the schools?"

She nodded. Yep. Her wall was up. He recognized that, too.

"This is intended as a tool for school guidance

counselors to use." Damn, this was harder than he had expected. The way she was looking at him…it was more like she was staring right through him. "I hope that it will help kids remember to not just stand there when someone is in trouble, but to act."

He realized that he was nervous as he turned the board around, showing her the acronym GET IN-VOLVED. Each letter of the words stood for an element of the program.

Christopher watched Kinsley as she read the board, her lips pressed into a thin line.

When she was finished, she simply nodded and said, "Get Involved, huh? That's good advice. Even if it is a little ironic coming from a man who seems to do everything in his power to avoid doing exactly that."

Chapter Thirteen

On Wednesday morning, Christopher still couldn't get Kinsley's face out of his head. The way she'd looked as she'd read the GET INVOLVED acronym.

She'd had good reason for looking so upset. The words obviously hit home.

Sitting at his desk, he rested his forehead on his palm. He was such an idiot. How could he not have seen the irony of the message before he brought it to her?

As soon as she'd read it, he'd seen it in her eyes. Sure, she kept a professional poker face, but she couldn't disguise the hurt. She'd told him it was perfect and then excused herself, saying she had a lunch engagement.

She'd walked out, leaving him sitting there with his presentation board on the desk and his foot in his mouth. He needed to practice what he preached.

GET INVOLVED?

His problem was that he was too afraid to get involved. So ridiculously terrified—of what? He had better figure it out because his fear was going to cost him the best thing that had ever happened to him.

They needed to talk about this. Even if he didn't know what to say. He needed to let her know it wasn't her; it was him. That she was smart and beautiful and deserving of so much more than he could offer.

He picked up the phone to call her office. But then he put it back down in the cradle. Maybe he should just go talk to her. Common sense told him he should wait until after work. He didn't want to upset her, but that seemed as though he wasn't giving her enough credit.

He got up from his desk and made his way into the reception area, but before he could get to Kinsley's office, Bev intercepted him.

"Mr. Jamison just called," she said. "He wants to see you in his office right away."

Christopher made his way to Emmett Jamison's wing of the building. His administrative assistant, Clara, was expecting him.

"Oh, good, there you are," she said. "He wants to see you but he has another meeting at 10:30." She glanced at her watch. "Oh, no problem. You have plenty of time. Go right in."

As Christopher walked toward Emmett's door, he heard Clara inform him that Christopher was on his way in.

For a fleeting second, he wondered if this had to do with the talk he had had with his father. But then that gave way to the guilt he felt over how things had turned out with Kinsley. Surely, she wouldn't have lodged a complaint against him, would she?

No, that would be completely out of character for her. But he couldn't ignore the little voice that jabbed at him and said she would be completely within her rights. He should've been stronger and not taken advantage of her while she was vulnerable, even though that's not at all what he had intended.

The same jabbing voice brought up words like love and feelings, but he ignored it as he rapped on Emmett's door.

"Come in."

Christopher opened the door and stepped inside. He was immediately set at ease by the broad smile that graced Emmett's face.

"Just the man I wanted to see," Emmett said. "Have a seat, please." He gestured to a chair in front of his desk.

Christopher complied.

As soon as he was settled Emmett picked up the display board that outlined the GET INVOLVED program. He tapped it with his finger.

"This is good work."

He paused, as if letting the praise ring in the air.

"You have done some impressive work in your short time here at the Foundation. I'm not the only one who has taken notice. But before I tell you what I have in mind, let me ask you, are you happy with what you're doing? Because you sure are doing a good job."

"I love what I'm doing. I truly feel like I've found my calling here at the Foundation."

"Great, that's exactly what I was hoping you would say. I have an opportunity I would like to talk to you about. We have discovered the need for a presence in New York City. I know New York is very different than Red Rock, but the work would be similar. We—the board, your uncle James, Lily and I—were hoping that you would be willing to take on the challenge. How would you feel about relocating to New York City and opening that office for us? We would love for you to be the man in charge. If anyone can do it, you could."

Emmett's offer caught Christopher so off guard, he couldn't even answer for a moment. He was truly stunned.

New York City? They wanted him to move out there and open the office?

But what about Kinsley?

"Would anyone else be in the office with me?" he asked. "Would I have a staff?"

Emmett steepled his fingers. "Not right off the bat. We would have to make sure that the new office was up and running and self-sustaining, of course—there's no mission without margin—before we could fully staff the office. But don't worry. We would pay to relocate you and give you a salary increase and housing allowance that would allow you to live comfortably in the city."

Of course, it would mean leaving behind everybody he had come to care so much about.

Kinsley's face was the first to flash in his mind again. Even before his newfound relatives and all the friends he had made since moving to Red Rock.

It was a tempting offer. It meant that they trusted him. It meant that they respected him and appreciated his vision. Uncle James, Lily and Emmett were the first people who had truly believed in him.

That inappropriate voice piped up inside him and reminded him that Kinsley had once believed in him too.

"I realize that this is a lot to think about," said Emmett. "I will have Clara draw up the specifics and get them to you by the end of the day. Why don't you take a few days to think about it before you let me know your answer? The sooner we can get you there, the better."

Christopher cleared his throat. "I want you to know how much I appreciate your confidence in me. I am greatly honored and humbled that you would entrust me with this position. I'll look forward to reviewing the details."

Emmett stood and offered Christopher his hand. Christopher stood and accepted it. What would Deke and Jeanne Marie think of this? His father had had a conniption when Christopher had accepted the job in Red Rock. If his father had thought this place was highfalutin, what in the world would he think of his son moving to New York City?

But Christopher reminded himself not to get too far ahead. He hadn't seen the offer yet. He had no idea what they intended in terms of dollars and cents.

Even though he wasn't anywhere close to making up his mind, he knew one of the biggest sacrifices he would be making would be leaving Kinsley behind.

Suddenly everything that had been so muddled and tentative seemed to snap into sharp focus. This job was everything he had ever wanted, except it didn't include Kinsley. But maybe time away from her in a place where he could focus on his job and not be distracted by her full lips and the way their bodies fit so perfectly together that it drove him nuts to even catch a glimpse of her in the office hallway was a good thing.

Maybe putting some distance between them was exactly what he needed. Then again, maybe this opportunity would cost him the one woman he had ever loved. But maybe that was case in point why he should go and not look back.

That evening Christopher sat at his desk reading—for the fifth time—the details of the generous New York City relocation offer that Clara had delivered to him just before five o'clock.

Among other perks, they were offering him nearly twice his current salary and a housing allowance that would afford him a comfortable apartment in Manhattan.

It was a far cry from Horseback Hollow and the life sentence on his family's ranch. This offer was a dream come true. And more than that, it was validation that he was good at his job. The board could've chosen anyone to head up this project, but they'd put their faith in him.

Christopher closed the file and leaned back in his leather chair, stretching his feet out in front of him and looking around his office. When he'd first gotten here, he'd thought this place was the be-all and end-all with its paneled walls, living room furniture and that view.

Now, he'd been handed the chance of a lifetime to write his own ticket.

So why was he hesitating?

The numbers checked out. It would be a long time before a chance like this would come along again, much less be dropped into his lap.

He needed to think about it. Sleep on it. Even if Emmett was pushing for a fast answer, Christopher needed a few hours to process everything. Then maybe this uncertainty would sort itself out.

In his head it was a no-brainer: only idiots passed up the chance of a lifetime for a woman. Especially when he'd had trepidations about their relationship before the deal was on the table.

However, now that the deal was on the table, his head and his heart were at odds.

He'd have to sort that out, and fast.

He put the file in his briefcase and clicked off his desk lamp.

It was after 6:30 p.m. The sun was painting the Western landscape outside his window in shades of gold and amber. Everything looked a little different in the light of this offer. As Christopher headed toward the elevator, the light that was still on in Kinsley's office drew him like a moth.

She was completely engaged in whatever it was she was reading on her computer screen. He stood there watching her, wanting to memorize the way she looked right now with her guard down and her hair hanging in soft curls around her shoulders. He owed it to her to tell her about the offer before she heard it from someone else.

"Don't you ever go home?" he said.

She startled and looked up at him. "Oh, Christopher. I didn't realize anyone else was still here."

"Just you and me," he said, his heart compressing at the words. "Do you have a minute?"

She pushed her mouse away and angled her body toward him. "Sure, come in."

He settled himself in the chair across from her.

"Everything okay?" she asked. Her hand fluttered to her blouse collar and she fidgeted with the top button, which, as always, was buttoned up tight.

Despite everything, he had to resist the urge to reach out and undo it and all the others and pull her into him so that he could lose himself in the Nirvana that was her.

And that was exactly why he needed to distance himself. He couldn't even think straight when he was with her. It was his own fault. Yep, it was all on him, and he needed to do something to regain his equilibrium.

"Everything is fine. More than fine, actually. I got a job offer today."

Her expression remained neutral. "Really? Where?"

"New York."

He told her how Emmett had called him into his office earlier.

"It's great money, and such an opportunity I can't see how I can refuse."

For a split second he thought he saw a flicker of regret flash in her blue eyes, and in that same split second he knew that if she said, "Don't go," he wouldn't. He'd turn down the offer and he'd take her home and make love to her until they'd finally figured out that this complicated thing between them didn't have to be so—

"How wonderful for you," she said, verbally slapping the sense back into him. "When do you leave for New York?"

* * *

Kinsley was happy for Christopher. Truly, she was.

And she had told him that yesterday when he stopped by her office. She said it with her most genuine a smile.

She wanted him to be happy.

Really, she did. And if she kept telling herself how happy she was that he was leaving, maybe she would start to believe it.

Even though she hadn't seen the specifics of the offer yet, Kinsley knew he would take it. The Fortunes were generous with their compensation. There was no way he would turn it down.

His leaving was probably the very best thing that could happen to both of them. He would relocate to a place where he could steep himself in big city, sophistication. She could keep her job here and maybe regain her concentration...and her heart.

Of course it would end up this way. Of course it would. This proved that it really was best that they hadn't committed to each other.

It was hard enough to know that he didn't want a relationship with her. The only thing that might've been harder was knowing that he did want a relationship and then him having to choose between her and his dream job.

She laughed to herself as she realized she had gotten it wrong. Women weren't Christopher's mistress; his work was.

She sat there trying to convince herself that this really was the best thing for both of them. If she said the words enough, surely she would begin to believe it. If not now, maybe by the time he made the move. Just then an email popped up in her computer inbox. Kinsley sat up a little straighter when she realized it was from Lily Cassidy Fortune.

The subject line read Surprise party for Christopher.

Kinsley clicked on the email.

Hello, Kinsley, I am calling on you for a rather large favor. Since you seem to be the colleague closest to Christopher, would you please take on the task of organizing a surprise going-away party for him? I was hoping we could do something nice for him— something a touch sentimental? I will leave it in your capable hands as I'm sure you will know exactly what to do to make Christopher realize how much he means to us and how grateful we are that he has accepted this challenge. We were hoping to have the party tomorrow, as he will be making the move this weekend. I know this is all terribly fast, but I'm sure Beverly will be happy to assist you with anything you need.

Kinsley fell back against her chair and her breath rushed from her lungs.

So it was official.

And he was leaving this weekend?

Christopher was leaving *this* weekend?

Her heart cracked open and filled with a leaden dread.

She wasn't surprised that he had accepted it. He'd all but made up his mind when they'd talked last night. She just hadn't realized he would leave so soon.

She fought the sudden urge to cry, blinking back the

unwelcome tears that clouded her vision. There was no use getting emotional. It was for the best.

Really, it was.

She needed to treat this the same way one would rip off a bandage—the faster the better. The sooner Christopher got on with his new life, the sooner she could get on with her life here in Red Rock without him.

She sat there for several minutes in her quiet office, listening to the whir of the air conditioner and the hum of her computer. Now that the tears were at bay, a strange numbness had overtaken her.

She picked up the phone and called Bev.

They had less than twenty-four hours. They would have to get this party planning rolling as soon as possible if they were going to pull it off.

The sooner they started planning, the sooner it would be over.

Chapter Fourteen

"*Surprise!*"

The chorus of voices rang out when Emmett opened the conference room door and ushered Christopher inside.

Christopher blinked once, twice, three times as he looked around at all of his coworkers who had crowded into the conference room, surrounded by streamers and helium balloons.

"What the heck is this?"

His uncle James stepped forward and clapped him on the back. "This is your party, son. We wanted to give you a good sendoff on your last day here in the Red Rock office."

A surprise party?

He glanced at Emmett and murmured something unintelligible. Emmett grinned back at him, obviously proud that his paper-signing ruse had worked to get him to the conference room.

Christopher *was* surprised. Surprised and genuinely touched that everyone would gather on a Friday afternoon—just for him.

There were steaming covered chafing dishes in the middle of the conference room table being tended to by catering staff in uniforms with the Red logo. His stomach growled as he inhaled the delicious aroma of Red's Mexican food—a mélange of savory dishes blending with the aroma of fresh corn tortillas, chilies and spices. There were platters of Red's famous corn roasted in the husk stacked on platters which were next to the biggest cake he had ever seen in his life. And there was champagne.

That's when he realized that everyone was raising a glass toward him. Lily stepped forward and handed him and Emmett each a flute, too.

Emmett and James, who were flanking Christopher, simultaneously touched their glasses to his.

"I would like to propose a toast," said James. "To Christopher Fortune, our golden boy. May you shine in the city as brightly as you do here."

"To Christopher!" someone shouted and everyone raised their glasses a little higher, then took a sip.

Christopher glanced around the room, taking in his family, friends and coworkers: Miguel and Marcos Mendoza were there. So was their cousin Sierra Mendoza Calloway. Standing next to her was Emmett's wife, Linda Faraday. She was talking to Susan Fortune Eldridge and Julie Osterman Fortune. Nicholas and Jeremy Fortune were there. Then he saw Tanner and Jordana Redmond and Sawyer and his wife, Laurel—

had they come all the way from Horseback Hollow to be here just for him?

As people surrounded him, offering handshakes, high fives and fist bumps, he realized how much he truly cared for these people.

It was a bit overwhelming.

Funny, before he got here, when he had first taken on the Fortune name, he had imagined them all to be so different than they had turned out to be. Not in a bad way. In fact, they were better than he could've ever imagined. They were all warm, loving, family-oriented people, and he was proud to be one of them.

And when Sawyer came over and shook his hand, Christopher experienced an inexplicable pang of homesickness for his immediate family in Horseback Hollow. Even Deke.

Especially Deke.

As the good wishes continued and people rallied around him—it was a good thing he wasn't claustrophobic—he found himself craning his neck searching for the one person he was desperate to see.

Finally, he saw Kinsley standing by the table with the champagne, refilling glasses, doing what she was so good at—helping other people.

His gaze was drawn to her like a pin to a magnet. He drank her in, trying to take a mental snapshot of her gorgeous face, her blue-blue eyes that were framed by eyebrows a few shades darker than her sun-streaked blond hair. Her finely chiseled cheekbones. The delicate slope of her neck. Her full lips.

He could still feel those lips on his. He could feel the way their bodies had fit so perfectly, as if they were made for each other. A surge of longing so deep and fraught with desire for her consumed him.

It was as if he were seeing her for the first time. Through new eyes. Now he wanted her even more than he had the first time he'd seen her.

Why was it that he never really appreciated what he had when he had it? Why did he always wonder if something better was around the corner? Standing here in the midst of the crowd, among all these well-wishers, his heart spoke loud and clear: there wasn't a better woman in the world for him than Kinsley Aaron.

He had to tamp down the urge to fight his way through the crowd and pull her into his arms. His heart ached for her.

As much as he loved the attention and the accolades and the thought that his uncle James and Lily Cassidy Fortune trusted him—*him,* the guy who never seemed to have the capability to do anything right back in Horseback Hollow—with opening their satellite office in a city like New York, and even though they had been more than generous with the compensation and benefits package that they had given him, moving to New York would mean losing touch with everyone that mattered to him.

And it would mean losing Kinsley.

Suddenly his future flashed before his eyes in a crystal-clear vision: he would have the money and the dream job and the prestige and everything he could ever want at his disposal in a big city where the world would be his oyster, but it would never be enough. He would never be satisfied with all of that because it was empty. Well, the work had proved to be fulfilling, but all the money in the world couldn't replace what he had found in Red Rock.

Being here, he had learned how to go home again.

He had learned the value of everything money couldn't buy.

Was he really willing to give up everything for... emptiness?

He excused himself from his colleagues and made his way over to Emmett and James, who were standing with Linda and Lily.

"This is a fabulous party," Christopher said. "I can't thank you enough."

Lily set a slender hand on his arm. "Oh, honey, I wish we could all take credit for this party. But this is all Kinsley Aaron. Is there anything that woman can't do? Didn't she do a lovely job?"

"There is absolutely nothing she can't do," Christopher said. "She's even taught me a thing or two since I've been working with her. So I'm not at all surprised to learn that she is the one responsible for this."

Christopher watched Kinsley as she cut the cake and put small squares on the colorful party plates. He watched her as she worked while everyone else was enjoying themselves. She was always willing to go the extra mile for somebody else. Always willing to sacrifice even if it meant standing back while somebody else shined.

How could he have been such a damn fool?

How could he have been willing to let go of the only woman in this world he would ever be able to love?

Christopher turned to James and Emmett. "If you don't mind, I need to speak to the two of you privately."

Both men did a double-take.

"Right now?" asked James. "In case you didn't notice, son, there's a party going on. Rumor has it it's in your honor."

"That's exactly why I need to talk to you now," said Christopher. "This can't wait."

Just keep yourself busy and it'll be over faster.

Kinsley was not in the mood to party. But she sure was good at playing the role of the hostess.

She reminded herself that this was not about her. It had nothing to do with her. She needed to keep smiling and keep her eye on the light at the end of the tunnel.

It would all be over soon.

So, Kinsley refilled the tortilla platters and the water pitchers. She brought out extra bottles of soda and champagne and replenished the paper goods, cups and the plastic utensils.

As she looked around, she caught a glimpse of Christopher. He was talking to Mr. Jamison, Lily Fortune and James Marshall Fortune. She looked away but not before she felt the heat of his gaze on her.

But then, when she glanced back, he was gone. Probably hidden by one of the one hundred balloons in the room. She breathed a sigh of relief and moved around the chafing dishes the catering staff had just replenished.

Good grief, these people were tough customers. From the way they were devouring the food you would think they hadn't eaten in days. But who could blame them? Red prided itself on delicious food. Today they offered beef brisket enchiladas, chicken mole and spicy lobster tacos. She was having to hustle now, but the more they ate, the less she and the staff would have to clean up later.

And the more work she would have to keep her hands busy and her mind off the reason for the party.

Christopher. The mere thought of him made her chest tighten and her heart squeeze.

Stop it.

But what good did fighting it do? She kept her head down and allowed herself to switch over to autopilot. To let the thoughts and feelings come and go as they would. Maybe if she leaned into the emotions she'd have an easier time of it.

Or maybe she would break down into a heaping, sobbing mess and really humiliate herself. She took a deep breath and released it slowly.

No, it seemed that the thoughts and feelings were hidden deep enough under the surface. Even so, everyone else in this room was so convivial and having such a good time that no one had a clue that her heart was breaking.

Scratch that. Her heart had already broken. Past tense. For days, she had been carrying around a bunch of bits and pieces of broken heart that she knew would never be able to fit back together again.

That was okay. She didn't have any use for her heart anymore. She just hoped the pieces didn't rattle.

Stepping outside of herself, she had to admit that Christopher had seemed astonished. It was always nice when a surprise party went off the way it was planned.

That's right. Focus on the good. There you go.

She resisted the urge to look up and search the crowd for him. So far, playing caterer had helped her to not moon over him, to not watch what he was doing or who he was talking to. It just hurt too much.

Plus, the last thing she needed was for someone she worked with to discover her secret: that she was brokenhearted because had slept with Christopher and the affair had gone horribly, disastrously wrong. *That* could be misconstrued in so many ways.

Normally, she didn't care what people thought of her. But this was a different case. She may have lost her heart, but it was imperative for her to walk away with her integrity and dignity intact. Because what had happened between Christopher and her hadn't been like that. She wasn't using him to get favors or a boost up the corporate ladder.

It was…

Yeah, it was.

And it was over now. She needed to get over it. But it had only been a week since she had given herself—body and soul—to him; her heart still felt tender and her pride was pretty raw.

What had she expected? She knew what she had wanted. But what you want and what you get were sometimes two entirely different things.

What she had gotten was a lesson. She didn't give her heart away easily. And she wouldn't do it again anytime soon. After all, who would want the bag of broken pieces she stored in the place where her heart had once lived?

She would feel better someday. It would just take time. Right now she needed to keep her chin up.

Chin up, buttercup. Her mom used to say that when they'd hit a rough patch. God, what she wouldn't give to be able to go to her mother right now. Not for advice, but for a shoulder. For the shelter of her hugs. She had been the one person in whom Kinsley had found unrequited love.

And if she'd learned one thing from watching her mother it was that sometimes when you loved too much your generous spirit became your undoing.

Unlike her mother, she had a second chance to reclaim herself. Rather than mooning, she would embrace the blessing in this narrow miss.

Right...

Forcing herself to look up, she glanced around the room admiring her handiwork—not looking for Christopher. Everyone was chatting, and the buzz of convivial energy filled the room. The helium balloons she had procured did a fairly decent job of hiding her—or hiding him. Either way, because they were clustered in the area where she had been hiding out, she had to make an effort to look for him. As if blatantly defying her, her eyes swept the room looking for him, but before she could pick him out she came face-to-face with a giant yellow balloon...well, what better caution sign could a girl ask for?

She was running the risk of driving herself crazy, so she made another conscious effort to refocus. She scanned the food tables in search of something to distract her, but it appeared that everyone was finally slowing down. Nothing needed refilling or replenishing or replacing.

She picked up a couple of empty cups and plates, realizing if she felt like the hired help, it was because she had put herself in that position. The catering staff would take care of this. She swiped the back of her hand across her forehead, then tucked an errant strand of hair behind her ear.

Maybe she would have a glass of champagne. She didn't really feel like celebrating, but that was no reason to boycott the bubbly. In fact, looking on the bright side, she should celebrate the fact that she'd pulled this off.

Who would've thought that planning a party would be one of the hardest assignments she'd ever faced?

The old adage what doesn't kill you makes you stronger definitely applied here.

She had just poured herself a glass of champagne when Mr. Jamison called everyone in the conference room to order.

"May I have your attention, please? Everyone, please settle down and listen. Christopher has something he would like to say."

Oh, boy. Here we go.

The room quieted down and everybody turned their attention to Christopher. For the first time that afternoon, Kinsley stopped what she was doing and gave him her ears.

Mr. Jamison turned to Christopher and murmured, "Are you sure this is what you want to do?"

Christopher nodded. "Actually, I've never been so sure about anything in my life." He glanced at Kinsley, and their gazes locked. She wanted to look away, but she couldn't. "Well, maybe I've been that sure about one other thing, and she's a big part of the reason that I'm going to say what I have to say. I appreciate this party. I appreciate everybody gathering here to wish me well and to give me such a great sendoff. However, turns out a funny thing happened on the way to the cake table. I realize I won't be moving to New York, after all."

Kinsley was frozen in place, desperately pulling back on the reins of her heart, which was hopefully anticipating a preposterous turn of events that would surely never be.

So just stop it.

Audible gasps mixed with surprised murmurs and astonished glances, but Christopher's gaze didn't waver from hers.

"It's always been important to me to be respected and regarded as an intelligent man. But it took a party like this, a gathering of my family and friends and one hell of a party planner—everybody please give Kinsley a round of applause for the wonderful job she did to bring us all together—to clarify some things for me."

Her hand fluttered to her collar. *Oh, why did he do that?*

She finally broke their gaze and glanced around at the people who were clapping for her. She really wished they wouldn't do that.

When they quieted down, Christopher continued. "Today I realize that I love Texas too much to leave. I have just gotten to know my Fortune family, and quite frankly I'm not ready to put that much distance between us. But most of all, there is someone special here I simply can't bear to leave behind."

Kinsley's heart stopped beating for what seemed like an eternity. When it resumed, it picked up double time.

"She has made me a better person. I haven't quite figured out how this happened, and I'm pretty sure I don't deserve her. But I love her. I love her with my entire being, and I can't imagine my life without her."

Kinsley's gasp was audible, surprising even herself. Heat crept up her neck and fanned across her cheeks as every gaze in the place turned to her.

She wasn't sure if she wanted to cry tears of joy or crawl under the table to escape scrutiny. The tears of joy definitely won out. This unusual proclamation of love certainly wasn't what she had expected when she thought about Christopher declaring his love, but had Christopher Fortune ever done anything by the book?

"I wouldn't blame Kinsley if she killed me right now," Christopher said, hoping he hadn't gone too far with this workplace pronouncement. "So if you see me with a piece of cake smashed in my face, it probably doesn't mean we've gotten married. It probably means she simply smashed that cake in my face, which I suppose I would deserve."

He was relieved when everyone laughed.

He couldn't quite see Kinsley, who had gradually worked her way to the back of the room. Hell, he didn't blame her—he probably shouldn't have gotten so carried away. It would serve him right if she told him to take a hike.

He remembered his initial vow to win her over no matter what. He fully expected to have to work harder than he'd ever worked his entire life to get her to commit to him. He'd never looked so forward to a challenge. Speaking of challenges, he still owed everyone the rest of the explanation. He turned back to the group and continued.

"Plenty of folks right here in this room are probably

better qualified than I am to open an office in the Big Apple. I was thinking about that while I was standing here enjoying everyone's company. So I offered Emmett, James and Lily a new proposal for the Fortune Foundation, but this one hits a little closer to home. With their blessing, I will be opening a satellite office of the Foundation in Horseback Hollow, with an anti-bullying/GET INVOLVED initiative. I will split time between Horseback Hollow and Red Rock. So, I'm sorry to say that you haven't gotten rid of me yet."

As his family and coworkers applauded this news, Christopher scanned the room for Kinsley, wanting to gauge her reaction, but he didn't see her. He wanted to go find her, but people approached and started the whole process all over again of shaking his hand, slapping him on the back and congratulating him—on the satellite office and on falling in love with a wonderful woman. They all seemed genuinely pleased for him. It was very moving, but he was starting to get a little anxious over Kinsley's absence.

Had she left?

He wouldn't blame her if she'd walked out. But if she had, he would fix it.

If it was the last thing he did, he would fix things between them.

He excused himself again from the knot of wellwishers and went to look for her.

He found her in the reception area standing quietly gazing out the window. It was a similar view as from his office, the one that had captivated him from the start. He'd thought the south Texas landscape couldn't look more beautiful. But he'd never seen it as a backdrop to Kinsley.

"I meant what I said in there," he said. "I'm in love with you. I may have changed my mind about the job, but I'm not going to change my mind about you. All I need to know is do I even stand a chance after all I've put you through?"

She turned and met his gaze. Her beautiful eyes were brimming with tears. In that instant he knew everything was going to be okay.

He walked over to her, pulled her into his arms and reached up and brushed a tear off her cheek.

"Don't worry," she said. "They're happy tears. I love you, too."

Kinsley was never so happy to leave a party—even one she'd planned. But she knew the two of them would have a much better time at the after party—in Christopher's bed.

With him, she was home, even amid the partially packed boxes that would now need to be unpacked. Yes, she was more than happy to help him with this task. It was the packing and the goodbyes she couldn't bear.

They spent a long, luxurious evening making love and snuggling and making love and snuggling. She couldn't tell if they were making up for lost time or living in the moment, but it didn't matter. They didn't need to define it. They already had when they had exchanged those three precious words that even twelve hours ago she feared she would never hear cross his lips.

If she had learned one thing about Christopher it was that when he said something he meant it. His word was golden, and Kinsley basked in the glow of it as he held her.

She splayed her hand across his chest, reveling in the downy-soft feel of his chest hair.

"So, speaking of being the last to know…" she said.

He pulled her closer, as if he were afraid she would get away.

"Oh, hell…here we go." He smiled and pretended to roll his eyes before he kissed her soundly. "I knew there would be hell to pay for what I did. May I make it up to you…again? Because I am perfectly willing to make love to you until you fully understand just how much I love you."

He shifted her to the side and then rolled on top of her.

"Oh, you have no idea how much trouble you are in, mister." She kissed his neck and then nipped at his earlobe as he nudged her legs apart and entered her again.

After they were spent and breathless, she managed to catch her breath. "As I was saying, I had to hear through the grapevine that you called your father. And that the two of you had a good talk."

He did a double-take. "Oh, yeah? Who is spreading such rumors?"

"I'm not telling."

He grinned at her slyly. "I thought we promised that there would be no secrets between us. Am I going to have to assign you penance?"

"Please do. I could be a very happy woman doing atonement with you." She traced his lips with her index finger, getting momentarily lost in the mix of masculine strength and male beauty that was Christopher.

She swallowed around a lump of love and gratitude that had settled in her throat.

Or maybe it was her heart that was so full it was spilling over. Whatever the case, she never wanted it to go away. She wanted it to keep bubbling up like a fountain.

She settled into the crook of his arm and rested her head in that place on his shoulder that seemed to be made just for her.

"Actually, it's not a rumor," he said. "I did call my dad. Deke said to tell you hello."

"Really?" she asked.

"No, but I do want to take you home to Horseback Hollow so that you can meet him and my mother. I know she'll love you. They will all love you. Maybe not quite as much as I do, but I don't know that that's humanly possible. But I digress.

"The call went great. Better than great. I underestimated my father. I learned that he and I are two different men, but that's okay. We have finally come to the point where we accept that and respect each other for who we are."

"I'm so glad," Kinsley said.

Gently, he rubbed her back in a slow, rhythmic motion that was almost hypnotizing. She couldn't remember the last time she had been this relaxed.

"I might not have called him—or at least not so soon—if not for you. Thank you for that. Thank you for always seeing the best in me."

"Well, not *always*— Remember, you still have a lot of penance before you're completely redeemed. But I can assure you that I do love what I see."

They were quiet for a moment. The air-conditioning

clicked on. Somewhere out in the world, outside the snug cocoon that had become their universe, a car door shut and a dog barked.

"So, who do you look like—your mom or your dad?"

"Everyone says I take after my dad. In looks and personality. My brothers say that's why Deke and I butt heads so often. That we're too much alike."

"I'd love to see a picture of him sometime. He must be a good-looking guy."

Christopher stretched. "My mama thinks so. She's stuck with him for forty years. Can you believe they've been married that long?"

"I think that's wonderful."

"Maybe that gives you a little hope for me. I don't commit easily, but once I do, I'm sort of like gum on your shoe."

"That's *so* romantic."

They laughed. She loved the way they didn't take themselves too seriously.

"At least I think I'll be the gum on your shoe. I've never loved someone enough to be their gum."

"Wow. How did I get so lucky?"

They laughed again, and when they stopped, she lost herself in his sigh of contentment.

"So, now, tell me again, how many brothers and sisters do you have?"

"I'm one of seven."

"Holy cow. Your poor mother."

"Nah, Mama loved her children. There are two girls and five boys, including me. A handful."

"Sounds like your mother should be canonized."

"Yup, pretty much. Wait—" he said sitting up suddenly. "I want to show you something."

Kinsley enjoyed watching him walk from the bed to the bedroom door.

"What a fine specimen you are, Mr. Fortune."

When he returned he was holding a photo album. The one she remembered seeing in his car that night they went to Mendoza's.

The night everything started.

"What's that?" she asked as he climbed back into bed beside her.

"It's a photo album my mother sent me to remind me of where I came from."

"And you're letting me look now? Remember that night before we went to Mendoza's? I thought you were going to smack my hand away from it."

He looked at her solemnly, momentarily sobering. "Besides loving you for the rest of your life, the other thing I can promise you is that I will never, ever raise a hand to you."

She inhaled sharply and nodded.

In that moment, she sensed that her mother was with her. That her mother, the angel, had quite possibly sent Christopher to watch over her. The kind of man she should have, rather than the kind of bad example her father had set.

Everything is going to be all right, Mom. Everything is fine now.

"Here," said Christopher. "Look at this picture. Here's my dad when he was about my age."

Wrapped in the sheet, Kinsley scooted up and sat next to Christopher on the bed.

She studied the picture, loving this new window into her love's world. "Wow, you do look like him."

"My dad's name is Jones. Deke Jones. I'm going to start using Jones in my name again. How would you feel about being part of the Fortune Jones family?"

"Hmm...Kinsley Aaron Fortune Jones," she said. "That's a mouthful. But it sounds like poetry to me."

When Christopher leaned in and kissed her. She knew that she was home, that she had finally found her family at last.

* * * * *

WHY RESIST A REBEL?

LEAH ASHTON

For Annie – who has always been way cooler than her big sister and then went and worked in film, just to rub it in.

Thank you for your endless help and patience as I researched this book. Any mistakes are mine.

You're awesome, Annie.

CHAPTER ONE

RUBY BELL ESTIMATED her phone rang approximately half a second before her brisk walk was rudely interrupted by an unfortunately located tuft of grass.

More fortunately, she'd had the presence of mind to hold onto said phone during her less than graceful swan-dive onto the dusty paddock floor. A paddock that had once housed a significant number of sheep, but more recently had become the temporary home of a ninety-strong film crew. Thankfully this particular patch of paddock showed no evidence of sheep occupation.

But, at such close range, Ruby had also learnt that the paddock floor was: a) lumpy and b) hard.

'Paul,' Ruby said, wincing slightly as she lifted the phone to her ear. Still lying flat on her belly in the dirt, she shifted her weight in an unsuccessful attempt to avoid the patches of grass that prickled through the thin fabric of her T-shirt and the seeping warmth that had once been her half-drunk cardboard cup of coffee. Just slightly winded, Ruby's voice was a little breathy, but otherwise she sounded about as efficient as always. Good. She'd built a successful career as a production co-ordinator that took her across the globe—regularly—by being sensible, unflappable, no-nonsense Ruby. Tripping over her own feet couldn't even begin to rattle her.

'I need you back at the office,' Paul said, even more flustered than usual. 'There's been a development.'

And that was it—he'd already hung up. Ruby knew it was

impossible to interpret her producer's urgent tone—it was quite possible the sky *was* falling, but about the same odds that one of the runners had simply screwed up his espresso again. Either way, Ruby needed to get her butt into gear.

'You okay, Rubes?'

Ruby glanced up at the worried voice, squinting a little against the early afternoon sun. But, even mostly in shadow— or maybe because of it—the very broad and very solid frame of Bruno, the key grip, was unmistakeable. Beside him stood a couple of the younger grips, looking about as awkward as they always did when they weren't busily carting heavy objects around—plus about half the hair and make-up department. Which made sense, given she'd managed to come crashing to the ground right outside their trailers.

'Of course,' she said, pressing her outflung hands into the soil and levering herself up onto her knees. She waved away Bruno's helpful hand as she plucked at her T-shirt, pulling the coffee-soaked fabric away from her chest. The parts of her not damp and clinging were decorated with a mix of grass stains and a remarkable number of dirt smudges.

Awesome.

But she didn't have time to worry about the state of her outfit just now. Or her hair—running her fingers through her short blonde pixie-cut confirmed only that it was somehow dusty, too.

A moment later she was back on her feet and her day carried on exactly as before—grass stains and the uncomfortable sensation she was covered in a head-to-toe sticky coating of dirt notwithstanding.

'Ruby!' A yell from somewhere to her left. 'Weather tomorrow?'

'Fine. No chance of rain,' she called out, not even slowing her pace. Paul, as always, would've preferred if she'd gained the power of teleportation. In its absence, she just needed to walk even faster than normal.

The cottage that temporarily housed the film's production office was only a few minutes away—tucked to the left beyond the final cluster of shiny black or white trailers and the slightly askew tent city that was catering.

She kept her focus on her path—already well worn into the grass in the two days since they'd set up camp—mentally crossing her fingers for nothing more serious than a coffee-related emergency. So far she'd already dealt with an unexpected script change, a sudden decision to relocate a scene, and an entitled young actress who'd gone temporarily AWOL. And it was only day one of filming.

'Got a minute?' asked Sarah, a slight redhead in charge of the extensive list of extras required for *The Land*—an 'epic historical romance played out in the heart of the outback'—from the top stair of a shiny black trailer.

'No,' Ruby said, but slowed anyway. 'Paul,' she said, as way of explanation.

'Ah,' Sarah replied, then skipped down from the trailer to fall into step with Ruby as she passed. 'Just a quick one. I've got a call from a concerned parent. They're worried about how we're going to get Samuel to cry in tomorrow's scene.'

By the time she'd reached the last of the row of trailers a minute later, Sarah was on her way with a solution, and Ruby had fielded another phone call on her mobile. Arizona Smith's assistant wanted to know if there were Ashtanga Yoga classes in Lucyville, the small north-west New South Wales country town in which they were filming.

Given the remote town's population was just under two thousand people, Ruby considered this unlikely—but still, with a silent sigh, promised to get back to their female lead's assistant asap.

Ruby broke into a jog as she turned the corner, her gaze trained downward—she wasn't about to hit the dirt again today—and her brain chock-full of potential 'developments' and their hypothetical impact on her already tight schedule.

Consequently, the first she knew of the very large man walking around the corner in the opposite direction was when she slammed straight into him.

'Ooomph!' The slightly strangled sound burst from her throat at the impact of her body hitting solid muscle. She barely registered her hands sliding up sun-warmed arms to grip T-shirt clad shoulders for balance, or the way her legs tangled with his.

What she *did* notice, however, were his hands, strong and firm at her waist, the fingers of one hand hot against bare skin where her T-shirt had ridden an inch or two upwards.

And the scent of his skin, even through the thin layer of cotton, where her face was pressed hard against his chest.

Fresh, clean. *Delicious.*

Oh, my.

'Hey,' he said, his voice deep and a little rough beside her ear. 'You okay?'

Slowly, slowly, embarrassment began to trickle through her body.

No, not embarrassment—the realisation that she *should* be embarrassed, that she *should* be extricating herself from this… *clinch*…as soon as possible.

'Mmm-hmm', she said indistinctly, and didn't move at all.

His fingers flexed slightly, and she registered that now she was moving. Then her back pressed against the cool metal of the shaded wall of a trailer, and she was sliding downwards. He'd been holding her—her feet dangling. Somehow she'd had no idea of this fact until her ballet flats were again responsible for holding her upright.

Had anyone ever held her so effortlessly?

She was medium height, far from tiny—and yet this man had been holding her in his arms as if she weighed as much as the average lollypop-thin Hollywood lead actress.

Nice.

Again his hands squeezed at her waist.

'Hey,' he repeated. 'You're worrying me here. Are you hurt?'

She blinked and finally lifted her head from his chest. She tried to look at him, to figure out who he was—but his face was mostly in shadow, the sunlight a white glare behind him.

But something about the angle of his jaw was familiar.

Who was he? He was fit, but he wasn't one of the grips. Some of the guys in Props were pretty tall, but Ruby honestly couldn't imagine enjoying being held in the arms of any of them. Which she was, undeniably, doing right now. Enjoying this.

She shook her head, trying to focus. 'Just a bit dazed, I think,' she managed. Belatedly, she acknowledged that was true. With every second, the fog was dissipating. But it was a gradual transition.

Right now, she found herself perfectly happy where she was. Standing right where she was.

'Are *you* okay?' she asked.

She could barely make out the slightest curve to his lips, but it was there. 'I'll survive.'

His grip on her softened a little as he seemed to realise she wasn't in any imminent danger. But he didn't let her go. Her hands still rested on his shoulders, but removing them wasn't even a consideration.

A cloud shifted or something, and the shadows lightened. Now she could make out the square line of his jaw, covered liberally in stubble; the sculpted straightness of his nose, and the almost horizontal slashes of his eyebrows. But even this close—close enough that the action of breathing almost brought her chest up against his—she couldn't quite make out the colour of his gaze.

A gaze that she knew was trained on her, exploring her face—her eyes, her lips…

Ruby closed her eyes tight shut, trying to assemble her thoughts. Trying to assemble herself, actually.

The fog had cleared. Reality was re-entering—*her* reality. Straightforward, straight-talking Ruby Bell. Who was *not* taken to romantic notions or embracing total strangers.

He wasn't crew. He must be an extra, some random guy minding his own business before she'd literally thrown herself into his arms.

Inwardly, she cringed. Too late, mortification hit. Hard.

Rational, no-nonsense words were right on the tip of her tongue as she opened her eyes.

But instead of speaking, she sucked in a sharp breath.

He'd moved closer. So, *so* close.

The man didn't look worried now. He looked almost...predatory. In a very, very good way.

She swallowed. Once, twice.

He smiled.

Beneath traitorous fingers that had crept along his shoulders to his nape, his overlong hair was coarse beneath her fingertips.

'You,' he said, his breath fanning against her cheek, 'are quite the welcoming party.'

Ruby felt overwhelmed by him. His size, his devastating looks, his nearness. She barely made out what he'd said. 'Pardon?'

He didn't repeat himself, he just watched her, his gaze locked onto hers.

Whatever she'd been going to say—the words had evaporated.

All she seemed capable of was staring at him. Into those eyes, those amazing, piercing...*familiar* blue eyes.

Finally it clicked into place.

'Has anyone ever told you, you look *just* like Devlin Cooper?' she said. Babbled, maybe. *God.* She didn't know what was going on.

One of his hands had released her waist, and he ran a finger down her cheek and along her jaw. She shivered.

'A couple of times,' he said, the words as dry as the grass they stood upon.

No, not quite like the famous Devlin Cooper. This man had dark circles beneath his eyes, and his darkest blond hair was far too long. He was too tall, surely, as well—she'd met enough leading men to know the average Hollywood star was far shorter than they looked on screen. And, she acknowledged, there was a sparseness to his width—he was muscled, but he didn't have the bulk of the movie star. He looked like Devlin Cooper might look if turned into one of those method actors who lost bucket-loads of weight for a role. Not that Ruby could imagine that ever happening—Devlin Cooper was more generic-action-blockbuster-star than the Oscar-worthy-art-house type.

But as the man's fingers tipped her chin upwards any thought of Devlin Cooper was obliterated. Once again it was just her, and this man, and this amazing, crazy tension that crackled between them. She'd never felt anything like it.

She was sure she'd never wanted anything more than to discover what was going to happen next.

He leant forward, closing the gap between their lips until it was almost non-existent...

Something—a voice nearby maybe—made Ruby jump, and the sound of her shoulders bouncing against the trailer was loud in the silence. A silence she was suddenly terribly aware of.

That rapidly forgotten wave of mortification crashed back over her, this time impossible to ignore. With it, other—less pleasant—sensations than his touch shoved their way to the fore. The fact she was covered in dirt and drying coffee. The fact her whole body suddenly appeared capable of a head to toe, hot, appalled blush.

She was still hanging off the man like a monkey, and she snatched her hands away from his neck.

'Hey. You're not going to catch anything,' he said, a lightness in his tone as he watched her unconsciously wipe her hands almost desperately against her thighs.

She stilled the movement and met his gaze. His eyes had an unreadable glint to them, and for the first time she noticed their thin spidery lines of bloodshot red.

'*Who are you?*' she asked in a sharp whisper.

His lips curled again, but he didn't say a word. He just watched her, steadily, calmly.

He was infuriating.

She ducked to her left, and the hand that had remained on her waist fell away. Ridiculously, she missed the warmth and weight of his touch immediately, and so she shook her head, desperate to refocus.

She put a few steps between them, taking deep, what-the-heck-just-happened breaths as she glanced to her left and right.

They were alone. No one else stood in this path amongst the trailer metropolis.

No one had seen them.

Relief swamped her. *What on earth had she been thinking?*

But then approaching footsteps made her freeze, as if who-ever walked around the corner would immediately know what had just happened.

Of course, it was Paul.

'Ruby!' her producer exclaimed loudly. 'There you are.'

'Ruby,' the man repeated, slowly and softly, behind her. 'Nice name.'

She shot him a glare. Couldn't he just *disappear?* Her mind raced as she tried to determine exactly how long it had been since she'd barrelled into the man. Surely not more than a few minutes?

It wasn't like Paul to come looking for her. Fume alone in his office if she were late, yes—but come find her? Definitely not.

It *must* be a real emergency.

'I'm sorry,' Ruby managed, finally, and meant it. But how to explain? She ran a hand through her hair; the movement dis-lodged a few forgotten blades of grass. 'I fell over,' she said, more confidently, then nodded in the man's direction. 'He was just helping me up.'

She smoothed her hands down her shirt and its collection of dust, coffee and grass stains for further effect.

There. All sorted, the perfect explanation for why she wasn't in Paul's office five minutes ago.

Out of the corner of her eye, the man grinned. He'd propped himself up against the trailer, ankles crossed—as casual as you like. A normal person would surely size up the situation, realise something was up and—she didn't know—do anything *but* act as if all he were missing were a box of popcorn and a choc-top.

'Thanks for your help,' she said, vaguely in his direction. For the first time she noticed the matching coffee-coloured marks all over the man's grey T-shirt, but she couldn't make herself apologise. He was just too frustratingly calm and oblivious. He could keep his smug smile and newly stained T-shirt.

She walked up to Paul, assuming they'd now go back to his office. 'So, what do you need me to do?'

Paul blinked, his gaze flicking over her shoulder to the man that *still* stood so nonchalantly behind her.

'You left in a hurry,' he said—not to Ruby, but to the man.

Ruby turned on her heel, looking from Paul to the man and back again—completely confused.

The man shrugged. 'I had things to do.'

Paul's eyes narrowed and his lips thinned, as if he was on the verge of one of his explosions.

But then—instead—he cleared his throat, and turned to Ruby. A horrible sense of foreboding settled in her stomach.

'So you've met our new leading man.'

She spoke without thinking. 'Who?'

There was a barely muffled laugh behind her.

The man. His knowing smile. The charisma that oozed from every pore.

Finally, *finally,* she connected the dots.

This was Paul's latest drama. *This* was why she'd been rushing back to the office.

They had a new leading man.

She'd just met him.

She'd just covered him in dirt and coffee.

Worst of all—she'd just nearly *kissed* him.

And he didn't just have a passing resemblance to Devlin Cooper. A passing resemblance to a man who commanded double-digit multimillion-dollar salaries and provided continuous tabloid fodder to the world's magazines and salacious television entertainment reports. A man who'd long ago left Australia and now was mentioned in the same breath as Brad, and George, and Leo…

'You can call me Dev,' he said, his voice deep and oh-so intimate.

Oh.

My.

God.

Dev Cooper smiled as the slender blonde raked her fingers desperately through her short-cropped hair.

Ruby.

It suited her. She was striking: with big, velvety brown eyes beneath dark blonde brows, sharp-edged cheekbones and a lush mouth. Maybe her elegant nose was a little too long, and her chin a little too stubborn—if she were a model his agent had picked out for him to be photographed with at some premiere or opening or whatever.

But, thankfully, she wasn't. It would seem she was a member of the crew of this film he was stuck working on for the next six weeks. And—if the way she'd been looking at him a few minutes earlier was anything to go by—she was going to make the next few days, maybe longer, a heck of a lot more interesting.

Ruby crossed her arms as she spoke to the producer—Phil? No, *Paul*. The man who'd owed his agent Veronica a favour. A really *big* favour, it turned out, given his agent had bundled him onto the plane to Sydney *before* she'd sorted out the pesky little detail of whether or not he had the role.

Dev guessed, knowing Veronica, that Paul had discovered he was replacing his leading man just before Dev had turned up in his shiny black hire car. Chauffeur driven, of course—his agent was taking no chances this time.

He shifted his weight a little, easing the pressure on his left leg, which throbbed steadily. Had it really only been a week?

The pancake-flat countryside where he now stood couldn't be further away from his driveway in Beverly Hills—the site of 'the last straw' as his agent had put it. Even Dev had to admit that forgetting to put his car into reverse wasn't his best moment. Ditto to driving into his living room, and writing off his Jag.

On the plus side, he hadn't been injured, beyond some temporary muscle damage, and, thanks to the fortress-style wall that surrounded his house, no one beyond his agent and long-suffering housekeeper even knew it had happened.

And, despite what Veronica believed, he hadn't been drunk.

Exhausted after not sleeping for four nights—yes. But driving, or attempting to drive, drunk? No, he hadn't slid that low.

Yet?

Dev scrubbed at his eyes, uninterested in pursuing the direction his thoughts had taken him. Instead, he refocused on Ruby and Paul, who had stopped talking and were now looking at him.

Ruby's gaze was direct, despite the hint of colour at her cheeks. She was embarrassed, no doubt. But she was brazening it out.

He liked that.

'I'm Ruby Bell,' she said, 'Production Co-ordinator for *The Land.*'

Her arm moved slightly, as though she was going to shake his hand before thinking better of it.

A shame. He was impatient to touch her again.

Maybe she saw some of what he was thinking, as her eyes narrowed. But her tone revealed nothing. 'Paul will give me your details, and I'll send through tomorrow's call sheet once I've spoken to the assistant director.'

He nodded.

Then Paul started talking, putting lots of emphasis on *tight timelines* and *stop dates* and *getting up to speed as quickly as possible*—all things he'd said in their abruptly truncated meeting earlier.

Lord, anyone would think he made a habit of missing his call...

He smiled tightly at his private joke, eliciting a glare from Paul.

Dev tensed. This film might have a decent budget for an Australian production, but it was no Hollywood blockbuster. He was replacing a *soapie star* as the lead, for heaven's sake.

No way was he going to take a thinly veiled lecture from some nobody producer.

'I get it,' he said, cutting him off mid-stream, the action not dissimilar to what had happened in Paul's office when he'd had enough of his blustering. 'I'll see you both,' he said, pausing to catch Ruby's gaze, 'tomorrow.'

And with that, he was off.

Six weeks of filming. Six weeks to placate his agent.

Six weeks working in a town out beyond the middle of nowhere. Where—he knew his agent hoped—even Dev Cooper couldn't get into any trouble.

A heated memory of chocolate eyes that sparkled and urgent fingers threaded through his hair made him smile.

Well, he hadn't made any promises.

CHAPTER TWO

IT TOOK ALL of Ruby's strength to follow Paul up the small flight of brick steps to the production office. She literally had to remind herself to place one foot in front of the other, as her body really, *really* wanted to carry her in the opposite direction. *Away* from the scene of unquestionably one of the most humiliating moments of her career. Her life, even.

How could she not have recognised him?

Only the possibility that any attempted escape could lead her back to Devlin Cooper stopped her. Oh—and the fact she kind of loved her career.

As they walked down the narrow hallway of the dilapidated cottage/temporary production office, Paul explained in twenty-five words or less that Mr Cooper was replacing Todd, effective immediately. That was it—no further explanation.

By now they'd made it to Paul's makeshift kitchen-cum-office at the rear of the cottage. Inside stood Sal, the line producer, and Andy, the production manager. They both wore matching, serious expressions.

It was enough to force Ruby to pull herself together. She needed to focus on the job at hand—i.e. coordinating this movie with a completely new star.

'I have to ask,' asked Andy, his fingers hooked in the belt loops of his jeans. 'How the hell did you get Devlin Cooper to take this role?'

Ruby thought Paul might have rolled his eyes, but couldn't be sure. 'Let's just say that the opportunity arose. So I took it.'

Despite the catastrophic impact on their immovable filming schedule, Ruby could hardly blame him. With Devlin's star
power, *The Land* would reach a whole new audience. Why Devlin *took* the role was another question entirely—did he want to
spend time back in Australia? Did he feel a need to give back
to the Australian film industry? A chance to take on a role well
outside his vanilla action-hero stereotype?

It didn't really matter.

Filming had started, and Dev's character Seth was in nearly
every scene. Tomorrow's call sheet had Todd's name all over
it—the guy who Dev had replaced. Unquestionably, they'd lost
tomorrow. Which was not good, as Arizona had to be at Pine-
wood Studios in London for her next film in just six weeks
and one day's time. They didn't have *any* time up their sleeves.

'Does Dev know the script?'

Paul just looked at her. *What do you think?*

Okay. So they'd lost more than just tomorrow. Dev would
need to rehearse. Ruby's mind scrambled about trying to figure out how the first assistant director could possibly rearrange
the filming schedule that she'd so painstakingly put together...
and she'd need to organise to get Dev's costumes sorted. And
his hair cut. And...

'Should I sort out a medical appointment?' she asked. A
doctor's report for each actor was required for the film's insur-
ance—everything from a propensity for cold sores through to
a rampant base-jumping hobby had an impact on how much
it cost.

'No,' Paul said, very quickly.

Ruby tilted her head, studying him. But before she could ask
the obvious question, Paul explained. 'He saw a doctor in Sydney when he landed. It's all sorted.'

Okay. She supposed that made sense.

'Accommodation?'

God knew where she'd put him. The cast and crew had already overrun every bed and breakfast plus the local—rather
cosy—motel.

'He's taking over Todd's place.'

Ouch. Poor Todd. He must be devastated—this role was widely considered his big break. He was being touted as the *next big thing.*

Only to be trumped by the current big thing.

She felt for him, but, unfortunately, the brutality of this industry never failed to surprise her.

This was not a career for the faint-hearted, or anyone who needed the reassurance of a job associated with words like *stable,* or *reliable.*

Fortunately, that was exactly why Ruby loved it.

Ten minutes later, the four of them had a plan of sorts for the next few days, and she was closing Paul's office door behind her as Sal and Andy rushed back to their desks.

For a moment she stood, alone, in the cottage's narrow old hallway. Noise spilled from the two rooms that flanked it: music, clattering keyboards, multiple conversations and the occasional burst of laughter. A familiar hum peppered with familiar voices.

To her left was Sal and Andy's office. Ruby didn't need to glance through their open doorway to know they'd already be busily working away on the trestle-tables that served as their temporary desks. The office would also be perfectly organised—notepads and pens all lined up, that kind of thing—because it always was. They were in charge of the film's budget—so such meticulous organisation was definitely a plus.

In theory, given her own role, she should be just as meticulous.

Instead, to her right was the room that, amongst other things, housed her own trestle-table desk, many huge prone-to-collapsing mountains of paper and only the vaguest sense of order. Or so it appeared, anyway. She had to be ruthlessly organised—but she didn't need to be tidy to be effective.

The room was also the home of the three members of the production crew who reported to her—Cath, Rohan and Selena. Unsurprisingly, it was this room where the majority of noise was coming from, as this was the happening part of the production office where all day every day they managed actors and scripts and agents and vendors and anything or anyone else needed to keep the film going. It was crazy, demanding, noisy work—and with a deep breath, she walked straight into it.

As expected, three heads popped up as she stepped through the door.

'I guess you all heard the news?'

As one, they nodded.

'Was kind of awesome when he walked out on Paul,' said Rohan, leaning back in his chair. 'Paul came in here and ranted for a bit before charging out the door in pursuit. Guess he couldn't find him.'

Ruby didn't bother to correct him.

Instead, she spent a few minutes further explaining the situation, and assigning them all additional tasks. No one complained—quite the opposite, actually. No one saw the unexpected addition of a major star to *The Land* as anything but a very good thing. It meant they were all instantly working on a film far bigger than they'd signed up for. It was a fantastic opportunity.

She needed to remember that.

Ruby settled herself calmly into her chair, dropping her phone onto her desk—fortunately no worse for wear after hitting the dirt for the second time today. She tapped the mouse track pad on her laptop, and it instantly came to life, displaying the twenty-odd new emails that had arrived since she'd last had a chance to check her phone. Not too bad given it seemed like a lifetime since she'd been busily redistributing those last-minute script revisions to the actors.

She had a million and one things to do, and she really needed to get straight back to it. Instead, her attention skidded about the room—away from her glowing laptop screen and out of the window. There wasn't much of a view—just bare, flat countryside all the way to the ridge of mountains—but she wasn't really looking at it. Instead, her brain was still desperately trying to process the events of the past half-hour.

It didn't seem possible that she'd so recently been wrapped around one of the sexiest men in the world.

While covered in dirt.

And had had absolutely no idea.

Inwardly, she cringed for about the thousandth time.

Work. She reminded herself. She just needed to focus on work. Who cared if she'd accidentally flung herself into Devlin Cooper's arms? It was an accident, and it would never happen again—after all, she wasn't exactly anywhere near Dev Cooper's percentile on the drop-dead-gorgeousness spectrum. And he'd hardly had the opportunity to be attracted to her sparkling personality.

Despite everything, that thought made her smile.

No. This wasn't funny. This was serious. What if someone had seen them?

She stood up, as sitting still had become impossible. On the window sill sat the antenna of their oversized wireless Internet router, and she fiddled with it, just so it looked as if she were doing something constructive. On a location this remote, they'd had to bring their own broadband. And their own electricity, actually—provided by a large truck that's sole purpose was to power Unit Base, the name of this collection of trucks and people that were the beating heart of any feature film.

Her job was everything to her, and a spotless professional reputation was non-negotiable. She didn't get each job by circling ads in the paper, or subscribing to some online jobs database. In film, it was *all* about word of mouth.

And getting it on with an actor on set… Yeah. Not a good look.

On the plus side, Dev would have forgotten all about the slightly mussed-up, damp and dusty woman who'd gang-tackled him by now.

Now she just needed to forget about how he'd made her feel.

I think some time away would do you good. Help you…move on.

Well. Dev guessed this place was exactly what Veronica had

been hoping for. A painstakingly restored century-old cottage, complete with tasteful rear extension, was where he'd be calling home for the immediate future. It offered uninterrupted views to the surrounding mountains and everything!

It was also a kilometre or so out of town, had no immediate neighbours, and, thanks to his agent, a live-in minder.

Security. Officially.

Right.

He needed a drink. He'd walked off a trans-Pacific flight less than eight hours ago. Even travelling first class couldn't make a flight from LA to Sydney pleasant. Add a four-hour road trip with Graeme-the-security-guy and was it surprising he'd had a short fuse today?

Please play nice with Paul.

This in his latest email from his agent.

He shouldn't have been surprised that the producer had already started updating Veronica on his behaviour. He'd even learnt exactly what she'd held over the prickly producer—knowledge of an on-set indiscretion with an aspiring actress ten years previously.

What a cliché.

And how like his agent to file that little titbit away for future use.

Good for her. Although he didn't let himself consider how exactly he'd got to this point—to where landing roles depended on tactics and calling in favours.

Dev had dragged an overstuffed armchair onto the rear decking. On his lap was the script for *The Land,* not that he could read it now the sun had long set.

Beside him, on one of the chairs from the wooden outdoor setting he'd decided looked too uncomfortable, was his dinner. Cold, barely touched salmon with fancy-looking vegetables. God knew where Veronica had sourced his fridge and freezer full of food from—he'd long ago got used to her magic touch.

Although the lack of alcohol hadn't gone unnoticed. *Subtle, Veronica.*

But she was wrong. Booze wasn't his problem.

He'd have to send good old Graeme down to the local bottle shop tomorrow or something.

But for now, he needed a drink.

Leaving the script on the chair, he walked through the house, and then straight out of the front door. Graeme was staying in a separate, smaller worker's cottage closer to the road, but Dev didn't bother to stop and let him know where he was going.

He'd been micro-managed quite enough. He could damn well walk into town and get a drink without having to ask anyone's approval.

So he did.

Walking felt good. For once he wasn't on the lookout for the paparazzi, as, for now, no one knew he was here. His unexpected arrival in Australia would have been noticed, of course, and it wouldn't take long before the photographers descended. But they hadn't, not just yet.

He had no idea what time it was, just that it was dark. Really dark—there were certainly no streetlights, and the moon was little more than a sliver.

His boots were loud on the bitumen, loud enough to disturb a group of sheep that scattered abruptly behind their barbed-wire fence. Further from the road nestled the occasional house, their windows glowing squares of bright amid the darkness.

Soon he'd hit the main street, a short stretch of shops, a petrol station, a library. He hadn't paid much attention when he'd arrived—a mix of jet lag and general lack of interest—but now he took the time to look, slowing his walk down to something approaching an amble.

Most of the town was silent—blinds were drawn, shops were certainly closed this late. But the one obvious exception was the pub, which, like much of the town, was old and stately—perched two storeys high on a corner, complete with a wide wooden balcony overlooking the street. Tonight the balcony was empty, but noise and music spilled from the open double doors. He quickened his pace, suddenly over all this peace and quiet.

It was packed. Completely—people were crammed at the bar, around the scattered tall tables and also the lower coffee tables with their surrounding couches and ottomans. It was the cast and crew, obviously, who'd taken the pub over. He'd seen for himself that Lucyville didn't exactly have a happening restaurant strip. This was the only place to drink—and eat—so here they all were.

The pub didn't go quiet or anything at his arrival, but he noticed that he'd been noticed.

It was a sensation that had once been a novelty, had later annoyed him to the verge of anger—and now that he just accepted. He could hardly complain…he was living his dream and all that.

Right.

He found a narrow gap at the bar, resting an arm on the polished surface. The local bartender caught his eye and did a double take, but played it cool. In his experience, most people did, with the occasional crazy person the exception rather than the rule. The paparazzi were far more an issue than Joe Public—no question.

He ordered his drink, although he wasn't quick to raise the glass to his lips once it was placed in front of him. Maybe it wasn't the drink he'd needed, but the walk, the bite of the crisp night air in his lungs?

Mentally he shook his head. Veronica would love that, be all smug and sure she was right to send him to Australia—while Dev wasn't so certain.

What was that saying? Same crap—different bucket.

His lips tightened into a humourless smile.

He turned, propping his weight against the bar. As he took a sip of his beer he surveyed the large room. It was a surprisingly eclectic place, with funky modern furniture managing to blend with the polished ancient floorboards and what—he was pretty sure—was the original bar. Not quite the backwater pub he'd been imagining.

The lighting was soft and the atmosphere relaxed, with the dress code more jeans than cocktail.

One particular pair of jeans caught his eye. Dark blue denim, moulded over elegantly crossed legs—right in the corner of the pub, the one farthest from him.

Yet his attention had still been drawn to her, to Ruby.

Only when he saw her did he realise he'd been looking for her—searching her out in the crowd.

He watched her as she talked to her friends, wine glass in hand. To all appearances she was focused completely on the conversation taking place around her. She was quick to smile, and quick to interject and trigger a laugh from others. But despite all that, there was the slightest hint of tension to her body.

She knew he was watching her.

Beside her, another woman leant over and whispered in her ear, throwing glances in his direction as she did.

Ruby shook her head emphatically—and Dev was no lip-reader, but he'd put money on the fact she'd just said: *No, he's not.*

Accordingly, he straightened, pushing himself away from the bar.

He liked nothing more than to prove someone wrong.

'He's coming over!'

Every single cell in Ruby's body—already tingling at what she'd told herself was Dev's imagined attention—careened up to high alert.

'It's no big deal. We met before.' She shrugged deliberately. 'Maybe he doesn't know anyone else yet.'

'When did you meet him?' Selena asked, wide-eyed. 'And how am I not aware of this?'

Ruby's words were carefully cool. 'When I was walking back to the office. We barely said two words.'

That, at least, was completely true.

Her friend had lost interest, anyway, her eyes trained on Dev's tall frame as he approached.

'Mind if I join you?'

Dev's voice was as gorgeously deep and perfect as in every

one of his movies. Not for the first time, Ruby questioned her intelligence—how on *earth* had she not recognised him?

With a deep breath, she lifted her gaze to meet his. He stood on the other side of the table before them: Ruby, Selena and a couple of girls from the art department. They'd been having an after-dinner drink, all comfy on one big plush purple L-shaped couch—now the other three were alternating between carefully feigned disinterest and slack-jawed adoration. Unheard of for professionals in the film industry who dealt with stars every day.

But, she supposed, this *was* Devlin Cooper.

Everyone else appeared struck dumb and incapable of answering his question—but Dev was looking at her, anyway.

To say *yes, she did mind,* was tempting—but more trouble than it was worth. So, reluctantly, she shook her head. 'Not at all.'

Dev stepped past the table and sat next to Ruby.

With great effort, she resisted the temptation to scoot away. Unlike the three other women at the table, she was *not* going to treat Dev any differently from anyone else on the cast and crew.

No adoring gaze. No swooning.

So, although he was close—and the couch definitely no longer felt *big*—she didn't move. Didn't betray one iota of the unexpected heat that had flooded her body.

'You shouldn't be embarrassed,' he said, low enough that only she could hear.

'Why would you think I am?'

Casually, she brought her glass to her lips.

Did he notice the slightest trembling of her fingers?

She risked a glance out of the corner of her eye.

He watched her with a familiar expression. Confident. Knowing.

Arrogant.

She sighed. 'Fine. I *was* embarrassed. Let me think: running into one of the world's most famous men, while covered in dirt and looking like crap—*and* then not even recognising said star...' Ruby tilted her head, as if considering her words.

'Yes, I think that pretty much sums it up. I reckon a good nine out of ten on my embarrassment scale.'

He didn't even blink. If anything he looked amused.

A different type of tension stiffened her body. Yes, her stupid, apparently one-track body was all a-flutter with Mr Hot Movie Star so near. But now she could add affronted frustration into the mix.

She didn't know what she wanted—an apology? Sympathy? A *yeah, I can see how that might've sucked for you,* even?

'But you only gave it a nine,' he said, placing his beer on one of the discarded coasters on the table.

'A what?' she asked, confused.

'On your *embarrassment scale,*' he said. 'Only a nine…' He looked contemplative for a moment, then leant closer, close enough that it was impossible for her to look anywhere but straight into his eyes. 'So I was wondering—what would've made it a ten?'

Immediately, and most definitely without her volition, her gaze dropped from his piercing blue eyes to his lips.

Lips that immediately quirked into a grin the second she realised what she'd done. What she'd just revealed.

He leant even closer again. The touch of his breath on the sensitive skin beneath her ear made her shiver.

Logically she knew she should pull away, that she should laugh loudly, or say something—*do something*—to stop this way too intimate moment. A moment she knew was being watched—and if people were watching, then people would gossip.

And there were few things Ruby hated more than gossip: being the subject of *or* the proliferation of it.

For she had far too much experience in the former. Enough to last a lifetime.

'You know,' he said, his words somehow vibrating through her body—her stupidly frozen body, 'I don't think anyone's ever been embarrassed when I've kissed them. In fact, I'm quite sure I've never received a complaint.'

Oh, she was so sure he hadn't…

'I was working,' she said, each word stiff and awkward.

So he had been going to kiss her—and she realised it was no surprise. Some part of her had known, had known there was no other way to interpret those few minutes, even though her rational self had had so much difficulty believing it.

But knowing she hadn't imagined it and *wanting* it to have happened were entirely different things.

'I kiss people all the time at work,' he replied, with a spark of humour in his eyes that was new, and unexpected.

Ruby found herself forcing back a grin, surprised at the shift in atmosphere. 'It's a bit different when you're following a script.'

'Ah,' he said, his lips quirking up. 'Not always.'

Now she laughed out loud, shaking her head. 'I bet.'

Their laughter should've diluted the tension, but if anything the air between them thickened.

With great effort, Ruby turned away slightly, taking a long, long sip of her wine—not that she tasted a thing. Her brain whirred at a million miles an hour—or maybe it wasn't whirring at all, considering all it seemed to be able to do was wonder how Dev's lips would feel against hers...

No.

'Well,' she said, finally, her gaze swinging back to meet his. Firmly. 'Script or otherwise, I don't kiss anyone at work.' She paused, then added in a tone that was perfectly matter-of-fact and perfectly polite, 'It's late. I need to go. It was nice to talk to you when I wasn't covered in dirt. And I'm sorry about your T-shirt.'

Ruby stood up and placed her wine glass on the table with movements she hoped looked casual. She glanced at her friends, who all stared at her wide-eyed.

She'd need to set them all straight tomorrow. Dev Cooper was so not her type it was ridiculous.

She managed some goodbyes, hooked her handbag over her shoulder, and then headed for the door. The entire time she risked barely a glance at Dev, but thankfully he didn't move.

Not that she expected him to follow her. She wasn't an idiot. He could have any woman in this bar. Pretty much any woman in the *world*.

For some reason she'd piqued his interest, but she had no doubt it was fleeting—the novelty of the crazy dusty coffee lady or something.

Outside, the early October evening was cool, and so Ruby hugged herself, rubbing her goose-pimpling arms. She was staying at the town motel, not even a hundred-metre walk down the main street.

Only a few steps in that direction, she heard someone else leave the bar behind her, their boots loud on the wooden steps.

It was difficult, but as it turned out not impossible, to keep her eyes pointed forward. It could be anyone.

'Ruby.'

Or it could be Dev.

She should've sighed—and been annoyed or disappointed. But instead her tummy lightened and she realised she was smiling.

Ugh.

She kept on walking.

In moments, following the thud of loping strides on bitumen, he was beside her, keeping pace with her no-nonsense walk. For long seconds, they walked in silence.

Really uncomfortable, charged silence.

'So—' he began.

'This isn't an act, you know,' Ruby interrupted. 'I'm not playing hard to get. I'm not interested.'

He gave a surprised bark of laughter. 'Right.'

Ruby slowed to a stop, her whole body stiff with annoyance. She stood beneath a street lamp that illuminated the gate to the *Lucyville Motel* and its chipped and faded sign.

'You sound so sure,' she said. 'That's incredibly presumptuous.'

'Am I wrong?'

Ruby sighed. 'Does every woman you meet *really* collapse into a pathetic puddle of lust at your feet?'

'You did,' he pointed out.

Her cheeks went hot, but Ruby hoped her blush was hidden in the shadows.

'I was light-headed. Confused. Definitely not myself.' She paused for emphasis. 'Trust me. You're wasting your time. *I'm not interested.*'

A little, nagging voice at the back of her mind kept trying to distract her: *Oh, my God, it's Devlin Cooper! The movie star!*

Maybe that was why she didn't turn and walk away immediately.

'You're serious?'

His genuine confusion was rather endearing. Unbelievably conceited, but endearing.

'Uh-huh,' she said, nodding. 'Is that so hard to believe?'

She knew he was about to say *yes,* when he seemed to realise what he was about to say. Instead, his grin, revealed by the streetlight, was bemused.

He shifted his weight to one leg, and crossed his arms. He still wore the same sexy ancient-looking jeans from before, but he'd traded his ruined T-shirt for its twin in navy blue. The action of crossing his arms only further defined the muscles of his forearms and biceps.

It also defined the unexpectedly sharp angles of his elbows and the lack of flesh beyond his lean musculature.

She knew she was not the only person to notice. The film set's grapevine was, as always, efficient, creating all sorts of theories for his unexpected weight loss.

Did you hear? His girlfriend left him—you know? That model.

I heard it's drugs. Ice. He's been photographed at every club in Hollywood.

He's sick. I know! That's why he's come back to Australia. To spend time with his family.

Not that Ruby believed a word of it. Gossip, in her experience, was about as accurate and true to life as the typical air-brushed movie poster.

What happened to you?

But of course the question remained unsaid. It was none of her business.

Dev studied Ruby in the limited moonlight. His gaze traced the angles of her cheekbones, the straightness of her nose and the firm set of her determined mouth.

Lord, she was...pretty?

Yes. Hot?

Yes.

But that, in itself, wasn't *it*...

And different. Very, very, different.

That was why he was standing out in the deserted, frankly cold, street. That was why he'd done something he couldn't remember doing in a very long time: he'd chased after a woman.

It was an unexpected novelty.

He liked it.

For the first time in months something—*someone*—had caught his interest. Ruby Bell—the cute little production co-ordinator on a dinky little Aussie film—intrigued him.

'So what is it, exactly, that you find so repulsive about me?' he asked.

She shrugged, dismissing his question. 'I don't know you well enough to form an opinion—repulsive or otherwise.'

'But isn't that why you're not interested?' he asked. Not that he believed her statement to be true. 'Because you think you know me?'

From his movies, from his interviews, from the rubbish they published in glossy magazines and newspapers that should know better. Devlin Cooper the star—the persona. Not the person.

She shook her head. 'This is the longest conversation we've ever had. How could I possibly know you?'

He blinked. She'd just surprised him—for the second time tonight. The first time had been walking out of that pub just as he'd been imagining how good she'd look in that big wrought-iron bed back in his cottage.

'Ah. So, it's not me, it's *you*,' he said, playing with that cliché line. Then, for the first time, the blindingly obvious occurred to him. She wore no ring, but… 'You have a boyfriend?'

'Oh *no*,' she said, her voice higher pitched and definitely firmer than before. 'Absolutely not.' She shook her head for emphasis.

Okay, now he was completely confused. And surprised, yet again.

Ruby wasn't following any script he'd heard before. How many women had he flirted with in his life? Some fawned, but most were clever, witty and/or sarcastic. But, he realised, normally he already sort of knew what was going to be said next—where the conversation, or the evening, was heading. In itself, that was part of the fun. The dance of words before the inevitable.

But this was undeniably fun, too.

'You think *I* want a relationship?' he asked, heavy with irony. 'Scared I'm going to want to settle down, get married…'

She laughed. 'No.'

'So what, exactly, is the problem? From where I stand this all seems pretty perfect. We obviously both like each other…' he held up his hand when she went to disagree '…we're both single *and* we're both stuck in an isolated country town for the next month or so. Is that not a match made in heaven?'

Ruby rolled her eyes. 'Weren't you listening back at the pub? I don't do relationships at work. *Especially* with actors. I'm not interested in becoming known as Dev Cooper's next conquest. *Très* professional, no?'

'I wasn't suggesting we make out on set, you know,' he said dryly. Ruby raised an eyebrow. 'I promise.'

She shook her head. 'Film sets are full of gossip. And my professional reputation is everything to me.' She paused, then repeated her words, almost to herself. '*Everything* to me.'

Commitment to your job—sure, Dev got that. Until very

recently, he'd practically been the poster child for the concept. But—really? Liaisons between crew and actors were not a crime, and far from uncommon. The world would not end.

But apparently, according to Ruby, it would. It was clear in every tense line of her expression.

They stood in silence for a while. Dev wasn't entirely sure what would happen now.

He was out of his element: he'd just been rejected. Inarguably so.

But rather than shrugging, comfortable in the knowledge that he had many other options, he found himself…disappointed.

And reluctant to walk away.

'Anyway,' Ruby said in a different, crisper, tone. 'You have an early call tomorrow morning, and I need to be at the office an hour earlier. So, goodnight.'

With that, she turned on her heel and walked away. Out on the street he watched as she walked down the motel driveway to an apartment on the bottom floor of the two-storey building. Then he waited until she located her key in her oversized handbag, unlocked the door, and disappeared inside.

Then he waited, alone on the street, some more.

It was odd. All he knew about this woman was that she was blonde, and cute, and felt pretty amazing in his arms.

What was the attraction? Why did he care?

How was she different from the many other women who he'd met in the past few, dark, blurry months? Months where no one had stood out. Where *nothing* had stood out.

Where when, a few weeks after Estelle had left, he'd attempt to chat to a woman—but his mind would drift. Where he'd find himself with suddenly no idea what had been said in the preceding conversation.

And didn't care at all.

That was why she was different.

Ruby pushed his buttons. Triggered reactions that had been lying dormant. Attraction. Laughter. Surprise.

So simple.

CHAPTER THREE

A LOUD BANG jolted Dev out of his dream.

He blinked, his eyes attempting to adjust to the darkness.

What time is it?

He lay on his back in the centre of his bed. Naked but for his boxer shorts, the sheets and quilt long ago kicked off and onto the floor.

He remembered feeling restless. As if he needed to get up and go for a run. Or for a drive. Or just *out*. Somewhere. Away.

Where?

It wasn't the first morning he'd asked that question.

Another bang. Even louder than before. Or maybe just now he was more awake?

The thick cloak of sleep was slowly lifting, and his eyes were adjusting.

It wasn't completely dark in here. Light was managing to push through the heavy curtains that he'd checked and double checked were fully closed the night before.

He shivered, and only then did he register it was cold. He had a vague recollection of turning off the heater on the wall. Why? The nights were still cool.

Obviously it had made sense at the time.

Another bang.

The door. Someone was knocking on the door.

What time is it?

He rolled onto his side, reaching across the bed, knocking aside a small cardboard box and a blister pack so he could see the glowing green numbers of the clock on the bedside table. There were none. He didn't remember turning it off, but it didn't surprise him that he had.

He had set that alarm last night, though. And the alarm on his phone. He had an early call today. He'd been going to get up early to read through today's rehearsal scenes.

Bang, bang, bang.

Dev swung his legs over the side of the bed in slow motion, then shoved himself to his feet. Three sluggish steps later, he discovered his mobile phone when he kicked it in the gloom, and it clattered against his closed bedroom door.

By feel he found the light switch on the wall, then rubbed his eyes against the sudden brightness.

His phone located, he picked it up to check the time. He pressed the button to illuminate the screen, but it took a while for his eyes to focus.

How long ago had he taken the sleepers?

He still felt drugged, still shrouded in the sleep that the tablets had finally delivered.

Seven thirty-two a.m. *Why hadn't his alarm gone off?*

Bang, bang, BANG, BANG, BANG!

'Mr Cooper? Are you awake?'

Graeme. Of course.

He twisted the old brass doorknob to his room, then padded up the wide hallway. Morning light streamed through the stained-glass panels of the front door around the over-inflated shape that was Dev's warden.

He took his time, his gaze trained on his phone as he checked that his alarm had been set. It had. So it had gone off.

Presumably he'd then thrown it across the room, given where he'd found it.

It shouldn't surprise him, but that wasn't what he'd meant to do today. Last night he'd felt…different. Today was supposed to be different. Different from the past ninety-seven days.

How specific.

He smiled a humourless smile. Who knew his subconscious kept such meticulous records?

The thing was, today wasn't the first day that was supposed to be different. But then, they never were.

Graeme was still hammering away at the door, but Dev didn't bother to call out, to reassure him that his charge was in fact awake and not passed out in an alcoholic stupor or worse—whatever it was that Veronica was so sure that Dev was doing.

In some ways Dev wished he could apply a label to himself. *Alcoholic. Drug addict.*

But he was neither of those things.

What about his sleepers?

He dismissed the idea instantly. No. They were prescribed, and temporary.

Definitely temporary.

Hollywood wasn't the shiny happy place people imagined. It was full of egos fuelled by intense insecurity. Stars that shone while simultaneously harbouring the intense fear that their light could be extinguished at any moment: at the mercy of their next role, of public opinion, of the whims of studio executives…always others.

So little control. It was no surprise that so many teetered over the edge. Fell into…*something.* It was just the label that changed.

But Dev had no label.

He just had…nothing.

He opened the door while Graeme was mid-knock. The other man started, then took a step back, clearing his throat.

'We need to leave in five minutes, Mr Cooper.'

Dev scratched his belly and nodded. He left the door open as he turned and headed for the bathroom. Four minutes later he was showered and had dragged on a T-shirt, hoodie and jeans. He pulled the front door shut and locked it as Graeme hovered nearby—impatiently.

When he was growing up, his mum had done the same thing—although not as silently. She'd tap her foot as she waited for her youngest and most disorganised son. The other two boys generally already in the family Mercedes, all perfect and consistently smug. *Hurry up, Dev! You're making us late!*

And just because he'd been that kind of kid, he'd taken his own sweet time.

This was why he didn't like having drivers. Why he insisted on driving himself to and from set for every single one of his many movies. He was a grown adult with a driver's licence—why the hell did he need a chauffeur? He was far from a child any more; he didn't need to be directed and herded and hurried. He was a professional—always on time. Always reliable.

Until now.

Today was not the first time he'd slept through his alarm. Or, of more concern: he'd heard it, switched it off, and deliberately rolled over and gone back to sleep. More than once the action of even setting his alarm had felt impossible. Weirdly overwhelming.

Other nights sleep had never come. Where his thoughts had echoed so loudly in his skull that even drugs had no impact. And those days he'd watched time tick by, watched his call time slip by, and switched his phone to silent as his agent, or the producer, or even the director would call, and call and call…

That had got him fired from his last film. The contract was pulled on his next after whispers had begun to spread.

So here he was.

And although he hadn't meant to—because of course he never *meant to*—it was happening again.

Without Graeme, he'd still be in bed, time passing. He hated that.

He sat in the back of the black four-wheel drive, staring unseeing out of the darkly tinted windows. Beside him was an insulated bag that Graeme said contained his breakfast, but he wasn't hungry.

You're not welcome here.

Closer to Unit Base, the bitumen road ended, and the car bounced amongst potholes on the wide gravel track. The irregular movements did nothing to jolt that memory. How long ago had it been? Ten years? No, longer. Fourteen. He'd been nineteen, home late—really late—after a night out with his mates.

He hadn't been drunk, but alcohol had still buzzed through his bloodstream.

'Where the hell have you been?'

His father stood at the very top of the staircase that rose majestically from the lobby of the Coopers' sprawling Sydney upper-north-shore residence. His mum had left a lamp on for him, and the soft light threw shadows onto his dad's pyjamas.

'Out,' he said. Grunted, really.

'You have an exam tomorrow.'

Dev shrugged. He'd had no intention of turning up. He dumped his keys on a sideboard, and began to head past the stairs to the hallway that led to his bedroom, tossing his reply over his shoulder. 'I'm not going to be an accountant, Dad.'

Patrick Cooper's slippered feet were still heavy as they thumped down each carpeted step. Dev didn't pause. He'd heard it all before.

He'd gone to uni to please his mum, only. But three semesters in, and he'd had it. He knew where his life was leading, and it didn't involve a calculator and a navy-blue suit.

His father picked up his pace behind him, but Dev remained deliberately slow. Unworried. Casual.

He was unsurprised to feel the weight of his father's hand on his shoulder. But when Dev kept walking, the way Patrick wrenched at his shoulder, spinning him around...yes, that shocked him.

His arm came up, his fingers forming into a fist. It was automatic, the result of the crowd he'd been hanging with, the occasional push and shove at a pub. He wouldn't have hit his dad—he knew that. Knew that.

But his dad thought he would. He could see it in his eyes, that belief of what Dev was capable of. Or rather, the lack of belief.

Dev saw the fist coming. Maybe he didn't have enough time to move, maybe he did—either way he stood stock still.

His father's knuckles connected with his jaw with enough

force to twist his body and push him back into the wall. And for it to hurt. A lot. He tasted blood, felt it coating his teeth.

But he remained standing, half expecting more.

But that wasn't going to happen. Instead, his dad fell to his knees, holding his fist in his other hand.

For long moments, it was perfectly silent. It was as if neither of them could breathe.

Then a clatter on the stairs heralded his mum's arrival. She gasped as she came into view, then ran to Patrick, kneeling beside him and wrapping her arm around his shoulder.

She looked up at Dev, her gaze beseeching. 'What happened here?'

'I'm quitting uni, Mum,' he said. 'I'm an actor.' His whole face ached as he spoke, but the words were strong and clear.

'That's a dream, not a career.' His dad didn't say the words, he spat them out.

'It's what I want.' What he needed to do.

'I won't support you, Devlin. I won't stand by and watch you fail—'

'I know that,' he interrupted. How well he knew that.

That his family wouldn't support him. That not one of them believed he'd succeed.

'Good,' his dad said. 'Then leave. You're not welcome here.'

It didn't surprise him. It had been coming for so long. His mum, the only reason he'd stayed, looked stricken.

He nodded. Then walked back up the hall the way he'd come.

He didn't say a word. No dramatic farewell. No parting words.

But he knew he'd never be back.

Graeme slowed to a stop at a paddock gate before a security guard waved them through. A dirt track wound its way over the smallest of hills, and then they were amongst the trailers that sprawled across Unit Base. The set was vast—yesterday the producer had told him it was the corner of a working sheep and canola farm. It spread across the almost perfectly flat countryside, overlooked by an irregular ridge of mountains. Yesterday, Dev's gaze had explored a landscape dotted with eucalyptus, rectangular fields of lurid yellow canola and paddocks desperately trying to hold onto winter hints of green. Today it was just a blur.

But something caught his eye as Graeme parked beside his trailer. Through the car window he followed that splash of colour with his eyes.

A woman in a bright blue dress, more like an oversized jumper, really, was barrelling rapidly along the path towards him. She was unmistakeable, her mop of choppy blonde hair shining like pale gold in the sun.

Ruby Bell.

She'd slipped his mind as soon as his nightly battle for sleep had begun, but now she'd sprung right back to the front, in full Technicolor.

He knew what she was: a distraction. A temporary focus.

But one he needed.

He was here. And thanks to Graeme—via Veronica—he'd be here on set each day, right on time. But right now he couldn't make himself care about the film, about his role.

Oh, he'd perform, right on cue, and to the best of his ability—as much as he was capable of, anyway.

But he wouldn't care. Couldn't care. Any more.

How was that for irony?

With his death, his father had—finally—got his way.

He was on time—just.

Ruby watched as he got out of the car, all loose-limbed and casual.

In contrast, she felt as stiff as a board. She kept making herself take deep, supposedly calming breaths as she gripped the papers in her hand, and reminding herself that she could do this—that this was her job.

It was just incredibly unfortunate it was *her* job. She shouldn't have been surprised, really, when Paul had taken her aside this morning and made her task clear: keep Dev on time and on schedule.

All the Dev-related rumours—a new one this morning hinting at a lot more than tardiness—should've made Paul's request a no-brainer.

Yet, she'd actually *gasped* when Paul had told her, and then had to make up some unfortunate lie about swallowing a fly, accompanied with much poorly acted faux coughing.

Once *again* Dev had managed to short-circuit her brain.

Because the task of babysitting talent was a perfectly typical request for the production co-ordinator, who, amongst other things, was responsible for organising actors' lives while on location.

Actors were notoriously unreliable. Putting together the call sheet was one thing—having anyone actually stick to it was something else entirely.

As she watched Dev watch her, a hip propped against his car, it was suddenly clear that getting him to do anything—at all—that she wanted could prove difficult.

This was not the man who'd smiled at her in the Lucyville pub last night, or who'd teased her on the street. Neither was he the man with the smug expression and the coffee stains on his shirt.

This man was completely unreadable.

'Good morning!' she managed, quite well, she thought.

He nodded sharply.

She thrust the portion of the script he'd be rehearsing today in his direction. 'Here are today's sides,' she said.

He took them from her with barely a glance. It was as if he was waiting for something—to figure something out.

'And?' he asked.

'I'll be taking you to be fitted by Costume, first,' she said. 'Then Hair and Make-up would like to see you prior to your rehearsal.'

'And you'll be escorting me?'

Ruby swallowed. 'Yes. I'll be looking after you today.'

It was immediately obvious that was the wrong thing to say. Something flickered in his gaze.

'I have my call sheet. I know where I need to be. I don't require hand-holding.'

'Paul asked that I...'

His glare told her that was another mistake, so she let the words drift off.

Then tried again. 'Mr Cooper, I'm here to help you.'

Somehow, those words changed everything, as if she'd flicked a switch. From defensive, and shuttered, his expression was suddenly...*considering?*

But Ruby didn't think for a moment that he'd simply accepted she was just doing her job. This was different—more calculating.

'Here to help,' he said to himself, as if he was turning the words over in his head.

Then he smiled, a blinding, movie-star smile.

And Ruby had absolutely no idea what had just happened.

It was dumb—really dumb—that he was surprised.

Heck—if *he* were the producer on this film, he'd have done the same thing.

It didn't mean he had to be happy about it.

He'd never been this kind of actor before; he'd never needed to be led around on some imaginary leash. Lord—he'd thought Graeme was bad enough.

And, of course, it had to be Ruby in charge of him.

It was a total waste of her time, of course. On set, he *was* fine, and not the fine he told himself he was whenever he was convincing himself to fall asleep.

He followed just slightly behind her. She was talking, quite rapidly, but he really wasn't paying much attention.

She was nervous, for sure. He *did* like that.

And he *did* like how the tables had turned. Last night she'd called the shots. Today—it was him.

Juvenile? Yes.

Fun? He thought so.

So Paul thought he needed looking after? No problem.

He'd be that actor, then. The ridiculous type who wanted everything in their trailer periwinkle blue, or who would only drink a particular brand of mineral water—not available locally, of course.

He'd prove Paul right—and irritate the self-important producer in the process.

A small win.

And it would push Ruby's buttons too—trigger that flare of response he'd already witnessed a handful of times, and was eager to experience again.

Dev smiled, just as Ruby stopped before a hulking white trailer and turned to face him.

Her forehead wrinkled as she studied him, as if she knew something was up.

He just smiled even more broadly.

Yes, this was an *excellent* idea.

Completely focused on the email she was reading—Arizona's agent, confirming that his client was available to attend an opening in Sydney the following week—Ruby picked up her loudly ringing phone from her overflowing desk without glancing at the screen.

'Ruby Bell.'

'Ruby.' A pause. 'Good afternoon.'

There was no point pretending she didn't recognise that voice. Her disloyal body practically shivered in recognition.

'How can I help, Mr Cooper?' she asked with determined brightness, her eyes not wavering from her laptop screen, although the email's words and sentences had somehow become an indecipherable alphabet jumble.

Even so, she tapped randomly on her keyboard. For her benefit, mostly, a reminder that she was a busy film professional who received phone calls from famous actors All The Time. She was working. This was her job.

No need for her mouth to go dry or for her cheeks to warm.

'Well,' he said, 'I have a problem.'

'Yes?' she prompted, with some trepidation.

He'd been scrupulously polite this morning. Allowed her to take him from appointment to appointment. He'd chatted inanely about the weather, and charmed every person she introduced him to.

But...

Occasionally he'd slant a glance in her direction that meant... she had absolutely no idea.

It wasn't about last night any more. She was sure. No question he'd long lost interest in perfectly average Ruby Bell by now.

Definitely.

'I can't figure out how to use the wireless Internet in my cottage.'

Oh. Her skin went hotter. Of course his phone call had nothing to do with her. *Of course it didn't.*

Hadn't she told him—what, three hours ago?—to call her any time?

Ruby took a deep breath. She really needed to pull herself together.

'I'm sorry to hear that, Mr Cooper,' she replied. 'I'll get that sorted for you straight away.'

'Appreciate it,' he said, and then the phone went silent.

Carefully, she placed her phone back onto her desk, darting her gaze about the room. She half expected everyone to be staring at her, to *know* exactly how flustered she was, despite all her efforts to not be. To somehow *know* that Dev had all but propositioned her outside the salubrious Lucyville Motel, even though she'd told her intrigued friends she hadn't seen Dev after she'd left the pub last night.

To *know* that chaperoning Dev around set this morning was stupidly difficult, despite her constant mental reminders that it was *so not a big deal,* and that she *was a professional* and *they were both adults* who could work together professionally despite the running-into-him thing, or the not-recognising-him thing, or saying-no-to-the-most-eligible-bachelor-in-the-world thing.

But no. Rohan worked quietly at his desk. Cath stood in front of the large whiteboard calendar, studying it with fierce concentration and a marker in her hand. Selena wasn't even in the room—she was out, busily signing in extras.

Ruby bit back a sigh. She was being ridiculous.

So she tilted her head left to right, rolled her shoulders a few times, wriggled her toes—and told herself she was cool, and calm and collected. *She was!*

And then she got back to work.

Less than an hour later, Dev stepped out onto the deck at the back of his cottage, sliding shut the glass door firmly behind him. Inside, one of the more junior members of the production office was busily fixing his 'broken' Internet.

He pressed his phone to his ear.

'Ruby Bell,' she said when she answered, sounding as brisk and polite as she had earlier.

'Ms Bell,' he said, ever so politely, 'thank you. I now have Internet.'

Well, he would once the guy inside realised the router had been unplugged.

'Oh, good,' she said. There was a beat or two of silence, and then she added, 'Can I help you with anything else?'

Dev's lips curled upwards.

'Yes, actually. I need a new hire car.'

'Is something wrong with your current car?' she asked.

No. Assuming you disregarded the fact that he had Graeme-the-warden driving him everywhere. Dev's suggestion he drive himself to set from now on was not warmly received. If Dev had access to the keys he never would've asked at all.

That would've made Veronica happy. About as happy as she'd been in her email this morning, and her many missed calls on his phone.

Turned out Graeme had passed on his trip to the pub.

Security—my arse.

'My current car is too…' he paused, as if in deep contemplation '…*feminine.*'

'Pardon me?'

'Too *feminine,*' he repeated.

The line remained silent. Was Ruby smiling? Frowning?

'I see,' she said, after a while. 'I'm sorry you find your *black four-wheel drive* so unsuitable. Can you explain to me what it is that you dislike about the car?'

There was nothing overtly discourteous in her tone—quite the opposite, in fact. Yet Dev heard the subtlest of subtle bites. He liked it.

'It's the upholstery,' he said. 'It has pink thread in it.'

'Ah,' she said, as if this were actually a valid complaint. 'Fair enough. Don't worry, I'll have a new car to you by tonight.'

'At the latest,' he said, just like one of the many delusionally self-important actors he knew who made these types of requests.

'Not a problem, Mr Cooper.'

'Appreciated, Ms Bell.'

Then he hung up with a smile on his face.

Ruby sat alone in her office, the Top 40 show on the radio her only company. It was late—really late, and she'd sent everyone else home fifteen minutes earlier.

But she had to get everything done—well, an hour ago, really—but Dev had really screwed up her day.

Losing Rohan for an hour to fix Dev's wireless had meant she'd had to run the call sheet alone; and unfortunately the runner she'd assigned to sort out the new hire car was young, and new, and seemed to ask Ruby a question every five minutes. Then, of course, there'd been Dev's email, asking for directions to every amenity in Lucyville. After she'd gritted her teeth and carefully replied to it—and therefore losing another thirty minutes—he'd blithely replied with one word: *Thanks.*

Thanks!

She'd silently screamed.

She'd had no idea Dev was like this—normally talent of the high-maintenance variety came with clear advance warning via the industry grapevine. Put two people who worked in film together, and guaranteed that stuff like 'Dev-Cooper-thought-his-car-was-too-girly' got talked about.

But—until the last twenty-four hours—she'd never heard a negative word about Devlin Cooper.

Oohing and ahhing about how he was *just* as gorgeous in real life—which she now knew to be true—yes, she'd heard that. But unreasonable, prima-donna carryings-on? Not a whisper.

Her phone rang, vibrating against the pile of sides—the scenes being filmed the next day—it rested upon.

Of course it was Dev, and reluctantly Ruby swiped her finger across the screen to answer the call.

'Mr Cooper,' Ruby said, setting the phone to loudspeaker so she could continue to work on the latest updates to a transport schedule. She was *not* going to let Dev distract her. 'How can I help you?'

'I was wondering,' he said, not sounding at all apologetic for calling so late, 'if you could recommend anywhere good to eat in Sydney.'

Ruby's jaw clenched. *Really?*

'Was it for a particular occasion?'

'A date,' he said. 'This weekend.'

Ruby determinedly ignored that irrational, disappointed kick she felt in her belly.

'Sure,' she managed to squeeze out. 'I'll get someone onto that for you tomorrow.'

'But I was hoping you could offer some personal recommendations.'

Had his voice become slightly deeper? More intimate?

Don't be an idiot! She typed the words on screen for good measure; maybe *then* it would sink in.

'Well,' she said, 'if you were thinking fine dining, then you probably can't go wrong with *Tetsuya's,* on Kent Street. Or *Quay,* at The Rocks.'

'Personal favourites?'

'No. I've heard the food is amazing, but I generally prefer somewhere a little less formal. Where people talk and laugh loudly and you don't need to book months in advance. You know?' Immediately she realised what she'd said. 'Although I'd imagine you don't have too many problems with getting a table.'

'Not usually,' he said, a smile in his voice. 'So where would *you* go for dinner this Saturday night in Sydney?'

She'd grown up in the outer suburbs of Sydney, but as an adult she'd spent little time there—aside from when she was working. And with twelve-to-fourteen-hour days typical on a film set, dining out—fine or otherwise—wasn't exactly a regular occurrence. Although, she'd crashed in the spare room of a set dresser between jobs last year...

'Some friends took me to a French Bistro right in the CBD when I was last in Sydney. It's a little fancy, but still relaxed. Plus, the Bombe Alaska is to die for.'

'Perfect. Would you be able to book me a table?'

Ruby gritted her teeth. *So not my job!*

'Sure!' she said, instead, with determined enthusiasm.

'Appreciate it,' he said, and the words were just as annoying the third time she'd heard them that day.

Then he hung up.

Ruby told herself she'd imagined the beginnings of a laugh before the phone went silent. As otherwise she'd need to drive to his place right now. And strangle him.

The next day was overcast, with rain forecast for the early afternoon.

Consequently, Asha, the second assistant director, was rather frantic when she rushed into Ruby's office just after eleven a.m.

'I need your help,' she said, running a hand through her shiny black bob. 'We have a situation in Hair and Make-up. Dev won't let anyone cut his hair, and we need him on set like *now*. We need to get this scene before the weather hits.'

Ruby sighed. She'd left him with hair and make-up not even

twenty minutes ago…but still—she really shouldn't be surprised.

A minute later, both women were striding across Unit Base.

'Dev isn't at all like what I expected,' Ruby said. She wrapped her arms tightly around herself as she walked, the breeze sharp through the thin cotton of her cardigan.

'You mean the whole "haven't slept or eaten in a month" thing?' Asha asked. 'Thank God Make-up and Wardrobe can work miracles is all I can say.' Then a long pause, and a conspiratorial whisper: 'I hear that he's nursing a broken heart. That Estelle van der something? She's already hooked up with someone new. Poor guy.'

Poor guy? Right.

'Yeah, that, I guess,' Ruby said. 'But I meant all of his demands? It's driving me nuts.'

Asha shot her a surprised glance. 'Really? Honestly, up until just now he's been a model actor. It's amazing how quickly he's learnt his scenes and he just nailed our rehearsals yesterday. His professionalism is the only reason we can shoot anything today.'

Ruby slowed her pace slightly. 'No complaints about his costume? Requests for a box of chocolates with all the soft-centred ones removed?'

Both were the type of requests that the Dev she'd been dealing with over the past day and a half would *definitely* have asked. Just this morning he'd asked to have new curtains installed in his trailer, as the current set let in too much light when closed. *Apparently.* Then he'd asked for a very specific selection of organic fruit. Rohan was wasting his time on that, right now. Ugh!

'No,' Asha said, coming to a halt outside the hair and make-up trailer. 'This random hair thing is it. But, it's only been a couple of days. Maybe he'll reveal his true self to all of us on set soon.'

'Hmm,' was all that Ruby could say to that. A niggling suspicion that she'd dismissed as ridiculous, impossible, was now niggling, well…louder.

But surely he wouldn't…?

She opened the door to the trailer, taking in the frustrated-looking hair stylist and his assistant—and of course Dev, sprawled ever-so-casually in front of a mirror, complete with two days' worth of—she had to admit—sexy stubble. As she stepped inside he met her gaze in the glass.

And winked.

Ruby dug her fingernails into her palms, then took a deep, calming breath. The action was not soothing in the slightest, but it did help her speak in a fair facsimile of an I've-got-everything-under-control production co-ordinator.

'Could I have a few minutes with Mr Cooper?'

It was a perfectly reasonable request—it was her job to fix exactly these types of hiccups—and so with quick nods and hopeful expressions aimed in Ruby's direction everyone filed out.

Ever so slowly—and Ruby now *knew* he was enjoying this—Dev spun his chair around to face her. His assessing gaze travelled over her, from her flat, knee-high leather boots, up to her fitted navy jeans, cream tank top and oversized, over-long wool cardigan. Then to her face—touching on her lips, her eyes, her hair.

Ruby wanted to kick herself for being pleased she'd made an effort with her make-up today. She'd done so yesterday too, not letting herself acknowledge until just now that it had—of course—been for Devlin Cooper.

God, she frustrated herself. She'd been sure she'd long ago got past this—this pathetic need for male attention. The need for anyone else to provide her with validation, other than herself.

No. That hadn't changed.

He opened his mouth, guaranteed to say something teasing and clever. He had that look in his eyes—she'd seen it in his movies, and definitely in person.

She didn't give him the chance.

'Who the *hell* do you think you are?'

Ruby had the satisfaction of watching his eyes widen in surprise. But he recovered quickly, as smooth as silk. 'I believe I'm Devlin Cooper.' He shrugged. 'You know, the actor?'

She shook her head. 'No way. Don't be smart. I'm onto you.'

'*Onto* me?' he asked, raising an eyebrow. 'What exactly are you *onto*?'

Ruby bit her lip, trying to hold onto the barest thread of control. Could he be any more deliberately oblivious? Any more *arrogant*?

'This,' she said, throwing her arms up to encompass the trailer. 'And the phone calls, the emails, the hire car, the chocolates, the fruit, the curtains…' Ruby started to count them off on her fingers. 'What next? What next trivial, unreasonable task are you going to lob in my direction?'

'You don't feel my requests are legitimate?' he asked. If he was at all bothered by her rapidly rising voice, his expression revealed nothing.

'I know they're not.' She glared at him when he tried to speak again. 'And I don't care why you've been doing it: I don't care if you're so shocked by the concept of a woman saying no to you that you need to be as irritating as possible in revenge, but—*please*—just stop.'

Dev blinked. 'Is that what you think I'm doing?' In contrast to even a moment before, now he looked dumbfounded—his forehead wrinkled in consternation. 'That's not it at all.'

But she was barely listening now.

'In case you're not aware, when you pull stunts like this, Paul—you know, my boss?—expects me to sort it all immediately. If I don't—if filming is held up, if we can't shoot a scene because of you, or if I need to ask Paul to call your agent to kick your butt into gear—it isn't *you* who looks like a massive, unprofessional loser. *It's me.*'

Dev pushed himself to his feet. He was in costume: dark brown trousers, a soft tan shirt with the sleeves rolled up, a heavy leather belt and holster, plus chunky work boots—he was playing an early nineteen hundreds Australian drover after all. Temporarily, her tirade was clogged in her throat as she digested the sight of him approaching her. He was so tall, so broad—and suddenly the trailer felt so small.

But then her frustration bubbled over again. Hot, famous movie star or not—*nobody* got away with treating Ruby Bell this way.

'You might have forgotten what it's like to rely on a regular salary, but trust me—I haven't. And I'm not having some entitled, full-of-himself actor think it's okay to stomp all over my reputation, my professionalism, my...'

With every word her voice became higher and less steady.

Dev had stopped in front of her. Not close enough to crowd her, not at all, and yet she found that words began to escape her as he studied her, his gaze constant, searching and...what? Not arrogant. Not angry. Not even shocked...

Sad? No, not that either. But it wasn't what she expected.

It had been silent for long seconds, and Ruby swallowed, trying to pull herself together.

'If you don't stop,' she began, 'I'll...'

And here her tirade came to its pathetic—and now clearly obvious—end.

What exactly would she do? What could she do? She'd just told him that she'd get blamed for any problems he caused, and that was pretty much true. And it wasn't as if she could get him fired.

Hmm. Let me think: Easily replaceable production co-ordinator versus the man who's starred in the world's highest grossing spy franchise?

She tangled her fingers into the fabric of her cardigan, suddenly needing to hold onto something.

Oh, God. What had she done? All he had to do was complain to Paul and...

Dev was still watching her.

'You'll what, Ruby?'

She made herself meet his gaze. 'I—' she started. She should apologise, she knew. Grovel, even—do anything to patch up the past few minutes as if they had never, ever happened.

But she couldn't do it—it would be like time-travelling ten years into her past.

'I'd *appreciate it*,' she said, deliberately mimicking him, 'if you could carefully consider your future requests, or issues, before contacting myself, or my office. We're all very busy at the moment.'

Even that was far from an appropriate request to make of a film's biggest star, but she just *couldn't* concede any less.

In response, Dev smiled. The sudden lightness in his gaze made Ruby's heart skip a beat. Alone in a room with Dev Cooper, Ruby would challenge any woman not to do the same—irritated beyond belief or not.

'It wasn't revenge,' he said, simply.

'But it was something,' Ruby prompted. What was all this about?

'I'm sorry that you thought I was trying to make you look bad in front of your boss and colleagues. I can assure you I wasn't.'

Even knowing he was a very good actor, Ruby believed him. Those eyes, in real life, were *nothing at all* like what you saw on celluloid. They revealed so much more—more than Ruby could even begin to interpret.

'It's much simpler than that. Much less exciting than some dastardly vengeful plan.'

Ruby crossed her arms, watching him stonily.

He sighed. 'Okay, bad joke. Look…' He looked down at the trailer floor for just a moment. 'It's simple, really. I don't need "looking after".'

Ruby narrowed her eyes. 'And the fact I'm the brunt of this behaviour is an unfortunate coincidence?'

'No,' he conceded. 'I just like…' He studied her face, then focused on her eyes, as if he was trying to work something out. 'I like seeing you react.'

She was not deluded enough to think that she stood out amongst all the other women she *knew* he surrounded himself with. She'd seen the photos of him with Estelle—a *supermodel,* for crying out loud. This juvenile game had *nothing* to do with her. Not really.

This was about his ego, his sense of the way things should be. She didn't come into it at all.

Ruby spoke very politely. 'Please carefully consider your future requests, or issues, before contacting myself, or my office,' she repeated.

He nodded, and for the first time in long minutes Ruby felt as if she was breathing normally.

'I'll do my best,' he said.

Every muscle in her body that had begun to relax re-tightened, ready for battle. Had he not heard a word she'd said? How could he possibly think—?

'No more stunts like this—I get it. I won't impact the filming schedule.'

But…

He grinned, but that brightness she'd seen—just for that moment—had long disappeared. Now there was a heaviness to his gaze, and the lines around his mouth were tight.

'I think I'm having too much fun with you.'

'I'm not interested,' she said, quick as a flash. But they both heard that she didn't really believe that.

Since when had she been this transparent?

He was so sure he knew where this was headed it made her want to scream. And simultaneously made her question her sanity. There was just something about the man, and the way he looked at her, that had her questioning herself. Had her questioning the rules she'd laid down for herself long ago…

She shook her head firmly.

'I'm going to tell Hair and Make-up that it was a misunderstanding and you're happy to go with the haircut as planned.'

He nodded sharply.

She turned to go, but paused at the trailer door.

'You do realise that the kid who threw sticks at the girl he liked in primary school never did get the girl?'

He laughed, the deep sound making her shiver. 'Not in my experience.'

Ruby slammed the door behind her as she left.

CHAPTER FOUR

'RUBY, CAN I HAVE a minute?'

Paul spoke from the hallway, barely poking his head into the busy office. He didn't bother waiting for an answer—as of course it wasn't a question—and so half a minute later Ruby was closing the door behind her as she stepped into the producer's office.

'Yes?'

Paul was rubbing his forehead, which wasn't a good sign.

'Are the drivers organised for tomorrow night?' he asked.

Paul was attending the premiere of his latest film in Sydney. Both Dev and Arizona would also be walking the red carpet—a bit of extra attention for that film, plus some early promo for *The Land*. 'Of course. All three cars are sorted.'

As was contractually necessary. *Must travel in own car* was a pretty standard condition for most actors. Quite the contrast to Ruby, who had driven up to Lucyville with her hire car packed full with everything she owned, Rohan *and* one of the girls from Accounts. Plus some miscellaneous lighting equipment.

Paul nodded sharply. 'Good, good.'

Then he went silent, allowing Ruby to start dreaming up all the potential reasons why he'd *really* needed to talk to her.

Right at the top of that list was Dev.

'So. I hear you had some luck talking Dev around, yesterday.'

Got it in one.

'Yes,' she said, far more calmly than she felt. 'He just needed a little time to understand what was required.'

'Excellent,' Paul said. 'As unfortunately neither his agent or I are having much luck making him *understand* that he signed a contract that specified he walk the red carpet at this premiere. He's refusing to go.'

Of course he was.

Ruby bit back a sigh. 'I don't think I'd have any more chance of talking him around than you would.'

'I have faith in you.'

Which meant: *Go fix this, Ruby.*

Paul had already reached for his phone, casually moving on to his next production crisis, now that—in his mind at least—this particular issue was sorted.

So Ruby walked out of his office, down the hallway, outside onto the dusty grass, then all the way across Unit Base to where the opulent, shiny black actors' trailers that housed Arizona and Dev were situated.

And knocked, very loudly, on Dev's door.

He was, Dev decided, becoming quite accustomed to people being annoyed with him.

There was Veronica, of course, all but breathing fire across the cellular network whenever she called. Her multiple-times-a-day tirades were exclusively for the benefit of his voicemail, however, as Dev considered Graeme a sufficient conduit for anything that Veronica really needed to know. He figured his agent could hardly complain. She'd planted her security guy/minder/driver/spy—she might as well get her money's worth.

Or, more accurately, *his* money's worth. As of course that was what all this was about—Veronica's much-stated concern for him was all about the money. He was her biggest star, and now she was panicking.

But he felt no guilt. He'd made Veronica very, very rich. He owed her nothing.

Then there was Graeme. The director. The producer. The rest of the crew. He gave them all just exactly what was needed—

whether it be his acting skills, the answer to a question, or simple conversation. But not one skerrick more.

Then his mother had started calling. In her first voice message, she explained she'd heard on the news that he was in Australia, and was hoping they could catch up.

He'd meant to call her, but then didn't. Couldn't.

And she'd kept calling, kept leaving polite, friendly messages, that always ended with a soft *love you*.

Each call made him feel like something you'd scrape off your boot, but, as he'd been doing lately, he just shoved that problem aside. To worry about later. Eventually...

Most likely at three in the morning, when he was so overwhelmed with exhaustion that he could no longer ignore the thoughts that caused him pain.

He clenched his jaw. *No.*

The woman on the other side of his trailer door, *she* was who he needed to be thinking about. Somehow, randomly, she'd grabbed his attention. With her, he forgot all the other rubbish that was cluttering up his head.

And she was, unquestionably, very, very annoyed with him.

He smiled, and walked to the door.

He opened the door mid-knock, triggering a surprised, 'Oh!' and she stumbled a step inside.

He didn't step back himself, forcing her to squeeze past him. Not quite close enough for their bodies to touch, but close enough that her clothes brushed against his.

Yes, he was being far from a gentleman, but no—he didn't care.

He found himself craving that flare in Ruby's gaze, that look she worked so hard to disguise.

But it was there—this heat between them. He knew it, she knew it—she just needed to get over whatever ridiculous imagined rules she'd created in her head and let the inevitable happen.

He let the trailer door swing shut behind him and turned to face her. She walked right into the middle of his trailer, in the 'living' section of the luxury motorhome. The trailer was practically soundproof, so now they both stood, looking at each other, in silence.

That didn't last long.

'I thought I made myself clear,' she said, frustration flooding her voice, 'how important my career is to me, and how you have *no right* to mess with it. To mess with my life.'

'But I haven't.'

She blinked. 'What would you call this? Refusing to attend a premiere that's in your contract?'

'Have I held up filming? Have I embarrassed you professionally?'

'You will if you don't go,' she said simply.

He smiled. 'Then you just need to get me to go.'

Her eyes narrowed. 'How?'

'Dinner.'

He hadn't planned this. Hadn't planned anything beyond saying no to Paul and seeing what happened next.

With Ruby there wasn't a script—things just happened.

But dinner, suddenly, was the perfectly obvious solution.

'That's blackmail,' she said, with bite.

He shrugged. 'Yes.'

No, he most definitely was *not* a gentleman.

She sighed loudly and rubbed her hands up and down her arms. 'So if I agree to dinner, you'll attend the premiere.' It wasn't a question.

'And make you look like a miracle-worker in front of your producer.'

She rolled her eyes. 'I'd rather you'd just gone to the premiere and never brought me into this at all.' She paused, meeting his gaze.

Her expression was sharp and assessing. 'Dinner at that French bistro on Saturday night—you booked that for...whatever *this* is.'

Maybe he had? At the time it'd been about riling her up, teasing her, irritating her with the idea he had a date with another woman. Childish, but he hadn't had a plan. Not consciously, anyway.

'Yes,' he said, because he knew she'd hate that answer.

'God, you're so, so sure of yourself, aren't you?'

He didn't bother replying. Instead he walked past her, then settled himself onto one of the small navy-blue couches. 'Why don't you take a seat? We can work out the details of our date.'

'No, thank you,' she said, very crisply. 'I need to get back to the office. I don't have time during my workday to waste on this. Call me later. Or even better, email me. More efficient.'

Lord, he liked her. So direct. So to the point.

She spun on her booted heel, then paused mid-spin.

'So this is your way of maintaining your one-hundred-per-cent never-rejected perfect score or something?'

'You can think of it that way if you like.'

She groaned. 'You think you're very clever, don't you?'

Considering he'd just achieved exactly what he wanted, he didn't consider it necessary to reply to this question either.

She continued her exit, but at the door she, just as he expected, had to deliver a final parting shot. Just as she had yesterday.

'You know what, Mr Cooper? Everything I'd heard about you before this week was good. Glowing even. Everyone likes you. Everyone loves to work with you. So, I reckon you must *really* be a great actor. Because, quite frankly, I don't think you're a very nice person.'

This time he had no pithy retort, so he just let her go.

After all, she was partly right. Right now he didn't feel like the Dev that everyone liked, as she said. The Dev that loved his job and that was beloved of many a film crew. The Dev with a million friends and a lifestyle that most could only dream of.

Right now he didn't know what type of person he was at all.

Ruby had laid out every single item of clothing she owned on her motel-room bed. Not just the clothing she'd brought with her for this film—everything she owned.

Years ago she'd got into the routine of selling her clothes before departing for a job overseas—eBay was brilliant for that purpose—rather than lugging it with her across the world.

She'd always thought it rather a flawless plan. She had a keen eye for an online shopping bargain, so she was rarely out of pocket, and, more importantly, she had the perfect excuse to buy an entirely new, season-appropriate wardrobe every six months or so.

The rare occasions she did date, it was always between films, so having a favourite, guaranteed-to-feel-awesome-in outfit was not really all that essential. She knew well in advance if she had a premiere to attend, so she could plan ahead—and besides, the full-length formal gowns were really only for the talent at those events, not the crew.

So. Consequently here she was, hands on hips—and not far from putting her head in her hands—with absolutely nothing to wear on her date with Dev.

It was tempting, really, *really* tempting, to rock up for her date in jeans and a ratty old T-shirt. So her clothing choice would make a very obvious statement about how she felt about the whole situation.

But, unfortunately, she just couldn't.

Turned out she was—much to her despair—incapable of being truly cool, and strong, and defiant. In this way, at least. Nope. Just as she'd been agonising over her clothing choices for work each day, she wanted to look her best on Saturday night.

Yes, it was pathetic. Yes, it didn't say a lot for her that, despite Dev's ridiculous manipulating of her and their situation, she still felt her body react at even the *thought* of him. And when they were together…well.

But then, he *was* basically the sexiest man on earth. She shouldn't be too hard on herself. Surely she wouldn't be human if she didn't wonder…

It was just a little galling to realise that she—who did know better—could still be distracted by looks over personality. As, really, there wasn't a whole lot about Devlin Cooper for her to like right now.

A long time ago, the Devlin Coopers of the world had been her type. Not that she had a life populated with movie stars, but at high school she'd gone for the captain of the footy team. And the captain of the tennis team. And the very charismatic head boy who every girl had been in love with. Then once she left school, it was the sexy bartender. Or the hot lawyer who ordered a latte every morning at the café where she worked. Or the son of the owner of the café. And...*and, and, and*...

She'd search out the hottest guy, the most popular guy, the guy who was the absolute least attainable for a girl like her—the rebellious foster child, abandoned by her teenage mother, with a reputation a mile long.

And then she would make it her mission to get him.

It was all about her goal, her goal to get the guy, to have him want her—*her*—Ruby Bell, who was *nobody*. Not popular, not unpopular. Not the prettiest, not the least attractive. And when she got him—and she nearly always did—she had that night, or nights, or maybe only a few hours, where she got to feel beautiful and desirable and valued and *wanted*.

But of course that feeling didn't last. She—and her temporary value—was inevitably dropped. She'd hurt and cry and feel just as worthless as she had before that perfect, gorgeous guy had kissed her.

Then the cycle would start again.

Ruby's eyes stung, and she realised she was on the verge of tears. Another memory—one that came later—was threatening, right at the edges of her subconscious.

But she wasn't going there—not tonight, and not because of Dev.

What was important was that she'd turned her life around. Never again would she need a man to make her feel alive—to feel worthy. Never again would she be sweet, and obliging and void of any opinion purely for the attention and approval of another person.

And never again would she be the girl that was whispered about. Who walked into a room only to have the men study her with questions in their eyes—and the women with daggers in theirs.

She'd grown up in a swirl of gossip and speculation, and her adult life had begun that way too—and way too early.

The sad thing was, at first she'd actually liked the attention. She wasn't the shy girl at the back of the classroom, she was a girl who people talked about, who people noticed. Suddenly *everyone* knew her name.

Maybe at first she'd fuelled the gossip. She'd been increasingly outrageous, telling herself she was in control, inwardly laughing at the people who looked at her with such disdain.

But at some point the power had shifted.

Or maybe she'd just never had any power at all.

Now she was all grown up. She was twenty-nine years old. She no longer needed anyone to validate her. She no longer harboured a fear it had taken her years to acknowledge—that if her mother hadn't wanted her, then maybe no one ever would. In men and their fleeting attention she'd received the attention and the *wanting* she'd so badly craved.

But now she knew she didn't need a man. She had her career, and her friends, and a lifestyle that she adored. If she dated, she chose men who were the opposite to the high-school football stars and Devlin Coopers of the world. And it was never for very long.

She was always in control. Everything was perfect.

And another beautiful man was not going to change any of that. She would not slide into habits long severed, or let their date impact her professional reputation: she had never been, and would never be, the subject of gossip at work. Gossip would never colour her decisions—would never control her—ever again.

She didn't hide her past from anyone—but it was the *past*. She couldn't let herself head down that path again. To lose herself while wanting something a man could never give her.

Ruby needed only herself. Could rely, *only,* on herself.

She turned, and flopped onto her back on her bed, uncaring of the clothing she squashed and creased beneath her.

Hmm. That was all well and good—and *right*.

But.

She still had a date with Devlin Cooper in two days' time.

An emergency shopping expedition was—most definitely—required.

Ruby had to spend a few hours in the office on Saturday morning, and so by the time she'd driven the four hours into the city, she was cutting it extremely fine.

Fortunately, one of her good friends was between films at the moment. So she was meeting Gwen, an exceedingly glamorous costume designer, at a boutique in Paddington, rather than hitting the department stores in a fit of mad desperation.

As she stepped into the store, complete with its crystal chandeliers, chunky red leather armchairs and modern, smooth-edged white shelving, Gwen squealed and trotted towards her on towering platform heels.

'Ruby! It's been for ever!' she announced as she wrapped her into a hug.

She'd considered sharing the identity of her date with Gwen, but had decided, on balance, that it was best if she didn't. Yes, she trusted her friend, but…it really was better if no one knew. It was only one date, after all.

In the same vein, she'd taken steps to ensure—as much as was possible—that their date remained firmly under the radar. When Dev had called her—she'd known he wouldn't email—she'd made it very clear that the gorgeous French bistro she'd booked was no longer suitable. It was not the type of place where privacy—and a lack of photography—could be assured. The last thing she needed was some grainy photo snapped on someone's mobile phone making it onto Twitter and, eventually, to the film set.

Yes, she was likely paranoid, and such a liaison with a film's star would not signal the end of her career. She *knew* that film sets could be the home to all sorts of flings and the more than occasional affair. It was natural in an industry where the majority of the crew were well under forty—the transient lifestyle was not ideal for anyone with a family, and roots.

She just didn't want to be that woman Dev had a fling with. She'd been *that woman* enough times in her life. Thank you very much.

So this was, she realised as Gwen unhooked a dress from a shiny chrome rack to display to her, more about how she perceived herself than about how anyone else would perceive her.

Which really was just as important… No. More important than her professional reputation.

But she'd fiercely protect that, too.

'What do you think?' Gwen asked, giving the coat hanger a little shake so that the dress's delicate beading shimmered beneath the down lights.

It was a cocktail-length dress, in shades of green. On the hanger it looked like nothing but pretty fabric, but of course she tried it on.

Ruby was bigger than the average tiny actress that Gwen was used to dressing, but still—her friend certainly had an eye for what suited her body.

As she stepped out of the change room and in front of the mirror Ruby couldn't help but suck in a breath of surprise.

She looked…

'Beautiful!' Gwen declared happily. 'It's perfect.'

Ruby twisted from side to side, studying herself. The dress was gorgeous, with heavily beaded and embroidered cap sleeves and a sweetheart neckline that flattered her average-sized curves. The silk followed the curve of her waist and hips, ending well above her knee. The beading continued throughout the fabric, becoming sparser at her waist before ending in a shimmer of green and flecks of gold at the hem. It was simple—but not. Striking—but not glitzy.

She loved it.

Twenty minutes later she'd parted with a not insignificant portion of her savings, and headed with Gwen to find the perfect matching heels and a short, sexy, swingy jacket.

And an hour after that she was alone in the hotel room she'd booked, only a short walk from the crazily exclusive restaurant where she would be meeting Dev. Really soon.

The dress sparkled prettily on her bed. She had her make-up and the perfect shade of nail polish raring to go in the bathroom.

But she paused, rather than walking to the shower. She looked at herself reflected in the mirrored hotel wardrobe.

There she was, in jeans and hair that had transitioned from deliberately choppy to plain old messy at some point in the day.

She wouldn't say she lacked confidence in herself or her looks. She didn't think she was hideously *un*attractive, but… *really?* When Dev could have anyone, why her?

It must be the challenge. It could be nothing else. And maybe he felt that he should be the one doing the rejecting, not her?

She nodded, and she watched the movement reshuffle her hair just a little.

Yes. That was it.

And after tonight—that would be that. He'd have achieved his goal, and in a week's time she'd be very, very old news.

Which suited her just fine.

Didn't it?

CHAPTER FIVE

Dev was late. Only a few minutes, but late, just the same.

He'd meant to be later, actually, having liked the idea of Ruby sitting alone at the restaurant, getting increasingly frustrated with him.

Simply because he enjoyed the flash of anger in her eyes almost as much as the heat of the attraction she was so determinedly—and continually—ignoring.

But, after a while, he began to feel like a bit of an idiot sitting alone in his penthouse suite, mindlessly watching the Saturday night rugby, when the alternative was spending time with a beautiful...

No, not beautiful. At least not on the standards that Hollywood judged beauty. But a compelling...intriguing woman. Yes, she was that.

Unarguably more interesting than his own company.

But when he was ushered into the private dining area of the exclusive restaurant by an impeccably well-mannered maître d', he was met by a table exquisitely set for two—but no Ruby.

His lips quirked as he settled into his seat. *Interesting.*

The restaurant sat right on the edge of Circular Quay, its floor-to-ceiling windows forming a subtly curved wall that provided a spectacular view of the harbour. To the right were the dramatic sails of the opera house. Straight ahead was the incomparable harbour bridge. Lights illuminated the mammoth structure, highlighting its huge metal beams.

He'd eaten at this restaurant before, and had certainly dined against a backdrop of the world's most beautiful skylines many, many times—but he wouldn't be human if he wasn't impressed by sparkling Sydney by night.

It was like nowhere else in the world.

However. Sitting alone in a dining room that could seat thirty—and which he'd had organised for tonight to seat only two—even a remarkable view could quickly become boring.

Which it did.

A waiter came and offered him a taste of the wine he'd selected, then after pouring Dev's glass he merged once again, silently, into the background.

Minutes passed. Slowly, he assumed, as he refused to succumb and check his watch.

He considered—then dismissed—the possibility that she wasn't coming at all.

No, she'd be here.

Almost on cue, the door to the private room opened on whisper-smooth hinges. He looked up to watch Ruby being ushered inside. And then kept on looking.

She wore a dress in greens and gold that caught and reflected every bit of light in the room. Her legs were long beneath a skirt that hit at mid thigh, and shown off to perfection by strappy, criss-crossed heels. When his gaze—eventually—met hers, he connected with eyes that were defiant and bold beneath a fringe that was smoother and more perfect than usual: not a golden strand out of place.

Her lips curved in greeting, but he wouldn't call it a smile.

He stood as she approached the table, and she blinked a couple of times as he did so, her gaze flicking over him for the briefest of instants.

The maître d' received a genuine smile as he offered Ruby her seat, and he then launched into his spiel, speaking—Dev assumed—of wine and food, but he really wasn't paying any attention. Instead he took the opportunity to just look at Ruby as she tilted her chin upwards and listened attentively.

This was, after all, about the first time she'd been perfectly still, and silent, in his presence, since their original *interlude* beside the costume trailer.

Then, she'd been veering towards adorable, while tonight she was polished and perfect. Different, for sure—but equally appealing.

After a short conversation, the maître d' repeated his vanishing act, and Ruby turned her gaze onto him.

'You're late,' he pointed out.

She nodded. 'So were you.'

He smiled, surprised. 'How did you know?'

'I didn't. But it seemed the kind of stunt you would pull. You've been very consistent in your quest to irritate me.' Calmly, she reached for her water glass. 'Not very chivalrous of you, however.' Another pause. 'Personally, I am never—intentionally—less than punctual. Time is everything in my job, and I see no reason why it shouldn't be in the rest of my life.'

Time is everything.

How true. Often, Dev had only recently discovered, you had a lot less time than you thought.

'So chivalry is important to you, Ruby?'

She took a sip from her water glass, then studied him over the rim. 'Actually, no,' she replied, surprising him. She looked out towards the opera house, her forehead wrinkling slightly. 'I mean, of course being courteous and honourable or gallant—or whatever a chivalrous man is supposed to be—is important.' She gave him a look that underlined the fact she clearly considered him to be none of those things. 'But it has to be genuine. Standing up when I approach the table, for example—' her words were razor sharp '—is meaningless. It has to mean something—have a basis in respect—otherwise I'd really rather you didn't bother.'

'I respect you,' he said.

She laughed with not a trace of pretention. 'I find that very hard to believe.'

'It's the truth,' he said. He wasn't going to bother explaining himself, but then somehow found himself doing so anyway. 'I was late because I like seeing you react, not because I don't value you and your time. I apologise if you feel that way.'

'I'm sure you agree that distinction is impossible to make from my point of view.'

Dev almost, almost, felt bad about it—but not quite. He was enjoying this—enjoying her—too much.

'You like pushing my buttons,' she said. 'You're very good at it.'

He shrugged, studying her. 'So is that what you're looking for? An honourable, perfectly chivalrous specimen of a man?'

Dev knew he was not that man.

Immediately, she shook her head. 'Absolutely not. I'm looking for no man at all.'

'You're focusing on your career?'

Almost silently the maître d' reappeared and filled her wine glass.

'Yes, but that's not the reason. I don't need a man. At all.'

'Need, or want?'

She rolled her eyes dismissively. 'Neither.'

He considered this unexpected announcement as their entrées arrived, but he wasn't about to question her further. Tonight was not for detailed analysis of their respective relationship goals.

For the record, his was—and had always been—to have no relationship at all. Estelle had been an unexpected exception, a relationship that had evolved, at times—it seemed—almost without his participation. Yes, he'd liked her. Enjoyed his time with her. Maybe considered the idea that he loved her.

But that night she'd left, she'd made it crystal clear that what he felt wasn't love. How had she put it?

Love is when you share yourself—reveal yourself. Your thoughts, your feelings, your fears. Something. Everything! Not nothing. Not absolutely nothing.

At the time he hadn't questioned her. But later, when he'd asked himself that question—if that *was* what he'd done, and who he was—he couldn't disagree.

They ate their salmon for a while in silence, their knives scraping loudly on the fine bone china.

'Is this really what you wanted?' she asked. She was still focused on her meal, her eyes on her plate, not on him.

She meant this date, this time alone with her.

'Yes.'

Now she glanced up. The harder edge to her gaze from before was gone; now she just looked confused. 'Seriously? Why on earth would you want to spend an evening with a woman who doesn't particularly like you?'

'I thought you said you didn't know me well enough to dislike me.'

She raised an eyebrow. 'I've begun to revise that opinion.'

He smiled. Maybe something resembling his *famous Dev Cooper smile,* as he didn't miss the way her cheeks went pink, or how eager she was to look away.

'You like me.'

Instantly, she met his gaze. 'Here we go again. It's getting tedious. Why on earth should I like you?'

'I'm charming,' he said.

She snorted. 'What exactly is your definition of the word? Blackmailing a woman into dating you? Really?'

'No. I must admit this is not my standard dating procedure.'

'For the sake of the thousands of women you've ever dated, I'm relieved to hear that.'

'Not thousands,' he said.

She waved her wine glass in a gesture of dismissal. 'Hundreds, then.'

No, not that many either. In hindsight, maybe Estelle was not the first to observe his relationship failings. Or, more likely, she was the only one he'd allowed close enough to notice.

A mistake, clearly.

'I'm not—' he began, then stopped.

I'm not myself at the moment.

No, there was no need to say that to Ruby. That was the whole point, wasn't it? For Ruby to be his distraction?

'You're not what?' she asked.

He gave a little shake of his head. 'It doesn't matter. All that matters is that we're here now.' He leant back in his chair a little, studying her. 'We're here, in this amazing city, at this amazing restaurant. And you, Ruby Bell, are wearing one amazing dress.'

The pink to her cheeks escalated to a blush, but otherwise she gave no indication of being affected by his words.

'Thank you,' she said, just a little stiffly.

'Here's an idea,' he said. 'How about we call a truce? For tonight. For argument's sake, let's pretend you don't hate my guts, or the way we both came to be sitting together at this table.'

She grinned, then looked surprised that she had. 'I don't hate you,' she said. 'You just haven't given me a heck of a lot to like.'

'I'll try harder,' he promised.

She held his gaze for a long, long while. Considering his words.

'Okay,' she finally conceded. 'But just for tonight.'

Belatedly, Ruby acknowledged that her dessert plate was completely empty—excluding some melted remnants of sorbet. She could barely remember what it tasted like—she'd been so focused on their conversation.

How had this happened?

A couple of hours ago she'd been dreading this date…

No. That was clearly a lie. Anxiously anticipating was far more on the mark.

But now, she found herself in the midst of a really fantastic evening. *Date.* A date with a movie star.

Although, oddly, she found she needed to remind herself of that fact every now and again. A little mental pinch of her arm, so to speak.

He was different tonight. Only for a moment earlier, and even then she was unsure whether she'd imagined it, had his gaze darkened. She realised that up until tonight there had been a kind of shadow to Dev. A…burden, maybe?

But tonight he was different. There was more of an openness to his expression. Oddly, as they chatted—initially about the industry but then, thankfully, about basically everything but—Ruby had the sense that the shadow was gradually lifting. She found herself wanting to find opportunities to make him smile again, to laugh.

It was as if he was out of practice.

Ruby gave herself a mental shake.

Oh, no. Now *that* was wishful thinking. She was putting way too much thought into this.

She needed to keep this simple: it was a date. One date. Only.

They'd just finished trading stories of their varied travel disasters. She'd noticed that Dev hadn't spoken of *that time I was mobbed by fans in Paris* or *this one time I was invited for afternoon tea with the Queen*—it was as if he was distancing himself from what made him so, so different from her. Somehow, he was making himself relatable. A real person.

Was he doing it deliberately?

Yes, for sure. He'd been right before—he *was* charming, and smart.

But also…it was working. She found herself questioning her opinion of him. She'd certainly relaxed. Something she knew was unwise, but the wine, the food, the lighting, and Dev… yeah, Dev… It was…he was…pretty much an irresistible force.

But not quite.

'Why film production?' he asked, changing the direction of their conversation yet again.

Ruby swirled her Shiraz in its oversized glass. 'Would you believe I'm a failed actor?' she asked.

'Yes,' he said, immediately.

She raised her eyebrows. 'Is it that obvious?'

He nodded, assessing her. 'Acting requires a certain…artifice. You—you tell it how it is. You're not pretending, not hiding what you think.'

She shifted a little in her seat, uncomfortable. 'You're saying I'm tactless?' she said, attempting a teasing tone but failing.

'Honest,' he said, disagreeing with her.

His gaze had shifted a little, become more serious. He was watching her closely, and it left her feeling exposed. She didn't like it.

'But,' he said, 'sometimes you try to hide what you're not saying: frustration, dismissal...attraction.'

Ruby had a feeling she wasn't being as successful in that goal as she'd like tonight. What could he see in her expression?

She decided it best not to consider that at all.

'You're partly right,' she said. 'At school I loved to act, but really I was only playing variations of myself. I wasn't any good at stepping into another character.' She laughed. 'But I still wanted to work in film—you know, delusions of glamour— and I couldn't wait to travel the world—so, I went to uni, then started at the bottom and worked my way up.'

'You were good at school?'

She shook her head, laughing. 'Not at all. I went to uni when I was twenty, after going back to finish Year Twelve. I had a... rebellious phase, I'd guess you'd call it.'

Dev's eyebrows rose. 'Really?'

She smiled, pleased she'd surprised him. 'Most definitely. A combination of a few things, but mostly I think I was just a pretty unhappy teenager.' She paused, not sure how much to share. But then, it was no secret. 'I was a foster child, and ended up going through a few different families as a teenager. For some reason I just couldn't stay away from trouble.'

He just nodded as he absorbed her words—he didn't look shocked, or pitying or anything like that. Which she appreciated. Her childhood at times had been difficult, but it could have been a lot worse.

'You were looking for attention,' he said, and now it was Ruby's turn to be surprised.

'Yeah,' she said. 'I figured that out, eventually.'

Although that really was too simplistic. It had been more than that.

She'd wanted to be wanted. To be needed. Even if it was painfully temporary.

'Don't look so surprised,' he said. 'I'm no expert in psycho-analysis or whatever—I can just relate. It's why I started to act. My family is overflowing with academic over-achievers. But I hated school—hated sitting still. But acting...acting I could do. It was the one thing I was actually pretty good at.'

He'd grown up to be a lot more than a pretty good actor.

'Your family must be really proud of you.'

The little pang of jealousy she felt, imagining Dev's proud family, was unexpected. That was a very old dream—one based on stability, and comfort and permanence. She'd dreamt up castles in the sky, with her own prince and toothpaste-advertisement-perfect family. But she'd traded it in long ago: for a life that was dynamic, exciting and unencumbered. *Free.*

'Not particularly,' he said, his tone perfectly flat.

His words jolted her out of the little fairy tale she'd been imagining.

'Your family isn't proud of their world-famous son? I find that hard to believe.'

He shrugged. 'I don't know. Maybe they are. I don't have that much to do with them.'

She was going to ask more, but he suddenly pushed his chair back, scraping it on the wooden floorboards.

'You ready to go?'

He didn't bother waiting for her to reply; he'd already stood up.

'I thought we'd agreed to leave separately?' she asked. All in aid of not being photographed together.

Dev shoved a hand through his hair, then, without a word, walked out of the dining room.

Ruby didn't have enough time to wonder if he'd just left, kind of balancing out being, well, *nice,* for the past few hours—when he returned.

'The staff assure me there's been no sign of paparazzi, so I reckon we can risk it.'

She nodded. Really, there was no reason to leave together at all. But still—they did.

As they left she was hyperaware of him walking closely behind her—down the stairs, then to a private exit that avoided the busy main restaurant. His proximity made her skin prickle, but in the nicest possible way.

It was probably the wine, but she felt a little fuzzy-headed as she shrugged on her coat, so she was careful not to look at him. All of a sudden the reasons why she'd refused the date felt just out of reach.

He held the door open for her, and he caught her gaze as she stepped outside.

Something of her thoughts must have been evident in her expression.

'What are you thinking?' he asked.

They'd taken a few steps down the near-deserted back street before she replied. 'You confuse me,' she said. 'I had you pegged as an arrogant bastard, but tonight you've—*almost*—been nice.'

The warmth of his hand on her froze her mid-stride. He turned to face her, his fingers brushing down the outside of her arm, touching skin when the three-quarter sleeves ended. His fingers tangled with hers, tugging her a half-step forward.

She had to look up to meet his gaze. They were between streetlights, so his face was a combination of shadows, the darkest beneath his eyes.

'No, Ruby,' he said. Quiet but firm. 'I think you had it right the other day, in my trailer.'

She racked her brain, trying to remember what she'd said— her forgetfulness a combination of being so red-hot angry at the time she'd barely known what she'd been saying, but more so just being so, so close to Dev. It was a miracle she could think at all.

'I'm not a very nice person.'

Then he'd dropped her hand, and was somehow instantly three steps away.

Her instinct was to disagree, to reassure him with meaningless words. But she couldn't, because he wasn't talking about blackmailing her for a date, or being deliberately late to dinner—he wasn't talking about her at all.

And because she didn't understand, and because in that moment there was something in him she recognised, she didn't say a word.

Instead she moved to his side, and together, silently, they started walking.

CHAPTER SIX

DEV WASN'T REALLY thinking about where they were going. He just needed to walk.

But soon the rapidly increasing light and numbers of people that surrounded them heralded the direction he'd taken—and he looked up to the many, many steps that led to the opera house. He came to a stop, and took a deep breath.

He didn't know what to make of what had just happened.

Mostly, he would've preferred it hadn't.

Tonight—and this thing with Ruby—wasn't supposed to be about any of that.

'So,' he said, sounding absolutely normal. He *was* a good actor. 'Where to now?'

This area was well lit, a flat, paved expanse between the string of restaurants edging the quay and the massive sails of the opera house. Even though it was late, it *was* Sydney on a Saturday night, so there were many people around: most near the water, although some sat in pairs or strings on the steps. But right now, where they stood, they were alone.

She lifted her chin and smiled brightly—but unconvincingly.

She really wasn't a very good actor.

'How about we just wander for a bit?'

'Perfect,' he said—and it was. He'd half expected sparky, fiery Ruby to reappear, to announce that their date was over, their deal was done, and to disappear into the distance.

At the back of his mind he was bothered that he was so re-

lieved, but, as he'd been doing so often lately, he filed that
thought away. For later—and there was always a later.

In unspoken agreement they walked slowly towards the
city—the wrought-iron railing that edged the quay to their
right, and a line of old-fashioned sphere-topped lamp posts to
their left. The breeze was cool off the water, but he welcomed
its touch, his body over-warm beneath his open-collar shirt and
suit jacket.

Ruby was talking, about *The Land,* about a play she'd seen
at the opera house one time, about the rumours of some action-
blockbuster sequel being possibly filmed in Sydney next year,
and how she hoped to work on it. At first she seemed comfortable with his contribution of nods and murmurs, but eventually
she started to draw him into the conversation. Asking questions
about Friday's premiere, about whether it was really as bad as
the papers had written today—that kind of thing.

'It wasn't my type of film,' Dev said. 'Maybe it was brilliant, just not for me.'

'So you thought it was boring?' she asked. He glanced at her,
noting the sparkle in her eyes.

'Pretty much.'

She laughed. 'So weepy family sagas aren't for you.'

'No. I'm more an action/thriller kind of guy.'

'What a surprise,' she said, teasing him. 'Although, I had
been wondering about that. Why *The Land?* Did you want a
change of direction?'

'No,' he said, automatically, and harshly enough that Ruby
slowed her pace a little, and looked at him curiously. 'I mean,'
he tried again, 'yes, that was it exactly.'

'You don't sound all that sure.'

He wasn't. Right now he should be shooting a role he'd
jumped at the opportunity to play. A negotiator in a smart, fast-
paced hostage drama, a twist on the action-hero-type roles he
was known for. But instead the role had been urgently recast,
and his contract for his next film, with the now-burnt producer,
had been torn to pieces. So here he was.

Only his previously stellar work ethic had prevented the story gaining traction. For now, the people involved had been relatively discreet, and Veronica had so far been able to mostly extinguish the—accurate—rumours.

But Ruby must have heard them—at least a hint of the truth. She watched him with curiosity in her gaze, but not the steeliness of someone determined to ferret out all the dirty details. She'd had all night to ask those questions—to push—but she hadn't.

He appreciated that.

'My agent had to twist my arm,' he said. That was the truth, at least.

He'd agreed only because he couldn't face another sleepless, pointless night in Hollywood. But he'd only traded it in for more of the same in north-west New South Wales.

Ruby was the only difference.

'You live in Sydney, right?' he asked, changing the subject.

They were walking amongst many people now—couples on dates, families, tourists with massive camera bags. If anyone recognised him, he hadn't noticed.

'Not any more,' she said.

'Melbourne?'

She shook her head. 'Not there either.' There was a smile in her voice.

Before tonight he hadn't been all that interested in getting to know the woman beside him. His interest in her had not been based around shared interests and the potential for meaningful conversation.

But at dinner, he'd found himself asking about *her,* and unsurprisingly that had led to him talking about elements of *himself* that he didn't share with his dates.

Maybe he was just rusty—it had been months since he'd gone out with a woman. Normally he had charming deflections of personal questions down to an art. He certainly didn't make a habit of welcoming them.

'If I name every city in the world until you say yes, we could be here a while.'

'And then you still wouldn't have an answer.'

They'd reached the end of the walk, and stood between the train station and ferry terminal.

Ruby was looking up at him, grinning—and waiting for him to do something with that non-response.

But he just left her waiting as he looked at her. Leisurely exploring the shape of her eyes, her nose, her lips. Beneath the CBD lights, he could see flecks of green and gold in her eyes he hadn't noticed before.

'You're beautiful,' he said, very softly, realising it was true.

Ruby took a rapid step backwards, and wobbled a little on her heels. He reached out automatically, wrapping his fingers around her upper arms to steady her.

For a moment her expression was soft. Inviting...

But then it hardened, and she shook his hands away.

'Nice try.'

'It's the truth,' he said, but immediately realised he was doing this all wrong as she glared at him. He didn't know how to handle this, why a compliment had caused this reaction.

'Look, it's getting late. Thanks for the lovely dinner. I'm going to head back to my hotel.'

She said all that, but didn't actually make a move to leave. If she had, he would've let her go, but that pause—he decided—was telling.

'If not Sydney, or Melbourne, or any other city in the world—where *do* you live?'

Ruby blinked as he deftly rewound their conversation. He could see her thinking, could see all sorts of things taking place behind those eyes.

'Wherever I feel like,' she said, slowly and eventually. 'I might stay where I've been working for a while. Or fly to stay with a friend for a few weeks. Or maybe just pick somewhere new I haven't been before, and live there.'

'But where's your base? Where you keep all your stuff?'

She shrugged. 'What stuff?'

'You don't own anything?'

'Nothing I can't keep in a suitcase.'

He took a moment to process this. 'Why?'

She smiled. 'I get asked that a lot. But the way I look at it, it makes sense. I've lived in some amazing places, seen incredible things. I'm not tied down—when I get a call offering me a job I can be on set, almost anywhere in the world, basically the very next day.'

'But don't you want a house one day?'

She wrinkled her nose. 'What? The great Australian dream of a quarter-acre block with a back pergola and a barbecue?' She shook her head. 'No, thanks.'

She spoke with the confidence of someone absolutely sure of their decision. He admired that—her assuredness. But he found it near impossible to believe. Could you really live your life the way she described?

'Most women your age are thinking marriage and babies. Putting roots down.'

'You're older than me,' she pointed out. 'Are you putting down roots? Is that what you're doing at your place in Beverly Hills?'

'Absolutely not,' he said. That was the last thing he wanted.

'Well, there you go.'

He must have looked confused, as she then tried to further explain.

'Is it so hard to believe? I told you before I'm a foster child, so my only "family" are the various sets of foster carers I called Aunty and Uncle. Nice people—great people—but, trust me, they couldn't wait to see the back of me, and I don't blame them. And nearly all my friends work in film, or did work in film, so they are scattered all over the place.'

He assumed he still looked less than convinced, as she rolled her eyes as if completely exasperated with him.

'No,' he said, before she tried again. 'I do get it.'

Didn't he, after all, live his life in kind of the same way?

Yes, he owned his home, but that was a financial decision, not one based on long-term planning—it wasn't a life goal or anything. He hadn't extrapolated that purchase into plans for the future: a wife, kids. Anything like that. In fact, he'd only ever had one goal: to act.

And now he wasn't even sure he had that.

'Do you want to get a drink somewhere?' he asked.

Ruby let the invitation bounce about in her brain for a moment.

'I should go,' she said. 'Like I said before. It's late, I—'

'But you didn't go.'

I know. She wasn't sure why. It had been the right thing to do—the right time to go. When he'd called her beautiful, she'd been momentarily lost. Lost in the moment and the pull of his warmth, and the appreciation she'd seen in his gaze. So, so tempting…

But then she'd remembered where she was—*who* he was—and why this was all a very, very bad idea.

'I should go,' she repeated. She'd meant to be more firm this time, but she wasn't—not at all.

'Probably,' he agreed. 'Based on what you've told me before—you should.'

He'd moved a little closer. *God.* He was good. He knew what he did to her when he was close. She could see it in everything he did—that arrogance, that confidence.

But unexpectedly, right now, it wasn't pushing her away.

Maybe because tonight she'd seen that confidence contrasted with moments of…not quite vulnerability, but *exposure.* He'd been raw, as if she was seeing Dev Cooper the man, not the actor.

And she'd found herself interested in that man. Oh, she'd always been *attracted* to Dev, by his looks, his charisma, by the persona his career had created. But that type of attraction was—with difficulty—possible to push aside. To be logical about. To walk away from, with the strict rules she lived by providing the impetus.

But *this* Dev. This Dev she couldn't so easily define. This Dev she wanted to know.

This Dev she wanted to understand.

No, thank you. But thank you for dinner...

It was suddenly impossible to say anything. She couldn't agree, but there was no other option.

So she was a coward and did nothing at all. But her expression must have portrayed her acquiescence, as he smiled—then grabbed her hand and tugged her after him.

They left Circular Quay, then headed a short way up Macquarie Street.

'Where are we going?' Ruby asked, belatedly.

He came to a stop. 'We're here,' he said. 'My hotel.'

They stood beneath a curved red awning—on red carpet, no less. A suited doorman stood only metres away, but when she glanced at him, he was carefully paying them no attention.

'This isn't cool, Dev, you said—'

'There's a bar on the ground floor, and the staff will guarantee we won't be disturbed—and certainly that no photos will be taken.' His lips quirked upwards—wickedly. 'I'm not inviting you to share a bottle of champagne as we roll about on my bed, Ruby.'

She knew she'd gone as red as the carpet. 'Oh,' she said. 'Of course not.'

'Shall we?' he said, gesturing at the brass-handled doors.

She nodded, and soon they'd made their way through the marble-floored foyer with its sumptuous oriental carpets to the hotel bar—a classic, traditional space. Full of heavy, antique wooden furniture, stunning silk wallpaper and chandeliers dangling with crystals, it was softly lit. A handful of people perched on bar stools, and a couple shared a drink at one table. Along one wall stretched a bench seat, upholstered in delicately patterned black and cream fabric. After Dev asked what she'd like to drink, she made a beeline in that direction, sinking gratefully into the soft cushioning, right in the corner of the room.

She watched Dev as he walked across the bar with their

drinks. He wore a dark suit, but no tie, and a crisp white shirt that was slightly unbuttoned. Somehow he made his outfit look casual and effortless, not formal at all. As if he'd happily wear the same outfit to do his grocery shopping, without a trace of self-consciousness.

The bar definitely was lit for mood, Ruby decided, but even so she was struck again by his unexpected gauntness. He didn't look unwell—just lean. But then, he'd eaten every bite of food in every course tonight…maybe he *had* been sick just like that rumour said? And now he was still putting weight back on. Or something.

She considered asking him, then immediately dismissed the possibility. Whatever had happened outside the restaurant—that moment—told her whatever was going on with Dev, whatever his private pain was, he would not discuss it tonight.

Besides—why would he? She was some random woman he'd even more randomly invited out for dinner.

She would never ask him those questions. They had this one night only.

He sat down, right next to her on the bench seat, rather than across the other side of the table as she'd expected.

Really? No. She hadn't honestly believed he'd do that. Of course he sat next to her, not quite touching—but touching was a very, very near thing.

He handed Ruby her wine glass, catching her gaze as he did so.

It was rather dark in this corner of the bar, she realised. Dark and…private.

His fingers brushed against hers and she jumped a little, making her wine splash about in its glass.

'Whoops!' she said, all nervous and breathy, and placed her glass firmly on the table, as if to somehow stabilise her thoughts.

The action was totally ineffective. She took a deep breath, but when she looked up—back into Dev's eyes—her mind went blank.

About all she was capable of at this moment, it appeared, was looking at Dev. And it *was* at Dev she was looking—not

Dev the movie star, but the Dev she'd just had dinner with. This Dev was an enigma—and this Dev, she liked.

He leapt from light to dark, revealing depth—maybe even pain?—that she never would have expected. And then he could slide so easily from teasing to darkly, insistently seductive.

As he was right now. Had he moved closer?

Maybe she had.

He knew she didn't want this, but in this way, at least, he was no gentleman.

He said he wasn't a nice person. Was this what he meant? This determined pursuit of a woman—of her—of what he wanted?

No, she decided. Not entirely. There'd been more, much more…

Ruby was losing herself in his eyes, his gorgeous, piercing blue eyes—but dragging her gaze away proved pointless, as she found herself staring at his lips.

It seemed the most natural, obvious thing in the world to lick her own lips in response.

Okay—now he *had* moved. When had he laid his arm across the back of the bench? She hadn't noticed at the time, but now it seemed a genius move, as it was so easy for his fingers to skim along the delicate, shivery skin of her neck.

Then up, up to her nape, his strong fingers threading through her hair, cupping her skull. But he didn't pull her towards him. Instead, he held her steady—but it really wasn't necessary.

As if she were going to duck her head, or look away now?

Then he was closer again, close enough that even in the dim light she could just see the red that was still in his eyes. For a moment she wondered what was wrong, felt a flash of concern for him…

But then that moment was gone, because she'd let her own eyes flutter shut, and all she could concentrate on was the feel of him breathing against her lips. So close, so close…

And then, finally, he kissed her.

For a crazy, silly moment her mind filled with images of Devlin Cooper kissing other women in movies. Of famous, romantic clinches, and of sexy, twisted sheets and picture-perfect lighting.

But then all that evaporated—as it was all make-believe. All utter Hollywood fantasy. This—this kiss—was real.

She was kissing a very real man. A man who had just teased her lower lip with his tongue. She leant into him, wanting more, needing more.

She needed to touch him, and she reached out blindly, her hand landing somewhere on his chest, then creeping up to his shoulders. His other hand was suddenly touching her, too, beginning at her waist, then creeping around to her back, beneath the little jacket she still wore. His hand splayed across her skin, not that she needed any encouragement to move closer.

He tasted like the wine they'd been sharing, like that crisp sorbet. Fresh. Delectable.

His kisses started off practised, but as she kissed him back, letting herself kiss him in the way he was making her feel, his kisses changed. They were less controlled, more desperate.

Ruby leant into him, matching him kiss for kiss, revelling in the feel and taste of his gorgeous, sexy, sinful mouth.

She felt incredible: beautiful, wanted.

She could sit here for ever, kiss him for ever…

But then his lips were away from her mouth, and trailing kisses along her jaw, up to her ear.

His breath was hot against her skin. So hot.

'Should we go to my room?'

Was that where this night had always been headed? Where they'd been headed since that dusty afternoon they'd first met?

Possibly? Definitely? Ruby didn't know—didn't care.

She just knew that standing now—on legs that would wobble—and leaving this bar for his room was the only imaginable option.

And so when he stood, and held out his hand for her, with that question still shining in his eyes, she knew what she was going to—what she had to—say.

'Yes.'

CHAPTER SEVEN

DEV LAY FLAT on his back on the sofa, staring up, in the dark, at the ceiling.

He was restless. Completely exhausted, but unable to sleep.

He'd tried pacing the considerable length of the penthouse's living areas, but it hadn't helped—from his experience pacing never did.

If anything his brain's wheels and cogs took the opportunity to whir ever faster, cramming his brain with all sorts of thoughts and ideas—leaving nowhere near enough room for sleep to descend.

He rubbed at his forehead, the action near violent. But as if he could simply erase all this crap away.

And it was crap. Useless, pointless, far-too-late-to-do-anything-about crap.

And so *random*. The stuff his subconscious was coming up with, that was building and festering inside him.

Snatches of time from his childhood.

Rare moments alone with his father.

Rarer words of praise—praise well and truly cancelled out with years and years of frustration and disappointment. At his failures—the straight As he never received, the sports he never mastered, the good behaviour he could never maintain.

And then memories of his brothers, so different from him, and yet who he'd admired so hard it hurt. Almost as much as he'd idolised his father—once.

Okay. Maybe not so random.

Of course he knew what this was about, it was as obvious as the watches his father had worn, the ones that had cost more than the average person's yearly wage, and that his father had made sure everyone noticed. But then, who could blame him? He'd worked *damn hard* for his money…

I worked damn hard, Devlin, and not so you could throw it all away. You know nothing about sacrifices—about what I would do for my family. Nothing.

He heard something—footsteps. Soft on the deep carpet.

He turned his head, and watched Ruby as she crept past. He couldn't see much in the almost pitch blackness, but she was most definitely creeping—her shoes dangling from one hand, each step slow and deliberate.

'Ruby,' he whispered. Then watched as she just about jumped out of her skin.

'Dev!'

He sat up and switched on a lamp, making Ruby blink at him in the sudden light.

She stood stock still, in her fancy dress and jacket—although her hair and make-up were somewhat worse for wear.

The reason for her déshabillé made him smile.

Although when he'd left his bedroom she'd been wearing only a sheet and a half-smile as she'd slept. *That,* he thought, was probably his favourite look for the evening. Or morning? Lord. Who knew what time it was any more?

'I thought you were asleep,' she said.

'Otherwise you would've said goodbye?' His voice was unexpectedly rough, rather than teasing as he'd intended.

'Yes—' she said. Then, the words getting increasingly faster, 'Actually, no. I mean, of course I would've said goodbye if you were awake, but I figured it was better if you were asleep. I didn't particularly want an audience for my walk of shame.'

His mouth quirked at her honesty. 'Shame, huh?'

She went pink. 'It's a turn of phrase. Of course I'm not ashamed. Just…' Her gaze flicked to the ceiling. 'This wasn't how I'd planned for the night to end.'

He didn't say 'me, either', because that wouldn't have been true.

It was just other elements of the night that had been unexpected, the moments where he'd looked at Ruby and felt...

He scratched absently at his bare chest.

He had no idea what he felt.

Her eyebrows rose, seemingly reading his mind. 'You are, at the very least, consistent in your arrogance.'

But there was a smile in her voice.

He shrugged unapologetically. 'I was right.'

She sighed, then readjusted the small gold handbag she had hooked over her shoulder. 'I should go.'

He nodded.

Dev went to stand, deciding he should at least be *chivalrous* enough to walk her to the door.

Maybe it was exhaustion. Maybe it was the way his legs had been bent on the too-short sofa, his left leg still weak from his accident—but either way, the result was that rather than ending up vertical, instead, he staggered.

Somehow Ruby was beside him, her arm wrapped tightly around his waist, just above the low-slung waistband of his boxer shorts.

'Careful!' she said, on a gasp.

Not that her slight weight would've made any difference if he'd been about to fall—which he wasn't. He'd tripped over his own feet—he was clumsy. That was all.

He went to shrug her off, annoyed at himself, and annoyed she'd thought he'd needed help.

'I'm fine,' he said. Short and sharp.

But she didn't let go, not completely. Her grip had loosened, but now her other hand traced over his skin, dipping into the slight hollows above and below his left hip.

'I didn't really notice before,' she said, very softly. 'It was dark and we were so caught up in the moment I didn't have much of a chance to look...'

Her fingertips trailed shivery trails across his belly, then up to the corrugation of his abdominal muscles—more defined than ever before. His trainer would be proud.

He meant to push her hand away, but didn't.

She looked up, straight into his eyes, and he was sure—absolutely positive—she was going to ask him what was wrong.

But at the last minute she didn't, and instead glanced away. Of all things, there was a grand piano in the corner of the room, and her attention appeared focused on its glossy black surface.

'I had a tummy bug a few weeks back,' he said, for some stupid reason feeling the need to provide an explanation. 'Lost some weight, and it's taking a while to put back on.' He shrugged. 'I have a fast metabolism.'

She looked up at him, and nodded, but didn't hold his gaze.

Her hand was still exploring, and she'd shifted slightly, so the arm around his waist was now more an embrace as she stood directly in front of him. Her fingers crept up one side of his body, tracing his pectoral muscle, over his flat nipple, then inwards to his breastbone. Then up, up, to the hollow at the base of his throat, across his collarbone, then curling, curling around to his neck.

But now her touch wasn't so gentle. She slid her fingers along his jaw, tilting his head back to her. His gaze connected with hers, darkest brown and startlingly direct.

'Is that why you can't sleep tonight?' she said, her words laced with scepticism.

'That's really none of your business.'

She closed her eyes for a long moment, then shook her head a little. 'No, of course not.'

He felt her begin to withdraw from him, her heat moving away.

His arms, that up to now hadn't moved from his sides, were suddenly around her, tugging her against him.

Her gaze fluttered up, her eyes widening. 'Dev?'

He didn't bother to explain—didn't even know how he would.

All he knew was that he wasn't ready for her to go yet.

So he leant towards her, and covered her lips with a kiss to silence her questions.

A crack between the heavy brocade curtains allowed the smallest slither of early morning light into Dev's bedroom.

Ruby lay on her side, her head propped up on one arm, staring at Dev's back as he slept facing away from her. Where the light hit his skin glowed a delicious olive: from the point of his shoulder it edged the side of his body, tapering gradually down from broad chest to narrow hips. There a sheet was bunched up, tangled around and over his legs.

He slept soundly, his breathing deep and regular.

Given their conversation of a few hours ago, she'd tried to wake him—to say goodbye. But he'd barely stirred when she'd gently touched—and later pushed—his shoulder, so she'd given up. Besides, given the shadows beneath his eyes that Hair and Make-up were spending so much effort covering up, he needed his sleep.

But she'd found getting out of his bed more difficult than she'd expected.

Before, when she'd woken alone, it had been easy. She'd basically leapt out of bed as her eyes had opened in the unfamiliar room—and reality had smacked her, hard.

What had she done?

No longer did a gaze she'd practically fallen into, or a touch that had made her whole body zap and tingle with electricity—let alone a kiss that was nothing like anything she'd ever experienced—cloud her judgment.

Now she could see the night for what it was. Not romantic, and surprising, and unexpected.

But a mistake.

Escaping had been the only option. Shoving the whole night somewhere right, right at the back of her mind where *one* day she might look back fondly and remember her date with a movie star.

Ha! More likely she'd remember what an idiot she was for falling for it.

Hadn't she gone beyond this? Beyond being impressed by looks, and a smile, and strength? Beyond decisions that were based on daydreams and chemical attraction—not sense and logic?

Apparently not—as she hadn't moved.

Dev moved though, and rolled onto his back.

In a flash Ruby was out of the bed, backing away until her heels hit the carpeted half-dozen steps that led to the penthouse's sunken bedroom.

But Dev slept on.

As she watched his chest rise up and down, Ruby felt like a complete idiot. So she didn't want him to wake up to see her still here but she *also* didn't want to leave?

She ran both hands through her hair in despair.

This was typical—there was *something* about Dev that had her thinking and acting in contradictions.

Maybe that something *is how he looked at me last night? The way he kissed me?*

Ugh! No, she wasn't going to do this to herself.

She was pretty sure she knew what she was doing—she was superimposing the heroes Dev had portrayed in his movies onto the man himself. Giving him traits that his characters—but not Dev—possessed. *Considerate, kind...or even brave, and mysterious...*

Naked, his leanness was blatantly obvious—with every breath each rib was brought into sharp relief. But maybe it was just what he said? A brief illness?

But none of the rumours rang true to Ruby. She didn't believe that he'd been sick, and if he pined for his supermodel ex, he was hiding it remarkably well. And party drugs? It just didn't fit.

She was sure there was something more—something darker. That there were layers to Devlin Cooper.

Or—maybe she should look at this more objectively.

He'd pursued her relentlessly, had arrogantly assumed he'd

get her into bed on the first night—and then promptly had, by being the perfect, charming date. In order to get just what he'd wanted, he'd become her ideal leading man.

He'd done what he was good at—act.

Yes. That was what had happened.

Here was no tortured soul—but simply an arrogant movie star.

So, silently, Ruby dressed, and, again in bare feet, made her escape.

She appreciated the lady at the concierge desk who raised not an eyebrow at her attire, and called her a taxi. Minutes later she was at her hotel, lying flat on her unslept-on bed.

She expected to be full of regret. She certainly should be.

She expected to be berating herself. Furious with herself.

And, she was—that was exactly what her brain was repeating in her head: that she'd made a mistake, that she'd been an idiot, what had she been thinking?

But instead all she could *feel* were memories of that moment she'd stared up into his eyes after he'd nearly fallen. Or out in the street outside the restaurant. Or the way he'd looked at her just before he'd kissed her in the bar.

Pain, passion. And lust, yes…but it had still been…special. In her heart—no matter what her brain was saying—she believed that she was different, that last night was special.

'And how stupid is that?' she said, aloud, and headed for a long, hot, shower.

CHAPTER EIGHT

WITH A LESS THAN elegant—but effective—movement, Ruby slammed the car door closed with her hip. She considered attempting to push the lock button on her key ring, but after thinking about how she would do that without putting down the pile of papers in her arms—and potentially seeing them fly off over the horizon in the stiff breeze—she decided her hire car was safe enough in a paddock in the middle of nowhere.

In her arms she balanced a reprint of this afternoon's sides, in blue to indicate they were the corrected versions. Today they were filming at the old farmhouse, a couple of kilometres from Unit Base. Really a farming family's actual home, they'd had to repaint the exterior to a less modern hue, and redecorate a handful of rooms—all of which would be returned back to their exact original state once filming was over. So, when she jogged up the wooden steps and through the propped-open front door, she walked into a home without a trace of the twenty-first century—at least not the parts that the cameras would see.

It was an aspect of filming Ruby had always enjoyed—this game of smoke and mirrors. When watching a finished film it never failed to amaze her that it made no difference she knew a staircase led to nowhere, or that a two-hundred-year-old stone cottage had really been built inside a sound studio. In the world of the film it was all real—and so she believed it, too.

Inside she stepped carefully over thick cables that criss-crossed the floor, the bright lights providing welcome warmth after the chill of the breeze outside. She squeezed between the crowds of crew until she found the on-set production assistant, who took the sides gratefully, and quickly filled Ruby in on the latest on-set dramas.

Of course Dev was there; she knew exactly which actors were filming today, so it wasn't a surprise to see him.

She'd been ready to see him this morning. To meet him at his car as had become customary. She'd practised talking him through his day, her standard nothing statements about being available to help him with anything—et cetera, et cetera. She'd been prepared, and totally fine about it—or at least had told herself that—but then she'd arrived at his car and he hadn't been there. And not in his trailer, either.

Graeme had been waiting, instead. To explain that Dev had arrived early, and would no longer require her assistance on set. Given his week of perfect punctuality—but mostly because *not* having to see Dev multiple times a day had massive appeal—she'd conceded.

So really, she should still be totally prepared to see him now. Yet, when she did—carefully only in her peripheral vision—she felt herself react, despite her best intentions. She wouldn't say her heart leapt—or anything so ridiculous—but there was definitely a lightness to her belly, and her skin went warm. She was unquestionably *aware* of him.

He sat at a rough-hewn kitchen table, his legs outstretched and his booted-feet crossed. He held a cardboard cup of coffee as he chatted to the director, that man's trademark baseball cap pulled down low.

If Dev was aware of her, there was absolutely no evidence of it. In his soft cream shirt, pushed up to his elbows and open at his throat, he looked the very epitome of relaxed. Not at all bothered that the woman he'd slept with not even forty-eight hours ago was five metres away.

Had he even noticed she was there?

Who cared if he did?

She was loitering—she'd done what she was here to do. She should leave.

So she did, circumventing the gaffer and the director of photography and their vigorous discussion about the room's lighting as she stepped out into the farmhouse hallway. The whole time—and it really bothered her she'd noticed this—Dev didn't as much as glance in her direction.

She made herself walk briskly to her car, as she really did need to get back to Unit Base, after all. She slid into her seat and slammed the door firmly behind her.

But instead of putting the key in the ignition, she found herself just sitting there for a moment, staring at the house.

What was she waiting for? For Dev to come charging out of the house, to wrench open the white hire-car door and pull her into his arms?

Certainly not. That was the last thing she wanted. No one could know what had happened between them. Ever.

It was good he'd ignored her. Perfect. Exactly what she wanted. She'd been relieved this morning when he'd cancelled her babysitting services—so what was different now?

Maybe because she was so much better at logical thought without Devlin Cooper in the vicinity.

She started the car, and drove carefully over a paddock rife with dips and potholes, her lips curving into a smile that was sadder than she would've liked.

Because really, this was laughable—that she cared that he'd so blatantly ignored her. That she'd created depth and layers and a *connection* with Devlin Cooper.

When of course, absolutely none of it—just like that early-nineteen-hundreds kitchen he'd been sitting in—had been real.

The unexpected creak of the cottage's front door opening had Ruby nearly leaping out of her chair. She glanced up at the loudly ticking clock on the production office wall: seven minutes past nine.

It was late. Very late. Even Paul had left twenty minutes ago.

It must be one of the security guards, checking up on her.

As she came to that logical conclusion she let out a breath she hadn't even realised she'd been holding, and smiled.

Who else would it be? The boogie monster?

'It's just me, Craig!' she called out to the slowly approaching footsteps. 'I'll just be a few more minutes.'

Her laptop made its little 'new email' pinging sound, and so her gaze was drawn in that direction as a man stepped into the doorway.

'Craig's having a beer with my driver, but I'll be sure to let him know.'

Ruby's gaze darted up—not that she needed the visual to confirm who that unmistakeable voice belonged to.

He'd propped himself up against the door's chipped architraving, as casual as you liked, in jeans and a black zip-up jumper.

For a moment her body reacted just as it had that afternoon in the farmhouse—every cell, every single part of her, suddenly on high alert. And for the same amount of time she was irrationally pleased to see him—long enough for her lips to form into the beginnings of a smile.

And then reality hit. The smile dropped, and Ruby stood up—abruptly enough that her chair skittered backwards on the floorboards.

'What are you doing here?'

He raised an eyebrow. 'Visiting you.'

'Why?'

Dev crossed his arms. 'Because I wanted to.'

Ruby realised she was wringing her hands and so pressed her palms down hard against the outside of her thighs. 'But today—' she began, then cut her words off as she realised where she was going.

He shrugged. 'I assumed the rules still applied—that you wanted no one on set to know.'

She shook her head. 'It doesn't matter. I mean, of course I don't want anyone to know, but I don't care that you ignored me. It was good, actually.'

Her words were all rambling and jumbled, and she sighed, resisting the urge to run her hands through her hair.

What was it about Dev?

Now Dev pushed away from the doorway. 'I wasn't ignoring you, Ruby,' he said, his voice low as he walked towards her. 'In fact, I don't think it would be possible for me to ignore you.'

He stood on the other side of her desk, watching her. He was so close, close enough that too many memories of Saturday night rushed right back to the surface, despite many hours of determinedly burying them all.

Most clear was the feel of his hands on her. Skimming across her skin, pressed against her back, gentle as they traced her curves.

She shivered, and that unwanted response snapped her back to the present.

'You should go,' she said. Very calmly.

He blinked, obviously surprised. 'Why?'

She laughed. 'Come on, we both know what Saturday was. You don't need to spell it out to me. I get it.'

'Get what?' he said, his forehead forming into furrows.

She sighed loudly. 'That it was a one-off.'

'You think I came here tonight to tell you that?'

'Why else would you be here?'

'I don't know,' he said, his gaze flicking to her lips. 'Maybe I was hoping for another kiss.'

It was so unexpected that Ruby was momentarily shocked silent. *Another kiss.*

It was…almost romantic. Somehow he'd taken what they had: a one-night stand—something you'd never associate with anything sweet or innocent, or meaningful—and ended up with that. A request for a kiss.

'That would be taking a couple of steps backwards, wouldn't it?' She spoke harshly, deliberately implying a tawdriness that the night they'd shared deserved.

He took a step back, as if she'd shoved him away with actions, and not only words.

His eyes were wide, and he went to speak—but then stopped. His gaze sharpened. Darkened.

'Don't work too late,' he said.

Then turned on his heel, and left.

All week, his mum kept calling.

And every time, he let it ring out. She left messages, but after a while he didn't bother listening to those, either.

Couldn't listen, maybe?

It didn't matter.

He knew what she was calling about. The funeral. It had been more than three months now.

That first call, the worst one, hadn't been from his mum, but from his eldest brother, Jared. He was a doctor, a surgeon, actually, and he'd been using his doctor voice when Dev had answered his phone. As always, Dev had been on edge, used to his brother's patronising calls, his regular requests to visit home more often. That his mum missed him.

Never his dad.

But this call had been different. The doctor-voice had been the thinnest of veneers, and it had taken no time at all for Jared to crack. And that was when Dev had finally understood that something was very, very wrong.

A heart attack. No warning. Nothing that could be done.

Dad's dead. The funeral's next week. You can stay with Mum. It would be good for her, she's...lost.

Except he wasn't going to the funeral. And he didn't.

He was pathetic not to answer her calls, or to listen to her messages. Pathetic and weak and useless.

But he just couldn't do it—he just couldn't deal with it. Not yet.

It was ringing now, as it had every day since he'd arrived in Australia. Dev couldn't stand it, so he pushed away from his dining-room table to where his phone sat on the kitchen bench, and declined the call.

Gutless.

That was what he was.

Eventually he walked to his bedroom, around his bed and straight to the en suite. The tray of sleeping tablets was looking bare. He knew he shouldn't be taking them every night, his doctor had warned him of the dangers, of the side effects—but he couldn't risk what happened on his last film again. Back then, each night, he'd had every intention of making it to set the next morning. He'd had his alarm set well before his call, he'd re-read his script—everything. Then sleep wouldn't come at all, or he'd wait too late to take the tablet that would lead to oblivion. And by the time he woke up it was too late. Or—worse—he did wake up in time, but in the raw of the morning, before he'd had a chance to wake up, to remind himself who he was, how hard he'd worked, what he'd achieved…he honestly didn't care. He didn't care enough to get out of bed, to get to set. He didn't care about anything.

But this film was different. The mornings hadn't changed, not really—more often than not he slept through his alarm, or threw it across the room—but when Graeme knocked on the door he'd drag himself out of bed, and with every step he'd get a tighter grip of what he was doing, where he had to be, what he was doing that day.

He had his pride. He was a professional, and a damned good actor. A whole film crew was waiting for him.

Or at least it had been different. These last few days when Graeme had knocked, getting out of bed had been harder. He'd needed even more coffee once he'd hit Unit Base—enough that his own coffee machine had materialised in his trailer.

He swallowed the tablet, then cupped his hands under the running tap to collect enough water to wash it down. Water trickled down his neck, then down his bare chest, forming damp, dark spots along the waistband of his tracksuit pants.

He leant forward, staring into his eyes. Under the harsh lights, his eyes were red despite all the drops that Hair and Make-up were giving him. His face was a jumble of sharp angles and shadows, his skin dull…

This had to end.

He was over this. Over it, over it, over it, over it…

Tomorrow would be different.

He switched off the lights and flopped onto his bed, his skin too hot and his legs too restless to cover himself with even a sheet.

Tomorrow would be different.

If he kept saying it, one day it would actually be true.

Ruby hammered on Dev's front door. It was a really lovely door, with panels of stained glass, and part of her worried that she'd damage it. Only a very small part, though. A much bigger part of her wanted Dev to get his backside to Unit Base. Pronto.

'Don't worry,' said Graeme beside her. 'It won't break.'

He stepped forward with an air of much experience and put her hammering to shame, rattling the door with his heavy-fisted knocks.

The delicate glass held. The noise was deafening. But there was still no sign of Dev.

'Do you have a key?' she asked, trying to peer through the multicoloured glass.

'No,' he said.

Ruby took a step back and put her hands on her hips as she surveyed the house.

Paul had called her to his office barely thirty minutes ago, and she'd shot out of her office and to Dev's cottage in record time. Unfortunately, Dev's call had been ten minutes prior to Paul's *'Where the hell is Devlin Cooper?'* rant, and with every minute that passed—and with a twenty-minute drive back to Unit Base…

Basically she needed Dev out of his house and into his car *now*.

There were only two windows on the front of the sandstone cottage, edged in dark red brick. Both were closed, and a quick test proved they weren't going to open easily. The white-painted veranda wrapped around the side of the house, and Ruby followed it, stopping at each window to check for an entry point. So far—no luck.

The back of the house was a modern extension, with the veranda opening out into a deck with views to the mountains—not that Ruby paid any attention to it. Instead she zeroed into a flash of pale colour—curtains that were flapping through a small gap in the sliding doors. It was only a small gap—did that mean Dev hadn't closed it properly when he'd left? Or when he'd returned?

Ruby hoped like heck it was the latter, because he certainly wasn't on set—her phone had remained silent—so if he wasn't in the house she had no idea where on earth to look for him next.

She had to push the door open to create a space large enough to walk through. She stepped through the curtain, pausing a moment to untangle herself from the heavy fabric. Inside it was dark—gloomy despite the sunny day outside. And silent—completely silent.

For the first time it occurred to Ruby that maybe Dev hadn't simply slept in. She'd immediately assumed he was lounging about, deciding he had more important things to do than—you know—his job.

'Dev?' she called out. Or meant to. Instead she managed little more than a whisper.

She cleared her throat, and tried again. 'Dev?'

Again—silence. This shouldn't be surprising given the noise she and Graeme had been making was infinitely louder, and had certainly elicited no response.

But still, only now did Ruby worry.

What if the rumours were true?

She knew many celebrities kept their addictions well hidden—many more did not—but Dev... She just couldn't believe it. She'd spent a night with him—surely she would've guessed?

She stood in the lounge room, and it was clearly empty. The hallway beckoned, and she broke into a run, throwing open doors as she went.

Bedroom—empty.

Study—empty

What would she know, or could she know, really, about Dev?

She thought of his gaunt frame, the sometimes emptiness in his gaze. Not all the time, and certainly not when he'd been looking straight at her—but there'd been moments when there'd been depth and flickers of so much…

No. She needed to stop that, needed to stop imagining things that weren't there. Romanticising no more than a forgettable collection of moments in time.

And she would forget them, eventually.

Right now she needed to focus—on her job, why she was here. She needed to find Dev and get him on set.

Her phone trilled its message notification, but she didn't bother to check. She knew what it was—Paul. Wanting to know where she was, and why she wasn't on set with Dev already. Five minutes ago, even.

Another room—a larger space, a sitting room. Also empty.

The next—a bedroom.

Occupied.

The door creaked on old hinges as she flung it all the way open, and rattled a vase on a side table when it smacked against the wall.

Then she was at the bed, kneeling on the soft mattress as she reached across the wide expanse to grab onto a bare male shoulder. And shake it—hard.

'Dev! Wake up.'

A sheet was twisted around his legs, and his skin was covered in goose pimples in the freezing room, the air-conditioning unit on the wall bizarrely turned on high.

She shook him again. 'Damn it, Dev!'

Her heart raced, her breath caught in her throat.

Then all of a sudden he moved, rolling effortlessly onto his back, his eyes opening slowly.

Ruby let out her breath in a huge sigh of relief, dropping her hands onto her knees. For a minute or so she just took deep breaths, staring down at her own hands as they gripped her jeans.

'You scared me half to death,' she eventually managed.

He reached up, rubbing at his eyes, his movements deliberate and heavy. He turned his head on the pillow to look at her, his lips tipping up into a smile.

'Good morning,' he said, all husky and unbelievably sexy.

'Oh, no,' she said. 'It is *not* a good morning, Mr Cooper. You're late.'

He blinked, obviously confused. Rather than reply, he reached for her, his fingers grazing along the denim covering her thigh.

'Come here,' he said.

She scooted back, but probably not as fast as she should. He grabbed her hand before she slid off the bed, tugging her towards him with a strength she hadn't expected. Or maybe it was just that she didn't resist.

Somehow she was right up beside him, leaning over him, her legs pressed up against the bare skin of his waist, and his hip where his tracksuit bottoms had slid down just a little.

She looked down at him, at his incredibly handsome face— even in the gloom and with pillow creases on one cheek—and forgot what she'd been about to say.

He still held her hand, clasped on top of her legs, and a finger traced hypnotic patterns across the delicate bones beneath her knuckles.

His other hand reached across his body, to touch her other arm where it hung uselessly beside her—neither touching him nor pushing him away. His touch slid upwards, feather light, following the shape of her wrist, her forearm, her elbow, then jumping across, and around her, to her back. And then—he pulled her against him.

She gasped as she fell, landing across his chest. He was warm now, hot, in fact, and her body was fast catching up as his hands travelled across her back.

Ruby looked directly into his eyes, eyes that were anything

but empty. A gaze that she found compelled her, questioned her, wanted her.

So she leant towards him, towards all that, then closer, closer, their kiss mere millimetres, mere milliseconds away…

And then she was gone—off the bed and metres away, her back to him as she took deep, deep, what-the-hell-am-I-doing? breaths.

She shouldn't be doing this. No. She *couldn't*.

Then behind her, he laughed. A low, unexpected sound that reverberated all the way down to her toes.

She spun around, her nails digging into her palms as her hands formed into furious fists. 'What's so funny?'

He'd sat up, his shoulders propped against the wrought-iron bed head. His gaze flicked over her, from her long boots and jeans up to her layers of vests and thin wool jumpers to keep her warm in the cool spring air.

'You,' he said. 'This. What *is* your problem?'

'*My* problem?' Ruby said, and then swallowed, trying to re-locate her brain—and, while she was at it, any sense of profes-sionalism she still possessed. 'The only problem I have is that you were required on set—' she pulled her phone out of her pocket to check the time '—over an hour ago.'

For the shortest of moments his eyes flickered, and his ex-pression shifted. He looked—surprised? Disappointed? Angry?

Then it had all disappeared to be replaced by a look she was all too familiar with—arrogance.

He tilted his head back, so it rested against the wall. Then slowly and deliberately, he turned his head towards her, every pore of his body oozing exactly how little he cared.

It was all very…*practised*.

Ruby's eyes narrowed as she met his, trying to see past this hastily erected façade, trying to figure out…*Dev*, really.

No. She didn't have time for this.

'I need you to get a move on, Mr Cooper. So we don't lose the whole morning.'

He nodded. 'Yes,' he said. 'I can see how you would need that.'

Dev didn't move.

Ruby stepped forward, and Dev's gaze dipped to her still-fisted fingers. 'Exactly what do you think you're going to do with those?'

Instantly her fingers were flat against her thighs.

'Are you unwell, Mr Cooper?'

He shook his head. 'I think you're quite aware how healthy I am.'

Ruby's cheeks went hot, but she pushed on, now right beside the edge of the bed. 'Then I really need you to get out of bed immediately. A lot of people are waiting for you.'

He shrugged. Then he looked pointedly at her hands—again fisted. But this time she made no move to relax them. Much more of this and she might well *actually* hit him.

'Mr Cooper. I'm sure you're aware of your contractual obligations.'

'Of course,' he said, with a nod. But then did not elaborate further.

Ruby swallowed a sigh. He knew the deal—this far into filming and with Arizona due to leave the country, there was *no way* that Paul could replace Dev. Besides, it wasn't as if there were a bevy of other A-list actors banging down the producer's door.

'Fine,' she said. 'Let's get to the point. I want you on set as soon as possible. You—for reasons unknown—have chosen to stay in bed today. And—inexplicably—despite the dozens of people relying on the success of this film, wish to stay here.'

'I'd agree with that assessment.' His voice was as dry as dust, his expression patently unmoved.

'So tell me,' she said, making absolutely no attempt to sound professional any more, 'what exactly do I need to do to get you out of this room?'

At this, he smiled. A real smile—a delicious smile. A smile that moved the heat still in her cheeks to somewhere low in her belly. It was a visceral reaction she couldn't have prevented if she tried.

And Ruby had the sudden realisation that this was where Dev had been heading the whole time. To this question.

'A favour,' he said.

He'd locked his gaze to hers. A gaze she didn't have a hope of interpreting.

Why did she even bother? Hadn't she decided he was just an actor, portraying whatever emotion or personality that would get what he wanted out of a situation?

'What type of favour exactly?'

Another shrug. 'I haven't decided yet.'

She gaped at him. 'You don't seriously expect me to agree to that?'

He didn't say a word, just looked at her. Then, after a while, slid down along the mattress until his head hit the pillow. Then, as calmly as you liked, turned onto his side. His back to her.

Ruby's mind raced, considering her options.

Could she go and find Graeme? Get him to somehow strong-arm Dev out to the car?

A quick glance at Dev, and his muscled physique and sheer size nixed that idea. No, that wouldn't work.

She could call Paul?

And…what? Her job was to solve problems. Paul expected her to solve things—once he gave her a problem, quite simply it ceased to be his. It was *her* problem.

'It can't be illegal,' she said, finally.

He casually turned over, to smile that devastating smile at her yet again, his chin propped on one hand.

My God. She was helpless to prevent the rapid acceleration of her heat—even at completely inappropriate moments, her body reacted to him.

'It won't be.'

'And it can't be a…' Ruby had to look away, staring at the elaborate cornicing above the curtains '…a kiss,' she said. Then faster, 'Or anything else like that.'

In seconds he was up, out of bed, standing right in front of her, forcing her to look at him. The emptiness had gone, but what he'd exposed was impossible to interpret.

'Is that how little you—?' he started. Then stopped.

Then in a different, heavier tone, the shutters firmly up again, he spoke. 'No.'

Ruby backed away, needing to put space between them.

'So you'll come now? Right this instant?'

He nodded.

'Okay,' she said. 'Fine. A favour. Done.'

She thought she'd get that smile again—but didn't. He just kept looking at her, revealing not a thing.

So she backed away even further, right outside the room and into the hallway.

'You've got two minutes to meet me out the front,' she said, briskly. Like Production Co-ordinator Ruby, not the Ruby who'd very nearly kissed Devlin Cooper again.

She didn't wait around for him to respond, she was just out of there. Away from him, away from the mass of confusion and attraction and questions and heat that was every encounter with Dev.

Outside, on the decking, she stared up at the cloudless sky. Just stared and stared and stared.

And wondered what on earth she'd just agreed to.

What on earth she'd just done.

CHAPTER NINE

DAYS PASSED. A week.

Nothing.

Ruby barely saw Dev at Unit Base, and the few times she did get out to set he didn't even notice she was there—or at least certainly gave the impression he didn't.

When she ate dinner at the pub a few times after work, she deliberately kept her back to the door and talked and laughed with her friends as normal—because it wasn't as if she cared if Dev arrived or anything.

And then she hated herself for looking over her shoulder whenever a footfall was somehow heavier or different or whatever. Just in case.

Occasionally she'd kid herself that he'd forgotten about their deal. That he was half asleep and didn't remember, or that he'd never meant it anyway.

But she didn't, truly, believe that.

So late on a Saturday afternoon, after a six-day work week and with every cell in her body desperate to crawl into bed and sleep straight through until Monday, it didn't really surprise her to see Dev sitting on the jarrah bench seat outside her apartment.

Equally, it didn't surprise her when her heart did a little somersault. Didn't surprise her—but she wasn't exactly happy about it either.

He wore jeans, T-shirt and a black jacket. A rugby team's baseball cap was pulled down low over his forehead, and dark sunglasses covered his eyes. He pushed himself to his feet as she slid out of her car.

Ruby locked the doors, and walked towards him as nonchalantly as possible, fumbling only slightly as she located her key.

'Is this your version of going incognito?' she asked as she stepped onto the small porch. 'As I don't think you're fooling anyone.'

'You'd be surprised how many people don't recognise me,' he drawled, catching her gaze with a pointed look.

For what felt like the hundredth time since they'd met, Ruby blushed, and she turned her head to give the task of opening the door her complete attention.

'You'd better come inside before the whole town starts talking,' she said as the door swung open. 'Apparently my motel manager tops even the local hairdresser in knowing all the Lucyville gossip.'

'That's a real issue for you, isn't it?' he asked, following her inside. 'People talking about you?'

Inside her apartment Ruby wasn't exactly sure what to do. After all, she had no idea why Dev was actually here.

'I would've thought you'd understand that,' she said, throwing her handbag onto the tiny kitchen bench. 'Given how much the world gossips about you.'

Tea, she decided. She'd make them both a cup of tea.

'For me, gossip's a necessary evil. I can't expect all the perks of fame without some of the crap.'

Ruby flicked the switch on the kettle, then found two coffee mugs that she placed onto the laminate counter. One had a chip on the handle.

Somehow, making tea for Dev in this simple little apartment seemed more surreal than anything else that had happened between them. She rubbed her thumb over the chip a few times, trying to pull her thoughts together.

Why was he here? What favour was he going to ask of her?

Dev was resting both his hands on the other side of the counter, watching her. 'Ruby?'

What were they talking about again?

'Gossip,' she said, reminding herself. 'Well. I'm not famous, obviously. So there's no real positive out of people spreading rumours about me, is there? Wouldn't it be more strange if it *didn't* bother me?'

'But you seem slightly more…obsessed with maintaining a lily-white reputation. Not one whisper of scandal is allowed when it comes to Ruby Bell. No hint of the slightest moment of unprofessionalism.'

Ruby snorted most inelegantly. 'My reputation is not lily white, I can assure you.'

Dev raised his eyebrows, but Ruby just shrugged as she flipped open a box of teabags and dropped one into each mug.

'I told you the other night that I had a bit of a wild youth. Well, unsurprisingly, that type of behaviour generates gossip. A lot of gossip. Some of it accurate, a lot of it not. According to the local grapevine, it's quite frightening the number of people I slept with as a seventeen-year-old.'

Ruby smiled as she reached for the boiled kettle and saw Dev's expression. 'Don't look so shocked. I wasn't as bad as people made out, but I did enough to deserve a good chunk of my reputation. I'm not proud of myself—but it's done now. I was very young, very naïve. But I've learnt, moved on—I'm not the same person any more.'

'You're not the type of person who gets gossiped about.'

Dunking the teabags, she looked up, pleased he'd understood. 'Yes, exactly. I had enough to deal with back then without the speculating glances, the whispers and the innuendo. In fact, gossip made my behaviour worse—I confused people talking about me with people actually giving a crap about me. Although, for a while, just being noticed was enough.' Ruby paused, and laughed without humour. 'And you know what? I was the one who figured out I needed to change, that I needed to grow up, and not one judgmental comment by some know-it-all busybody made one iota of difference.'

Too late she realised she'd raised her voice, and tea was now splashed in tiny droplets across the counter.

'Oh,' she said, in a small voice. Then stepped away, snatching up a tea towel and blotting ineffectually at the hot liquid.

Dev was now in the kitchen with her, and he reached out, taking the towel from her.

'What happened?' he asked.

She looked down at her feet, and wiggled her toes in her ballet flats.

'I didn't say anything happened,' she said.

'But it did.'

She looked up abruptly, her lips beginning to form the words and sentences to explain…

Then she realised she was standing in a two-and-a-half-star holiday apartment with peeling vinyl flooring with one of the most famous men in the world.

No, he really didn't need to know about any of what happened.

So she remained silent.

For a long minute she was sure he was going to push—but he didn't.

Instead he calmly picked up the coffee mugs and tipped their remaining contents down the sink.

'We don't really have any time for a drink, anyway,' he said, his back still to her.

'Why's that?' she replied, for a moment, confused. Then, in a flash, she remembered—the only possible reason why he was here. She swallowed. 'The favour.'

He turned slowly, then leant his hips against the cabinets. Belatedly, he nodded.

'Our plane leaves in just over an hour.'

Ruby knew her mouth was gaping open, but was helpless to do anything about it.

Dev smiled. A devilish smile that was becoming so, so familiar.

'We have a party to attend. In Sydney. No time to drive so I chartered a plane.'

As you did.

'A party?' Ruby asked, when her jaw had begun functioning again.

'It's just casual, at a private home. A birthday party of a—friend.'

He said it as if that was all the information she could possibly need. When she stood, just staring at him, his eyes narrowed impatiently.

'You really need to go pack.'

'What if I have plans tonight?' she asked.

He shrugged. 'You agreed to the deal.'

'I didn't agree to put my life on hold at your whim.'

He grinned. 'Lord, Ruby, I do like you.'

She shook her head, dismissing what he said. 'I have plans tonight.'

Plans involving instant noodles and a small pile of romantic comedy DVDs, but still—plans.

'Well, you should've thought of that at the time. Negotiated appropriate methods of notification of the favour or something—but, you didn't. So—here we are. And I'd like to cash in my favour. Tonight.'

Ruby considered continuing her argument. Or just flat out refusing to go. He wouldn't, after all, drag her out of her apartment against her will.

Maybe he saw what she was thinking in her eyes.

'It's just a party, Ruby. Nothing sinister, I promise. You might even have fun.'

But still, she hesitated. He was so brash, so sure of getting his way...

'I really don't want to go on my own.'

That sentence was said much more harshly than what had come before. But oddly, without the same self-assurance. Quite the opposite, in fact.

And so, somehow, she found herself packing her little red carry-on suitcase.

Then minutes later she was sitting beside him in the back seat of Dev's four-wheel drive, zipping along as Graeme drove them to the airport. And to the mysterious party beyond.

The luxurious Cessna took less than an hour to cover the four hundred and fifty kilometres between the single-runway Lucyville airport—the home of the local aero-club and certainly no commercial airlines or chartered jets—and the private terminal adjacent to Sydney International airport.

Unsurprisingly, Ruby had asked a lot of questions in the drive to the Lucyville airport. Dev had responded carefully with as few words as possible:

Whose party is it? *Ros.*

And she was? *A friend.* He'd managed to say this more confidently this time—regardless, Ruby had still raised an eyebrow.

How many people could be there? *Fifty?* He had no idea.

Where was it? *Her house.*

Why don't you want to go alone?

To this, he'd simply shrugged, and by then they'd arrived at the small strip of tarmac amongst the patchwork paddocks—and there was no more time for questions.

Take-off was taken up with a safety demonstration by their stewardess, plus a bit of oohing and aahing by Ruby over their plush leather seats that faced each other and the glossy cabinetry in the little food and beverage galley behind the cockpit.

'This is completely awesome,' she'd said at the time. Dev agreed—money made life a lot easier and, at times like this, a lot more fun.

Fortunately, in this instance, it also distracted Ruby from her quest to discover exactly where they were going.

During the short flight she was ensconced in the jet's tiny bathroom, courtesy of his explanation that they would need to drive direct from the airport to the party. This had earned him yet another glare, and then later another—from freshly made-

up eyes—as she'd buckled up next to him for landing, plucking
at the fabric of her jeans.

'I really didn't have anything suitable to wear.'

'You look fantastic,' he'd said—sincerely—running his gaze
over her brown leather heeled boots, dark blue jeans, creamish
camisole and navy blue velvet blazer.

She'd just rolled her eyes. Which—again—she'd repeated
when he'd quickly changed on arrival in Sydney.

'Two minutes to look like *that*? Really?'

But she'd smiled, and he'd been stupidly pleased that she'd
approved of how he looked.

Now they sat in the back seat of another black four-wheel
drive, this time with a new driver, Graeme having been left a
little flabbergasted back in Lucyville. But then, he couldn't do
much given Dev hadn't booked him onto the flight.

Which hadn't been a difficult decision. No doubt he'd hear
all about it from Veronica—sooner rather than later. But right
now, it was all about tonight.

Ruby made a few attempts at conversation, but all fell flat.
Instead Dev found himself staring at nothing out of the window, Sydney passing him by in a multicoloured blur of lights.
As their destination became closer, even the lights failed to register as his eyes completely unfocused.

Then he didn't know what he was looking at, or thinking
about. *Nothing* he told himself, but of course he wasn't.

Snatches of voices, bursts of laughter, moments of anger,
conspiratorial giggles. Memories. None fully formed, more a
collage, a show-reel of moments in time. All set in one place,
at one house—at one home.

When the driver pulled into the familiar ornate gates, Dev
waited for the crunch of flawlessly raked gravel—but there was
none. The tyres rolled across a driveway that had been paved
perfectly smooth some time in the past fourteen years.

The driver expertly negotiated the cars parked along the
semi-circular curve, pulling to a stop directly before the tiered
garden steps that led to the front door.

Ruby opened her own door, stepping out of the car almost the moment the car rolled to a stop. Hands on hips, she stood, surveying the house, the gardens—and the guests who flowed around them, walking up from the street in couples and groups.

Dev sent the driver on his way and joined Ruby, watching her watch what was happening around her.

Up until this moment she'd displayed not one hint of nervousness about the evening. Yes, she'd been a little bothered about the lack of time to prepare, and had sighed loudly at his halfway answers to her questions. That she was frustrated with *him,* there was no doubt.

But otherwise she'd been typically no-nonsense Ruby. Just as she was on set, she'd been calm, and focused. He'd almost been able to read her thoughts: *It's just a party. No big deal.*

Now they were here, however, he could see sudden tension in her posture.

She turned towards him, tiny lines etching her forehead.

'Who am I?' she asked.

It took him a moment to figure out what that meant.

'You mean if anyone asks?'

Her answering nod was terribly stiff.

Lord. He didn't know. He barely knew why *he* was here, let alone how he should describe his unexpected guest.

'My—'

He was going to say *date,* for the reward of that flash to her eyes—that delicious reaction of heat tinged with anger.

But tonight he found riling her was not on the top of his list of things to do.

So no—he wouldn't push, he wouldn't call this a date when he knew in her head she'd so stubbornly decreed that they would never, ever date again.

'—friend,' he finished.

It sounded lame—and like a lie. As much of a lie as calling *Ros* a friend.

And somehow it was also the wrong thing to say, as Ruby took a big step back, then looked away, staring up at the moon.

'How about we just go with work colleague?' she said, with a razor-sharp edge.

He didn't have a chance to respond, or to even begin to figure out what he'd done wrong, when she began to stride towards the house.

He caught up with her well before they reached the door, where a smartly dressed man—but still obviously a security guard—widened his eyes as he recognised him.

He opened the door for them without a word, and inside, in a redecorated but still familiar foyer, a small crowd of guests mingled.

Ruby looked at him curiously, and he knew what she was thinking. The guests were all older than them, by a good twenty or thirty years.

But then the enthusiastic chatter stilled, and one by one people turned to face him, replacing their cacophony with whispered speculation.

Then, from amongst it all, out stepped a women with silver-blonde hair styled in the sleekest of bobs, and an elegant dress that flattered a figure still fit and trim at—as of today—sixty.

Her eyes, so similar to his, were wide, and coated in a sheen he didn't want to think about too much.

As dignified as always, she approached them politely. Although her smile went well beyond that—it was broad. Thrilled.

Dev felt his own mouth form into a smile in response—not as wide, not as open, yet he still had the sense he'd been holding his breath for hours.

He reached for Ruby, wrapping his hand around hers in an instinctive movement.

'Ruby, this is Ros,' he said, 'my—'

'Mother,' she finished.

Ruby didn't look at him, she simply smoothly accepted the hand that his mum offered, and wished his mother a happy birthday.

'I'm Ruby,' she added, 'a colleague of Dev's.'

His mother glanced to their joined hands, then back to Dev, questions dancing in her eyes.

But no, he wasn't about to explain.

A long moment passed, and Dev realised he'd made a mistake. He should've hugged his mum, or something...but he'd felt frozen. Out of practice.

Then it was too late, and his mum said something that was terribly polite, and trilled her lovely, cultured laugh, and disappeared back into the crowd. A crowd now full of disapproving expressions, all aimed in his direction.

Yes, he knew who he was—the son who'd blown off his father's funeral.

This is a mistake.

He still held Ruby's hand, and he would've tugged her outside, straight back to their car, if more guests hadn't filled the space behind them. Instead, he pulled her into one of the front rooms—'the library', his mum called it, with its walls of multicoloured books and oriental carpets.

Or at least he thought he'd drawn Ruby into the room—belatedly he realised it was more Ruby doing the directing. Inside, she dropped his hand, and pushed the door shut behind them, hard enough that it verged towards a slam.

'This is your *mother's* birthday party, Dev?' she said. Then on a slightly higher pitch, 'You invited me to your *mother's* birthday party?'

He nodded, because there was nothing else he could do.

Her hands were back on her hips again, and she took a long, deep breath. 'Okay. So, do you want to hurry up about telling me *what on earth* is going on?'

Ruby was doing her absolute best to hold herself together. What she wanted to do—desperately—was throw something in Dev's direction. Something hard, preferably.

What the hell was he playing at? Just who did he think he was?

A floor lamp glowed in the corner, and flames flickered in

the fireplace, throwing soft light across the room and making the dark leather of the button-backed chesterfield lounge suite shine.

Into that shininess, Dev sank, stretching his legs out long before him. He tilted his head backwards, resting it along the back of the sofa, and stared upwards, as if the delicate ceiling rose suddenly required his full attention.

'We can go in a minute,' he said, just before she was about to speak again.

The low words—quiet and so unexpected—had her swallowing the outburst she'd had ready.

All of a sudden the fight went out of her—and all she could remember was the reason she'd agreed to come here in the first place: *I really don't want to go on my own.*

'Go?'

He looked at her. 'Yeah. There's a restaurant I like, at Darling Harbour. I won't have any trouble getting us in.'

Ruby had been standing near the door, but now she crossed the room, perching on the edge of the single chesterfield armchair directly across from Dev, her booted feet only inches from his distressed leather loafers.

'Why would you want to leave your mother's birthday party? I bet it's a milestone, too, given all these people.'

'Her sixtieth.'

Ruby nodded. 'So why leave?' she repeated.

He stood up abruptly, and shoved both hands into his pockets. 'It was a dumb idea to come. I don't know what I was thinking.'

'How was it a dumb idea to come to your own mother's birthday party?'

Dev's gaze was trained on the fire, and he stood perfectly still.

'It just was. Is.'

Now he looked at her, but in the uneven light she couldn't read a thing. 'I'm confused,' she said.

He shook his head dismissively. 'You don't need to understand. Let's go.'

His fingers wrapped around the door handle, but before he had a chance to twist it open Ruby was on her feet.

'I don't need to understand?' she asked, far from politely, stepping closer so they were almost toe to toe. 'You're telling me I'm supposed to just accept that you whisked me across the state *and* deliberately concealed our exact destination—and ask no questions?'

'Yes,' he said. 'That would be ideal.'

Dev rubbed his forehead, not looking at her. In the flickering shadows, the darkness beneath his eyes was suddenly even more pronounced.

Without thinking, Ruby reached out, running a finger whisper-soft along the top edge of his cheekbone.

At her touch, his hand dropped to his side, but otherwise he didn't move a muscle.

'Does tonight have something to do with *this?*' she asked, her fingertips tracing across to the smudges of black beneath his eyes.

For long moments, their gazes met, his momentarily open and revealing above her exploratory touch.

That his unspoken answer was *Yes,* was obvious—but there was more. A lot more.

His eyes revealed a depth of emotion she'd only seen before in glimpses. But now, right this second, he'd set it all free—for her to see.

But what was she seeing? Sadness, she knew. She recognised. And loss. Guilt?

But then it was all gone, gone as quickly as he gently but firmly took her wrist and pushed it away.

'Let's go,' he said. Again, he reached for the door.

Ruby touched him again, covering his much larger hand partially with hers.

'I think we should stay.'

He was staring at their hands. Ruby could feel the tension beneath her palm, the rigid shape of his knuckles.

'Why?'

'Because you want to stay.'

He looked up, his eyebrows raised. 'And how, exactly, do you know that?'

She had no idea. But she did.

She shrugged, deciding it best to say nothing at all. She stepped away, lifting her hand away from his, conscious that she really had no idea what was going on here. That she was the last person in the world who should be advising anyone on their own family issues.

Dev was right, really—there was no reason she needed to understand any of this. Not why Dev brought her here, not why he wanted to leave—and certainly not why Dev's beautiful mother would look at her son with such a mix of instantaneous joy and pain.

She shouldn't *want* to understand. There was no point.

She was no one to him. *A friend,* he'd said, for the evening. That wasn't even true, and yet still she'd felt a stupid, stupid kick to her guts when he'd said those words.

Work colleague was the accurate term. The only term to describe them.

She stepped away, suddenly terribly uncomfortable. As she knew all that, believed all that—and yet all she could think about was Dev, and those dark eyes, and that sorrow behind them.

'I think we should stay.'

Ruby's head jerked up at the deep, firmly spoken words. As she watched, Dev opened the door, holding it open for her.

He looked relaxed and utterly unbothered. As if he'd always been the one who'd wanted to stay the whole time, in fact.

He motioned towards the door. 'Ready?'

Ruby just nodded in response, and then he followed her out into the hallway.

The party spread from the three-storey home's expansive entertaining areas through concertinaed bi-fold doors to the garden. Tall stainless-steel patio heaters dotted the grass, and fairy lights wound their way through the ornamental hedges and carefully pruned gardenias. The thirty-metre high Ironbarks and Turpentines of the adjacent Sheldon Forest—imposing even at night—formed a towering backdrop to the evening.

It was—clearly—yet another fabulous party hosted by Ros Cooper.

For about the twentieth time in the two minutes since he'd walked out of the library, Dev changed his mind.

He'd been right. He should go.

'Devlin!'

Dev bit back a groan, but turned to face that familiar voice.

'Jared!' he said, as forced and false as his eldest brother.

He blinked as his gaze took him in. How long had it been? Two years? Five?

Jared had softened just a little around the middle, and his temples sported new sprinklings of grey. But his expression—anger mixed with frustration mixed with judgmental dismissal—that was remarkably unchanged.

Actually, not remarkable at all. Jared, like his father, wasn't known for his swift changes of opinion.

It took barely a minute for Jared to introduce himself to Ruby, to make some irrelevant, meaningless, small talk—and then get straight to the point.

'Mum's pleased you're here.'

Dev nodded. 'You're not.'

'No. You'll just end up upsetting her.' His brother casually took a long sip of his beer.

'That's not the aim.'

Jared shrugged. Over Dev's shoulder he mouthed *hello!* at someone behind them. He was always so smooth—always so perfect. The perfect son—one of two both equally, differently perfect: at school, at sport, at socialising.

Then along came Dev. Not even close to perfect.

'You shouldn't have come,' he said, as friendly as if they were discussing a footy match. 'I wish you hadn't.' Now he bothered to catch his gaze. 'But as you're here, at least try not to ruin tonight for Mum, okay? It's her first party since...' Jared swallowed a few times, and the pain of his loss was clear even in the moonlight.

Dev reached out—but he didn't know what to do. So he let his hand flop back uselessly to his side. Jared was oblivious, his stare becoming hard.

'Just don't let her down again.' Jared pushed the words out between clenched teeth—and then wasted no time waiting for a response.

'Lovely to meet you,' he murmured to Ruby, and then Dev found his gaze following his brother's suit-jacketed shoulders as he walked away, across the limestone paving and back inside the house.

A hand brushed his arm. 'Dev?'

Ruby was looking up at him, questions in her eyes. 'You okay?'

He nodded sharply. 'Do you want a drink?'

She raised her eyebrows, but let him go. When he returned a few minutes later, she'd found a small bench nestled in the garden. A man he didn't recognise sat beside her, and something he said made her laugh. A beautiful, genuine, honest, Ruby laugh.

'She's with me,' he said, sounding about as caveman as he intended as he came to a stop before them.

The guy looked up and Dev could see the exact millisecond he realised who he was. And that was all it took—the man stood up without a word, and left.

Ruby looked at him disapprovingly as he sat. 'That was rude—and inaccurate.'

He handed her her champagne. 'It's what they all expect of me. And, also, it was technically correct. You did come with me.'

She smiled, just a little. 'That's not what you meant.'

He shrugged. 'I've got other things to worry about than some guy who doesn't have the guts to stand his ground.'

She took a sip of her drink, looking out across the garden. 'Yeah, I'm getting that feeling.' Another sip. 'Are you going to tell me about it?'

'No.'

She shifted on the wooden bench, and recrossed her long legs so they were angled towards him. 'Then why, exactly, did you bring me here tonight?'

'I don't think I know,' he said, deciding she deserved honesty—even if he couldn't provide answers.

I really don't want to go on my own.

That particular moment of honesty in Ruby's apartment had definitely been unplanned. Until that moment, even he hadn't known it was true. He'd told himself that she'd make the night more fun, that she'd be—his favourite word when it came to her, it seemed—a distraction.

Looking at her now, at her eyes that were wide with concern for him, *distraction* didn't really cut it.

Because Veronica could've organised him a distraction, a stunning accessory for his arm who wouldn't have asked a single question.

But he hadn't wanted that; he'd wanted Ruby. He'd used that stupid *favour*—something he'd dreamt up in some desperate attempt to gain control of a humiliating situation, a favour he'd never thought he'd use—to get her here.

He'd manipulated her—for the second time.

And once again, he just couldn't feel bad about it.

He was glad she was here. *Ruby.* Not anyone else.

'I heard that your father died,' she said, very softly. 'Someone mentioned it, on set.' A pause. 'I'm really sorry.'

'We weren't close,' he said, dismissive. 'The opposite, in fact.'

'I'm sorry,' she repeated.

'I didn't go to the funeral,' he said, suddenly. Unexpectedly.

'You couldn't make it?' she asked, and he liked that she'd jumped to that conclusion, as erroneous as it was.

'He wouldn't have wanted me there. You could say we didn't agree on a lot of things.'

An understatement.

Dev waited for her to judge him on that decision. To tell him he'd made a mistake.

'Is that why your brother is so angry with you?'

Dev managed a tight smile. 'Brothers. And yes, that's partly why. The rest has been a lifetime in the making.'

'You're the odd one out.'

A small, harsh laugh. 'Yeah.'

'Are you close to your mum?'

He nodded.

'But you haven't seen her much recently.' He must have looked at her curiously. 'She was shocked to see you tonight, I could tell. So I guessed you hadn't popped by for dinner in a while.'

'I haven't been here in years. Ten years or more. When I saw Mum, it was somewhere else. A restaurant or something.'

'Because of your dad?'

Another nod.

For a while they were both silent, and little snippets of unintelligible conversation drifted across the breeze to them.

'That really sucks, you know,' she said, finally. 'That you have siblings, parents—and you're estranged from them all.'

He knew what she meant. That she'd had none of that. No family to be estranged from.

'Sometimes I think it would've been better if I didn't have them.'

All he associated his family with were guilt and failure—his. And disappointment—theirs. Except for his mum—but then, she got the consolation prize of worrying about her youngest son all the time.

'Now that,' Ruby said, 'was a very stupid thing to say.'

Her matter-of-fact words made him blink. 'Pardon me?'

She didn't back down—but then, she never did.

'You heard me.'

She spoke without anger, and something—something about how sure she was of his apparent stupidity—made him smile.

'I like you, Ruby Bell.'

'You keep saying that.'

He stood up, holding out a hand for her. 'I think I just figured out the reason I invited you.'

'Invited? Is that what you call it?'

But she was smiling as she wrapped her fingers around his. They were just slightly cool, but where they touched his skin they triggered instant heat.

'I reckon we go enjoy this party.'

Whatever Ruby might think, right now he didn't need to talk. But then, he didn't want a mindless distraction either.

Quite simply, he wanted Ruby.

CHAPTER TEN

LATER—MUCH LATER—Ruby leant against the mirrored walls of the penthouse's private elevator, and grinned at Dev.

'That was fun,' she said. She felt good, buzzing with a touch of champagne, her toes pleasantly sore from hours of dancing.

'Yeah,' he said, with a slightly bemused smile. 'I know.'

The elevator doors slid open, and Ruby stepped out, her boot heels loud on the foyer's marble floor. A lamp on a spindly-legged side table glowed softly, only partially lighting the room.

But two steps later, she stopped dead.

'Where am I sleeping?'

Dev laughed behind her, and Ruby turned to look at him. He'd propped his shoulders against the wallpaper beside the shiny elevator door, and he looked at her with a sparkle to his eyes.

He pointed at the floor. 'I booked you a suite on the floor below.'

'What's so funny?' she asked. But the narrowing of her eyes was more a habit now. At some point he'd stopped being *quite* so irritating.

Come to think of it, for at least half the night—more if she disregarded the whole favour debacle—he'd been quite the opposite.

'This is a private elevator. You'll need to go all the way back to the lobby. When we arrived I didn't think.'

'Oh,' she said, nodding.

Dev didn't move. His jacket was thrown haphazardly over

his arm, and part of his shirt had untucked itself. He should look like a mess. Instead he looked…rather appealing.

Dishevelled. Yes. That was the word for it.

Ruby blinked, and attempted to refocus. She needed to go to her room.

As she walked to the elevator Dev didn't move. He just stayed where he was, looking at her with an unreadable expression.

She pushed the down button—the only button on the shiny brass panel.

And waited.

Not for the elevator door to open—as it did that immediately—but for…*something.*

The doors had opened fully now, and Ruby could see herself reflected in its walls. She looked into her own eyes, trying to determine what was going on here. Why she was still outside the elevator.

Her gaze wasn't so unsure though. Her gaze was…

The doors shut again, and now all she could see of herself was the blurriest of silhouettes.

'You're still here,' Dev said.

Out of the corner of her eye she knew he hadn't moved. But he was watching her. Waiting.

Now all she could hear was the sound of her own breathing—definitely faster than was normal.

She turned, a slow, deliberate movement.

And then Dev was there, standing right in front of her. *So close.*

She tilted her chin upwards to catch his gaze.

'I'm still here.' There was a long pause. 'You're very difficult to resist, you know that?'

His gaze, already warm, flickered hotter.

She reached out, her fingers toying with the untucked hem of his shirt, then travelling upwards, tracing his buttons in slow, irregular movements. 'Maybe it's the whole world-famous-movie-star thing.'

She felt him tense beneath her fingertips. 'Maybe,' he said. But his tone was flat.

Her exploration had reached his collar, skimming across its sharp, starched edge. Then she was touching skin: the cords of his neck. His jaw. Hot beneath her touch.

'Or maybe not,' she said. Then she looked up again, looked up into those blue, blue eyes.

Who was she looking at? At Devlin Cooper, Hollywood star? Or Dev, the man who made her heart flip, and who managed to make her smile just as regularly as he pushed her buttons? Who made her breath catch when he allowed her a glimpse of his true self? The man who'd calmly cleaned up her kitchen and who'd reached for her hand in his mother's front hall?

Could he tell that for her there really was no question?

Yes, she thought as he leant towards her, and as she stood on impatient tiptoes.

Yes, she thought as their lips finally met, and as he pulled her tight against him—and before the incredible touch of his mouth obliterated the possibility of any further thinking at all.

Dev woke, gradually. It was dark—very much night still.

As his eyes adjusted in the blackness, Ruby's shape materialised before him. She slept on her side, facing him. He liked the way the sheet followed her shape, up along the long length of her legs, over the roundness of her hips, then down to the dip of her waist.

She was asleep, her breathing slow and regular.

How long had he been asleep for?

He turned over, reaching for his phone on the bedside table. Pressing the button to make the screen illuminate simply confirmed what he'd suspected: it was two in the morning. He'd slept for less than an hour.

He bit back a groan. What had he expected? One visit to see his mum and suddenly life would be back to normal? He'd finally be able to sleep?

Well—yes. That was exactly it.

It was exactly why after all these weeks he'd finally sat down about twenty-four hours ago—once again unable to sleep—and listened to every single one of his mother's voicemail messages, no matter how much it hurt.

The decision to charter a flight and attend the party had come much later the next day, out of the blue. He hadn't questioned it at the time, nor his decision to take Ruby with him.

And he didn't regret either decision. Tonight had been…he didn't know. Something good. A step forward maybe.

To where he had no idea, but the sense of moving in any direction was certainly a welcome contrast to the past few months.

Except—he still couldn't sleep.

He wasn't magically cured.

It made him want to hit something.

Instead, he pushed himself off the bed in jerky, frustrated movements, and headed for the en suite. He shut the door carefully behind him before switching on the light, not wanting to wake Ruby.

Someone had ensured his zip-up bag of toiletry supplies had made it into the bathroom, and he barely had to look into it to find the familiar tray of tablets. A moment later he'd pushed a couple out onto his hand, but, rather than transferring them to his mouth, he found himself just staring at them.

He was reluctant to take them with Ruby here. They lasted a good five hours, and if Ruby tried to wake him before then he'd be groggy, a mess.

Last time she stayed with him, he'd lain on the couch, wanting to put distance between himself and Ruby. Then, after her aborted attempt to leave, he hadn't thought twice about his tablets. He'd known she'd be gone in the morning, and told himself he didn't care—that it was exactly what he wanted.

But tonight that option held no appeal. He didn't want to retreat to another room, and he didn't want to be a drugged-out lump beside her.

Was it so much to ask? A night where he got to be normal again? Where he could sleep beside a beautiful woman with only thoughts of *her* in his stupid head, and not useless things he could do nothing about?

He just wanted to sleep beside Ruby. To wake beside her and not feel as if the weight of the world were on his shoulders, or that getting out of bed was an impossible option.

He dropped the tablets into the sink, then twisted the tap so hot water chased them down the drain.

Decision made, he switched off the bathroom light, and climbed back beneath the sheets.

But once there, even the gentle in and out of Ruby's breathing proved no use.

Sleep was as elusive as always. Tonight was no different from the many nights before it.

Finally, hating himself, he surrendered—to the pills, and to the necessary oblivion of sleep.

Dev was still asleep when Ruby stepped out of the bathroom. She wrapped her arms around herself as she watched him, cosy in the thick terry-towelling robe she wore. He slept just as he had that morning—was it really only last week?—when she'd agreed to the silly deal that had landed her here. Which was like a log, basically.

Now what?

Briefly she considered repeating her exit from a fortnight earlier—and simply disappearing.

But this morning, that just didn't seem right. Or, at least not an option she was letting herself think too much about.

She'd get dressed, then figure out what would happen next. After all, that would fit the theme of the last twenty-four hours—making decisions without pretty much any thought of the consequences.

Her clothes were puddled on the floor, and as she bent to gather them in her arms her familiar red carry-on suitcase caught her attention. It lay on its back, right beside Dev's backpack, in front of a wardrobe.

Disappearing was suddenly a *very* viable option, she decided as she stalked on bare feet to their luggage.

Had he really even booked her another room? How dared he assume—?

But just before she snatched the bag up, an unevenly folded note drew her attention, balanced atop the red fabric.

She'd barely read the single handwritten sentence, when she heard a sleepy laugh behind her.

'I had the concierge organise for your bag to be brought up here after you fell asleep.'

Oh.

'I thought you might want your things.'

She turned to face him. He'd raised himself onto his elbows, the sheet falling low to reveal the delicious strength of his chest.

She glanced down at Dev's note again, his neat all-capitals script.

'Cross my heart,' he added, into her continued silence.

She believed him—that wasn't the issue. It was just taking her a moment to absorb the thoughtfulness of the gesture—firstly that he'd thought to organise for her bag to be delivered, and secondly that he knew her well enough to guess her reaction at the bag's discovery.

It felt…nice.

'Thanks,' she said.

He rubbed at his eyes, his movements slow and heavy-looking. 'How does breakfast in bed sound? Room service here is exceptional.'

And just like that, she'd decided what she was doing next.

They ended up spending the day in Sydney.

With no driver—and Dev in dark glasses and a baseball cap—they headed for Bondi beach.

Ruby had pointed out an advertisement as she'd read the paper, the many Sunday sections spread like giant colourful confetti across the bed. *Sculpture by the Sea.*

Dev couldn't say he was a regular visitor to art exhibitions, but he figured he could do a lot worse than walking from Bondi along the coast down to Tamarama—with Ruby. So yeah, he was sold.

It was a mild October day, and yet keen sunbathers still dotted the beach. They both held their shoes in their hands as they walked, the sand smooth beneath their feet and the ocean as perfect a blue as the sky.

'Where's the art?' Dev asked.

Ruby smiled and pointed vaguely ahead of them, the slight breeze ruffling her hair. 'I think it starts down there somewhere?'

But really, neither of them was too worried about the sculptures.

During the short drive from the city, they'd chatted easily—a continuation of their easy breakfast picnic-of-sorts on his bed. It all stayed very light, which suited him just fine.

No talk about anything serious. No talk about last night, and certainly no talk about tomorrow.

But now, in Bondi, they'd gone quiet.

Not an awkward silence—quite the opposite. But still, Dev didn't like it.

'What's your favourite movie?' Ruby said—all in a rush, as if maybe she didn't like the silence either. 'I mean, of yours. That you've been in.'

As she walked she stared at a spot somewhere on the sand ahead of her.

'*Now You See Her,*' he said, immediately.

She looked up at him, her eyes squinting a little in the glare. 'I've never heard of it.' She paused a second. 'Sorry.'

He smiled. 'Good. It's awful. I had about two lines in it, a straight-to-video effort filmed on the Gold Coast when I was twenty.'

'And so it's your favourite because?'

'I got paid for it. My first paid role in a movie.'

They'd reached the end of the beach and paused to step back into their shoes before walking up a small ramp to the footpath.

'That's interesting,' she said. 'Not your first starring role, or first blockbuster, or first Golden Globe nomination?'

'Nope. It was the money in my bank account—as small amount as it was. Proved it wasn't just a dream—but that it could be my career.'

They walked a little further without speaking, past the famous Bondi Icebergs swimming club. Dev had been here a few times—not to swim in a pool so close to the ocean that the Pacific's waves often broke straight into it, but to the bar. For a few promotional events, the occasional dinner...

Irrationally he imagined coming back here with Ruby, in summer, to swim. For a moment he could almost see it—her hair slicked back just as it had been after her shower this morning, smiling at him across the water...

But he quickly erased that idea—he wouldn't be in Australia in summer, he'd be in Hollywood.

By then, everything would be back to how it was. And Ruby would be off working on her next film, along with all her rules about dating cast and crew, and her refusal to ever settle down in one location.

'Dev?'

Ruby had asked him a question, he realised. 'Sorry, I was...' He ran a hand through his hair. 'What did you say?'

'I was worried I'd offended you,' she said. 'Don't worry, it was a stupid question.'

He slanted her a look. 'You do know you have to ask me it now?'

But they'd reached a little temporary marquee—the start of the sculpture walk. A few minutes later, equipped with a catalogue, they'd descended a series of stairs to reach the first set of sculptures, scattered across the tiers of rocks that lined the cove and spread their way into the ocean.

Ruby stood in front of one—a giant red nail that appeared to have been hammered between the rocks, tall enough to loom above them both.

'What was your question?'

She sighed. 'It was nothing. I was just saying I was surprised that the money meant so much to you.'

'Given my background,' he finished for her.

She shifted her weight awkwardly. 'As I said, a stupid thing to say.'

'I'm not that easily offended,' he said. At least, not with her. But then—if she was someone interviewing him—he never would've answered the original question honestly, anyway.

Actually, he wasn't entirely sure he'd told anyone the truth before.

Not that it meant anything—it was a trivial thing. Meaningless.

'Having a privileged background doesn't mean I don't have an appreciation for hard work, or for money.'

'Of course not,' she said, very quickly.

He knew he could've left it at that, but as they walked further along the path he found himself explaining. 'My dad was a self-made man,' he said.

Ruby didn't say anything, but her pace slowed.

'He started with absolutely nothing—as a labourer, actually. Mum met him back then. He worked his way up, he became a builder. Then began his own construction business, and started to buy and sell property. Sometimes to renovate and sell, other times to hold, or to rent.'

They'd walked straight past the next sculpture, Dev realised. But he didn't want to stop; if he did, the words would, too.

'All he wanted for us boys was security. A secure career. A good income. A good family.'

'So he didn't want you to be an actor,' she said.

He lips quirked, but it wasn't a smile. 'No.'

Ruby didn't even glance at the next sculpture. Stairs rose above them, leading out of the cove, and they walked up side by side, Ruby's fingers brushing against the hand rail.

'I was supposed to be an accountant.'

'No!' Ruby said, and it was such an exclamation that Dev had to grin.

'That's what I thought, too. I wasn't as good at school as my brothers—Dad said it was because I didn't apply myself, and he was probably right. I just didn't like sitting still, I didn't like being quiet and studying in my room.'

'I believe that,' Ruby murmured. 'I bet you were a trouble-maker, too.'

'Yeah,' he said, smiling fondly at a million memories. 'Dad didn't like that, either.'

To their right, greenery and grass reached up to the road above them. Tiny painted totem poles decorated the slope—but Dev wasn't really paying any attention.

'So, yeah, earning my first pay cheque meant something. A lot.'

She nodded. 'Your dad must have been pleased.'

'I doubt it. I'd moved out by then.'

She looked at him, with questions in her eyes—and as they walked he found himself telling her everything. About that night when his dad had been waiting for him; when he'd been drunk—and arrogant; when he'd felt the crunch of his father's fist against his cheek.

How he'd never gone back.

Ruby just listened, letting him talk.

'You were right the first time,' he said, after a while. 'About your surprise that a wealthy kid would appreciate a pay cheque so much. Six months earlier, I wouldn't have. I *was* spoilt. I did take my life for granted. I'd never have admitted it—maybe because I didn't even realise it—but deep down I *knew* I had a safety net. I'd subconsciously given myself the option to fail.'

The footpath ended, and grassy flat parkland spread before them. Large pieces of abstract art—some whimsical, some just bizarre—attracted groups of people. A pride of lions made out of what looked like straw; a delicately balanced collection of chairs topped with two metallic acrobats, and even an over-sized mixer tap.

'But you didn't fail,' she said.

'I couldn't,' he said.

No way would he let his dad be right.

'So you did achieve what your father wanted for you: a career, financial security.'

'Not the way he wanted.'

They'd left the park, the footpath leading them to another cove, the blue-green waves splashing across tiers of huge, smooth rocks.

'Did that matter?'

He didn't know. That was the problem, *his* problem.

And now it was too late.

So he didn't answer the question. They just walked, and Ruby didn't ask again. They followed the edge of the ocean, in silence, until they hit the white sand of Tamarama beach. Ruby quickened her pace a little, and led him between sculptures—finally flopping cross-legged beside a giant turtle constructed of tyre rubber.

He sat beside her, his legs stretched out, the sand warm beneath his skin.

'A miscarriage,' she said, out of the blue.

'Pardon me?'

She was looking at the ocean. Surfers bobbed just beyond the cresting waves.

'Yesterday you asked what happened. And that's it. What made me take my life in a less scandalous direction.'

There was a deliberate lightness to her words that she didn't come close to pulling off.

'I'm sorry, Ruby.'

She nodded. 'Thank you. I'd been seeing this guy—a nice guy. From a good family, very smart, very handsome. He had his choice of anyone. I wouldn't say he chose me, though. Or at least, he didn't mean to.'

Dev held his tongue, although it was near impossible.

'It was an accident, me getting pregnant. I hadn't meant it to happen, although of course that isn't what people said.'

People. People gossiping about Ruby, judging her.

She shifted a little on the sand, so she faced him. 'But I

was *so* happy. I didn't expect it, but it was like—' she bit her lip, looking down for a moment '—like finally I'd have a family. I didn't care if it was just me and my baby, but then the father surprised everyone and decided to stay with me. He was a good guy.'

She was tracing a hand through the sand, drawing illegible scribbles that instantly faded away.

'So I had everything: my baby, a guy. It was perfect. Finally I felt like I had a purpose. That I belonged. I wasn't the girl who people whispered about, I was going to be a *mother,* and I had a boyfriend who said he'd stand by me. A *family.*'

Her hand moved from the sand, to her stomach. Somehow Dev knew she was unaware of what she was doing, the way her fingers lay across the perfectly flat line of her T-shirt.

'I was stupid, and I told people as soon as I knew. I was showing off, I guess. Over-excited—proving them all wrong. I never considered the possibility of miscarrying, and I certainly didn't understand how common it was so early in a pregancy. And then one day I started bleeding, and when I went to the hospital they told me I'd lost my baby. I felt like my world had ended.'

He couldn't just sit still any more. He reached for her, wrapping his arm around her waist and pulling her close against him. She pressed her cheek against his chest.

'That's when I figured it out—figured out that I had it all wrong. I dumped the guy—a relief for him I'm sure—and quit my dead-end job to go back to school. I decided I was all I needed in my life—that I didn't need some guy, or a family, or *anyone,* to be happy. I just needed me.'

She was so sure, her voice so firm.

But her body shook, just a little.

She tilted her chin up, to look at him, finally.

He didn't know what to say. Or maybe he knew that there wasn't anything he could say, anything that would make a difference.

Besides, that wasn't what she wanted. It wasn't what he'd wanted, either, when he'd told her about his dad.

So he did the only thing that did make sense—and kissed her.

But it was different from their kisses of before—this wasn't flirty, although it was certainly passionate. It was…beautiful, and sad, and he was suddenly *sure* there was something different between them, some connection, something special. And he was the last guy to think anything as fluffy and romantic as that.

But with Ruby, on the beach, beneath the sun and beside the giant friendly tortoise, it was unlike anything he'd ever experienced.

'Oh, my *God,* it's *Dev Cooper!*'

The shriek tore them apart. Immediately Ruby retreated, shrugging off his arm in a brutal motion, and jumping to her feet.

He glanced up to see a group of teenage girls approaching him, all pointing and chattering loudly. Across the beach people were twisting on their towels to have a look, to see what all the fuss was about.

Earlier today he'd seen a few curious, wondering glances, but he'd been lucky. No one had approached him, no one had burst the little bubble that he and Ruby had so inadvertently created. After a while he'd stopped even noticing, he'd been so wrapped up in Ruby.

But that bubble was gone now—destroyed. Ruby was looking back towards the houses and the road above the beach, as if determining her escape strategy.

Not from the rapidly approaching crowd—but from him.

He was on his feet. 'Ruby—'

She had her phone in her hand. 'I'll sort out a car. You won't be able to walk back to Bondi, now.'

Not *we won't,* but *you.*

She spoke in her work voice, as professional and false as it got.

And as the girls slowed their charge to look at him almost shyly, momentarily lost for words, his pasted-on smile was equally plastic.

But then he *was* a good actor, so he submitted to the autographs, and the photos, and the screaming—while the whole time all he wanted to do was to yell and shout and tell them all to go away. To leave him alone.

Although even if they did it would be too late. Ruby was only metres away, her arms wrapped around herself, watching.

But that moment had passed. Their moment.

He told himself it was for the best, that it wasn't something he wanted, or needed.

Just like Ruby, he'd long ago made his own path.

And he walked it alone.

CHAPTER ELEVEN

ON MONDAY EVENING, Ruby nosed her hire car up the long gravel driveway to Dev's cottage. Even as she pulled to a stop she wasn't entirely sure what she was doing.

She'd been driving home from another long day, already planning what she was going to order at the pub for dinner. And then—unexpectedly—she was here.

No. That wasn't completely true.

It wasn't at all unexpected. Given the amount of time her subconscious had allocated to Dev today, her arrival here could even be considered foreseeable.

That fact didn't make it any less a bad idea.

She held the car key in her hand, and made a half-hearted attempt to reach for the ignition before stopping herself.

She was here now. She might as well go talk to him—clear the air.

Yesterday's flight home had been awkward. There was no other word for it. It was obvious neither of them had intended what had happened at the beach.

She should regret it, she knew. Why would she share something so personal with a man she barely knew?

A few times, during that long hour in the jet, she'd meant to say something. To somehow laugh off what had happened.

But it was impossible. She couldn't very well tell him: *Look, I've never told anyone else—ever—what I told you today. Just forget it, okay?*

Right.

Last night she'd lain in bed, telling herself she'd made the sensible decision to back away. That her immediate reaction to that dose of reality—as shocking as if someone had dumped a bucket of salt water on top of her—was appropriate.

He was *Devlin Cooper.* She needed to remember that. It was so easy to be seduced into reading something more into the situation, imagining so much more than there was between them, or would ever be.

He wasn't looking for for ever, and she certainly didn't want it.

So today, her mind had wandered for the hundredth time to little flashbacks of how Dev had looked as he'd leant against the wall beside the elevator; or the way he'd looked at her, that moment before he'd kissed her, down at Tamarama…

She shoved open her door, stepping out into the cool evening.

Belatedly she realised the front door was now open. Dev stood, propped against the doorframe, watching her.

Waiting for her.

'Looked like you were doing some serious thinking there,' he said as she stepped onto the veranda.

'No,' she lied, quickly. 'Quite the opposite. I was thinking we've been spending way too much time being serious.'

His lips quirked. 'How so?' he asked, a little gruffly.

Where he stood, half in the shadows and half illuminated by the hallway light, she couldn't read his gaze.

She stepped closer, attempting what she hoped was a flirtatious, happy-go-lucky, I'm-totally-cool-about-all-this smile.

He took a step backwards, gesturing for her to come in.

But she didn't. She needed to get this sorted first. They needed to both understand what this was.

'Maybe you were right,' she said. Dev raised his eyebrows. 'A few weeks ago, outside the pub. When you said we were just two single people stuck in a country town. How did you put it? A match made in heaven.'

He nodded. 'You said you didn't date anyone you worked with.'

'Too late now,' she said, with a bit of a laugh. 'Besides, some-how we've flown under the radar. No gossip.'

'Except for Graeme. Graeme thinks you're great, by the way. You should hear him on our drives into set.'

Ruby smiled. 'Well, then, Graeme is very discreet. I'll have to thank him.'

They both fell into silence.

'So what you're saying is?' Dev prompted.

Ruby narrowed her eyes. 'Isn't it obvious?'

'Not at all,' he said. But was that a sparkle in his eyes?

She gave a little huff of frustration. 'Fine.' And she closed the gap between them, and before she had the chance to lose her nerve—and just because she wanted to—she kissed him.

Not tentatively, not questioning.

When, after an age, they broke apart, she needed to take a few long breaths to pull herself together.

'That's what I want,' she said.

He was reaching for her again. 'I like this plan.'

'Just until the film is over,' she clarified as he almost carried her inside, slamming the front door behind them.

Maybe it was the sound of the door, or the distraction of Dev kissing her neck, and the shiver it triggered through her body—but her words weren't as firm, or as clear, as she'd like.

But she didn't have a chance to repeat them, as now Dev had swept her up into his arms and was carrying her to his room.

And really, now wasn't the time for talking.

Ruby had dinner with him every night, and they took advantage of all the food in his fridge—which magically doubled in volume, thanks to Graeme.

It was easy, and fun. He continued to pay her no special attention on set, although it was difficult. Especially when Ruby broke her own rules—just once—when delivering an updated copy of the day's script.

It had been a genuine, work-related visit—but the kiss behind his very firmly closed trailer door was far from professional.

The memory made him smile as he stretched out along his couch. Ruby walked back from the kitchen, a glass of red wine in her hand.

'Now don't you look comfortable?'

He smiled, and tapped the space in front of him on the striped fabric. Her eyes sparkled as she sipped her wine, then placed the glass carefully on the coffee table.

She came into his arms easily. How long had it been now—a week? A week since she'd turned up at his front door, still with her rules, but with him, and this film, a temporary exception.

But he could live with this, especially when she kissed him. When Ruby was kissing him, *that* was all he thought about, all that filled his mind.

But when she left—and she always did—then he would think.

She'd leave around midnight. Ruby said it was because sometimes she gave members of the crew lifts to set—which sounded plausible.

But it wasn't the real reason. She was keeping this light, and simple. Waking up together, or breakfast in bed, or conversations where they bared their souls—no. They were not things they wanted, not what this thing they had was about.

They both knew that.

Did she guess he still wasn't sleeping? Sometimes he thought so. She'd look at him with concern in her eyes, and occasionally he'd be sure she was going to start asking questions.

But she never did.

On set, the rumours had dissipated. Dev had done nothing to perpetuate them—excluding that one morning, he'd never missed his call, had never been anything but prompt and professional. Everyone seemed to love Dev Cooper.

And, thank goodness, there were no *new* rumours. This was Ruby's nightmare, the niggling fear at the back of her mind that suddenly All Would Be Revealed somehow, or that the paparazzi that occasionally bothered to make the trip out to Lucyville would snap a photo of her and Dev together.

Which would be difficult—given their relationship existed entirely within the walls of his cottage. Graeme got rid of any loitering cars anywhere near the property, and so far it was proving remarkably effective.

But still—Ruby worried.

And not just about becoming the subject of gossip once again, but about Dev.

She needed to go. She lay curled on his couch, her back to Dev's chest, a warm blanket covering them both. Earlier they'd been watching a nineteen-fifties Danny Kaye musical they both loved—but not enough to be rather easily distracted. It had long ago ended, the TV screen now black.

Dev was breathing steadily behind her, but she knew he wasn't asleep. She seemed to have a talent for dozing off, but not Dev. Except for that morning in the penthouse, she'd never seen him sleep. Not once.

He mustn't be sleeping. Not well, anyway. She knew that whenever she saw the red in his eyes and his skin after he washed off his day's stage make-up. She'd seen a packet of sleeping tablets in his bathroom, but she had no idea if he took them. She'd never asked.

She'd never asked about anything.

She could guess what was wrong. Extrapolate from what he'd told her at the beach that day. All the rumours had been way off. Her guess was that Dev was still processing his father's death, and his own grief. That was the cause of his weight loss, his problems sleeping, the sadness in his gaze.

But that was all it was—a guess. So many times she was tempted to ask him about it. Like right now, in this darkened room, and in this intimacy they shared.

Did he want to talk to her about it? Did he want to share something so personal with her?

Did she want him to share something so personal?

No.

On the beach, it had all been too intense. Too much, too over-whelming. He'd felt the same way, too.

She didn't want that. She couldn't want that—not when they had only weeks together.

What would be the point?

So she turned in his arms and kissed him goodbye. And, as she did every other night, drove home to her own, lonely bed.

And she told herself she was doing the right thing.

Ruby woke up with a start, blinking in the unfamiliar room.

Dev's place.

She'd fallen asleep. Her handbag was still out in the lounge room, so she turned over, planning to reach across Dev to where she knew he left his phone on his beside table, so she could check the time.

But Dev wasn't there.

She crawled across the bed, wrapping herself with a sheet before she checked his phone. Three-twelve a.m.

Far too late to drive back to her place.

She realised she didn't mind.

A thin crack of light glowed beneath the en-suite door. 'Dev?'

No response. She stood, arranging the sheet like a towel. She felt faintly ridiculous for her sudden modesty—Dev had, after all, seen her naked.

But still, just walking about his house in the nude felt like a step too far—a dose of reality in their perfect little world.

She knocked on the door, but the slight touch pushed it open.

Dev sat on the closed toilet lid, in boxer shorts only. His head had been in his hands, and as he looked up at her he raked his fingers through his hair, making one side stand up on end.

He looked—awful. Worse than she'd ever seen him, despite the much-needed weight she'd noticed he'd put on in the past few weeks.

The shadows beneath his eyes were verging on black, and his eyes were rimmed red.

He looked exhausted. Broken. Ruined.

Of course it wasn't a surprise.

But she'd made herself ignore it. She hadn't wanted to know.

It didn't fit with what she'd decided was allowable between them. This was far, far too serious.

'Oh, Dev...'

She went to his side, automatically wrapping her arm around his shoulder. She crouched awkwardly beside the cistern but didn't care. She had to do something.

But he shrugged her off.

'I'm fine,' he said, angrily. Much louder than she expected. It made her want to back away, but she didn't let herself.

'No,' she said, 'you're not.'

He looked away—at the towel rail. At nothing.

'I'm just having trouble sleeping,' he said, all dismissive. 'That's all.'

She glanced at the sink. A tray of tablets lay almost empty on the counter top.

'It's not good for you to use those for too long,' she began.

He stood up abruptly, crossing the room. 'I *know* that,' he said. He was looking at himself in the mirror, as if he hated what he saw.

Ruby straightened, but didn't go to him.

'Without them I just don't sleep. I can't.'

'Okay.'

He looked at her, his gaze unbelievably intense. 'If I don't take them, I don't sleep. And if I don't sleep, I can't—'

Act.

He snatched at something. Two tablets, she realised, sitting on the ceramic counter.

Right in her line of sight. As if he'd been staring at them.

For how long?

He tossed them at his mouth, then wrenched the tap on, gathering water in his cupped hands that he tipped haphazardly down his throat.

Everything inside her screamed at her to leave.

She'd decided she didn't want this. This was supposed to be fun, and flirty, and temporary.

Nothing that was happening right now was *any* of those things.

'Can you please leave?' he said, meeting her gaze in the mirror.

Because he asked, she nodded.

But she didn't go very far. Not to her car, and certainly not back home to her apartment.

Instead, she shut the bathroom door behind her, and crawled straight back into Dev's bed.

She didn't know what she was doing, or what she could offer him.

But tonight, she was not walking away.

After Ruby left, Dev spent long minutes in the bathroom, waiting for his whirring brain to slow.

He'd known she hadn't meant to stay, but when she had, he'd been glad.

Really glad.

Stupid, really.

Because what did it matter? Filming ended in two weeks, and then he'd fly back to LA. And Ruby would… He didn't even know. *That* was how transient this relationship was.

But even so, he'd tried again. Tried to sleep like a normal person. To fall asleep beside Ruby.

Predictably, just like last week in that fancy penthouse, sleep hadn't come. But tonight he'd really resisted the tablets.

Tonight he'd thought it might be different.

Why?

Just like how the mornings hadn't been any different? The one single variation from the murky fog that was his mornings was last Sunday, when he'd woken beside Ruby. And even that had only worked because he'd been fortunate she'd slept in so late. He'd been nearly normal.

He'd hoped that would become the norm, but it hadn't. Nights were hard. Mornings even worse. It was a constant, awful cycle of frustration—and in between he managed to be to all appearances a fully functional human being.

A miracle, probably, that on this film at least he could hide whatever the hell was wrong with him. He could hide it from Ruby.

Until tonight. Tonight he'd done a really crap job of hiding it.

He didn't think Ruby would be coming back tomorrow night. This wasn't what she'd signed up for.

He pushed the door open, not bothering to switch off the light. The bathroom light flooded the room, and the obvious feminine shape on the bed.

For a minute or more he just stood there, then gave his increasingly blurry head a shake, and switched off the light.

In the gloom he slid onto his side of the bed, and without letting himself think too much—and quite frankly with the drugs unable to do much thinking anyway—he reached for her.

She wasn't asleep, he realised, and she turned to face him in his arms.

'I'm fine,' he whispered into her hair.

'I want you to be,' she said, her breath tickling his chest.

And then his eyes slid shut, but a moment before the thick blackness of drugged sleep enveloped him he made a decision.

Tomorrow things would change. Not because he'd crossed his fingers or shouted into his brain that it would, but because he'd just lied to Ruby.

And he didn't want to do that again.

I want you to be.

Finally, he slept.

CHAPTER TWELVE

LATE ON WEDNESDAY afternoon—two days later—Dev knocked on his mother's front door. He shoved his hands in the pockets of his jeans to stop himself fidgeting, but it was a pretty useless gesture.

He was nervous.

He'd chartered another jet, and the entire flight he'd bounced his legs, or tapped his toes or *something*. Now he turned around on the spot, looking out onto the manicured front garden and his nondescript hire car, taking deep, relaxing breaths.

This really wasn't a big deal. It was his mum, and—despite everything—he knew she loved him.

Behind him the door rattled—the sound of the brass chain lock being undone, the click of the deadbolt, the twist of the door handle.

By the time the door opened, he was staring at it, waiting.

'Devlin!' his mum exclaimed, once again with a smile broader than he deserved. Then she paused. 'Is everything okay?'

She looked momentarily stricken, and he wanted to kick himself. Was a disaster the only reason she could imagine him visiting her unannounced?

Well, given the past fourteen years—probably.

'Everything's fine. Everyone's fine, as far as I know.'

She nodded, then opened the door wide. 'Well, come in! I was just going through the photos from my party. It was so wonderful to have you there.'

He nodded automatically, then reached out, grabbing his mum's hand and holding it tight.

'Mum, I'd like to talk to you about Dad.'

Instantly he saw the pain in her eyes, but she squeezed his fingers tighter.

'Good,' she said. 'Because I've got something I want to show you.'

Dev had cancelled dinner last night, and as Ruby walked to his front door late on Wednesday evening she wasn't sure what to expect.

Tuesday morning had been…eye-opening. When his alarm went off Dev just kept on sleeping, and it wasn't until she'd given him a decent shake that he'd finally woken.

He'd looked unhappy to see her, though. As if he'd wished the night had never happened, that she'd never seen him like that.

She'd felt like such an idiot, as the final pieces of the puzzle had fallen into place. That morning a few weeks back when she and Graeme had nearly bashed the front door down, Dev hadn't been sleeping in. He hadn't been so arrogant to believe his needs were more important than the rest of the cast and crew.

Something serious was going on with Dev, and she'd been at first oblivious—and then later deliberately dismissive—of the signs.

She'd been scared by how close she'd felt herself get to him, so she'd kept her distance.

Yeah, that was the word: scared.

But now what was she to do? All she could offer him was two more weeks. That was all she had. And she desperately wanted to help.

Now wasn't that a contradiction? So worried for Dev her heart ached, but so sure she had to leave.

He'd left the front door ajar, so she pushed it open, her heeled boots loud on the hallway's floorboards.

'Dev?'

He called out from the kitchen, and so that was where she

headed. He sat at the rustic dining table, cutlery, a bottle of wine and two glasses set out neatly. On his placemat only, however, lay a battered-looking notebook. He stood as she walked into the room.

'What's all this for?' she asked, taking in the soft lighting, and the scent of something delicious bubbling on the stove.

'I cooked,' he said, then added when she must have displayed her scepticism, 'Really. I make a mean puttanesca.'

She smiled, his enthusiasm completely infectious. 'Lucky me.'

He bent to kiss her, his lips firm. It was more than a quick hello kiss, and when they broke apart Ruby's heart was racing. Without thinking she brought her hand to her chest, and his lips quirked at the gesture.

'Me, too,' he said.

Dev wouldn't let her help as he confidently moved about the kitchen, so she propped a hip against the bench, and watched him as she sipped her wine.

They chatted about the day on set—about the temporary disaster of Arizona falling off the horse she was riding, the director's latest tantrum, and even the glorious cool but sunny weather.

But not the little notebook on the table.

Ruby would glance at it every so often, and after a while Dev grinned. 'I was going to explain while we ate—but you can go grab it if you like.'

She didn't need to be asked twice.

She sat at the dining table, facing Dev. But he'd slowed right down, his gaze regularly flicking in her direction.

The notebook had a brown leather cover, with Dev's surname embossed in a corner. Ruby ran a finger over it, already sure she knew who it once belonged to.

'It's your dad's, right?'

Dev nodded, but he kept his eyes focused on the pot he stirred.

Ruby opened the book. The first page was covered in numbers and dollar symbols. As was the next. A quick flick through the entire book showed it was nearly full with almost identical pages—dollar amounts. Some huge. Tens of millions of dollars. Hundreds of millions.

'What is this?'

Dev was carrying two plates piled high with pasta to the table. He placed them down carefully, then waited until he was in his seat before looking at Ruby—straight into her eyes, his gaze crystal clear.

'All I wanted, growing up, was for my dad to be proud of me.'

His voice cracked a little, and Ruby wanted to reach for him, but knew, instinctively, that now wasn't the time.

Dev swallowed. 'A cliché, I know. When I failed at that as a kid, I told myself I'd stopped caring what he thought. I used to tell myself that I wanted to become an actor because Dad would hate it, not because, deep down, I knew I was good at it. And that maybe, eventually, he'd see that.'

He kept twirling his fork, the same strands of pasta wrapping tighter and tighter.

'But he didn't. Then I left, and that was that. No more caring what Dad thought about me, no more looking to him for praise and approval. Except, then he went and died. And I realised that was all absolute crap. I've been waiting fourteen years to speak to my dad.'

'You still cared what he thought.'

Dev nodded, but then shook his head. 'Kind of. Of course I still wanted the slap on the back, the *good job, son,* all that stuff. But most of all, I just wanted to hear his voice. He worked so hard to achieve his goals, and he reached every single one. I should've swallowed my pride.'

His tone was so different from that afternoon on the beach. Now he spoke with near reverence—it was such a contrast. 'He could've called you, too,' Ruby pointed out. 'You're his son just as much as he's your father.'

Dev smiled. 'Of course he should've. But he was a stubborn old guy. Mum said he never even considered calling me.

Or coming with her when I visited. But then, I was exactly the same. As stubborn as him.'

He reached across the table, and took the notebook that was still in Ruby's hands. 'You know what this is? It's the takings at the box office for each of my movies. Every single one, right from that stupid one up at the Gold Coast that bombed. If he could find how much I was paid, that's there, too.'

He flipped through the pages, running his fingers over the print.

'Isn't that a little...?' Ruby struggled to find the right word.

'Harsh? Brutal? Mercenary? Yes. But that's Dad. That's what he understood: cold, hard cash. He could relate to that in a way he couldn't relate to my career.'

'Doesn't it bother you that this is what he focused on?'

Dev handed her back the book. Ruby opened it on a new page, now understanding the scribbled letters and numbers. It was meticulous: the box office takings across the world, DVD sales—everything.

This wasn't something thrown together in minutes—it was hours of work. Hours of research over months—years even. Crossing out numbers, updating them, adding them together.

'No,' she said, answering her own question.

'No,' he repeated.

'I went to a doctor today,' Dev said, later, in bed.

Ruby's back was to him, his body wrapped around hers.

She was silent, long enough that he thought she might have fallen asleep.

'Yes?' she said, eventually.

Her head was tucked beneath his chin, and her blonde hair smelt like cake, or cookies. *Vanilla-scented shampoo,* she'd told him, when he'd asked.

He hadn't been going to tell her this. Stupid, really, when he'd told her all that other stuff.

He hadn't even told his mum. He'd driven straight from his doctor's appointment in the city to the house where he'd grown up. Not on the advice of the GP, but because he'd planned on doing it anyway.

He'd made his decision the night before. Things had to change—*he* had to change—and no one but Devlin Cooper could do it.

'He thinks I could be depressed,' he said. Then he said the rest much more quickly, before he second-guessed himself silent. Ruby deserved to know. 'The trouble sleeping, the loss of appetite, the horrible mornings, it's all textbook, apparently.'

Had she tensed in his arms?

'I thought depression was...I don't know. When people lock themselves in their house all day. Can't work, can't function, can't...feel.' Her words were very soft, almost muffled in the sheets.

'It can be, I guess. My doctor explained the different types to me, and their symptoms. It just all fits, and the cause is pretty damn obvious. To be honest, I'm not all that surprised.'

She turned, pulling herself up a bit in the bed so her head rested on her pillow and she faced him. It was late, but enough moonlight filtered through the curtains for Dev to make out her expression; for once it was completely unreadable.

His palm felt cool against the fitted sheet, no longer touching her.

'I knew something was wrong, right from when I first met you.'

She reached for him, tracing the line of his jaw, across to his lips.

'I should've asked more questions, I should've pushed harder.'

Dev blinked, confused. 'I wouldn't have said anything. Not until now.'

She shook her head against the pillow, and carried on as if he'd never spoken. Her touch reached the fragile skin beneath his eyes, just as she had in his mother's library. 'I ignored this. I went back to my place each night *knowing* something was wrong.'

'You didn't do anything wrong,' he said. 'You *did* ask, but it wasn't the right time for me to say anything. No time was right.'

Her fingers fluttered away from his skin, and she twisted her hands awkwardly together in front of herself.

'I'm sorry,' she said.

He smiled, but she was too busy staring at her hands to notice. 'Don't be. I used to call you my distraction. I did feel when I was with you.'

In different ways. To start with it was very simple, very basic: lust. The thrill of the chase. His competitive nature to win the girl who rejected him.

But it was still heady, still an abrupt contrast to the beigeness of the rest of his days—and certainly the blackness of his nights.

And even her presence hadn't been enough to take him away from that.

But later, maybe even the first time she'd been in this room—when she'd been willing to do *anything* to get her job done, to get him to set—what he *felt* had shifted.

Oh, the lust was still there. There was something about Ruby, something about her smile, her laugh, her eyes…

But now there was more. Now there were moments of quiet that were the opposite of awkward. Times he looked at her and felt more connected to her than he could ever remember being with anyone. More comfortable but simultaneously completely off balance by his lack of familiarity with the emotions he felt around her.

'A distraction,' Ruby said, very, very softly.

Automatically he reached for her, but she moved, and his hand slid from her hip. 'In the very best possible way.'

Her lips curved into somewhat of a smile, and he knew he'd made a mistake.

'You're more than that, you're—'

But she cut him off.

'So what happens next?'

He needed a moment to refocus. 'With my depression?'

Her gaze flicked towards the ceiling. So she didn't like that word. He was the opposite—the label, in its own way, was powerful.

'The doctor gave me some pamphlets to read, and told me to have a think about it, and we'll meet again in a few weeks' time.'

'When *The Land* wraps.'

'Yeah,' he said.

'That sounds…'

'Anti-climactic?' Dev said, and she nodded. 'Kind of. We talked for a while, and even though I'd already decided to visit my mum, what he said just made it even more obvious. Depression is the symptom—I needed to resolve the cause.'

'And you think you have?'

Dev shifted his weight a little. 'Maybe. I hope so.'

Would he sleep tonight? He had no idea.

He expected Ruby to ask more questions, but she didn't. Instead they just lay there together, not touching.

More than anything he wanted to touch her, to pull her close against him again.

But if he did, she'd leave. He could as good as hear her excuses in his head.

It made no sense, none at all.

But Dev wanted her here, even at arm's length—so he didn't reach for her, and he didn't say a word.

And, eventually, he slept.

Ruby didn't sleep. She might've dozed, just a little, but mostly she just lay there, watching him.

Could it really be that easy? One visit to his mum, one battered leather notebook—and Dev was all better?

She didn't believe it.

Something had changed, though. A switch flipped, a corner turned…something like that. Not once tonight had she glimpsed a bleakness in Dev. No more little moments where he'd leave her, leave whatever they'd been doing, and retreat to wherever it was where his sadness, his regret, his guilt and his doubts lay. A weight had lifted.

She *was* happy for him. Thrilled. For him. Watching him sleep like this—*really* sleep, a true, natural sleep—was kind of wonderful.

No, just straight wonderful. Now she knew what she'd seen before, that drugged nothingness masquerading as restfulness—and the difference was undeniable.

What confused her was how *she* felt.

She felt restless, and she fidgeted as she attempted to sleep, her legs tangling in the quilt.

Finally she gave in to the compulsion to move, and climbed out of bed, walking on silent feet out of the room to avoid disturbing Dev. In the kitchen she automatically poured herself a glass of water, but she didn't drink it—just set it down on the granite bench top and walked away.

Her laptop sat on the dining-room table, from when she'd needed to make some changes to the script for Paul. She settled in front of it, flipping it open and blinking at the sudden brightness of the screen in the darkened room. She'd barely noticed the darkness, the moonlight flooding through the open kitchen blinds more than enough illumination for her to find her way.

She reopened an email that had arrived yesterday. A contact in London, who'd recommended her for a role. A great role, on a huge movie—big budget, already one confirmed big-name star.

She had to smile as she realised she was excited at the prospect of working with such a famous actress, given she had an even more famous star sleeping no more than ten metres from her right now.

Funny how quickly his job became irrelevant. At least—when they were together.

Other times, it seemed it was *all* he was. A movie star.

On set, or at Unit Base, that was who he was. Devlin Cooper, Hollywood star. Heartthrob. Sexiest man on earth. All those things.

But alone, particularly tonight, but at other times too—he was just Dev. Just a normal person. Far from perfect. The opposite of perfect, maybe.

That should be a good thing, right? That he was as normal as everybody else. As normal as her.

She sat back in her chair, stretching her legs out in front of her. It was cool, and her skin had goose pimpled where it wasn't covered by the oversized T-shirt she wore. She should really go back to bed.

She let her eyes blur, so she couldn't read the actual words of the email. But she knew them all, almost off by heart.

A request to send her CV. Such a simple thing. In this case, it was little more than going through the motions—if she wanted this job, it was hers.

And yet yesterday she hadn't sent it. Not today yet either.

Her eyes flicked to the time on the microwave. Well. Now it was tomorrow, and still she'd done nothing.

Pre-production began in three weeks, after *The Land* wrapped. The perfect amount of time to get herself sorted, maybe book herself into a hotel room for a week somewhere fun in Europe—France maybe, or Croatia—before she needed to get to London. She even knew where she'd stay—a tiny shoe-box of a room at a friend's place that she rented whenever work took her to London.

It was beyond easy. Exactly what she wanted.

She drew her legs up to her chest, wrapping her arms around herself, her chin propped where her knees touched. And just sat like that, thinking.

There was a noise, the sound of a tree branch scraping against the tin roof. It was loud in the silence, and her body jolted.

She was being ridiculous. What was she waiting for? For Dev?

Now *there* was a waste of time. He left in two weeks too, back to LA, a place where the unions could make it tricky for a foreigner to work—even if she was silly enough to daydream about things that would never happen. And that she didn't want to happen anyway.

She loved her life; it was perfect as it was. Dev just didn't fit.

And as if Dev would want her to fit into his life either.

If that thought rang a little hollow she ignored it.

Instead, she leant forward in her chair, and made the few clicks necessary to reply to the email and attach her CV. Then another to press send.

She walked back to Dev's bedroom. He still slept, flat on his back now, his chest rising and falling steadily.

She'd wanted to leave, before. She wanted to leave, now.

She should, she knew.

Dev didn't need her. He had his life back on track—there was no more need for her. No more need for her to be his distraction.

Had she ever thought she was anything more?

Yes.

That was the problem. That was why she'd tried, and failed, to keep her distance.

But she wasn't about to disappear in the middle of the night.

Tonight she'd sleep in his arms—just this once.

Because, she didn't really want to leave. That was the problem.

CHAPTER THIRTEEN

THE FLASH OF blonde hair was unmistakeable.

Dev tripped, the toe of his boot catching in the uneven dirt, and he took a moment to steady himself.

'You right, mate?'

Dev nodded. A moment ago he'd been in the middle of a conversation with the young actor as they led their horses in readiness for their next scene. Now he had no idea what they'd been talking about.

He smiled. This was crazy.

He watched as Ruby flitted amongst the crew, as busy and efficient as always.

And, as always, not as much as one glance was thrown in his direction.

His smile dropped. Up until today it hadn't bothered him, her obsession with keeping their relationship private. Of course he understood.

But after last night, it just didn't sit right.

This wasn't just some fling; he knew it.

So what was it, then?

His horse shoved his head against Dev's side, rubbing his ears against his shoulder.

It yanked his attention back to what he should be doing— running through his lines.

Right now he needed to focus. Tonight, he'd talk to Ruby.

He ended up talking to her a lot earlier than that.

Dev opened his trailer door in response to angry hammering, and Ruby flew into the tiny space. She stalked straight past him, and then kept on pacing, not even catching his gaze.

'I thought we were past this?' she asked, agitation oozing from every pore.

He held up his hands in surrender. 'I have absolutely no idea what you're talking about.'

She spun about, getting right up close to him. He knew she was frustrated, but his reaction to her closeness, to the fire in her eyes, was obviously not what she'd intended.

She shoved one of his shoulders. 'This isn't funny!'

'I have no idea if it's funny or not,' he pointed out.

Ruby took a deep breath, then one big step back.

'The Australian Film Association Awards? Does that ring a bell?'

He nodded. 'Sure. Paul spoke to me about them about an hour ago.'

'And?'

'I said I'd get back to him.'

She put her hands on her hips, and just stared at him—as if that explained everything.

Ruby sighed. 'Do I seriously need to remind you about your contract? You walking the red carpet at the awards is all about generating early buzz for *The Land*.'

She then muttered something about arrogant overpaid actors under her breath.

He reached out, wrapping his hand around Ruby's. 'I said I'd get back to him. And I will—once I speak to you.'

She blinked, then glanced down at their joined hands. 'What do I have to do with it?'

He squeezed her palm, but she didn't respond. Her gaze was now wary, and he watched as she shifted her weight from foot to foot.

He grinned. 'Normally I'd hope for more enthusiasm when I'm inviting a woman to a red-carpet event.'

Her eyes narrowed. 'Is that what you're doing?'

He nodded.

'Why?'

This wasn't the reaction he'd expected when he'd had the spur-of-the-moment idea. He'd forgotten all about the awards night, but once Paul mentioned it it seemed perfect.

'Because I want you to come with me.' Then, he added, before she could say what he knew was on the tip of her tongue, 'I *want* people to know we're together.'

She tugged on his hand. Hard. He let her go, but he didn't understand why she was doing this. *He* wanted to wrap his arms around her, to kiss her. To tell her how amazing it was to realise what he had right in front of him—what he had with *her*.

But she didn't want to hear it.

Ruby wrapped her arms around herself, rubbing her fingers up and down the woollen fabric of her oversized cardigan. 'What if I don't?'

'Why wouldn't you?' he asked, slowly. Confused.

She rolled her eyes. 'I don't know, maybe because I don't want people to know about…' she threw her hands out in front of her, vaguely encompassing them both '…whatever this is.'

'What do you think this is?'

She shrugged. 'Something fun. Temporary. *Private*.'

He shook his head. 'How can you believe that? I've spent more time with you in the past few weeks than I've spent with another woman *ever*.'

He ignored yet another eye roll, his blood starting to simmer in anger. Why was she doing this? Why would she deny what they had?

'I've told you more than I've told anyone. I've revealed more of myself to you—*given* more of myself to you—than I thought I was capable of.'

More than Estelle—or anyone—had thought him capable of.

She was staring out of the window, through a tiny crack in the curtains.

'You've gone through a tough time,' she said, as if she was choosing her words carefully. 'I was just the girl who happened to be here. The distraction.'

'That's just a *word*,' he said. 'It's meaningless, and it isn't true when it comes to you—not any more. Not since that morning you came into my room prepared to bodily drag me onto set.'

She wasn't listening. 'When you go through really emotional events, it's natural to attach yourself to someone—'

'You're just making this up as you go along,' he said. 'You don't know what you're talking about.'

She crossed the trailer, putting more space between them. 'No,' she said, 'I think I do. This was never supposed to be anything serious. And it isn't.'

'Is that the issue, Ruby? *You* don't want serious, so you're ignoring what's happening right in front of you? I didn't think I wanted it either, but I can't pretend this isn't happening. I won't.'

Ruby just shook her head, still avoiding his gaze.

'You told me on the beach the other week that you learnt you didn't need anyone, years ago. I get that. I definitely get that. But I'm not like the men from your past. I won't let you down.'

Now she turned to him, her gaze suddenly sad. 'How, exactly, will you manage that?'

'To not let you down?' he repeated.

She give a sharp nod. 'Yes. What exactly have you planned for us beyond this film, and beyond this awards night?'

He was silent. Honestly, he hadn't thought beyond that. He just knew he wanted Ruby.

She smiled, very slowly. Dangerously. 'Let me guess—we'd go back to Beverly Hills.'

'I guess—' he began. It made sense, he supposed.

'And I would work where?'

He knew this wasn't leading anywhere good, but found himself helpless to change the direction of the conversation. 'I don't know. I live in Hollywood. So—'

'So that's where I'd work.'

He ran a hand through his hair. 'Damn it, Ruby—I was just inviting you to the AFAs. That's it. We don't need to plan out every second of our future together.'

'That wasn't what I was asking you to do,' Ruby said. 'Not at all.'

She walked towards him—past him—to the trailer door.

He couldn't let her leave, not like this, and in two strides he was in front of her, blocking her exit.

'Ruby, I'm new to this, too. I don't know what I'm doing.' He managed a dry laugh. 'Obviously. But—I just know that things feel *right* with you. Different right, special right. I haven't felt this good in for ever. And don't you dare attribute that to my dad.' She snapped her mouth shut. 'I can't describe it, Ruby, but I'm not ready to let it go. I can't let you walk away from this.'

She caught his gaze, her eyes a richer brown than he'd ever seen them. 'Try and describe it,' she said, so softly he leant closer to catch the words.

'Describe it?' he repeated, then, gradually—he understood what she was asking.

'Yeah,' she said. 'Describe what we have, what it is that you expect me to give up so much for—my privacy, my independence, the career I love, a lifestyle that suits me perfectly.'

Love.

That was what she was asking. Was this love?

His mind raced, whipping about in circles but coming to no meaningful conclusion. It was a word he rarely used, that he'd never said to anyone but a blood relative.

Was it even possible to love someone after so little time?

Little vignettes of their time together mish-mashed in his brain. At the beach, in bed, alone together on set, talking, laughing, loving.

He cleared his throat. 'I never said I wanted you to give up anything for me.'

She twisted the door handle, and it clicked open loudly in the heavy silence.

Then, without a word, she left.

And Dev was powerless to say the words that might bring her back.

* * *

Ruby walked briskly back to the production office, deftly handling the standard peppering of questions and minor dramas that always accompanied her progress across Unit Base.

She sounded totally normal. Totally like herself.

And why wouldn't she?

She'd known they'd reached the end of their thing. Their fling.

Fling. Yeah, that was the perfect word. Disposable.

Love.

Ruby dug her fingernails into her palms as she jogged up the steps to her office.

No, it wasn't love.

But still, it was the word she'd been waiting for him to say.

How silly, how delusional.

Besides, she should be angry with him. Angry with him for not understanding how far she'd come, and how important—how *essential*—her independence was to her. She could never give up her career, or her nomadic lifestyle. Not for anything, and certainly not for anyone.

At the doorway to her office she paused. Inside, her team were working busily away. They didn't even look up, all so used to the frantic comings and goings of the office.

Everything was just as she'd left it. As if Paul had never called her into his office, as if she'd never stormed over to Dev's trailer, and as if she'd never so vehemently refused his invitation.

And yet everything had changed. Right in the middle of all that, right in the middle of doing what she knew she'd had to do, what she'd known had been inevitable, she'd paused. For that one moment she'd reconsidered, she'd tossed everything up in the air that she'd worked so hard for, waiting on bated breath for Dev to say the words that would…

What?

Mean that she and Dev would live happily ever after?

No way. Ruby had long ago thrown away her dreams of a knight in shining armour, of the one man that would wake up in the morning and still want her—and then again the next day and for ever.

Love was for fools, for the foolish girl she'd once been.

It wasn't for her.

Dev brought the hire car to a stop in the familiar driveway.

There weren't nearly as many cars as his mum's birthday party, but there were enough to let him know he was the last to arrive. Typical—his older brothers were *always* early.

The front door was unlocked, so he followed the buzz of conversation and squeals of children to the back of the house. In the kitchen both his brothers stood at the granite bench, beers in hand, talking to his mum as she busily chopped something. Beside Brad stood a woman he didn't recognise—a girlfriend perhaps. Outside was Jared's wife who he *did* recognise from the wedding photos his mum had emailed him years ago. Two children raced across the paving on tricycles, shrieking with exuberant laughter that made him smile. But the smile fell as the adults' conversations stalled—his presence had undeniably been noted.

He strode with determined confidence to his mum and kissed her on the cheek.

Once again she looked thrilled at his appearance, as if she'd expected a no-show, or a last-minute cancellation.

Neither of which were unprecedented.

He was ashamed of his behaviour. The worst had been most recently—skipping the funeral, avoiding her calls. He'd been incapable of processing his own emotions, telling himself he'd be no use to his mum, that he'd just cause more tension, more trouble, more hassle. That his dad wouldn't have wanted him around, anyway.

Which was all total rubbish, of course.

But well before that—the decade before that—he'd neglected his mum. His visits home to Australia were limited, and always due to work, never specifically to see her. Now he suspected it was because he'd wanted to completely box away and forget his family, a family he considered unsupportive and just completely different and disassociated from him. In his family he had always felt like a square peg in a round hole.

Not that he'd done anything at all to test that theory since he was nineteen.

Or at least, not until now.

A Sunday afternoon barbecue—a simple thing, and, he hoped, a step in the right direction.

His brothers were not exactly effusive in their hellos, but they were cordial enough. Samantha, Jared's wife, and Tracey, Brad's girlfriend, were much more welcoming—if not a little star-struck, despite doing their best to hide it. It made him smile. In this kitchen, where he'd been forced to eat his vegetables and load the dishwasher, he didn't feel even the slightest bit like a movie star.

They ate lunch outside, the table piled high with barbecued everything—prawn skewers, sausages, steak, fish. Dev didn't say much, allowing the conversation to happen around him.

'I heard you're filming in New South Wales,' Samantha asked, catching his eye from across the table. Beside her, Jared eyed Dev warily.

He nodded. 'Yeah, a romantic drama, something a bit different for me.' Dev then spent a few minutes describing Lucyville, some of his co-stars, and making generic comments about how much he was enjoying working again in Australia—which, he realised as he said it, was actually true.

Beside Sam, Jared slowly relaxed before Dev's eyes.

What had Jared honestly expected him to do? Say something inappropriate? Grunt a response? Throw food across the table?

He realised he'd tensed his jaw, and that his back had become stiff and unyielding.

As Sam chatted away, asking questions about the film industry and about LA, Dev forced himself to relax.

He couldn't get angry with Jared. Or Brad.

They were just protecting his mum, and had absolutely no

reason to believe that today was the start of something new. That he wouldn't let her down—let them all down—again.

If this was a movie, the script would probably call for him to dramatically jump to his feet—to declare his grief for the loss of his father and for the loss of more than a decade of time with his family. For never meeting his niece and nephew before today. He'd use words and phrases like *a tragedy* and *regret* and *I can only hope you can forgive me* and that type of thing, and then all *would* be forgiven, and the camera would pan back, and they'd all be one big happy family. The End.

But life didn't work like that, at least not in the Cooper household.

Today was not the day for dramatic declarations, and it was not the day to expect a magic wand to be waved and for everything to be okay.

It was, and remained, simply a step in the right direction.

He needed to earn a conversation without tense undertones. And he intended to.

Ruby was the first person to tell him he was being stupid to wish the family he had away. The words had resonated more than he'd realised—when he'd been unable to sleep, when the words had been piled on top of all the other snatches of memory and guilt that filled his subconscious to the brim. Even now they still resonated, even when sleep came—mostly—much more easily.

That was a very stupid thing to say.

So to the point, so straightforward. So Ruby.

It was why he was here. She was why he was here.

'How is Ruby?' his mum asked from the head of the table, reading his mind.

'The blonde from Mum's party?' asked Brad, and Ros nodded.

'I liked her,' she said.

'Me, too,' Dev said, without thinking. Then he cleared his throat. 'She's well, I think. I don't really know—we're just colleagues. She's the Production Co-ordinator.'

As of three days ago, it was all true, but still the words felt just like a lie.

Three days since whatever had happened in his trailer. Even now he wasn't sure what had really taken place—or what he could've done to ensure a different ending. Sometimes he was angry at her, and frustrated at the crazy assumptions she'd leapt to; how unfair it had been of her to put words into his mouth, to assume the worst of him—and to fast-forward their relationship to a point where they needed to consider anything beyond the next night, or next week.

But other times he was furious with himself. Furious for letting her walk away, for not running across Unit Base—screw what anyone thought—and saying whatever he needed to say to get her to stay. Furious for not considering how she'd react, not considering what a public relationship with him might mean to her—a woman still scarred by the gossipmongering of her past. Of course she didn't want to open her life up to the world for a fleeting fling.

But would she do it for something more?

Because what they had couldn't be on her terms any more— no more secrets, no more end dates.

And she hadn't wanted to hear that, hadn't wanted to consider it.

Until *love* had come into it. Out of nowhere. And love just wasn't something he was familiar with. That he knew how to do.

The conversations around him had moved on, but he barely heard a word.

Had it been out of nowhere? *Had* it been so shocking, so unexpected?

Yes, he'd told himself.

But now—it was a no. An honest, raw, no.

Everything he'd told her in that trailer, about what he'd shared with her, what he'd revealed—that came from a place of trust, of intimacy, of connection.

A place he'd never gone before—that he hadn't been capable of going to before.

A place of *love*.

In his mother's back yard he was surrounded by his family, and he was here because of love. Love he'd tossed away, not appreciated, and now was hoping to win back, slowly and with absolutely no assumptions. It was going to take time.

And he was doing this because in his darkest moments, when the darkness had sucked the world away from him so that he was left isolated and so, so alone, *love* was what he had craved. Love from his father, but also from his family. Love and respect were all that he'd ever wanted.

In his rejection of his father, he'd tossed away a family who loved him. And they must love him, to allow him to sit here after so long.

He'd let himself believe he'd failed his father, and his family, with his chosen career.

But he'd been wrong.

His failure was in being as stubborn as his dad. For closing himself off from the possibility of love—from his family, or from anyone. He'd rejected love, because he'd been too scared to risk it—to risk failing in the eyes of someone he loved again.

Now he wanted love back in his life, regardless of the risks.

He'd wasted a huge chunk of life alone, even if he had been surrounded by people and the glitz and glamour of his career.

But enough was enough.

He wasn't letting Ruby go without a fight.

CHAPTER FOURTEEN

RUBY PADDED TO her front door in bright pink fuzzy bed socks and floral-printed pyjamas, a mug of instant noodles warming her hands.

It wasn't late, not even nine p.m., but it had been a long day and the lure of her couch had been far stronger than that of the pub and the rest of the crew.

Whoever was at the door knocked again as she opened the door just a crack, and the insistent pressure pushed the door to the limits of the short security chain.

'Settle down!' she said, 'I'm here.'

'You're not really in a position to complain, you know.' The all too familiar deep voice froze Ruby to the spot. 'I've learnt my door-knocking technique from you. Loud and...demanding.'

She ignored that.

'Why are you here?' she said, trying to sound calm. She considered, and dismissed, pretending to assume this was work-related. Or simply closing the door and walking away.

Option two had the most merit, but...well...

It was Dev. He just didn't do good things to the logical, sensible, decision-making part of her brain.

'We need to talk,' he said.

He'd stepped up right close to her door, so he could peer through the opening at Ruby. A dim globe above the door shone weak light over him, throwing his face into angular sections of darkness and light.

He met her gaze, and his was...too hard to make out.

She told herself that was why she mechanically reached upwards to close the door temporarily to unhook the chain, and then to swing it wide open and gesture him inside.

He paused for a moment, as if gathering his thoughts or taking a deep breath, and then strode into her tiny living area. He stared at her couch and its piles of blankets and magazines, and the small collection of DVDs she'd hired from the motel's surprisingly extensive supply.

Ruby swallowed her automatic apology and the compulsion to fuss and tidy. He'd just turned up uninvited—he could stand.

'So?' she asked, crossing her arms across her chest. 'Talk.'

If he was ruffled by her abruptness he revealed none of it.

'You don't have to live in Beverly Hills,' he said. 'Or work in Hollywood. I wouldn't expect you to.'

Ruby walked back to the door. 'I think you should go.'

He raised an eyebrow. 'Why did you let me in? What else did you think I was here to talk about? The film?' He laughed. 'No. You knew this was about us.'

She shook her head, but he didn't move. He just looked at her.

Now she could interpret his gaze. It was…just Dev. Honest, with not a shred of the actor's artifice that had fallen away as their time together had lengthened.

But right now, she didn't want to deal with that. She wanted to deal with the arrogant actor she'd originally thought him to be, the man who always got his way, who manipulated people—manipulated her—to get what he wanted.

As hard as she tried, she couldn't now believe any of that was true.

She didn't know what to say, but she did walk away from the door. She remained standing, more than an arm's length away from Dev, too far away to touch.

'Ruby?'

She picked a spot on the wall to stare at—a crack in the plaster beyond Dev's shoulder. 'There is no us,' she pointed out.

'There could be,' he said. 'I want there to be.'

'I don't do relationships,' she said.

'Neither do I—don't you remember?'

That night out on the main street, under the street lamp.

'We'd need to figure out the details—find a way for our careers to work together—but they can. I don't care where I live, and I don't need to cram a million films into each year.'

Ruby sniffed dismissively. 'So you'll just hang around whatever place I end up, waiting for me to come home each day from work? Right.'

He shrugged. 'Why not? I could do with a break. I've been filming back to back my whole career. And who knows? I've always been interested in production. Maybe I could look into funding a few projects, having a go at being an executive producer or something.'

Ruby tried hard to hate him for having enough money to have these choices. But couldn't.

Besides, logistics weren't the real issue. Not at all.

'No,' she said. 'This isn't what I want.'

Now she met his gaze, so he knew she wasn't talking about career decisions.

'Isn't it?' he said. He took a few steps forward. Now touching would be really easy—all she had to do was…

She curled her nails into her palms, hoping the tiny bite of pain would bring her back to her senses.

'No. I like my life. I'm happy just as I am.'

His lips quirked, and the small movement shocked her. 'Now you're just being stubborn.'

Her eyes narrowed. 'I am not. I—'

Then he was closer, really close. Still not touching, but crowding her, as he had the day they'd met.

This wasn't fair. He *knew* what he did to her, how his nearness loosened her hold on lucidity.

She felt herself faltering, felt herself tilt her chin upwards, her fingers itch to reach out and touch him, regardless of the contradictory indignation that rushed through her veins.

No. She couldn't let this happen—she couldn't let her hormones have so much control over her. She was right. She'd made the right decision to walk away. This could never end well; this was all wrong; she didn't need this; she didn't need Dev; she didn't…

'Love.'

The single world stopped the tumult in her brain. It stopped everything, actually. Ruby's whole world went perfectly still.

Automatically she opened her mouth. To what? Question? Deny?

But Dev was too quick for her.

'I figured it out today,' he said, really softly. 'That you were right. That is the word to describe this, to describe us. *Love*.'

'I never mentioned love. I don't do love.'

She sounded just as stubborn as Dev had accused her of being. She squeezed her eyes shut, trying to regroup.

She didn't know how to deal with this. How to deal with any of this.

She was tempted to repeat what she'd said before, something about the stress that Dev had experienced, about his depression, about how it was natural for him to read more into his feelings for her at such a vulnerable time.

But she couldn't say that. Firstly because she didn't believe any of it, but secondly because that neat little explanation didn't explain *her*.

It didn't explain why she'd so haphazardly and unwisely spoken in his trailer. Words she hadn't planned and a concept she didn't even know she was capable of considering.

It also didn't explain the rest. Sharing her past with Dev— not just the version she rolled out to everyone just to get it over with: her foster child upbringing, a hint of her rebellious past. But the real stuff—the stuff that mattered. The stuff that had hurt, that had changed everything—and continued to hurt.

And it didn't explain why, despite her fear of what was happening with Dev and her ingrained habit of distancing herself from men, she hadn't run away from him. Not when it counted.

So did that mean she loved him? That she was in love with Dev?

Ruby opened her eyes, incredibly slowly. She looked up at Dev, catching his gaze and holding on tight.

Did he love her? The way he was looking at her right now, it was tempting to believe it.

To imagine that finally it was actually real.

That he was her fairy-tale prince, about to carry her away into the sunset.

Away from her life as she knew it.

To her happy ever after.

That was a fantasy.

Ruby took a deep breath, and straightened her shoulders.

With great difficulty she took a step backwards, the action suddenly the hardest thing she'd ever done.

'I don't do love,' she repeated. 'This isn't love.'

Eventually, he nodded. A sharp movement.

The next thing she knew he was gone, and she was standing alone in her tiny apartment. So she walked to her kitchen, and turned on her kettle. Then, with fingers that shook only slightly, she found a new mug, and tore open a packet of noodles.

And the night continued on exactly as she'd planned.

It had to.

The Riva, Split, Croatia—two weeks later

Ruby strolled across the wide, smooth tiles that paved Split's Riva, a line of towering palm trees to her right, the Adriatic Sea to her left.

Beside her was—*Tom?* Maybe. Some guy who'd been on the walking tour of Diocletian's Palace that she'd just completed. She'd paid little attention to the tour, to be honest, and hadn't even noticed the tall, blond thirty-something guy who now walked beside her.

Accepting his invitation for an ice cream and a walk had been a reflex action. She needed to move on—needed a *distraction,* she supposed. The occasional times she did date, it was always somewhere like this—somewhere exotic and amazing where everything was light and, importantly, temporary. No hopes, no expectations.

She hadn't touched her ice cream, and it had begun to run in rivulets down the waffle cone as it melted, trickling stickily onto her hand.

The breeze whipped off the ocean, and she shivered despite the warm autumn sun.

Tom was talking about what he did back in Canada.

'I'm sorry,' she said, cutting him off mid-sentence. 'I shouldn't have accepted your invitation. I'm…' What? Getting over a break up? That didn't sound right in her head. Too…trivial. So she just finished lamely: '…not interested.'

Ouch. Quite rightly, Tom was less than impressed. He plucked her cone from her fingers, and dumped it, along with his, in a bin, before walking away.

Ruby felt a little bad, but mostly relieved. Not her proudest moment, but she just couldn't pretend any more.

This little side trip to Split for a week before pre-production began in London was *not* exactly what she needed. It was *not* the perfect distraction.

It was not helping her relax and gain some perspective and just, well…get over it.

Get over Dev.

She'd been standing looking at nothing out at the ocean, so now she turned away, heading for the small apartment she was staying in, on the second floor of a local family's stone cottage, right at the end of the Riva.

Maybe she should move her flight forward. Choosing to be alone was obviously her mistake. Surely her friend Carly wouldn't mind if she moved in a few days early? And she was fabulous at entertaining her guests. A few nights out with her and then Dev and *The Land* would all be a distant memory…

Right. Kind of like how she'd told herself that working for Dev for another week wouldn't be so bad, even though she'd then spent every hour of her work day preventing herself from throwing herself at him and babbling something ridiculous about having made a terrible mistake...

It had been most frustrating. She had done the right thing. For her.

She didn't need Dev. She'd been absolutely happy before she'd met him. She didn't need Dev to make her life complete, to give her anything in life she wasn't perfectly capable of achieving herself. Her life was full and lovely and gorgeous—and she didn't need a partner, and certainly not a husband, to finish it off.

And she'd hate herself if she ever let herself believe differently.

It wasn't peak tourist season in Croatia, and so around her people dotted the Riva, rather than cramming it full. Some were obviously tourists—couples holding hands, families with small crowds of children. Others not so much. An older couple walking in companionable silence, a group of women chatting enthusiastically away.

I wish Dev were here.

The thought came out of the blue, and Ruby walked faster, as if to escape her traitorous subconscious.

The thing was, now wasn't the first time she'd wished such a thing.

Like on the plane to Heathrow, where one of the movies was so awful she'd turned in her seat to list all its flaws before realising that it was a stranger snoring softly beside her, and not Dev.

Or waking up in her gorgeous little Split apartment, the sun flooding through gossamer curtains onto her bed, and she'd turned and reached out for familiar, strong, warm, male skin.

But all she'd touched was emptiness.

She really needed to get over this.

She'd never spent every night with a guy like that—never in her whole life. That had been her mistake. She'd got too used to him, and now he was like a habit. A bad habit.

That theory didn't even begin to convince her.

Ruby undid the latch of the wrought-iron gate that opened to the series of stone steps leading to her apartment.

As she unearthed her keys from her handbag she remembered her sticky ice-creamy fingers, tacky against the smooth metal.

What a waste of a perfectly delicious ice cream.

The random thought made her smile, but she noticed that something was blurring her vision.

Not tears, at least, not proper ones. These stayed contained within her lashes. Mostly.

In the bathroom she washed away the remnants of vanilla and caramel, and made the mistake of meeting her own gaze.

She looked pale, and blotchy—but mostly just miserable.

Like a woman who'd just walked away from the love of her life.

And who had absolutely no idea what to do next.

The sleek, low-slung car slid to a stop at the end of the long red carpet.

It was still daylight—late afternoon actually. Dev bit back a sigh—these awards nights started early and went notoriously late. He could think of another billion or so places he'd rather be right now.

Outside, temporary metal fencing kept rows of fans a good distance away, but he could already hear them calling his name. Other cars arrived around him, and women in dresses every colour of the rainbow emerged into the sunlight in front of the glamorous, sprawling Darling Harbour hotel. Their partners in monotonous black provided little more than a neutral backdrop.

Dev watched as each couple walked only a few metres before television cameras and shiny presenters swooped. Dev knew the drill; he'd been here—or at events just like this one—a thousand times. He knew this stuff, knew the name of the designer of his suit, exactly the right thing to say and how to smile enthusiastically for every single fan's photo.

He could do this.

Graeme twisted in his driver's seat to look over his shoulder at Dev. Graeme, Dev had decided, was his new Sydney driver. He was a good guy—and he still hadn't breathed a word of his and Ruby's relationship. In this industry, such loyalty was very nearly unprecedented.

'Ready?' he asked.

Dev shook his head, but Graeme was already climbing out of his seat. 'I'll just be a minute,' he said. Not that another minute would make him look forward to the next handful of hours any more.

Besides, he was perfectly capable of opening his own door.

But—it was too late, and he straightened his shoulders, and brushed imaginary lint off his extremely sharp designer suit.

He could do this, he repeated, looking towards the red carpet, and the many ascending steps it richly covered.

Then the other door opened—the door across from him, facing the street—and he twisted around, surprised.

'Graeme, you may need a bit more practise opening—' he began, but the words stuck in his throat as a woman slid onto the leather seat beside him, and Graeme shut the door firmly behind her.

Ruby.

'Hi,' she said, very softly.

She wore a long dress in red—a deeper red than the carpet— a red that matched her name. It flowed over her body, slinky in all the right places, and with a V neckline that was…remarkable.

Her blonde hair was perfectly sleek, her make-up immaculate, her lips—of course—ruby red. It was Hollywood glamour—red-carpet glamour.

'Hi,' he managed, although it took quite a bit of concentration.

Her lips curved into a smile, but it was only fleeting. She caught his gaze with hers, and didn't look away.

Her gaze might have been rock steady, but uncertainty was obvious in her chocolate eyes, in her shallow breathing, and her fingers that twisted themselves in the delicate fabric of her dress.

'I thought that if I was with you, that if I *needed* you…' she took a deep breath '…that I would lose myself.'

He nodded, knowing now was not the time to speak.

'I used to confuse sex with intimacy, and I've worked really hard not to make that mistake again. And I haven't. But now I've made a different one—I've confused intimacy with just sex. A fling. It's taken me a few weeks to figure that one out.'

He could see the depth of emotion in her eyes, and he desperately wanted to move closer—to reach out—to touch her. But he didn't move. He needed to let her finish.

'I tried to ignore it, even when it was happening. I tried to pretend that I didn't care, that I didn't worry about you more than I can remember worrying about anyone—ever. I kept a distance between us, I closed my eyes and pretended you weren't hurting, because then I wouldn't need to admit that I hurt, too. For you.'

And for herself, too.

'I'm not familiar with love, you know?' Now she looked away, but only for a moment. 'I don't know how to recognise it—how to filter it out from my ancient habits—to distinguish it from misguided infatuation or fantastical daydreams. But when I wasn't with you, when I walked away from you—that didn't make it easier. What I felt didn't go away, not even a little bit. What I was feeling for you ruined *everything*.'

But she was smiling, and he realised he was smiling, too.

'I don't want this, you know?' She nodded out of the door, towards the hordes of people and the observant cameramen who were trying to peer through the black tinted windows. 'But I didn't want this even without the movie-star thing. Even if you worked in Props, or wrote scripts, or didn't even work in film at all.'

'Me either,' he said. 'I thought I was good at going it alone. That I had it all sorted, the best way to live my life.'

'Me too!' she agreed, and laughed briefly. 'And it's risky changing direction.'

'What if I decide this way is better? Then what happens if it doesn't work out?'

Ruby nodded, her eyes widening in surprise. 'Exactly. It's scary.'

Dev shrugged. 'I decided it was worth the risk.'

And it was. Even when she'd said no, it had still been worth it. Even though it had sucked. Really, really sucked.

His life wasn't going to be about regrets any longer. Except—even then, when he'd laid his heart on the line—he hadn't been entirely an open book. He'd still withheld one thing.

'I love you, Ruby Bell.'

Quick as a flash, she replied, 'I love you too, Devlin Cooper.'

Then for long moments they smiled huge, idiotic grins at each other.

Over her shoulder a camera flash momentarily stole his attention, bringing him abruptly back to reality—to *his* reality.

'What about the paparazzi, Ruby? The gossip and the rumours? With me, it's as good as guaranteed.'

She shocked him when she shrugged. 'I used to think that I had to prove something to the gossips—prove them right or prove them wrong. But you know what? I don't care any more. You arrived on set amidst a storm of rumours, and you didn't change one thing—you didn't react, you didn't engage, you didn't deny. You were just you.' She paused, then reached out to grip his hand. 'People can say whatever they like about me, or you, or us—but I know the truth. We do. And I've decided that's all that matters. I'm in control of my life, no one else.'

She was amazing. If he hadn't fallen long ago, just that would've pushed him over the edge.

'Do you want to walk the red carpet with me, Ruby?'

She nodded, and amongst a sea of camera flashes he opened his door, and stepped out, only to turn and offer her his hand.

She slid across the seats, and swung her gold stiletto heels onto the red carpet. He bent closer to whisper in her ear.

'This is serious, you know that? For ever stuff. Happy every after, like in the movies.'

'No,' she said, so firmly he went still. He caught her gaze as she looked up at him from the car's leather interior. 'Not like in the movies,' she said, 'and not like in fairy tales.'

Finally she reached out to take his hand, letting him pull her to her feet.

They stood together, side by side, the red carpet before them, fans screaming, cameras as good as shoved in their faces. But all he was aware of was Ruby, of her hand in his, and the look in her eyes as she looked up at him. With love, and with everything she had to give.

He knew he was looking at her in exactly the same way.

'This is real life,' she said.

* * * * *

LET'S TALK
Romance

For exclusive extracts, competitions
and special offers, find us online:

- facebook.com/millsandboon
- @MillsandBoon
- @MillsandBoonUK

Get in touch on 01413 063232

For all the latest titles coming soon, visit
millsandboon.co.uk/nextmonth

MILLS & BOON

THE HEART OF ROMANCE

A ROMANCE FOR EVERY KIND OF READER

MODERN

Prepare to be swept off your feet by sophisticated, sexy and seductive heroes, in some of the world's most glamourous and romantic locations, where power and passion collide.
8 stories per month.

HISTORICAL

Escape with historical heroes from time gone by. Whether your passion is for wicked Regency Rakes, muscled Vikings or rugged Highlanders, awaken the romance of the past.
6 stories per month.

MEDICAL

Set your pulse racing with dedicated, delectable doctors in the high-pressure world of medicine, where emotions run high and passion, comfort and love are the best medicine.
6 stories per month.

True Love

Celebrate true love with tender stories of heartfelt romance, from the rush of falling in love to the joy a new baby can bring, and a focus on the emotional heart of a relationship.
8 stories per month.

Desire

Indulge in secrets and scandal, intense drama and plenty of sizzli, hot action with powerful and passionate heroes who have it all: wealth, status, good looks…everything but the right woman.
6 stories per month.

HEROES

Experience all the excitement of a gripping thriller, with an intens romance at its heart. Resourceful, true-to-life women and strong, fearless men face danger and desire - a killer combination!
8 stories per month.

DARE

Sensual love stories featuring smart, sassy heroines you'd want as a best friend, and compelling intense heroes who are worthy of the
4 stories per month.

To see which titles are coming soon, please visit

millsandboon.co.uk/nextmonth